Prospect Hill

Prospect Hill

Richard Francis

FOURTH ESTATE · *London*

First published in Great Britain in 2003 by
Fourth Estate
A Division of HarperCollins*Publishers*
77–85 Fulham Palace Road
London w6 8jb
www.4thestate.com

10 9 8 7 6 5 4 3 2 1

A catalogue record for this book is available from the British Library

ISBN 0-00-714109-2

Typeset by Rowland Phototypesetting Ltd,
Bury St Edmunds, Suffolk
Printed in Great Britain by
Clays Ltd, St Ives plc

For Jo

This novel takes place in 1970, and is set in a large town called Costford, which is hooked on to the south-east corner of Manchester in exactly the position occupied by Stockport in the real world. The substitution seems to have warped history a little. While the rest of the country went to the polls in June of that year, the inhabitants of Costford find themselves heading for a general election as winter approaches.

Part 1

One

May only saw her house occasionally, really saw. Same as her face: she'd lived in both since the year dot. Her house was big and comfortable-looking on its corner plot in Harper Moor, but its windows seemed threateningly black. Black as bowler hats, though her own bowler, in its big brown paper bag, was maroon. The windows were all shut, despite it being August and quite close, the grey sunshine only just strong enough for shadows.

She left her Imp in the road in case Cherry wanted a lift back, and walked up her path. It had been poor Hub's idea to have it done in crazy-paving. Typical of him always to want things that bit extra. It was like walking on a jigsaw, and she noticed one of the pieces was riding up. She stamped on it a few times to see if it would settle, but no such luck. She'd have to get somebody in to see to it before the postman went head over heels. Since Eric, her old odd-job man, had developed shortness of breath she'd been in limbo, and there was a patch of damp on her bedroom ceiling that was getting bigger by the week.

She became aware of her mother's little gossamer voice coming through the glass, singing 'Silent Night'. For a moment she closed her eyes and sighed. Then resolute, in town councillor mode, she plodded up the rest of the path and pushed her key in the lock.

'Hello,' she called from the hall. There was no reply, and the singing carried on. They would be in the back room. Still, she remained where she was for the moment, rearranging the spider plant that tumbled from a big blue pot beside the telephone table. 'Hello-o-o,' she called again.

'Oh, May!' came Cherry's voice, from the back room sure enough.

She took a breath and went in, glad for once she'd been born with thick ankles and sensible shoes, needing to feel solid and unflappable.

Her mother and Cherry were sitting at the dining table. They each had a Basildon Bond writing pad in front of them.

'We're writing letters,' Cherry said, putting on one of those bright and breezy teacher faces.

'Oh. Good,' May replied.

'We got a bus into the middle of Costie, and bought them from W.H. Smith's.'

'You could have got them from Band's round the corner.'

'We wanted a trip out, didn't we, Nan?'

May didn't like the word Nan, but Cherry didn't have a lot of choice, given she already had a gran and a granma of her own. It would hardly be appreciated if she called her Hilda. 'Were you served by someone on the small side?' May asked. 'Quite buxom with it?'

'I don't know. Probably not my strong point, other people's bos-ooms.'

'Oh well.'

'I'm writing to a friend of mine I was at college with,' Cherry said. 'Noreen Hallett. Imagine that. You have to start off, Dear Noreen.'

'And who are *you* writing to, Mother?'

Her mother didn't look her in the face, and just carried on singing 'Silent Night', but a silly little smile on her lips showed that she was listening.

Smirk was the word. A silly little smirk, exactly the same expression as that young criminal had had on his face when he came up before her on the bench, trying to look as if he thought it was clever to have stolen somebody's television set.

'She's writing to Auntie Alice,' Cherry said. 'I said she should invite her to tea.'

'That'll be nice.'

As a matter of fact, it *would* be nice to invite her to tea, in reality not just let's pretend. May didn't know how Cherry had the patience to play those silly games, but of course she'd been an infant school teacher, and it was no doubt much the same dealing with somebody's second childhood.

Cherry must have been one of the few people in the history of the human race to give up teaching in order to become a waitress. A quick sidestep and down she'd fallen into the bottomless pit, one of those career moves you couldn't reverse.

It hadn't taken her long to realise that waitressing was not all she had hoped it would be, though what she had hoped it would be May couldn't imagine. She'd given up that in turn, and now didn't have a job at all, except babysitting Mother. The arrangement suited May down to the ground, and of course she reimbursed Cherry for it, being as Mother was only her step-grandmother in the first place, hardly an obligation. But she worried about the outlook. Cherry might be waiting to get wed, like girls did in the old days, but it wasn't the old days, and Cherry wasn't a girl any longer.

But, anyway, it would be a good idea to have Auntie Alice over to the house again, even if Mum failed to recognise her, or more likely, pretended to fail.

'Do you want a lift back?' May asked Cherry.

'No, walking will be quite nice.'

Fill in the time, too, May thought.

After Cherry had gone May tried to engage her mother in conversation. 'I went to the hat factory this afternoon, Mother,' she said.

In order to avoid having her attention snagged Mother began to draw on her Basildon Bond. May craned her head sideways to see what. A stick man with a face shapely as a potato, carrying an animal of some kind, a cat judging by its whiskers. She gave her mother a sharp look.

'You know, where they make the bowler hats for London businessmen. And for butlers. For members of the horse-racing fraternity as well.' That's how the manager had put it to her, in reverent tones, 'horse racing fraternity'. 'If there's one thing that can turn a man into a fool, it's a horse,' May had told him, wiping the pompous look off of his face. She'd been thinking of Uncle George. It had been a great release to poor Alice when he got summoned to the golden bookie's in the sky.

'The men plunge their hands in boiling water to mould them,' she went on. 'The council are thinking of having a museum of hatting, now the trade's on its last legs. They make a few women's hats too, with a different rim and different colours, more feminine. They gave me one.' She opened her bag and got it out to show her. 'They don't seem to have caught on much, though.'

May pushed the hat between her mother's face and the writing pad, to make sure it interrupted her drawing. Her response was to start singing again, 'In your Easter bonnet', which at least showed something had gone in.

'Yes, Mother, thank you very much.'

May set about getting tea. She had bought a bit of lamb's liver that morning at Eatmore's, and cooked it with onions, mashed potatoes, and some runner beans Joe Patterson down the road had given her from his allotment. While doing so, she ran over what she ought to get on with after tea. Mother meanwhile continued working on her pad of Basildon Bond.

A note to the planning officer, on behalf of the Bradburys, was the most important thing. She'd popped round to their house just before going to the hat factory, after Mrs Bradbury had come into her surgery last Tuesday, full of grief. She was a sharp-nosed woman with a put-on accent, well adapted to whining.

There was a patch of land behind the Bradburys' house, their detached house, which had been unused for nearly twenty years, to their knowledge. They woke up one morning and it had suddenly become full of mechanical diggers. How they'd managed to creep in in the middle of the night, May couldn't picture. But they were there all right, she'd seen them for herself, like a lot of big yellow animals in a zoo. Perhaps the Bradburys were sound sleepers.

Their house wasn't as detached as all that, it was squashed in with a lot of semis of the same vintage. Apparently the land behind the houses had been used by the original builders, and never distributed among the properties as intended. Now it had been bought by a civil engineering firm called O'Briens, to keep machinery in. There was a tiny alley by the Bradburys' house down which they'd had to squeeze the JCBs, scraping their wall as they did so.

'My husband's a teacher,' Mrs Bradbury had told May in the surgery. Maybe he was, and maybe he wasn't. May noticed a driving-school car scuttling shamefacedly out of their driveway as she arrived.

The woman next to the Bradburys had her own story to tell when May knocked on her door to test the local mood. She'd got up one morning to find her goldfish had flipped out of its bowl on to the floor.

'Frightened by the throbbing of the engines,' Mrs Bradbury put in. She was hanging round the rear of May like a wasp round a pot of jam.

That hadn't been the point the neighbour was trying to make. Apparently her fish was prone to flipping in that fashion. But this time it had been on the carpet longer than it should, and when she returned it to its bowl it had just floated there like a peeled carrot, without a sign of life.

The neighbour remembered what she had read in some magazine: how to give a goldfish the kiss of life. She fetched a drinking straw from the kitchen, shoved it in the bowl, and blew. While doing so she happened to glance up and saw a line of digger drivers peering over her fence at her.

'That's how it's going to be from now on,' Mrs Bradbury said. 'No privacy whatsoever. My daughter's studying for her A levels.'

'You can't even revive your goldfish in peace,' May had agreed. As it happened the goldfish had died, or rather, stayed dead.

Just when May was on the point of serving up, Mother's sharp little voice took up a song once more.

> 'I'm the sheikh of Arabie
> Your love belongs to me
> At night when you're asleep
> Into your tent I'll creep.'

For two pins May would have poured molten liver over that fluffy white head of hers. Her mother's general dottiness was depressing enough, but this penchant, as old Hub would have put it, for singing drove May completely up the wall. The mindlessness for one thing, songs being trotted out for the most part without any sense of occasion, without any sense of the words at all; but also the quality of her voice, a thin relic of how it had been but in a funny maddening way possessed of a reedy beauty in its own right. It made her want to scream.

And this time there was something else. Her mother hadn't sung this particular song before, not to May's knowledge, and it caught her on the raw.

How dare you? she thought. How dare you take *everything* from me? My future, which is now my past. My life as a whole. My tent.

My one and only, long-ago, little tent.

The tent came from a church outing she'd gone on with a group of young people before the war. They spent a weekend at some sort of hostel in the Lake District, a kind of Christian guest-house or retreat. What she was doing there May could hardly remember. She had always believed in God, still did, but not to excess.

After an afternoon ramble the party stopped off for tea at a place that turned out to be a pub, and, feeling very daring, installed themselves there for the duration. May was drinking half a pint of beer even though the steadier girls had lemonades or sherry. Perhaps as a result, her evening took an unexpected turn for the better. A young man started talking to her; not from the church – a young man from anywhere at all, in fact from Nottingham. He was a steeplejack, or so he said.

If he was fibbing it was almost as good as being one in reality. To want to tell a girl like her that he was such a thing, scampering up gas holders and church towers, to want her to see it in her mind's eye. He was small and curly haired, and bobbed his head as he talked. After an hour or so he asked her if she'd like a cup of coffee in his tent.

> At night when you're asleep
> Into your tent I'll creep . . .

The song was probably old hat even then. Wasn't it to do with Rudolph Valentino, in that silent film? Perhaps not – you could hardly have a song in a silent film. But it couldn't have been far off that vintage.

Now, stirring the liver in its onion gravy, May imagined the song going through her head as the young man from long ago made his suggestion, and in sympathy with the memory, if it was a memory, mouthed the words to herself, out of time with her mother's ghostly voice.

When she stood up she'd felt massive, like one of the very towers he was supposed to climb. She followed him out of the pub taking big gas-holdery steps, hoping he wouldn't turn round. She was conscious, as always, of the thickness of her ankles. Her dress suddenly seemed to her to be just material, hanging from her with no proper shape, like a curtain. She could feel all the eyes on her back, hot little jealous eyes, thinking to themselves, what kind of a girl is she after all, going off with just anyone? wishing that anyone would ask *them*. One of them said, 'Don't forget, lights out at ten o'clock.'

He didn't have a car, he had a motorbike. Years later she could still remember what a jolt it was seeing it parked in the roadhouse car park, resting on its little elbow. I'm getting into deep water here, she'd realised.

He got on first, so she had his tactful back to look at, with his leather jacket riding up a touch and revealing a manly, almost invisible, bottom. She had to hoik her frock up further than you would ever think, almost as far as going to the loo, just so as to swing her leg over the seat. It reminded her of tucking her skirt into her knickers in PT at school. She looked around fearfully as she did it, but there was nobody in the car park except a couple of children drinking pop in the back seat of an open-topped touring car.

When she was on, she tugged her hem down as much as she could, but it would only go an inch or two. In for a penny in for a pound, she suddenly thought. When they were whooshing along on the bike, passers-by would hardly have time to notice.

The young man's jacket had little leather epaulettes and she wondered for a moment if she should hold on to them. No, she'd seen what people, what girls, did when they were riding pillion. She had to have the courage of her convictions. She slid her arms each side of his chest. It was funny how on certain occasions you were allowed to do that sort of thing, at a dance for example, but other times you would be considered really forward. She shuffled up the seat and leaned her head towards his shoulders. Afterwards she thought of him smelling of leather as if that's what men smelled of, but of course it was just his jacket.

As they drove off she felt her hair go loose in the wind, which made up for pink goose-pimply legs. She had to hold on tight to his chest to stop herself slipping off the back of the bike while it climbed up the mountain. She could feel her bosom squashed against his back, and wondered if he could feel it too, through the leather.

They were soon high up. He drove the motorbike on to a little track, and there was his tiny tent, on a patch of grass with a flat bit in front and then the ground dropping down and down to the green valley below where the grazing sheep looked the size of cottonwool balls in Aspro bottles. She thought the wind was from the ride, but when they stopped it was still blowing, only warmer, right in the mouth of the tent so that the canvas was curved and hard. The thin bright air made her feel drunker than the half-pint. Inside the tent was like being in a balloon.

He boiled water just outside the flap, on a little primus, leaning forward to tend it. They were sitting on his sleeping bag. The tent smelled of grass. Her heart was thumping so that she could feel it in her ears. When his arm suddenly reached towards her she thought, Now we're for it, but he was only giving her a little tin cup of coffee, and she felt half relieved, half sorry, as she took it from him.

He talked about wanting to climb mountains, like some of his steeplejack friends did. They had gone to a climbing club where the famous mountaineers went, but weren't allowed in.

'You know,' he said, nodding despondently.

She nodded back. She knew: too common. She had every sympathy now she had ridden, more or less bare-legged, on a motorbike, and was sharing a tent with a young male friend.

The steeplejacks had got drunk. Then they got their climbing gear, went back to the club, opened the door of the room where all the upper-class climbers were, bundled in and began climbing along the floor, just as if it was a sheer rock face, getting purchase on the feet of the Alpine mountaineers as they went.

'They were fine about it. Thought it was a bit of fun,' he told her.

She guessed it might have worked out better if they hadn't been fine about it. She pictured the real mountaineers laughing at the antics of the steeplejack ones. Her instinct told her that wasn't the outcome to have aimed for. She didn't know at the time what instinct it was that told her so, but later she would have the word for it: political.

'He was a perfect gentleman,' she told a voice that came at her out of the darkness of the hostel dorm. She tried to say it in such a way it would sound like a lie, but it was the truth. They had sat on his bed thing and drunk their coffee. It wasn't that he was disappointed about how she looked, surely, because he had seen what she was like in the pub. In any case her legs were safely tucked under her, out of sight, though it meant gyp when she tried to walk on them back to the bike. All they had done was drink coffee and talk, which was what they were supposed to be doing, but as they drove back she found herself crying a little into the wind. Even her dress, on the return trip, felt longer and less reckless.

Afterwards she realised she didn't remember his name. Perhaps he hadn't told her it. She thought it was Bob, but maybe she'd christened him in retrospect. When, subsequently, she imagined a time when her life felt light and airy, the ride up the mountain came back to her, the sensation of bobbing along above the valley, and their arrival at the little tent.

But it was Mum who was the light one now. Always had been from one point of view, a tiny creature to have had a big daughter like her, cuckoo in the nest, she used to say. And with age she had gone so she didn't weigh anything at all, with her ghostly little slightly out of tune singing voice threading the air.

While they were eating their dinner Mother suddenly asked: 'When's Alice coming over, then?'

May looked up at her. She was looking attentively back. These moments of shrewdness and focus always caught May on the hop, even though they came quite often. They reinforced the sense she had that her mother couldn't really be as doolally as she seemed, that she was playing tricks on her, putting on an act.

Sometimes, even worse, May would have a vague, uncomfortable sense that her mother's moments of lucidity were the act.

'How about Sunday week? It'll be quite a to-do. I'll have to drive out to Waveney Bridge and fetch her back in. And then drive out again to take her home.'

Her mother thought for a bit, building a forkful of beans, liver and potato. She continued to be a neat eater, no matter how raggedy she became in her mind. Her little mouth was shut tight as she chewed. Then she said, 'It's a lot of trouble to go to. Best leave her be.'

'She's your sister, Ma.' Ma was like Nan, not a nice word. May only used it when she wanted to hector. It suddenly occurred to her that nowadays she wanted to hector a great deal. Her mother's senility filled her with rage, not the sort that made you shout and bluster, but the kind that created a permanent background hum. Perhaps, oddly, Mother might be the same way herself, suffering a kind of deep-rooted impatience with life, singing whenever she was in danger of saying the terrible things that had crept into her mind.

'You would stick up for her,' she answered, with a sour look, and then was off again, this time warbling about seeing you in old and familiar places.

Not if you had the choice, you wouldn't, May thought to herself as she cleared the plates.

Luckily Mother was happy to go to bed, or at least to her bedroom, early these days. May took her up the stairs at about seven, then sat in the front room for an hour or two, writing to the planning officer about the Bradburys, doing other constituency letters and then reading council papers while the TV was on in the background. There wasn't a peep from above, and she was so relaxed that it gave her a start to hear someone knocking at the door.

It was a constable.

He filled the door frame. They're very large in real life, May thought. She remembered her Imp was still in the road. Perhaps it was facing the wrong way. But it was still light, and anyway she wasn't sure if that was against the law these days.

'Are you Mrs Rollins?' the constable asked.

'Miss Rollins, yes.'

He gave her the long, slow look of a child who'd passed only woodwork. 'Miss Rollins, yes,' he muttered on the in-breath, as if committing it to memory.

'And you?'

'Me?' he asked, flummoxed. He raised his eyebrows so they disappeared into his helmet, and pointed at his own chest.

'Are?' she prompted.

'Constable Aitkin.'

'How do you do.'

'Do you know a Mrs Baxendale?'

'I should do. She's my mother.' May wondered if she should explain that the difference in names was because her mother had been married twice, while she herself had reverted to her maiden name after Hub died, but forbore. No point in giving the lad any more cud to chew on, given the heavy weather he was making as it was.

Suddenly she shivered. 'What about her?' she asked.

'Do you know her present whereabouts?'

'Her present whereabouts are in her bedroom.'

'She's at the police station.'

She opened her mouth but had nothing to say. Then she turned and ran upstairs.

Even in moments of crisis, there's room for vanity. It's funny how those charging animals on the TV, she thought, the big ones like elephants and rhinoceroses, always had dreadful baggy bottoms beneath their fat little tails.

Mum's bed raunged about on, but currently empty. Her wireless tuned to some drivel, music for the seaside organ by the sound of it, but nobody listening, even not-listening. What on earth had she done – thrown herself from the window?

May drove to the station in her Imp while the constable turned his pedals in the rear-view mirror; cranked his velocipede, as Hub would have said. Despite the warm evening he seemed to have put on some sort of cape, presumably stored in his saddlebag, and it made his hunched form look like a musketeer who'd been demoted to the ranks.

She always kept a tube of peppermints on the passenger seat, and she took one out now, digging for it with blind fingers in a half-satisfactory, half-disagreeable fashion that reminded her of the nose-picking days of early youth. The taste cut across the smell of perfume that seemed endemic to her car, though goodness knew she didn't use any on herself.

Perhaps the process of firkling out the Polo used up more concentration than it should have, because suddenly she was bearing down on a lollipop lady at the awkward junction of Priory Road and Edgemere Street. She too, as if in some sort of hidden conspiracy of weather, was wearing a long white mackintosh, one of those that seem to be made out of the same substance as gumboots. The hand that wasn't holding the lollipop was stretched out palm forward in a 'stop' gesture, and May stopped in the very nick of time.

The woman was red-faced, as one would be on an August evening wearing a coat made of boots, but it could be fear at the sudden proximity of May's Imp. In the heat of the same moment May herself had almost inhaled her sweet without even realising until she felt it arrive back in her mouth.

She sat, getting her breath back. Nobody attempted to cross the road.

After a few moments the lollipop lady retreated to the pavement where a group of her friends and relatives seemed to be waiting to greet her. She gave May a final dark look over her shoulder. Annoyingly, the constable had used the opportunity to catch up, but May accelerated smartly away and got to the police station without him tagging at her heels.

She strode up to the reception desk where there was a tired old sergeant she vaguely recognised. A motorcycling type of lad, all in leather like a uniform, was sitting on a chair in the corner giving a fishy eye to the room at large. He looked no better than he ought to be, a far cry from her steeplejack of long ago. She recognised his type but not him. There were so many of them, lads of that ilk, that was the trouble.

'You are?' she asked the sergeant.

'Sergeant Begley, Madam.'

'Good evening, Sergeant Begley,' she said.

'Yes,' he replied, as if confirming a fact. He had one of those heads that had been stood in front of a low heat, so his face was slowly melting off. The bags for his eyes had slid halfway down his cheeks. He consulted a clipboard on his desk for inspiration. 'Councillor Rollins,' he read.

'The same.'

He leaned confidentially across the desk. 'Your mother's with a WPC. She's having a nice cup of tea.'

'Oh. Good-oh.'

'Did you bring the . . . ?'

She leaned back towards him. 'The what?'

'Dressing-gown,' the sergeant mouthed, presumably so as not to get the scallywag going. His breath was warm and sweetish, tea-smelling.

'No, I did not. What – oh, I see.' Her heart hit her boots.

'Never mind. We'll see what we can do.'

'Constable Aitkin didn't say to.'

'No, I don't suppose he did. Probably a bit shy. Tell you what, you take a seat, and I'll go up and tell them you're here.' He inclined his head towards a chair as far as possible from the motorbike youth.

She sat on it and he trundled off. The youth looked ahead but she could feel his eyes peering at her. She pictured her mother singing 'Silent Night', distraught and in her nightie, with uniformed police all round her.

Then, almost overwhelmingly, she pictured something else.

That lollipop lady, in the middle of a Costford street, at 8.30 p.m. of a late August evening.

She, May, had hit the brakes for her. She had nearly swallowed her Polo.

May wrapped her arms round her front as if to hold the shock in. She must have been seeing things. God forbid I'm going the same way as mother, she thought.

The constable came in.

'Constable,' she said.

'Ah,' he replied. He gave the youth a bit of a look and stepped over to her. Somehow he seemed more sure of himself after his ride. 'Everything all right?'

'I want to ask you something.'

'Oh yes?'

'On the way here –'

'Funny that. I stopped and asked about it. That's why I was a time getting here. It was a new lollipop lady. They were trying her out, type of thing. Seeing if she's got what it takes. They don't like to do it with real children, in case. Can't afford to flatten one of them, just on a try-out. They need to have a bash at twilight, practise for the winter afternoons.'

'I thought that must be it,' May said. 'That's why I went for her. Put her on her mettle.'

'I'll go on up, see how they're getting on.' He winked, or as near as he could get, puckering the side of his face but not closing his eye, and went.

May felt trembly with relief as she resumed the wait. After a few minutes they came down, the sergeant, a policewoman, her mother. The constable wasn't with them, but funnily enough her mother was wearing his cape over her nightie. She wasn't singing, and looked lost and forlorn.

'Here she is,' said the sergeant. 'Safe and sound. We'll just get the formalities done. Won't be a tick.'

He went to his desk and wrote something on his clipboard. Then, to May's surprise, he pointed his head towards the youth and made a tugging movement, like you do if you're trying to bite through a thread. The young man got up and went over to the desk. They talked for a few moments and the young man signed something. He looked impertinently back at May and left the station.

'I'd have felt a lot safer with him under lock and key.'

'Oh, we couldn't do that,' the sergeant said.

'They're given too much rope to hang themselves, these days. Don't I know it, being a JP.'

'Thing about it is, is in this case he was the plaintiff, you could say.'

'In which case?'

She had got up and was over at the desk by now. Sergeant Begley leaned over as he had before. 'Do you know how your mother got out of the house?'

'I'm afraid I haven't the slightest idea. I was in the sitting room, doing some paperwork. Council business.' How *had* she done it? She must have tiptoed down the hall and let herself out the front door.

The sergeant reached under his desk, and felt about. 'Thing is,' he said, bringing a wicked looking jack-knife to the surface, 'does this object ring a bell?'

May looked at it in horror. What had the old monster been up to now?

'I have –' She was going to say never seen it before in my life, but suddenly realised that would make matters worse, true though it was. 'It's one my late husband had. We were very fond of camping.' She saw, in her mind's eye, poor Hub revolve in his grave. One evening, in a bright and breezy tent, had been all she'd ever had of that experience, or wanted of it. Where the knife had come from in real life, Lord alone knew. All May could think was that Mother must have slipped the leash when out with Cherry earlier on today, and hopped into the Army and Navy to buy it. They wouldn't have scrupled at selling one to an old dear like her. Perhaps she'd told them some fiddle-faddle about a nephew in the Scouts. Perhaps she'd even stolen it.

'She was running down the street waving it at people,' the sergeant said. 'Caused a bit of a ruckus, I can tell you.'

'Oh my God.'

May pictured passers-by scattering. She spent half her life deal-ing with juvenile delinquents, and now she had a senile one of her own. 'She's – quite harmless,' she said lamely, not having the faintest notion whether she was harmless or not.

'I'm sure she is, deep down. But she did try to stick this knife –' the sergeant held it up to her so she could catch the nasty smile of its blade – 'in that young man that just left. Couldn't get it through the leather, as luck would have it.'

'Oh dear, oh dear, oh dear,' May muttered.

'Not to worry. He could see there was no point pressing charges. He said the same as you, the old dear is harmless deep down. Probably be a good idea to keep a sharp eye on her in future, though but.'

What do you expect me to do, chain her up like a goat? she wanted to say, but nodded instead.

'And better keep this out of harm's way,' he said, pushing the knife at her across the desk.

'Oh, I don't want it.' She remembered it was supposed to be hers, reached a hand to it, then pushed it away. 'Back.'

'Thought it might have sentimental value. Being –'

'No, no, I don't need a knife to remind me of times gone by. Give it to . . .' She nearly said the deserving poor, but on reflection they were the last people who ought to have it. She shrugged her shoulders instead.

'Don't trouble your head,' he told her. 'We'll dispose of it safely.' He leaned across further. 'Experts,' he added, tapping his nose.

Mother had begun to sing 'The Teddy Bears' Picnic'.

'It's very kind of you all,' May said to the room at large. 'And the cape.'

'Proper knight in shining armour, that young copper,' the sergeant said. 'Sharp as a knife along with it.' He realised what he'd said. 'Bright as a button,' he added by way of correction.

'But won't he need it?'

'Not this weather. Just drop it in when you're passing. Part of the service.'

As she drove back, her mother caterwauling in the passenger seat, May thought to herself: the trouble is, she's becoming more horrible than ever. She's turned into a kind of murderer. If she keeps plugging away at it, she'll become one in truth. She's been fairly horrible all along, but I was the only one who ever seemed to notice. Everyone else has always thought she was the salt of the earth. It's her fault that my life turned out the way it did, not just the fact that I was born ugly and left on the shelf all those years, at a time when you had to marry to get anywhere, be anything.

That night, as she lay in bed, May thought of the youth who'd come up before her for stealing a TV set. He seemed to merge with the young man in the police station, who in actual fact didn't look anything like him but who had the same insolent eyes. She began to feel frightened, and stirred under her blanket uneasily. She didn't like it when it was too warm for an eider-down: not enough cosiness. The boy in court had had a funny name, which she couldn't remember. She kept picturing him in her mind's eye threatening her with her own mother's jack-knife. Why she should fear him in this way, she couldn't quite think. The bench had found him not guilty, after all – he had no reason to bear a grudge. The old man who'd chased him from his house had thought he recognised him, then wasn't sure. The man who bought the TV in a pub did the same. So he'd got away with it.

But in the dock he had looked at her with hatred all the same, for some reason she couldn't quite fathom, though she felt she knew in her heart of hearts what it must be, if only she could put her mind to it.

Two

Jack Kitchen, the caretaker, always looked round the edge of the Town Hall door as if he expected an angry mob outside.

'Only me, Jack,' May told him. Who would it be, the Queen of Sheba? A different matter on a Saturday night, with the hop going on and rat-faced young crawling over the shop, but on a wet Tuesday?

Seeing Jack peering out like that reminded her of the way that young police constable had arrived on her doorstep, when she'd done likewise. He was still without his cape after nearly a fortnight. It was hanging on the coat-stand in the hall. That would teach him to be nice to mad old ladies.

She glanced down the street at the wet Costie road and pavement. The clouds were purple above the viaduct over the way, the same purple some fat noses of her acquaintance had gone with age and alcohol.

Hub used to greet Jack in French, '*C'est moi,*' saying it like a password.

Jack never did cotton on, but would just look blankly back. Born to be a doorman when all was said and done.

Now Jack nodded, and stepped to one side to let her in, jingling with keys as he did so. He shut the door and then hared along the corridor till he overtook her, liking to lead the way. She'd always had the feeling he had a leg missing but had never managed to get the topic to crop up naturally. Surely you'd need a wooden one to get along as nippily as he did, spinning a quick semicircle with every other stride.

It was Committee Room B tonight. Ted Wilcox, Tory leader and chairman of the meeting, was in position at the head of the table, and most of the others were standing around making chit-chat. Jack pulled the door shut behind her.

Ted wagged his head as a signal for her to approach. His long white hair shone softly even when there was no obvious source of light. Hub once told May he applied unguents from faraway places.

Hub had also said, 'Ted's native lingo is *sotto voce*.'

Too true; at least it was when she found out what it meant. Ted had a way of speaking to you in a voice like glue, with fat moist insincere eyes to go along with it.

'How's your mother?' he asked.

I think the word you're looking for is father, she thought grimly. They all said that that was indeed what he was after, though not of course with her.

'All right?'

In his concerned smile there was a world of meaning. I understand she's been rampaging through the streets of Costford in her nightie, stabbing people, was what he was really saying. She could be an embarrassment if you don't keep her in check. And if you want me to turn a blind eye you'd better be a good girl, one way or another. Toe the line.

'Who told you?'

'I'm on the police committee, don't forget. Sergeant Begley had to make a little report, just in case anybody comes to harm in the future. We've all got to keep our backs covered, you know that, that's what life's about. But in the meantime, not a dicky-bird. You know me, May. I'm a man who plays his cards close to his chest.'

He patted his chest, by way of illustration, then looked across at hers. There was something sarcastic about his gaze. No man had ever looked at her bosom in a serious light, not even horrible Uncle George when he did his grab.

'You know how it is,' she said. 'Nothing worth watching on the television. A girl needs a bit of fun.'

'I respect you for standing by her, don't get me wrong. Just as I'll stand by you. Just as we always stand by each other. And one thing I've always enjoyed: your ever-ready sense of humour.'

She knew what that remark was about, too. Ted couldn't *sotto* the least titbit without it being as loaded with freight as a goods wagon. It was about her indiscretion at the last meeting of the Planning and Redevelopment Committee.

It had been the first meeting, if you wanted to be pedantic about it, given the Planning Committee had just amalgamated with the Redevelopment and Civic Buildings Committee to pro-vide a beefed up decision-making body, at least according to Glen Parsons, planning officer and new broom, as Ted labelled him. A young man who talks my language, Ted had said, practically rubbing his hands. True, perhaps: he seemed fresh and clever enough, though May noticed a haunted look in his eyes from time to time, as of someone who'd been catapulted into a snake pit. Which he had been, given the endless aggravation caused by the Prospect Hill council flats development.

It was one of those issues that cropped up in local government from time to time, that just seemed to get more complicated and more insoluble with every passing day. The project had been approved by the council years ago, when it had a tiny Labour majority rather than the tiny Tory one it had now. All the fund-ing had been gone into. There were to be four tower blocks, providing 297 flats, two-thirds of them earmarked for one- or two-person households. The Ministry of Housing in London had given the go-ahead. And then, a week later, the Ronan Point disaster had happened.

Oddly, May had been in London that day. She was at Waterloo Station, on her way to visit an old chum who'd moved to Woking. Hub wasn't long dead and she needed a change. They had a sort of electric thing at the station which uncoiled news at you. May could remember watching it as it spelled out BLOCK-OF-FLATS-COLLAPSE-AT-RONAN-POINT-GREAT-LOSS-OF-LIFE-FEARED. She also remembered the disgruntled feeling she'd had: what was all the fuss about people dying? People died all the time. If it was good enough for Hub, why shouldn't it be good enough for *them*? He hadn't had *his* death announced on an electric news uncoiler – how he would have loved it if he had!

But Ronan Point was a disaster that cast a long shadow, as Ted Wilcox had said at the meeting last month, that very one at which May took it into her head to liven the proceedings up a little.

Whitehall had suspended all building of tower blocks pending the outcome of the official inquiry into Ronan Point. During the two years that followed, residential blocks for public housing began to go out of fashion in any case. May herself had gone on a jaunt to Exeter, at ratepayers' expense, to see how the council there had taken a couple of diddly little streets of slum terraces, given out grants to do them up, and compulsorily purchased several of the properties in the rows, which they pulled down to make room for little parks with benches where little Exeter people could sit and rest their weary limbs. It just wouldn't do in Costford, where there were six thousand slum dwellings to cope with. It was a southern solution. Up here in the big bad north of England, surgery was the only answer, as she'd said on one occasion. Amputate the diseased limbs.

Poor choice of language, as it turned out. Bert Colley, the Independent, or Rate Payer, as he preferred to be known, had immediately gone hugger-mugger with Trevor Morgan, Labour, with the result that Trevor asked whether the blocks should be regarded as prostheses. Fortunately, not enough councillors knew what the word meant to make much hay with it. Falsies would have been more effective and was probably the word Bert had used, but that wouldn't have been Trevor's style.

The rethink after Ronan Point wasn't as difficult for most other councils, who were less heavily committed to tower building, but Costford was already at the point of no return. All the funding, at both local and national level, had been approved, contracts entered into. A complicated transaction to acquire the necessary land had been signed, whereby the final instalment wasn't payable until after building work was started. The rate-payers were gaining from the delay in this one respect at least, but the property developers involved were howling with fury, and helping to create an atmosphere of disillusion and panic about the whole business. Until the work was under way the council couldn't advance them their cash by law, even if they wanted to.

The problem was compounded when the Tories took overall control of the council. Ted Wilcox had had no choice but to press on with the development. Then the local Labour Party saw an opportunity to capitalise on public disillusionment with high-rise building, and decided to oppose it. In other words, the Conservatives were backing a Socialist policy which the Socialists themselves were attacking at every opportunity.

And last month the Planning and Redevelopment Committee had met to give the building work its go-ahead, despite the fact that even though the public inquiry had established the ground rules for future projects, the government itself had not given its formal consent. The long jam had to be eased, Ted had said, being a close companion of certain of the logs involved himself. And it was at the consequent difficult meeting that May had committed her indiscretion. You had to allow yourself a moment of madness from time to time, or at least you did if you were her. What Ted would never understand as long as he lived was that you shouldn't be careful all the time. Politics needed a touch of spice, same as anything else. One can't spend one's whole life as a baked bean.

Trevor Morgan had spoken to the topic, with that smile of his going not simply from ear to ear but further, all about our duty to provide our poorer brethren not just with subsidised housing but with the trappings of a civilised way of life along with it. 'It's not even a matter of ethics but of aesthetics, too,' he'd said at one point, to a low growl from Ted. 'We shouldn't be talking just about shelter, but about pleasant surroundings as well,' he added by way of translation.

RICHARD FRANCIS

Aesthetics was a word definitely missing from Ted's vocabu-
lary, along with love, honour, obey, and quite a few others. The
week before, May had been with him at the unveiling of a statue
in the precinct, a spindly, spiky thing. 'Don't ask me what it is,'
Ted had said fiercely, to the grief of the sculptor who was standing right by him, nodding ingratiatingly. 'I'll tell you what it is.
It's another what-is-it? sculpture. I suppose it's better than that
other thing,' he added bad-temperedly, pointing to a sculpture at
the far end of the precinct that seemed to be all circles but turned
out to be the work of the same individual. 'I don't know why
people stopped doing ones of ladies with no clothes on,' he added
regretfully. 'That's my idea of art.'

While Ted was still shaking his head at Trevor's remark, May
got to her feet. 'You know what happens when I go on a binge?'
she found herself asking. There was nervous laughter, especially
from Ted.

What am I saying? she asked herself. No, it's all right. They
know I don't go on binges. They understand it's a flight of fancy.

'Next morning, I wake up and I wonder, Where am I? I
wonder *Who* am I? And the next thing I think to myself is, Oh
Lord, please don't let me be working class.'

Desperate laughter from fellow Conservatives, especially Ted.
What a one, he seemed to be saying. He looked from side to side
as if inviting his colleagues to join in his amusement, his eyes like
daggers.

An Oh I say, from Labour. Bloody hell from the Rate Payer,
Bert Colley, who was more Labour than Labour was.

Trevor Morgan's cheekbones pinked up. He was the only one
of the lot of them with the gumption to work out what she was
up to. He didn't go on binges any more than she did, but the
difference was, it wouldn't occur to him to pretend to. And he
knew it. It was beyond his ken to be no better than he ought to
be. Put that in your pipe and smoke it, she thought, giving him
a look.

'I think that's a gratuitous –' he said, making matters worse.

26

'You can't have it both ways,' she told him. For a dizzying second she all but added, As the actress said to the bishop, but decided in the nick of time that that would be taking the mad moment too far. 'You can't talk about offering subsidised housing to our socially deprived fellow citizens, and at the same time pretend that you would like to be socially disadvantaged yourself,' she went on. 'That's not sympathy, that's humbug. You don't live in a council house yourself, nor, I imagine, do you intend to.' He lived in a little house on an estate in Edgemere, not good enough quality to be council. 'All I'm suggesting is that we keep the debate to practicalities, and steer clear of sentimentality. That's the way we'll get things done.'

'Sailed a bit close to the wind that time, duck,' Ted had muttered as they left the chamber. It was funny how he could give the word duck a threatening edge.

And now he was warning her, before his evening's meeting got under way: no more talk of binges.

Norman Forrester came up, wanting a word with Ted. Rumour had it he was one of the money men behind the Prospect Hill developments, so he probably had a lot to say to him. May took her chance and walked away from the table straight into the company of, guess who? Trevor Morgan himself.

He looked at her before he saw her and his face was sharp, almost cheap looking, with pale skin that looked as if it might erupt into adolescent eczema any second. His eyes were anxious behind thick lenses.

And then they saw her. It really was the most ridiculous effect: that smile of his came like a rabbit from a hat, completely out of proportion. His mouth wasn't generous enough, his nature wasn't expansive enough, yet there it was. Caught her wrong-footed each time, along with everybody else. Somehow or other you wanted to begin your conversation saying thanks very much, which was the last thing you should be doing in this game, especially to one of the other lot. It was the sort of smile you could build a career on, which was exactly what he was doing.

'Hello, May.'

'Good evening, Trevor. You well?'

'Yes, thanks. Right as rain. How's your mum?'

Not another one. 'She's hunky-dory, thank you very much.'

'Good-oh.' Still the smile. It made you think of what they said on holiday, Come on in, the water's lovely.

Perhaps he meant nothing by it. Ted would never have come over all secretive if it was general knowledge.

Suddenly a chill hit her stomach. Ted had said that he had heard through the police committee. Who wasn't on the police committee, May excepted?

But no, that rigmarole he'd put her through, no point in it if everyone had been told what had happened. Sergeant Begley would have shown Ted his little report in confidence. A word in your ear, all that claptrap. Just covering himself in case the old dear killed somebody for keeps, somebody a bit less forgiving than the last young chap she'd had a go at. That's what life was all about, keeping your back covered.

'Mrs Morgan all right?'

'She's hunky-dory as well,' he said, still smiling away as if that was the most wonderful joke, Mrs Morgan hunky-dory, Mrs Bax-endale the same, what do you know? 'You'll be speaking to it tonight?'

'Make no mistake.'

'Worse luck for me.'

'I'm sure you can look after yourself, Trevor,' she told him.

'I'd sooner have you looking after me.'

'You've only got to cross the floor, and you're welcome to me.'

'If they were all like you, May, I would.'

'Touch me not, me name's temptation.' Her eyes switched back to Ted, who was still deep in conversation. Norman was bent over him like a mother giving suck to her young.

'You're seeing what I'm seeing,' Bert Colley said suddenly in her ear.

'Don't *do* that, Bert. You made me jump out of my skin.'

Trevor had shimmied off already, and was standing over the far side, talking to the Labour leader, Dick Hardy. Even from this distance his smile still flashed at her, like Morse code. What a one. He could walk backwards across a room without his feet ever touching the ground.

'I'm just saying,' Bert said.

Ted, Ted, she thought. You worry about me watching my p's and q's, you should be a bit more careful with your own.

She walked over to the table, conscious of Bert's look on her back. 'Norman!' she said, as if she'd just noticed his existence.

Norman looked round with a start.

'Hello, May,' he said glumly.

'I wanted a word. I'm having a spot of bother with a leak in the roof somewhere. I've got a wet patch in the ceiling of my small back bedroom.'

'I don't do wet patches nowadays. Not been in that game for a long while.'

You're telling me, May thought. You do whole tower blocks, that's what you do. But only when nobody's looking.

Ted had got the message. 'Enough of this socialising,' he said. 'I think I'd better be calling us to order.'

'That isn't what I think it is,' May said. 'Oh, dear dear.'

'Sorry,' Cherry replied, as if it was her fault.

'For heaven's sake.' Why Cherry had had a helmet cut, goodness only knew, with a fringe straight across her forehead. It made her hair look as if it was pulled on of a morning like a balaclava. But it wasn't her fault if May's mother was up in her bedroom singing 'Nelly Dean'. 'She sounds like a public house at closing time.'

'She's been singing it the whole evening. It's as if –' Cherry shrugged her shoulders. 'As if she's only got room in her head for one thing at a time.'

'Two things. Knowing how to get on your nerves is the other one.'

'I got used to it in the end.'

It wasn't, on reflection, that Cherry shrugged her shoulders exactly. It was more she compacted them. Something in her movement reminded May of the studio couch they'd had in the lounge in Hub's day, the way its legs used to stow themselves away when you folded it over to turn it into a settee again. One additional movement and Cherry's whole body could vanish into thin air, leaving behind just her hairstyle like a discarded hat.

'Would you like a cup of tea?' Cherry asked.

'My house. Let me make you one.'

May made tea, brought the cups in and handed one to her. No TV on, no book open, no knitting on the go. What did the girl do with herself, when Mother didn't want to play? What worried May was what she did when she was by herself in that little house of hers. If anything.

'What have you been doing with yourself, then?' she asked her.

'Do you remember how Daddy always called a teapot a tea po?'

'Oh, your father.'

Cherry was as bad, with her own mannerisms. She huddled around her cup as if protecting it from a strong wind. 'I'm going out with someone.'

'You were going out with someone last time I saw you.'

'Not the same one. Well, I'm still going out with him too.'

Two at once: May felt mildly irritated. Couldn't the girl get anything right?

'What I mean is, Ben's all – he's all mind, in a way. Don't get me wrong. I like mind. I like mind a lot.' She waggled her head and did a kind of grin that made her eyes pop. 'Mind, mind, mind. But you know, sometimes you need a rest from it. Phew.'

'Nelly Dean', which had been dormant for a while, resumed up above.

'So what's this one, all body?'

'Quite a lot. Not all body, obviously. But, you know. Substantial amount.'

'What does the mind one think about it? Does he know?'

'Oh yes.' Cherry sounded shocked at the suggestion he might not. 'They get on fine. The body one's pointing his wall. Dave.'

'Dave?'

'Is pointing his wall. The mind one's wall.'

'Perhaps he could have a look at my leak.'

'He only does it as a sort of hobby. He's in the Merchant Navy. He's between ships.'

'That sounds like a good way to fall in the water,' May said sourly. Surely it was time Cherry thought about growing up. She was not far off thirty.

I can talk, she suddenly remembered, I was thirty-four when Hub came along.

'What about you?' Cherry asked.

'Me?'

'What have you been up to? Was it a good council meeting?'

'It passed the time. I'd better see if I can settle Mother. I'll nip you home first.'

'I'm happy to walk.'

'It's still tipping it down. And you don't know who might be skulking about out there.' Like my mum, she thought, should she manage to climb out of her bedroom window before I arrive back, with a dagger in her teeth.

In bed May thought about Aunt Alice's fingers.

It had been a shock when she saw them last Sunday, on Alice's visit. Her fingers seemed to have shortened and gone knobby. Worst of all, the nails were ragged and unpainted.

Alice used to have lovely long narrow fingers, with long, properly manicured nails on the ends of them. In the days when she lived with her, May would wonder how she could do her seamstressing with nails like that. May had been a lodger with Aunty Alice and Uncle George all through the war years, after being offered a secretarial post at a little clothing factory out in Waveney Bridge. Her boss was an elderly man who still wore wing collars and insisted on referring to her as a typewriter, like they did in the old days. Mother had never forgiven her for leaving the nest, constantly writing postcards to inform her about jobs available in Costford or Manchester. At that time Alice herself worked at a clothing and haberdasher's shop. Her real trade was dressmaking, but there wasn't a lot of call for handmade ones during the war, so in those days she was mainly doing alterations, along with curtain-making and furniture upholstery.

In the mornings, when Alice had done all she had to do, which was a lot since she liked to get through her chores first thing, she'd fetch out her little bottle and brush and paint her nails bright pink, three quick strokes to each one. Then open the front door with just the pads of her fingers and flutter off for the bus, waving her nails in the breeze as she went. When she remembered it subsequently, May always had the same thought: anyone who can paint her nails like that can do anything. One thing she believed: being able covered big things and little. If you're good at being a surgeon, you'd probably be good at being a cleaner. And the other way around.

That was one of the reasons she was a Conservative. People were different from each other. And some of them were better than others. Better at being, when all was said and done, people. Alice could do you a dress without a pattern. Without even taking a measurement. Just one look at you from her sharp intelligent eyes, and she was off.

But there was another look too. Halfway through the manicuring she would glance up for a second, as if coming up for air, and catch your eye. And for an instant you could see something deep inside her. May had known that for years but never put her finger on it till now. It's because I've become acquainted with final things, May realised, with my mother going potty. That look, which used to come and go, had never left Alice's eyes during the Sunday visit.

It was horrible unhappiness. Or it was just a blank, a nothingness. The two things seemed the same. In the depths of her bed, May thought: that's why people are so unhappy in hell. There's nothing there. It isn't anywhere. There's no such place.

Alice's hell had been being married to Uncle George. It had been like keeping a complicated machine in working order – you had to constantly oil the moving parts and make sure the cogs clicked together. And when you'd got it going, what did it do but clank out of the house down to the betting shop to spend all the money. Or pub. She pictured him swaying from side to side as he waddled down the road, like the tin man in *The Wizard of Oz*, though in Uncle George's case he'd really lacked a heart. He'd got worse as the years went on, and it was a blessed relief for all concerned when he finally passed away.

But last Sunday Alice had brought a book with her, something she'd been working on for months. It was like a photo album, only with long descriptions round each picture. It was all about Alice's life in Waveney Bridge over the years.

May couldn't bear to watch her try to turn the pages with those stumpy fingers of hers. Or to see the spidery uneven writing where a few years ago there would have been the sort of copperplate you could eat your dinner off. Worst of all was the fact that fat ugly useless George seemed to be in pride of place, with a hanky knotted in each corner on his head, or holding a cat, or puffing his pipe, with that funny remote look dead people always achieve in photos, as if the sunlight shining on them comes from a different sun than yours.

May had wanted to say: But he's the one who spoiled it all, who held you back, he's the villain of the piece. He didn't even give you any children. Though God alone knew, he probably tried hard enough. He was just that type. The only thing he'd put his back into would be that and downing pints of beer. He'd even got his hands on May one day. He grabbed her breast and squeezed it till her eyes watered. 'It's just a bit of fun,' he kept repeating. What struck her, as she thought about it afterwards, was that most of the time she felt despondent because men showed no interest in her, but George's grab had made her feel even worse. The blind fierce way he did it made her remember the saying: all cats are grey in the dark. What a waste of Alice, May thought: George would have been happy to make do with any woman, so long as she wore a skirt. Even me. And now she's trying to resurrect him, make him a proper husband in memory.

As she neared sleep May thought of Alice's fingers as they used to be, not the hands or the rest of her, her fingers in the wind on their way to catch the bus. They were pink, with pinker tips, like interlaced twigs of cherry blossom.

It was not loud knocking, just one degree louder than sleep, so it took time to wake her. The sound found its way into a dream for a while, though she couldn't remember anything about it when she surfaced. Then she lay for a time with her eyes open, thinking of this and that, aware of the knocking in the background, like you are with the wireless sometimes when you're not listening to it.

Next she thought: Mother.

Then she realised she had got ahead of herself, and what she was hearing was a gentle tap-tap on the front door, a kind of knocking on tiptoes.

She went down on tiptoes herself, as much as she was able, didn't even turn on the light. Perhaps, she thought, if she didn't make anything of it, he wouldn't really be there. She didn't dare check whether her mother was in her room.

For a moment she gathered herself behind the door. At least I can give him his cape back, she thought. Then she pulled the lapels of her dressing-gown together with one hand and turned the knob with the other.

It wasn't the constable.

It was a man. A man at whatever-time-it-was in the dead of night. It was very dark, but there was faint light on his face from a street lamp, and she realised she knew him. Oh God, she thought, it's the one who gave me that look in court.

Even though the bench had found him not guilty she'd recognised a look when she saw one: there was unfinished business in his vicinity. Her heart thumped. Bentley, that had been his name, same as that youth who'd got himself hanged that time. Something, some strange name, then Bentley. Perhaps it was even *because* they'd found him not guilty that he'd put so much hatred into that stare. He'd interpreted their verdict as a sign of weakness, and like some predatory animal he was motivated to attack anything that seemed vulnerable.

She was just about to speak, or moan, or cry, she didn't know which – she was just about to *utter* – when he moved his face slightly and the arrangement of his features seemed to shift. It wasn't Bentley.

She did know him, however. But still, for a second, she didn't know who it was she knew.

Then she did. Trevor Morgan.

She hadn't recognised him because he had no reason being on her front step in the middle of the night. But perhaps she should have. The knock had been a politician's knock, exactly loud enough.

For a moment her heart still thumped, as if she'd forgotten certain facts, just as she'd pretended to in that story about going on a binge: how old she was, what she looked like; who she was, and always had been.

Her stupidity made her blush, but luckily those big red cheeks of hers would be lost in the dark.

'I nearly broke my neck,' whispered Trevor.

How funny, she thought, that he should come this time of night to tell me that. Then she remembered. 'Sorry,' she whispered back. 'It's my crazy-paving. It's a bit crazier than it's supposed to be.'

They stood in silence for a moment. 'I didn't realise you were so tall,' she told him, still in a whisper. It was those lofty town hall ceilings, they reduced everybody. Also, of course, he didn't have a tall way with him. He always gave the impression of being a handy-sized politician – by instinct no doubt, so as not to put people off. Only when it was called for did he loom. It was a talent, just like that overwhelming smile of his, the ability to acquire stature or shed it like a chameleon changing its colour. 'Come in,' she told him.

They stumbled together in the hall after the door was shut and the darkness was complete. Since that night in the tent May had guessed no man would ever desire her, but part of you lives in hope. That part cheered up for a second. Putting out your hands and encountering each other was like nothing so much as being at a teenage party. That saying came into her mind again: all cats are grey in the dark. But this time she thought, thank gawd for small mercies.

'Didn't want to disturb Mother,' she explained, still in hushed tones, 'with the light.'

'Heigh-ho,' he replied. It was a catchphrase he had, meaning yes. They were words that lent themselves to whispering.

She grabbed him by somewhere, probably a shoulder, and tugged him towards the lounge. She felt for the switch with her free hand and found it straight away. It had been there all her life, after all.

The second the light came on, he smiled, as if that was electric too.

Then he did something she'd never seen him do before. He vibrated his lips, like you do when you are going brrrr with cold and she realised he wasn't far from bursting into tears. Possibly he was in a state of shock.

'Tell you what,' she said, 'you sit down and I'll go and make us a nice cup of tea.' Then she scarpered as fast as her legs would carry her.

Fool, she thought as she did so, I should have given him a cuddle.

Of course, it would only have been like your mum doing it, or your aunty. But why not? Better than nothing. She might have been a mum or an aunty to him, but she wouldn't have been one to herself. It might have been a quite different cuddle on the inside. Another opportunity lost, she thought sadly.

But what on earth's amiss? she asked herself while she made tea in the kitchen. It can't just be that rising slab. Something had brought him along to her house in the first place, in a state of woe.

She thought back to the meeting. Nothing there to make a grown man blub. It was the usual old business of the flats at Prospect Hill. Work had already started, in fact. You could tell it had by the fact that there was talk of a strike. The workmen were agitating for 'dirty money', though goodness knows why. True, they had to dig four big holes, for the foundations of the four blocks, but that was their job, after all. There was nothing dirty about dirt, which she'd said, even getting a twitch of a smile from Ted. Nothing was going to stop the development at this stage. True, the government had still not rubber-stamped it, but what they *had* rubber-stamped was a plan by the Minister for Housing to demolish 1,796 houses in the borough in the next two years, a plan that was utterly dependent on the Prospect Hill development if it was to work.

She had tried to counter the argument Morgan had raised last time, and get rid of any after-effects of her unfortunate remark about amputation. 'What they'll be like,' she said, 'they will be like terraced streets on their hind legs.' Same values, same sense of community, only one on top of another instead of side by side. The modern way. Yanks been at it since goodness knows when. The whole point of being a Tory was to know when to adapt old ways to new. Nothing lonelier than living on a bleak modern estate if you were a one- or two-person household. Neither practical nor sociable, it would be like those little corrugated iron sties scattered over a field, one pig in each, each pig the same as the one before. Being up higher would help people think bigger, it stood to reason.

The reference to pigs was a bit of a chance, but it was her job not to be boring.

Trevor had presented the opposition case. Doing it on the cheap. People crammed together. The tide had turned against tower blocks. Architects fed up with them. Sociologists disapproved of them. Tenants complained about them. The general public felt dwarfed by them.

May, getting back on her feet: But it was your lot who put these plans forward in the first place. Labour councils have erected these erections all over the country.

It could have been better phrased but the important thing is to get up and at them while the whites of their eyes are still visible.

Trevor: That was then. And it's a question of the space available. Some of those Labour boroughs had more crowded conditions than here in Costford. Costford is hardly Manhattan Island.

May: Well, let's take the chance of becoming a little more *like* Manhattan Island, that's what I suggest.

All over, bar the shouting. They were only going through the motions in any case, being the development was on its way. All Trevor could come up with, after her riposte, was a warning that tall buildings were a hazard for aircraft, particularly as Prospect Hill was below the approach to Manchester Airport.

What's happening to Harold Wilson's technological revolution? May wondered, when my Labour colleague shies away from becoming like Manhattan Island, and then expresses doubts about the safety of air travel?

But none of this had been worth nearly crying about.

Three

For years, from the age of sixteen, Trevor Morgan had bought himself a paperback book every Friday lunchtime. It was a routine he decided on during his very first morning at the bank.

In he'd walked. His suit felt too big for him. He'd told Mum before leaving the house, and she'd done something quite funny, but typical. She'd come up right behind him, right right up, and then marched forwards, so with each swing of her arm his in-front arm swung too, with each step of her leg, his stepped as well. It was like being a robot. Left right left. 'Where we going, Mum?' he asked. She said nothing, just breathed in rhythm. Huff puff.

Through the sitting room. Across the hall. Turn right, on to the staircase. Up the stairs. 'Too risky, Mum!' he called out when they were a few steps up, because they were teetering. They had to be on the same step, or rather steps, as each other on the way up or their legs and arms would have stopped fitting, but there wasn't really room for their two feet at a time. He kept having the feeling they would fall backwards. 'We'll break our necks, I bet you.'

On to the landing. They were going to his bedroom.

Nope, sharp right turn. Into hers. Sharp left through the door. Up to the wardrobe. Stop. His legs felt shivery with the strain of not having known where on earth they were going.

Now his mum trotted round in front of him. She pointed at the wardrobe mirror. Then at him. She was acting as if she'd gone dumb. Also Chinese, the way she moved, with a big Chinese smile on her face. She trotted round him as if he was a tailor's dummy, twitching his suit then displaying her hand in the direction of the mirror, like a magician who's just performed a trick, putting her Chinese head on one side. He said that thing Japanese people are supposed to say, 'Ah, so.' It sounded a bit like arse hole.

The suit fitted. Perhaps it was the bank that was too big for him.

It had marble pillars and a gold ceiling, and a mezzanine floor with wrought iron railings to stop people falling off it, or throwing themselves over when their accounts went haywire, and a big staircase cascading down to the lobby. As Mr Thomas said, nothing but architecture from bottom to top. And, of course, he couldn't escape the feeling that he didn't deserve to be there.

Mum had never known. She had helped him with his application form, but he'd put that bit in afterwards, in the dead of night: pass in French.

He'd crept downstairs to the kitchen table to do it. He had English and maths but to get a proper traineeship they wanted a language as well. Mum thought they would overlook it when they met him in person. 'What use is French in a place like Costford?' she asked. 'I've lived here all my life and I've never met a French person yet. Best I can do is Mr Duxfield, who comes from Brighton.' Trevor wasn't so sure, not sharing his mother's confidence about what effect he might have on people he met. Anyway, he had a feeling he'd not get to meet them at all if he didn't fulfil their basic requirements. So he did his deed of darkness. They never checked.

Even many years later his mind would sometimes return to that fiddled application form. His career was like a house that had one tiny brick missing, somewhere in the foundations. But, he would think to himself, it's still standing. And anyway it's only an imaginary brick. The trouble was, it's one thing having an imaginary brick, quite another imagining one being missing.

Imagining *not* having an imaginary brick. Sometimes, almost feverishly, he would think: but that's a good thing, isn't it? It's *all* just imagination. Nobody else in the world knows my French was a fib. If nobody knows about it, doesn't it become the truth? Or same as? Anyway, once I was in the bank I did just as well as all the others who passed their French. Better. And for all he knew the others had lied about French as well. Or maths, or English. People are always lying about something. Mum was right about one thing. You didn't need to speak French in a bank in Costford.

The immediate effect of forging his pass in French was to make his suit sleeves feel too long, as if they slid ape-like over his hands, though when he looked they ended only a fraction past his wrists, which was fair enough.

That first morning he was shown around by Mr Thomas. Mr Thomas was middle-aged, with a harelip that seemed to cause him to talk in a dry, witty way, as if each word was valuable. After he died, Trevor remembered him as having grey skin and more particularly, a grey tongue, flicking over his lips like a lizard's. Funny thing was, he liked him being grey. It went with his grey suit and grey hair.

Mr Thomas had a desk in the floor space behind the tellers, and Trevor was given a second chair at it. The next desk along belonged to a big bloke called Mr Cartwright. He was big but not quite big enough. By an odd coincidence his suit really was too large. It was one of those double-breasted ones, and sagged off him. The trousers had been built for someone with a huge horse's groin, so that they hung in a large flap between his legs when he stood up, which he did to shake hands gravely with Trevor. His round face with slightly goofy front teeth made him look as if he was laughing at himself all the time, and he wore thick glasses. Almost the first thing he'd said was, 'The big drawback is, I've recently had a colostomy, you know.'

'Oh,' Trevor said. He didn't dare ask what it was. 'Drawback to what?' he said instead.

Mr Cartwright looked a bit taken aback. 'Life, that's what. The whole kit and caboodle.'

'Ah.' Trevor grimaced as sympathetically as he could. 'Sorry.'

'As a whole.'

'Oh.'

'It puts you off your stride, that's the main problem. You do know what it is, don't you?'

It was too late to admit it now. 'I've a fair idea.'

'Bloody bag, that's what it is.' His forlorn expression, in conjunction with his goofy teeth, made him look as if he wanted Trevor to laugh, but luckily Trevor didn't.

Back at the desk, Mr Thomas explained in a low voice: 'It's what happens when your bottom goes out of action for good. You know: bum. Gives up the ghost, type of thing.'

'Blimey.'

'They have to reroute through the front. Make an outlet.' He nodded his grey face which almost seemed to have a slight smile on it, but that could have been the effect of his harelip. 'He's a lovely lad all the same,' he added.

Suddenly Trevor had a passionate desire to please Mr Thomas, and Mr Cartwight for that matter. This was a world where there were middle-aged people working the same as you, calling each other lad; where someone could tell you about his colostomy bag. He wondered how many of the teachers at school had worn them.

He had been in limbo all his life and was now in the real world. People going past you in the street – perhaps a lot of them had bags, but you would never know. Working in the bank they told you, the men anyway.

Main thing was, Trevor wanted to please them, be one of them. He felt a sharp need to qualify in some way, make up for that pretence about French. I know what I'll do, he thought, I'll buy a book every week. He'd never been interested in reading before.

Friday lunchtime turned out to be the ideal opportunity for it.

Every other day the staff had their food together in a little room on the first floor. It had a gas ring in it, and Miss Waite, the senior teller, would heat up her lunch in a little saucepan that she kept there. The others brought sandwiches. Miss Cottrell, who was a timid little clerk of about twenty, and who funnily enough had a harelip just like Mr Thomas, ate the smallest sandwiches Trevor had ever seen, paste ones always, two quarter rounds, adding up to a slice of sliced bread in all, with the crusts cut off. Even a person with a small mouth could eat them in a single bite, but she took tiny nibbles, holding each sandwich to her lips in her two paws like a hamster, and made them last as long as the others did theirs.

But on Fridays it was a tradition that Mr Thomas and Mr Cartwright went out to a fish and chip restaurant together, and to his joy Trevor was invited to come along too. He sometimes had fish and chips with his mother, but what they served you in the café seemed different, bigger and more golden. He told Mum: 'I think it must be whale.' He had peas too, which he never did when they had fish and chips at home, and a cup of tea.

What Mr Thomas and Mr Cartwright always did after their Friday lunch was go to Woolworth's and look at tools and electrical fittings. That's when Trevor went to W.H. Smith's and bought his book, which he would set himself to read by the end of the following Thursday. Fat ones meant he had to get a long way through by the end of the weekend. He read lots of novels. Despite the difficulty of finishing them in time, he liked books you could weigh by the pound, such as *The Grapes of Wrath* and *The Herries Chronicle*. After a while he started buying history books too.

This was how he got to know Christine. She worked at Smith's, and after a few Fridays she spoke to him: 'You buy a lot of books.'

He hadn't thought about her except as someone to pay, and when she spoke it came as a shock. But then he thought, Oh, *right*, like you do when the penny drops. A couple of weeks later he asked her out. He just did what he'd heard people do, said, 'I wonder if you'd like to go to the pictures?' and she said, 'Yes.' If I'd realised it was this easy, he thought, I'd have done it sooner, though the opportunity had never arisen before.

It was only when he'd left the shop that he had an attack of nerves. He felt himself shaking, even though it was a warm day. He began wondering what she looked like. I saw her about twenty seconds ago, he thought, but I can't remember her at all. They'd arranged to meet outside the cinema, and his stomach churned as it occurred to him he might not be able to recognise her. What shape face has she got, he asked himself. Round? No, that was fat people. She wasn't fat, she was ordinary sized. Oval. Trouble was, everybody in the world, who wasn't fat, had an oval face. He tried to remember the bits of her one by one. Ears. Nose. Eyes. Mouth. It was no good. It was like trying to draw a face when you can't draw, which was what he couldn't do either. Body. She wasn't tall, that was all he was sure of. When she stood behind the till you could only see the till, which of course made it even harder to picture her.

Body. He remembered something one of the teachers at school had said, when showing them how to fill in forms for jobs. Name: John Brown. Age: sixteen. Sex: Yes please. On that note he tried to picture her bust. No luck. You probably couldn't get much idea anyhow, with her clothes and uniform and stuff. He wondered if she wore a uniform, but couldn't even remember that.

One thing, he realised, she would have a bust of *some* kind, whether or not. That thought was impossibly sweet. It seemed too much to expect from life: going to the pictures with a girl, the girl having a bust in her own right. It seemed such a valuable thing. He felt almost jealous, to think girls were entrusted with them.

Perhaps he ought to turn and go back into the shop. Tell her that he'd just remembered something he wanted to say, give himself another chance to get her fixed in his mind. He imagined standing there trying to take her in. It would be like just before French O level, when he had a bit of paper with tenses written down on them, which he was forlornly trying to memorise as they stood outside the exam room. But he would have to say something. What? He imagined thinking of a good excuse, going in, then before he could trot it out, accidentally saying, 'I just came back because I wanted to commit your bust to memory.' Her eyes, whatever sort of eyes they were, opening wide with surprise. Her mouth, whatever mouth it was, going white with anger or disgust. Anyway he'd be late back at the bank if he didn't go straight there now.

That evening he told Mum he was going to the pictures the day after tomorrow.

'What're you seeing?' she asked.

'*Witness for the Prosecution.*'

'Oh, I'll come with you,' she said. 'I like the sound of that one.'

They did sometimes go to the pictures together, always had since Trevor was small. In recent times he felt a bit ashamed of standing in the queue with her and would try to look as if he just happened to be positioned behind this person who was a perfect stranger, but she would spoil it by talking to him. He'd answer in monosyllables, out of the corner of his mouth, and once she noticed and said, 'Why are you talking in that funny way, Trevor? You look like an ostrich that's swallowed a tin can.'

He felt like one now. 'No. I'm. Going,' he said. He shrugged his shoulders.

'What did you say? Oh, I see. Oh, my goodness. Do you mean – you're going with a girl?'

He nodded. His eyes were as wide as they could possibly be, so as not to miss any of her response, but it was his ears he made use of first. She made one of those funny giggles down her nose, the sort that seem to rattle inside your nostrils so they sound nearly like a snore, and waved her hands as if she'd burned them. Then she patted the air as if she was patting a real live girl into place just there. 'Ooh,' she said, 'I think she's a beauty.'

'I can't remember what she looks like at all,' he told her. 'Off hand.'

She clapped her hand over her mouth and burst into laughter. He laughed too, but his face felt as if it had been boiled.

After the pictures they went to a milk bar. He'd never been in one before. It was such a white place: white walls, white milk in a sort of aquarium on the counter, a white tinge to the air. He had coffee and she had a milk shake. She had a Wagon Wheel too. He would never have ordered one for himself but he didn't mind buying it for her. She had insisted they go halves at the pictures, because she was earning too.

She took off the paper and held it in front of her face for a moment. It was so big it made her look as if she had a blank brown disc for a head. While she was eating it he wondered why he wouldn't have dared eat one. He used to have one after swimming with his mum at Redford Baths, so probably he thought of them as childish. Sure enough, although Christine seemed a quiet, serious type of person, she said 'Yum yum,' in a little-girlish voice just before she took her first bite. You were allowed to be childish sometimes, that was the point. You couldn't talk about people's colostomies the whole time.

'Want a bite?' she asked.

'No, it's OK,' he replied, wishing even as he said it that he could bring himself to say yes. An idea crossed his mind: taking a bite of a girl's Wagon Wheel would be like having a kiss in biscuit form. He despised himself for being chicken but at the same time he thought: perhaps the sort of person I am, I stand on the sidelines and have ideas about life. A kiss in biscuit form: he couldn't have worked that out if he'd actually had a bite. Then he remembered that what he was supposed to be doing was memorising what Christine looked like. It had been all right meeting outside the pictures because she'd recognised him the moment he caught sight of her. In fact she hadn't given him time to tell whether he was recognising *her* or not. Perhaps he was just seeing himself reflected in her eyes. There's still work to do on this subject, he told himself. In the cinema he had stolen glances at her, but the dim film light left her face a blur. Once she noticed he was looking at her and not the screen, and had leaned over and whispered 'Silly.' Quickly he switched his head back to the Old Bailey, with Charles Laughton looking like a crafty white blancmange.

Now he looked again. Her glass was at her lips so only the top of her nose and her eyes showed. Her eyes looked straight back, and seemed to hold his fixed, as if she was a hypnotist. He smiled at her to try and break the trance. The glass left the bottom half of her face. Then her head rose, and approached him across the table, almost as if it wasn't attached to the rest of her, like a balloon. As it grew near he saw she had a little white moustache from the shake. At the last moment her face tilted so that their noses didn't collide, and then her lips touched his. They tasted of ice-cream and lipstick.

Even as he sat there, heart pounding, while she finished off her shake, he thought to himself: she really is difficult to fix in the memory. Her face is just there, less than two feet from mine. We've just kissed. But if she suddenly vanished from the face of the earth would I be able to get her back again, in my mind? It was exactly the same problem he'd had with those French words.

'*Bonjour Tristesse*,' he said.

'I beg your pardon,' May asked, looking up from pouring the tea.

'Book I read years ago. In translation, of course. I ate books in those days.'

'I suppose that's why you're so thin. Nearest I got was the grapefruit diet. Fat lot of good it did me.' She shook her head so sharply that her hand, pouring the tea, shook too in miniature.

Trevor remembered a thing his mum had given him when he was small, zigzag wooden struts with a pencil at each end. You drew with one and the other pencil copied it, bigger or smaller according to how you concertinaed the zigzags.

'Hello sadness. That's the title.'

'Just as well. I thought for a moment we had a stranger come in.'

'It is a stranger to me. Or was. Before Mum died, anyway.'

'My mother will live for ever.'

'Love her!' he suddenly said, his voice hard in the middle and trembly with stupid emotions all round the outside. 'While you can,' he finished feebly.

May gave him a stern look and shoved a cup in his direction. 'Hilda? Love Hilda? Easier said than done, I'm sorry to say,' she told him.

He took the cup. There was something so – what word? large about May. Fat, even.

When he was eleven years old his feet had suddenly bolted. 'What's going on?' his mum said. 'You're about four feet tall, with size nine feet.' Her comment had come out of the blue and it gave him a shock, so much so he sobbed outright. He had a sudden terrible fear it might be fatal, his feet feeding off the rest of him like a pair of enormous leeches.

Mum had clasped him to her bosom. Had to kneel down to do it. 'Now, mardy pants, don't worry yourself. The rest of you will catch up. And in the meantime . . .' – she pulled her face away from his and gave him a cunning look – 'just think, nobody will be able to push you over, no matter how hard they push.'

May was unpushoverable in a completely different way, like a sideboard is; no, like a bed, a bed where you want to crawl in and sleep. All at once he felt ill with tiredness.

'I'm so sorry,' he said. 'I've no business, poking.'

'Oh well, we all poke a bit, in our trade.'

'But that's not. What I came about.'

'You're not worried about those flats, surely? They were always going ahead, whether or no.'

'No, of course not.'

'It's only the usual rough and tumble.'

'May, I can rough and tumble with the rest of them. In fact it's going sweet as a nut. I meant to tell you earlier, before Bert butted his way in, they've asked me to put my name forward as the Labour parliamentary candidate. You know Jock Granby's resigning his seat?'

'The way I see it, his seat's being pulled out from under him.' May seemed to relax, basking in the prospect like a frog on a lily pad. 'Tell you another thing.' Her expression changed and she pursed her lips. Trevor noticed she had a ginger moustache: it brought to mind the milky one on Christine's lip those years ago. One piece of the jigsaw, he thought. No it wasn't. All he was remembering was a moustache Christine didn't have. It was May who had the moustache. 'It may be a poisoned chalice.'

'Oh, come on. Don't tell me you're jealous?'

'I'm too long in the tooth for that game anyhow. But you've got to remember, when Jock first won the seat Costford was Labour. Now us Tories are ahead of you lot in the council. It'll be touch and go. That's why they're weeding Jock out. People don't go for his type any more, hopping from one whisky to the next. Remember what happened at the Town Hall Christmas do last, when Jock got so pie-eyed he tried to dance with the Bishop of Manchester? From behind, the cassock looked like a frock, so he said. Final nail in his coffin. It doesn't bear thinking of, if the Pope would ever visit.' She laughed silently at the thought, shook her head, and raised her cup to her mouth while it was still laughing.

'I don't have that problem, at least.'

'What you'll need to do: hide behind that smile of yours all the way to Westminster.'

'I'm not in much of a smiley mood, to be honest with you.' Though it was funny how you could forget for a while. The day he buried his mum he'd nearly burst into laughter while the service was going on, when a funny thought struck him.

'What is it, Trevor?'

By the power of suggestion he could feel his mouth grinning, like dead bodies do. 'She's leaving me.'

There was a long silence. Finally he managed to look up at May. Her face was blank, as though waterproofed against what he'd told her.

Then she said: 'She's leaving you.'

He nodded.

'Good heavens.'

He almost wanted to argue, to say, well, why not, she's got a right to if she wants. Instead he just said yes and shut his eyes tightly. He wasn't quite sure if he was trying to rein tears back or to squeeze a couple out. He felt as if he was acting even though he was completely sincere.

'Another man?'

'I think so.' He knew so, but it seemed harsh to say it outright. He'd spent so many years being on Christine's side that he felt a stupid desire to defend her against May's disapproval.

For her part, Christine had been quite direct with him.

He'd arrived home after the planning meeting, let himself in and gone into the lounge, where he could hear music playing. She was sitting on the settee, feet tucked under her. She seemed relaxed. She looked up at him with a slight smile on her face, a sad one, he realised afterwards. She was sweet and soft.

'Hello, Trevor.'

'Hello. Do you want a cup of tea?'

'No. I want to tell you something.'

'Oh? Has something happened?'

'No. But something's going to happen.'

He felt his heart leap. What he thought it was, was what he wanted, had for years. And the timing was perfect. He would be able to let it slip out at the constituency selection meeting. But of course, that's not the point. It really isn't the point. It's just a happy coincidence. It's an extra. But why not enjoy an extra as well, if it comes running up and waves its arms at you?

'Chris, I'm so –'

'No, Trevor, hear me out. You do all the talking in this household and it's my turn for a change. Trevor, I'm very very sorry, but I'm going to leave you. There's no point in arguing about it. There's someone else. Another person has –' For the first time she was stuck for a word. 'Impinged,' she said eventually, and shrugged her shoulders, as much as to say, you know what I'm getting at.

'Is that what you call it?' he said glumly.

'There's no need to try to be clever. You're not at the council now.'

'I'm sorry.' My God, the selection. What chance would he have if his wife had run off? He could lose the lot: career plans; home life. The whole house, with its missing brick, would come tumbling down around his ears, in punishment for fiddling his French, all those years ago.

Poor Mum, he thought.

She wouldn't have wanted to see his marriage break up. Perhaps, perhaps, she hadn't really liked Christine, in her heart of hearts. He got the impression she was disappointed that Christine wasn't wilder, though if she had been she would perhaps have regretted that as well. Anyway, Christine had proved fairly wild after all, for what that was worth. But what Trevor didn't like was the idea that he was moving on without Mum knowing, going into a different stage of his history. The fact that it was for the worse was neither here nor there. He imagined Mum walking along a street, poor ghost, looking for their home and finding no door to knock at.

'There it is,' Christine said.

'Heigh-ho,' he said bleakly.

'I wish you would remember you are not a bloody donkey.'

'You make me feel like one.'

'Oh Trevor, there's no need.' She got to her feet, stepped up to him, ran a hand through his hair. 'It's been good, I promise you it has. It's just that it's . . . stopped. It's come to an end.'

'I didn't think it would ever come to an end,' he said quietly. When a very large thing happens it proves to have all sorts of angles and aspects: that was what his brain was coping with. Why had she thought it necessary to tell him it had been good? Because all those hours, days, weeks, all that life, had gone nowhere. You couldn't put it into a glass case in a museum and walk up to it and say, 'That was good, that was. A lovely object.' It was not good, it was gone. It hadn't amounted to anything. It had been a waste of time. All that time.

'Is he . . . ?'

'I don't know. We haven't gone to bed yet. I'm sorry if that disappoints you.'

He stared at her, to see if she was being sarcastic. But no, she looked genuinely apologetic. What a fool he'd been! He'd pushed her towards this. There was no denying it. It was his fault.

He continued to stare at her, appalled. He'd only been going to say handsome, or nice, something of that sort. She'd imagined he was making reference to what was inside the bloke's trousers. He'd thought it was something you could be drily adult about, the way Mr Thomas had been adult about Mr Cartwright's colostomy. The possibility of sharp, imagined detail had never crossed his mind.

'I couldn't be unfaithful to you, Trevor. Pathetic, isn't it?'

'How can you say that when –'

'I mean sleep with somebody behind your back.'

'I don't want you to sleep with anyone in front of my front, either. I don't want you to sleep with anyone at all.' He lowered his head and spoke in a croaky voice. 'Except me.' What a complete weed I am, he thought.

'Well, I'm sorry about that. It's not how you felt before.'

He needed to commit her to memory. A waste of time was

one thing but if he couldn't picture her in his mind's eye at all it would never have happened in the first place. Their life together would have left no footprints behind. The nearest he would ever be able to get to proof would be knowing what ice-cream and lipstick tasted like, together.

She backed off to the settee and sat down again. Even while he looked at her he couldn't remember her. It was as if he had to see her each second for the first time. He wished he had one of those zigzag things of long ago, fitted up to his inner and outer eye, so that as the one took in her features, the other could draw them in miniature on the inside of his head.

'She's a silly girl,' May said.

'Oh no she's not.' What was he doing telling May in the first place? She was his political opponent, could make hay with this. Not that she would. That was the point: she was on his side. But he didn't want her to be on his side if that meant being hostile to Christine. He wasn't ready for that. He cast about in his mind for something to say by way of riposte. She's book manager at Smith's. She uses the word impinge.

'I mean she's silly to leave you, if that's what she's doing. Sensible to marry you. Silly to leave. That's all. My guess is, she'll come to her senses.'

She was talking as if it was after all a dry, adult business. It probably was for her, living as she must in a dry, adult world. She could probably discuss colostomies, mastectomies, adulteries, without batting an eyelid.

'No she won't. I know her. I can tell.'

'Don't be too sure.'

'She won't.'

'All right then, she won't.'

'What am I to do?'

'Say nothing to the selection committee. Tell them it's all hunky-dory. Ask Christine to play the game until then. Thing about politics, you have to learn to take one thing at a time.'

'I suppose so.'

'Take my word for it. Oh botheration.'

'Nelly Dean', in a thin but carrying voice, had started up again.

Four

The culprit was Art Whiteside, estate agent. Not good news.

'I suppose everybody knows,' Trevor said glumly.

They were sitting in the headmaster's office in Broad Green Primary. The whole school smelled of wee, this office included. Did not one of the little tykes ever get to those miniature loos on time? May wondered. She'd had to use them herself when the other governors were taking up all the staff facilities, holding her posterior above the target like some sort of Lancaster bomber, but they had no excuse with their short legs and tiny rear ends.

It was so strange about Trevor. She had never met anyone else with his promise of going the distance, yet he seemed to have no grasp of day-to-day politics whatsoever. As if he was immune, above it all almost.

'That doesn't matter. It's not what you do. Or are done unto. It's –' She remembered Cherry telling her something that her young man Ben, the mind one as she called him, had told her, about the fact that we go through life surrounded by colours we can't see and noises that we can't hear, because they're beyond our range. We do our business in the middle of a sort of jungle. It had impressed Cherry no end, though not enough to prevent her from needing to supplement mind in due course with body, so-called. Perhaps she felt the need of some jungle she could see. 'You do things by the book, and let the rest go hang. It's – it's protocol, that's what it is. There's a lot to be said for protocol.'

'Then they *know* you are a hypocrite.'

She tried to find a way of saying it. You have your cup of tea, like they do in Crumpsall's, with the waitresses in their black frocks and frilly aprons, and for all you know there's bedlam swirling all round you: according to Ben, anyway. But it doesn't matter. There's a gap between you and it. You're having your cup of tea by the book. It's not hypocrisy, it's playing the game.

'Anyhow, you've got nothing to be ashamed of,' was all she said in the end. He was right of course. In politics everybody always knows everything, except perhaps for Trevor Morgan himself, the man destined for the top. And above all, in politics you take the blame not for bad behaviour but for bad luck. It had to be that way or everything would grind to a halt, men in particular being what they were. When she thought of the womanising ones she knew they seemed like a herd: Art Whiteside, Ted Wilcox, Uncle George, not of course that Uncle George had been a politician – he'd found it enough of a strain just walking on two legs. But men being men, protocol had to be what it was. A veil was drawn.

But in this case, where it was a wife who'd gone off the rails, Trevor could very well find himself penalised for not keeping his house in order.

The headmaster, Mr Lowe, came in. He was a young man who drove a motorbike, but too chubby to be a descendant of her long-ago steeplejack. May began to argue with Trevor about council support for another school in the borough, Costford Grammar, which was direct grant. That wasn't hypocrisy either, even though it was for Mr Lowe's benefit. They took opposite sides on the subject, and it was their job to argue. Mr Lowe gave them a disapproving look and shoved a couple of cups of tea at them.

'We'll be on the go in ten minutes,' he said.

'Bang on,' May told him cheerily. Trevor just turned on that smile of his.

'Well, I'll leave you to it, in the meantime,' Mr Lowe said, losing confidence, and went off.

'How do things stand, then?' May asked.

'What things?'

'What things do you think?'

'I thought you might be talking about Costford Grammar.'

'My dear boy.'

'Much the same, I suppose you could say.' He lifted up his cup, and drank. 'She's still at home. She won't leave me till it's official.'

'How're you going to make it official, then?' It sounded as if they had some sort of equivalent of an engagement party in mind. 'Surely she doesn't expect . . .'

'No no, she's ready to be the guilty party. She just doesn't want to, you know, *do* anything, do anything drastic until we all know where we stand.'

'That's what I was getting at, protocol.'

'Which bit's the protocol? Her not . . . ? Or her being willing to say she did?'

'Both of them. It's all protocol. What I was saying. As far as the horizon.'

'I think that's called being a Tory,' he said, and smiled again.

It really did warm the room. It made everything seem important and unimportant at the same time. Bugger protocol, she thought. Bugger being a Tory, for that matter. When you looked at Trevor in a certain light he was unstoppable. He had to be. 'Did *you* know about Art Whiteside?' she asked.

He hadn't. He really hadn't. It was like money in the bank, the way he could not know what everybody knew. Who everybody knew. Leave it to his wife to be acquainted with Arthur Whiteside. She was just a member of the human race, like the rest of us.

'She's been learning golf,' Trevor said. 'She met him through that.'

'You're the one who should be playing golf.'

'Haven't got the patience.'

'It can stand you in good stead, golf. It didn't do President Eisenhower any harm.'

'Oh well. I'll make do without. It's not very socialist, in any case.'

'Harold Wilson plays it.'

'Good luck to him. Football's more my game. Specially as things have turned out.' His face fell. 'Art Whiteside gave her lessons, as I understand.'

Taught her her swing, without a doubt. It must be a very cuddly technique to pass on, the swing. Like teaching the serve in tennis. If women ever started to learn to play cricket there'd no doubt be some fellow in a bristly moustache all ready to help them with the bat.

May had seen Art Whiteside swing, and sure enough he was good at it, to her untutored eye at least. It was a site meeting of the planning committee when the golf club wanted to extend its clubhouse. Art was fussing over certain councillors like a fly on a cow pat, and was part of a golfing demonstration on the first hole. There was a deal of yabber about free trial memberships and whatnot, next best thing to bribery as far as she was concerned, but it wouldn't be sporty to mention such a possibility.

Art stood there on the first hole, one eye screwed up, the other like a marble, glaring at the ball on its little cup. Then he raised his club, his big eye and little eye still fixed on the ball. He remained like that for a long moment, then with a rush of wind he swung. He stood without moving while a perfect circle made of blurred club and arms appeared alongside him. There was a sound like a pistol shot and the ball had vanished goodness knew where. He shut his eyes as if he needed to rest them after all that staring, and smiled.

It was impressive in its way, or would be for a young fool like Christine, anyhow. The club got its clubhouse, needless to say.

'Have you seen his leaflets?' she asked Trevor.

'His what?'

'You know, where he advertises houses for sale. He goes in for funny ones. He says, this is a charming little house, well you bet it is, you didn't expect it to be a bunch of flowers, did you? –

I'm not a florist. That type of malarky. Being that the firm's called Penrose. With a rose on their sign.'

'Oh well, I suppose he prospers.'

'He prospers all right, but that's not the reason.'

Mr Lowe came in, and summoned them in to the governors' board.

It was planning review a couple of days after the meeting at Broad Green Primary, not an official session, just an informal one to arrange the order of business, check out what was in the offing, arrange site visits and the like. May had a word after with Joss Carpenter, who had been on the committee since the year dot and who knew everything there was to know. He had a big round head like a melon, and tonight it looked oddly pale.

'You all right, Joss?'

He looked up at her. 'Just the ticket,' he said, his voice faltering.

'What's up with your ticker, then?'

'No, ticket. Just the ticket.' His voice tailed off again, and he repeated, 'Et.'

'I heard. But you don't look it. Something the matter?'

He shrugged. 'Your mum all right?'

'You won't get away with it that easy. My mother's completely cuckoo, for what it's worth.'

'Oh May,' he said. Poor chap, he had such a big face to look sad with, an upside-down smile like a clown. 'I've got trouble with my waterworks.'

'That's only to be expected, in a man of your age.'

'Do you think? I'm telling you, it's given me the willies.'

She gave him a look, just in case a sense of humour was at work, but not a hope. There wasn't a spark at the best of times in that head of his. 'Hub was a martyr to it, and look at him.'

He looked at her like a rabbit caught in headlights. 'But Hub died,' he said in a sad little voice.

'Oh yes, I suppose he did. But that wasn't his waterworks. It was his ticker, matter of fact.' Joss's face went blank as a search-light as he tried to take that in. 'In my experience the heart and waterworks are not connected, more's the pity.' Might as well be good old May while I'm about it, she thought.

Joss went so far as to turn his smile the right way up, and nodded wonderingly. 'I suppose not.'

'I wanted a word in your ear,' she went on.

'Oh yes?'

She mimed the words: 'About Art Whiteside.'

Straight away he regained his interest in life. That was what she was trying to explain to Trevor before the governors' board the other day, on the subject of protocol and playing the game. This wasn't an affectation but the stuff of life. A man could be worrying himself silly about his waterworks, but if he's a politician at all you only had to address the right question to him and he entered another realm altogether. Her own grandmother had tried to explain the secret of onion gravy while she was on her deathbed. Nothing hypocritical about that, it was playing along with the rules you had gone by, the priorities you had learned. That was the trouble with Mother. She had surrendered entirely to wispiness, like the girl in Shakespeare who floated off. Had become light and flighty, lacking something solid to hold on to.

'Art, eh?' His little yellowing eyes looked shrewdly into the middle distance.

'Whether he's got a finger in a particular pie.'

'Question is, whether there's a pie he *hasn't* got a finger in.'

'I was wondering about the proposed council flats, the ones we're going to build on Prospect Hill.'

'Funny you should mention that. I did hear he had acquired some of the land up there, in the course of business like, a few months before the go-ahead. The original go-ahead, I mean. Bit of a nowhere place I thought at the time, but of course that was before it got earmarked.'

'I don't suppose nowhere cost him much by the acre.'

'I don't suppose it did.'

'And he hasn't been lurking around? With his hand out for his money?'

'There are one or two speculators and contractors getting very restive about that. Several people have got their fingers burned, one in particular. I won't tell you his name, but if you should happen to say Norman Forrester it wouldn't be far off the mark. I expect you noticed how he was bending Ted Wilcox's ear a week or two back. I'm sure Art'll be glad when it's all over OK, howsomever he's a shrewd enough fellow, and I'll bet he's a man to keep his investments well spread out. I haven't seen him socially since that golfing do.' His face clouded. 'I took out one of those free trials but I haven't had the chance to make use. What with one thing and another.'

She left him as glum as she found him, not wanting the mither of trying to snap him out of it all over again. Golf wasn't a good game for a chap with a jumpy bladder, unless he was willing to piddle behind a nearby tree. But what he'd given her was food for thought, and no mistake.

When she got home Cherry had her body chap with her, Dave by name. May had told her she could entertain while babysitting her nan. It was a thankless enough chore and the girl had her own life to live.

It was the first time she, May, had met him. He seemed friendly enough, though the word body might have been a bit of an exaggeration. He was a dark-haired, dark-complexioned chap, with a big-featured face. His forehead was low enough to stop you being in danger of mistaking him for the mind one.

'I had a look at that bit of damp you've got, Mrs Rollins,' he said, 'on your bedroom ceiling.'

'Miss.'

'Miss.'

'Stage name. I used to be Mrs Hammond when my husband was alive. Cherry's dad.'

'Oh, right.'

'Funny you should mention my damp. I was just thinking about it. Got let down by a colleague of mine, who turns out to have too many fish to fry.'

'I can come round some time and sort it out. Won't take two ticks.'

'That's very kind of you. You'll have to let me make it worth your while.'

'No, it's OK, promise.'

I suppose you'll be reimbursed in favours from my stepdaughter, she thought. A funny kind of transaction, but no worse than happens in politics.

After they'd gone she thought about the possibility Joss had opened up. One of the things you had to watch was being too clever by half. Over the last months Trevor had established himself as the leading opponent of the flats scheme. He had a wife who'd got restless at home all those evenings when her husband was at council meetings. Art Whiteside had wanted the scheme to go through in order to realise his investment. He had a proud record as a lady-killer. He could have lured Christine off the straight and narrow so as to put himself in a bargaining position *vis-à-vis* Trevor.

No, too neat and pat. It relied on too many things falling into place. Also the deal wouldn't be important enough to Art to entail so much strategy. It would be just one of a number of pies at any given moment. He could hardly slap and tickle his way through each and all of them.

Unlike me, she thought, who donates my late husband's daughter's body in exchange for getting a damp patch in my ceiling fixed.

But whether or not, it was food for thought.

She went into the hall and dialled Trevor's number.

The phone rang. It was quite late, and would have given Christine a start if she hadn't felt so numb. Perhaps it's Art, she thought, ringing to wish me goodnight, but she knew it wasn't. He was not that type of a man. Not at all sentimental: too grown-up, somehow. She watched her hand grasping the phone. It reminded her of manoeuvring those cranes you get in amusement arcades, trying to make the claws pick up a present.

'Hello. Can I speak to Trevor, please?'

That May woman, who never seemed to leave Trevor alone, despite being a Tory. You could almost imagine her being sweet on him, except she was so old and such a battleaxe. 'He's out, at a meeting.'

'Please could you ask him to get in touch with me.'

'Yes, of course.'

Christine put the phone down. The old girl sounded very cold and disapproving. Let her. Let them all be. Even her mum and dad had gone cold and disapproving. Her dad had looked up from his chair and said, 'I don't understand what's got into you, our Christine.' He didn't take his pipe out of his mouth while he spoke.

'I see you don't want to miss a puff of your blimming tobacco,' she told him, suddenly reckless.

He went red. 'Thank you very much, young lady,' he said, and sure enough puffed. It was one of those horrible gurgly ones too. She almost laughed but didn't dare, partly because it would be so rude, and partly because she was frightened she would burst into tears. Several times since this business with Arty started she had intended to laugh and had sobbed instead, as if the buttons for laugh and cry were next to each other like letters on a typewriter keyboard, and you could easily press the wrong one.

Her mum said: 'Give me a hand in the kitchen, love.'

In the kitchen, Christine said, 'Oh Daddy, Daddy!'

'What about him?' her mother asked.

How could she say it? The way he sat in his comfy worn-out armchair, wearing his comfy worn-out slippers, smoking his comfy worn-out pipe, thinking thoughts in his comfy worn-out brain. She just shrugged.

Her mother whispered, 'Has Trevor been . . . you know?'

'I know what?' she replied, deliberately obtuse. 'What do I know?'

'You know. Playing about. I suppose in politics you can have your pick.'

'He's a local councillor, Mum, not the Prime Minister of England.'

'There are plenty in these parts ripe and ready, let me tell you.'

'Well, that includes me. It's me who's been ripe and ready. I've been the one trotting about all *ripe*, as you call it.'

'Keep your voice down, my girl. Your dad'll have a fit.'

Christine pictured him rolling about on the carpet, having his fit, while the puffs rose in steady sequence like Indian smoke signals. She felt near hysterics.

'I don't know what's got into you, Christine. You were always straight as a die.'

That was the whole trouble.

It had come out of nothing, in that horrible period after Trevor's mother died. All Christine was trying to do was cheer him up.

'You've still got me,' she said.

'I know.'

He was abstracted and she wanted to jerk him out of his abstraction. 'All of me. That's what you've got. All. Of. Me.' You couldn't ever have said that about your mother, was what she was thinking: not *all* in that sense of the word.

He nodded.

'Just think,' she went on, determined to get his attention. 'I've never been to bed with anybody else.'

'I wouldn't have minded if you had,' he replied, still looking miles away. He said it in a funny monotonous hollow-sounding voice, very unlike his usual expressive one.

She was dumbstruck. She felt her mouth open and close like a fish's. She looked at their chrome and corduroy Habitat furniture and wondered if it would date. All sorts of thoughts flooded through her head. I've been swindled: I could have sowed my wild oats and didn't. It was as if *he'd* been unfaithful to *her*. She was sure he had never been with another woman, and yet he could say such a thing. She felt her whole being had been contradicted in some way. Her marriage must have been a sham all along, even while she'd been under the impression everything was going swimmingly. Only the problem in their particular case had been *lack* of other men, the absence of affairs, not the presence of them, a kind of inside-out sham.

She asked him about it later, when he seemed more himself.

'You know what you said?'

'About what?'

'About not minding if I'd been to bed with somebody else.'

'Oh that.' He suddenly seemed to snap to attention. 'Why, have you?'

Again, she felt the breath leave her body. He was giving her a hopeful look. 'No, I have not,' she managed to say, shaking with indignation. It wasn't just that she felt she was being falsely accused, it was also that the accusation was that she had been loyal and honest and innocent. She'd been had both ways at once.

'Oh well,' he said, shrugging.

'Why don't you mind if I had?' she asked. 'I would have thought –'

'I would have liked you to have. I would have preferred it.'

'Trevor,' she said, her voice trembly. 'What's got into you?' She realised that part of the tremble in her voice was caused by an odd new excitement creeping into the corner of her mind, a feeling that anything could happen.

'Nothing's got into me,' he said irritably. 'I just wouldn't mind if you had a secret, that's all. If you had a part of your life that I didn't know about. It would make you more . . . of a mystery, I suppose.'

'Less boring, you mean.'

'No,' he said testily. 'Anyway, I don't want to talk about it. I've got other things to think about.'

'Well, I blinking well want to talk about it. Boy, do I. I've never wanted to talk about anything so much in my whole life. Isn't it enough for you that I'm . . .' She nearly found herself saying, a manager at W.H. Smith's, but stopped in time. That wasn't anything much, compared to being a councillor and an assistant manager at the bank, even though it was a lot to her. She had a little cubby-hole at the back of the shop for her office, and sometimes she would look out the window, especially when it was raining, and think, well, here I am. The one time when she wasn't pleased with her job was when her mum and dad told her what a good job it was. Then she became all bitter and twisted, out of the blue, and told them she didn't even earn as much as a policeman did. 'What's *that* got to do with the price of fish?' her father had asked. She couldn't tell him. 'At least you don't have to lock people up,' her mother told her.

'Isn't it enough that I'm a woman?' she said, finally, to Trevor.

'A woman what?'

'A flipping, bloody woman, that's what. Isn't that enough of a . . . mystery in itself?' She felt herself blushing, it seemed such a silly, stuck-up thing to say. For heaven's sake, what was so clever about being a woman? It wasn't even as original as being a manager at Smith's. 'We're different from each other, that's what I mean.'

'Are we?'

'How can you say, *are we*? Of course . . .' She trailed off again. A picture had come into her head, quite unlike anything she'd ever thought of before. She imagined his thing, that tube coming out of his body, her stuck on one end of it, him on the other.

Perhaps it *was* very samey after all. Perhaps Trevor was right.

'Everybody's got a secret,' Trevor said. 'Except you.'

★　　★　　★

A friend of hers, Mary Hogg, had decided to sign up for introductory membership at the golf club, which was expanding its female list, and she wanted Christine along for moral support. Trevor wasn't interested – too busy in any case – and Mary's husband was a non-starter, having not long ago lost a finger of his right hand. It was only the ring finger but meant he couldn't grip a club properly. 'When he gives me a feel,' Mary whispered, 'I look down and there's his finger, gone. It makes me go all of a doo-dah, honest to God.'

Art Whiteside took them under his wing. He was a friend of the Hoggses, apparently, and certainly seemed very friendly with Mary. Christine watched his hands as they held the club. No fingers missing there – a few extra if anything, big strong ones that obviously gripped like a vice. She didn't like him much – he seemed crude and obvious. Trevor was like quicksilver in comparison.

Art's attention switched when he saw what a bad golfer Christine was. His arms came round her so tightly that her shoulders were pressed inwards, plumping her breasts together. She wasn't sure what he smelled of but it was something. A phrase came into her head from Sunday School years ago: a mote in your eye. Art was like having a mote in your whole body, your whole world, filling up all the available space.

Far from helping with her swing, the pressure from him made her wag her club feebly, and there was something delicious about that. She found herself wanting to be small and ineffectual.

She remembered when she and Trevor had first gone out together, and she had had to initiate the kiss. And now Trevor had the nerve to accuse her of not being promiscuous enough, of not being promiscuous at all. His quicksilveriness seemed to change into a sort of sliminess: he was a politician, after all. There was something weak and feminine about it. Him wanting her to have adventures when he didn't have any himself: what a bloody nerve!

She found herself pressing backwards into Art's rank presence, and immediately, to her horror and triumph, felt an answering lumpy pressure against the top part of her right buttock. The force from his hands on hers went up her arms and into her body, ignoring the club altogether, which now flopped about like a broken limb.

'I can't do this,' she said, suddenly breaking his grip and turning to face him. His moustache looked harsh and bristly, the texture of scrubbing brushes when she was a girl. She felt a swoony desire to feel its roughness on her skin, to be made sore by it. She glimpsed his thin red lip under the tufts.

She tugged her eyes away from Art's mouth and their gazes locked together. A kiss hung in the space between them like a balloon about to pop.

They hadn't actually *done* anything, but there was an atmosphere of violence in the air. It was how the weather feels when thunder has just rolled. Mary understood what had gone on; anyone within range would have picked it up.

'The main thing wrong with your drive,' Art said, 'is, you didn't make any contact with the ball.'

Oh yes I did, Christine thought. My husband would be proud of me.

Trevor came in nearly an hour after May's phone call. He'd been in discussion with Dick Hardy, the leader of the Labour group, after the council meeting ended. He was one of those people being tired didn't suit. It made Christine feel impatient just to see his shoulders sag. It was as well that they didn't have to be nice to each other any more.

'Have you had anything to eat?' she asked.

He looked at her as if waiting for the penny to drop. 'I don't know,' he said in the end, sounding puzzled.

'Well, are you hungry, or what?'

'I'm a bit hungry, I think.'

'All I had was a sandwich. I didn't feel like cooking anything. Do you want me to get you one?'

'No, no. Don't worry. I'll do it myself.'

That wasn't to save her work or be independent. It was because his favourite sandwich was so disgusting that he was ashamed of it. He sloped off into the kitchen. God, she thought, I know him so well. It almost seemed a waste, leaving him. But of course, that was why she wanted to leave him, because she knew him so well.

Oh no, she thought: that's his complaint about *me*. That's why I started leading another life.

The trouble was, once you started leading another life, you left your original one behind.

She remembered the phone message, and followed him into the kitchen. Sure enough, he was opening a tin of marrowfat processed peas. She watched him from the doorway as he carried the tin over to the sink, pressed the gawping lid back into place, turned the tin over and drained it. He'd already put margarine on a slice of bread. He used a fork to scrape peas on to the slice, then squashed them down so they wouldn't roll off. He reached over for the vinegar.

'I forgot to tell you,' she said. He stopped in mid-reach, like a schoolboy who'd been caught out. 'It's all right, it's your house. You're allowed to eat pea sandwiches if you want to. Our house,' she corrected as an afterthought, recalling the imminent parting of the ways. Wise to keep your claim staked. Obediently his hand collected the vinegar bottle and shook it over the lumpy surface of peas. 'May Rollins rang. Wanted you to call back.'

'I suppose it's a bit late now,' he said.

'I expect she's sitting there, waiting for the phone to ring.'

'Maybe.'

'One thing I always wanted to ask you,' she said. He turned towards her. She oughtn't to have put it like that: it was too redolent of farewells. 'What does marrowfat mean?'

'I haven't a clue,' he said. 'Just fat, I suppose.'

'Fat?'

'You know, fat peas,' he snapped. He strode off into the hall.

She stepped up to the side, spread another slice of bread, and put it on the top of the peas. Make an honest sandwich of you yet, she thought. Or near as dammit. She pressed it into place just hard enough so the peas didn't squirt out. 'Rather you than me, sonny Jim,' she said.

'Oh hello, Trevor,' May said.

'I'm sorry it's so late.'

'Not to worry. There's no point in me going to bed yet awhile. Can you hear her?'

Tinnily, in the distance: 'There's only one thing worse, in the universe, and that's a woman, yes, it's a woman . . .' The faint voice had managed to take all the bounce out of the song, so it sounded sad and haunting.

'Oh yes.'

'What I wanted to say – is your young lady in earshot?'

'I don't think she's – no, she's not.'

'Good-oh. All it is: don't do anything too final. Don't go past the point of no return.'

'I think we've gone past that already.'

'What I need to know: all things being equal, would you want to give it another try?'

'What?'

'Your marriage, what do you think?'

'Oh. Yes, I suppose.' A pause. 'Yes, I would.'

'In that case try to stay put for the time being.'

'All right,' he said obediently and put the phone down. Instantly it was replaced by a plate with his pea sandwich on.

'Oh, thank you,' he said to Chris.

She gave him a quick faraway smile and went into the lounge. He followed.

'Do you remember getting these chairs?' she asked, sitting on one. 'We worried about the shit brownness of the corduroy. You put them together with that little key thing that came with them.

We thought, Oh God, is the lounge going to have an overall effect of shit? Please come to a party in our lounge. We've gone in for the bog look.'

'Allen key,' he said, sitting down on the chair opposite.

'Allen key, that's right. Funny to have a key with a name. Allen key. Jeremy key. Little Ruthie key.' She looked at him, wide-eyed. 'When you'd finished assembling them, you said: "And the bonus is they're not bad to sit on."'

'Well, that's true,' he said, feeling irritable. He wished his teeth were sharper, to chomp through the pea sandwich without squelching it.

'Daddy doesn't think so. He sat on one as if it was solid granite. You could practically hear his bottom crying out for the comfort of home.' She rested her head in her hands and looked sadly at the carpet. 'I wish he was more of a man.'

'He seems all right to me.'

'You would say that. You always think the best of everybody.' She said it as though it was an insult.

It was.

'If you had your way,' she went on, 'you'd prefer people to be *worse*, I don't know why. I suppose it's so you could have the pleasure of forgiving them.' Suddenly she burst into tears, and ran out of the room.

When May had finished the call she thought to herself, I don't know why I told him to stay put. Where else could he go? He's not got anywhere else to stay but put.

She said it out loud: 'Nowhere to stay but put.'

She went up to the bathroom and had a strip wash. Then into her bedroom and put her nightdress on. She looked at herself in the mirror. The nightie hem was just below her knees, then there were her shiny white legs and two blue slippers with pom-poms on that Cherry had given her for Christmas. She sighed. I sit by the telephone all evening waiting for a man twenty-odd years my junior to call, a man of a different political persuasion, a man who can be the bees' knees when he's so minded; and look at *me*.

She obeyed her own command and looked a bit more. Give me a candle and I'd be Florence Nightingale, she thought. Wheelchair parade came into her head, a party trick her dad and her Uncle Cyril used to do on high days and holidays. They'd sit side by side on kitchen chairs and spin imaginary wheels. Uncle Cyril would begin: 'By the right, quick march!' and both of them would pump at their right wheel, then at the left, faster and faster until at a certain point they would turn both their wheels at the same time, like when a horse changes from a canter to a gallop. 'Left turn!' – right wheel pumped forward, left wheel backwards, till you thought they *had* left-turned. Even more so for 'About turn!'

That was the trouble with not being pretty enough to attract a mate when you were still young enough to have children. Family fun went off into the grave. Uncle Cyril really did end up in a wheelchair for the last few years. Now all May had was her potty mother and Cherry.

Mother. She suddenly realised silence had fallen.

She tiptoed along the landing and into her mother's bedroom. She'd tucked herself up as nice as pie. She still looked pretty as she lay asleep on the pillow. May's heart contracted as she looked at her, not with love, but with sadness that she couldn't feel any.

Back in her own room she was on the point of getting into bed herself when she thought: no, I'll do it now. Nothing like causing the maximum inconvenience for getting your point across. She thought of Trevor knocking on her door in the dead of night. It gives a sense of occasion, that's what it does.

She got up, slipped her dressing-gown on, went down to the hall, and dialled.

The phone rang and rang. Good, she thought, he's in bed. Finally it was picked up. Sure enough the voice at the other end was full of sleep, and testy at the same time. 'What's up?'

'Mr Whiteside?'

There was a pause. May listened intently in case she heard sounds in the distance, a rival to Christine, but all that came through was Art's breathing, still in its slumber rhythm.

'Who is this?'

'It's May Rollins.'

'Oh.' He was changing his demeanour. She could almost see it: the pyjama trousers being hitched up, the whiskers unteased. 'Yes, councillor.'

'I'm sorry to trouble you at this late hour.'

'Not at all. It's always a pleasure to speak with you.'

'I thought we ought to have a few words. In strict confidence.'

'Indeedy.'

I'm not about to sell my house, May thought, so there's no call to smarm. She didn't say it but tried to put it into her tone of voice: 'Not on the phone, all things considered. Perhaps we could meet.'

'My office all right?'

'Oh no. I'd prefer a public place. There's more privacy.'

'How about the golf club?'

'That would be just the job. Shall we say tomorrow at one?'

'I think I've got an appointment then.'

'It's quite urgent, Mr Whiteside. Perhaps you should cancel it.'

'Oh.'

May wondered if it was with Christine. She left him a moment to consider whether to try to put her off or not, said: 'I'll see you then, then,' and put the phone down.

Back in bed her thoughts returned to Trevor. She wondered if she was becoming a doting old fool, scheming on his behalf in this way. At my age you're entitled to have a protégé, she told herself. It was strange how Trevor's political magic had nothing to do with ability on a detailed level. He would never be able to plot as she had done for him. That was part of the unfairness of life: that she could be as busy and complicated as she liked, but

73

would never possess his flair. It's me who can't stay anywhere but put, she thought. *He'll* be off goodness knows where.

Even as she thought it she knew where he'd be off to, but she didn't dare let herself use the words.

Five

It was a small terrace in Mill Park. They'd been workers' cottages in the old days, and still went for a snip, but a more professional type of people had moved into some of them, not the sort who made real money but a couple of school-teachers he knew of, and a midwife he personally had sold one to.

Art had wondered about the midwife, given it was the nursing profession, and also she wasn't a bad looker, in a large sort of way. But a few warning bells had rung. A midwife, unmarried, pushing forty: it suggested leanings in another direction altogether. And maybe it was all that gynaecological knowledge put him off his stride a bit, being a gifted amateur himself.

No such temptations on this occasion at number seven, though in any case he had just got himself well and truly fixed up, once and for all it looked like. It was only an old biddy who answered the door. She seemed a bit ill at ease, however.

'My husband's gone out,' she said. She was wearing a thick purple dress with white spots that went halfway down her legs and made her look like a poisonous toadstool.

'You told my secretary it would be convenient in the morning.'

'Oh.' She said it in a funny tone of voice, not disagreeing, but as if that was news to her. As if yesterday when she made the appointment she had been a different person altogether. 'He goes to the park in the mornings.'

'I won't be two ticks.' He could have told her the valuation then and there, after one quick look from the outside – even from his office, just being given the address: £2,800. But that wasn't the way it was done. You had to have a professional standard. 'There's no commitment, of course.'

'He'll be back later on. Sure as eggs is eggs.'

'I can't manage later on. I've somewhere I've got to be.'

'I don't know,' she said, shaking her head. She took a step backwards, obviously to get away from him, but he decided to take it as a cue and stepped into the hall.

'Nice house,' he was going to say, but as he opened his mouth to speak he found that all the breath had left his body. It wasn't a nice house at all. The temperature in the hall had plummeted by fifty degrees; he'd walked out of a sunny day in early September into a meat store.

He turned back to look at the biddy. She was fastening the front door. Then she turned to face him, and gave a little smile. He stared at her, trying to make it out. It could have been the secret smile of a witch; or the shy one of a little old lady.

He took a deep breath, trying to calm his thumping heart down. 'Bit of a chill in here,' he said.

'It's always been a coolish house,' she told him. 'But it's easy enough to heat,' she added.

Praise be, he thought, at least she's still wanting to sell it. And I'm an estate agent; which means it's in her interest for me to stay alive.

He felt the tips of his ears go red with embarrassment at the thought that he'd had anything to fear from her. 'Let the dog see the rabbit,' he said, and took out his tape measure.

Ten minutes later he was finished. He'd gone through the house like a dose of salts. It had carried on being as cold as a nun's fanny, but nothing untoward had happened, though he'd had another bad moment by the wardrobe in the second bedroom. 'I'll send you my estimate in the post,' he told the biddy, which he never normally did, believing it better policy to give customers a price then and there and see if he couldn't get a signature on the dotted line. But she would want to consult her old man in any case.

'I was down on all fours in the second bedroom,' he told Wendy, who did the office work.

'Doing what you know best, by the sound of it.'

'I was measuring up from the corner, when I had this funny feeling. I thought somebody was in the room with me. Not the old lady. She'd stayed downstairs. That's why they want to sell: buy a bungalow. More likely to be a shed, with what that place'll fetch. Anyhow I look up over my shoulder, and there he is, standing there. In a suit, with a hat on his head.' He paused, to let the picture sink in. 'Then I realise: no head. Zip, I got up pronto, I can tell you.'

'Goodness me, Mr Whiteside,' Wendy said, 'you'll put me off my lunch.'

She didn't believe a word. Well, fair enough. It wasn't true anyhow, though he'd believed it for a moment. 'The wardrobe door had swung open. The suit was on a hanger, hanging from a hook. It was a double hook, and the hat was on the one above it. They must have separate bedrooms.'

'That's my plan.'

'You what?'

'If I ever get hitched up. A bedroom all on my lonesome.'

'Wouldn't that be missing the point?'

She gave him a long, pitying look.

'Suit yourself.' He never tried it on with office staff: too much like trouble. Unethical, was the word.

'As a matter of fact,' Wendy said, 'the old man popped his clogs a year or two back.'

'I beg your pardon?'

'Her niece rang yesterday from Southport, while you were out of the office. She wants Mrs Barker to buy something near her. She said she's never been the same since her husband died. The niece can speak for her. She's got . . . what's-it.'

'Power of attorney?'

'Yes, power of attorney.'

'My God.'

'That's what she said.'

'She told me he'd be back from the park, sure as eggs. Sure as eggs, she said.' Art shook his head and stayed silent for a moment. 'It was the coldest house I've ever been into.'

'Maybe we should leave somebody else to handle it.'

'What do you mean?'

'Give a low estimate. Get shot of it.'

'Blow that for a game of soldiers. I'm in business to sell the bloody things, not live in them.'

'Do-on't sa-ay you've not been wa-arned,' Wendy said in a ghostly voice, waggling her head from side to side.

'I won't. Talking of warning, I'm off out again now. You'll have to expect me when you see me.'

'Where shall I say?'

'Nowhere.'

'The golf club, then.'

'It's not what you think. Tell them I popped *my* clogs as well.'

'This is supposed to be a going concern.'

'I'm going, aren't I?' he asked, and went.

May Rollins came into the clubhouse with a tapestry handbag you could carry your clubs in, a dress like a sack of spuds, and a hat akin to a bowler on her head, except it was maroon and had a sort of guttering round the edge where a man's one would have a level rim.

He didn't expect a woman of her years to be an invitation to forbidden pleasures, but there was something profoundly depressing about the way she looked plain and fussy both at once. She wasn't the sort of councillor he liked to socialise with as a rule, preferring younger ones with the rest of their lives to look forward to. On the make, in other words.

'Let me get you a drink, Councillor Rollins.'

'A G and T will do the trick.'

He got the G and T, and a Scotch for himself.

'Something I've been meaning to ask you,' he said. In his game you learned not to start a meeting on the receiving end.

'Oh yes?'

'One of my customers wants to buy a house through me that's got an old air raid shelter in the back garden. He's said he's heard the council won't let people demolish them nowadays. I told him that couldn't be right.'

'It is, I'm afraid.'

'What on earth's that about?'

'Nuclear war, that's what it's about.'

'You're joking.'

'I'm afraid not. The council has civil defence obligations, and under them it's not allowed to get shot of any of its current defences. I had a constituent chewing my ear off about it just the other day. "The council must think we're all dumb," she said. "My shelter wouldn't survive a small knock, let alone a nuclear blast." I said to her, "Don't let yourself get so aereated. There's a solution to every problem. In this case: get rid without letting them know."'

'I see,' Art said. He'd already told his bloke the same thing. 'What can I do *you* for, then?' he asked.

May Rollins raised the small glass in her large hand and took a sip. The lemon slice bobbed against the pale hairs above her upper lip. She put the glass down on the table. 'Oh no,' she said, 'oh no no no.'

He rubbed his own moustache, suddenly nervous.

'You'll be doing it for yourself,' she explained.

Blackmail was what it was. She put it to him that he stood to make money out of the Prospect Hill flats project, and that Trevor Morgan opposed it. Therefore he had stolen Morgan's wife to get influence over him or alternatively reduce *his* influence in the council and discredit him at the MP selection committee. If he, Art, didn't let her go, May Rollins would make sure the story got to the press.

'Let her go?' he said. 'You make it sound as if she's in prison.'

'Let her go,' May repeated, looking at him with a pair of sharp teasing ginger eyes. The maddening part was it was all untrue. He hadn't thought for a moment of Trevor Morgan's opposition to the flats. The project had been on the shelf for years but it was all but signed and sealed at last, and there were too many important people not wanting to get their fingers burned. You might as well be opposed to Mount Everest.

'Prospect Hill's got nothing to do with it,' he told her.

'Oh yes?' she said. 'What are you saying, Art? Are you in love with her?'

He looked at her, appalled. How could he say it? How could he, Art Whiteside, say that? It was the most unlikely explanation, the most obvious lie in the book.

May took another drink of her G and T. When she lowered it there was a little smile on her lips. Maybe it was just where they had lined up with the curvature of the glass. He remembered that biddy's smile this morning. The chill of her house came back on him, and he shivered.

No, May's eyes were smiling as well as her lips. It was a trick, a trap. She knew he hadn't been plotting. But she also knew he couldn't deny it, because his only explanation would make everyone laugh their socks off. Truth is stranger than fiction, like they say in books.

And her accusation being untrue gave it more bite than ever. The gossip people didn't want believable stuff, too boring. They wanted stories that stretched belief. He tried to get his head around what the old girl had worked out on his behalf. Her story was ideal. It was untrue, which made it interesting; but the lie couldn't be proved, which made it true. She was laughing all the way to the bank.

The cleverness of it made his head ache. 'You ought to be in the business of selling houses,' he told her.

'I have enough trouble keeping my own in good repair,' she replied. 'I've got a leak through my bedroom ceiling.' Then she leaned forward over the table, almost knocking over her empty glass. He thought she was going to whisper something. For a mad second he imagined she was going to give him a peck. What did they call it? The Judas kiss. A little smacker to say, Got you. A girl he was getting nowhere fast with once did something similar to him, poked her lips out as if she was going to stretch them through the air to reach him, till he was on the point of shoving his own lips out in response, heart beating like a fisherman catching a fish; and then he'd understood it was just her way of telling him to get lost. Another half-second and he would have found himself in limbo, lips dangling. Gave him a wink as she went off, to rub it in.

But all May was doing in point of fact was shifting her weight forward so her bottom could rise from her seat, on the cantilever principle. Once her rear was safely airborne, she pushed her hands down on the table top to get her upper half erect. Then she gave him a little nod, as if they had just met casually, and went.

Art watched through the window as her Imp drove away. Bertie from the bar came over and deposited a small bowl of silverskin onions on the table.

'You looked a bit peckish,' he said.

Art popped three of them in at a go and immediately regretted it. Last thing he should eat. For two pins he would have fired them across the room like miniature white cannon-balls, but he swallowed them whole as next best thing, and looked up at Bertie, eyes streaming. 'Thanks, old man,' he croaked.

'Do yourself a mischief,' Bertie said in his grumpy way, and scuttled back to the bar.

Art looked at his watch. Nearly half-past one. Nothing for it. He picked up his whisky, drank it off, and washed it around his mouth to get the oniony taste away. He even gargled a little with it as he swallowed. Nothing like that for making your tonsils catch fire.

★   ★   ★

Wednesday was early closing at W.H. Smith's, which often gave
Christine and Art the latitude to stretch their lunch hour a bit. If
he was free he would pick her up at the bottom of the precinct
and whisk her off into the hills for a while. There was a little car
park just beyond Waveney Bridge, overlooking a valley with a
canal and railway line in it, and Moundle Hill beyond. Sometimes
there was another car parked but they would avert their gaze
and hope that the occupants would do likewise. This is a place
for assignations, she would think. It's for bosses to take their
secretaries. How demeaning. And she would feel a little tingle of
excitement. She thought of the A6 murder case, and James Han-
ratty being hanged. People get killed in places like this, she
thought.

Not that she and Art got up to a lot. That was the golden rule.
They kissed and cuddled till she almost felt she would explode.
She'd ask herself: am I enjoying this? Am I looking forward to
when it goes further?

The answers were contradictory. She wasn't enjoying it much
but at the same time she was quite looking forward to going
further.

A lot of the time they just talked and ate their sandwiches. It
was then she would ask herself what she really thought of him.
He was coarse-grained compared with Trevor, but intelligent,
also big and quite manly. He'd told her he used to be a Teddy
boy in his youth and she could still see a bit of it in him: his hair
was bushy with a hint of duck's arse, and his jackets were just a
touch longer in the body and bigger across the shoulders than
most people went in for nowadays. Perhaps his trousers were
narrower too, without flares. They were certainly as bumpy in
the region of the crotch as she had initially thought when at the
golf club.

He was practical and commonsensical, he appreciated her, and
he was nicer than . . . than you might have any right to expect.
He was an awful Tory, of course, but then she was fed up with
politics. Trevor being Labour hadn't stopped him from wanting

her to have gone to bed with other blokes. Art could be what he wanted as far as she was concerned, as long as he didn't become a councillor.

Her mother had had a conversation with her in the kitchen the other day. Christine knew she was trying to make the peace. She had asked: 'Are you looking forward to, you know, being with him all the time?'

'Oh yes,' Christine answered, and then her heart sank to her boots. The prospect of being with Art all the time, not just for sex but day to day, going shopping, eating together, perhaps having children and being a family, filled her with dread. It wasn't that there was anything wrong with him exactly, at least that she could identify: it was just that it would be a journey into the unknown. Strangely, as she thought about it, she said it out loud.

'That sounds exciting,' said her mother, and gave a little shiver. 'A journey into the unknown, eh?'

Christine coloured up. It was a silly thing to say. Art was an estate agent, not the continent of Africa.

What's that got to do with it? she asked herself. She thought of what Trevor had said about wanting her to be mysterious. That was the whole point. Being with Art would make every-thing mysterious. He would be an unknown quantity, and she would be too. He would influence her to be different from what she was. He's a new man: I'll be a new woman, she thought. Other people changed you. I hope you're satisfied, she thought, in relation to Trevor.

But when she was in bed that night (Trevor was sleeping in the spare room) her heart contracted with fright. I don't want to be a new woman, she thought. I like being me. She remembered going to stay with a cousin when she was young, and sharing a bed with her. In the middle of the night she had woken and been aware of her different smell. It wasn't that her cousin smelled bad or anything – she just smelled of herself, but it filled Christine with desperate longing for her own little room, with its safe smells, and everything in its place. She hadn't been able to stop herself from having a silent cry out of sheer homesickness, even though she was only there for the weekend.

As she'd lain in bed remembering that long-ago time, her stomach churned at the thought of what lay in store for her in the near future: a big strange man in her bed for ever, rank swampy smells just at the very moment when you wanted to feel snug and cosy. I'm not cut out for this caper, she'd thought sweatily. Just as she slipped into sleep, she was telling herself that the prospect of living with Art was like the dread you might experience waiting for an operation, when you knew there was nothing you could do to prevent it, but you felt completely panic-stricken at the prospect. She had only ever had her appendix out but that had been bad enough.

The following morning she'd felt different. Trevor's done nothing to stop it, she told herself. Serve him right. He was the one who *started* it, in actual fact. It had made her feel better, putting the blame for the situation where it belonged.

One thing Art didn't believe in: beating about the bush.

He pulled into his office briefly on the way to Christine's. It was one of a small row of businesses on an unadopted road that led to St Andrew's Church and then went all round the church and back again, so that the glum Victorian building was on a sort of island. Outside the businesses the road was in sets but as it went round the churchyard it was simply hard earth, with straggly buddleias and rosebay in the verges. Art imagined coaches and horses galloping around it.

He pulled up outside the next shop to his office, Jack Eatmore, Butcher, which had been there since the year dot. When he was a lad he'd believed the shopkeeper was really called Eatmore, and was repeatedly amazed at the good luck of it, but that had gone out the window about the same time as Father Christmas. The current Jack Eatmore was about ninth in line – it was like what Lord Home called the Prime Minister: the fourteenth Mr Wilson.

Jack was just closing the shop up for the Wednesday afternoon. He looked like skinned cattle in his own right, with blood points and wormy veins all over his fat cheeks. He turned as Art came up.

'I saw that young lady of yours go past a bit ago,' he said.

'Wendy?' Art said in surprise.

'No, no, not Wendy. The one that works in Smith's. On her way home, I dare say. Tell you what, she's got what it takes to fill her blouse.'

God knows how he'd heard about it. 'That a fact? I thought you were talking about Wendy.'

'Not the same shape at all. Good-looker in her own way, mind, if you like the daddy-long-legs type.'

'I wouldn't know. She's staff.'

'That's why you have to look further afield, is it? Man of principle. What I say is, all the more for the rest of us.' Jack screwed his features up and wheezed out a laugh. His face went like a beetroot. Lose your sense of humour or die, thought Art, and nipped into his own office.

'That was quick,' Wendy said, looking up from her desk.

'I'm not back yet.'

'Oh really? I thought ghosts in this part of town didn't have heads. You seem to have yours still. Big one and all.'

'Not just my head. Tell you what, the butcher man next door would like to invite you out. He confided.'

She gave Art a long look, then shuddered from the soles of her feet to the top of her head. Art could have sworn he saw a distinct ripple pass up her body. He found himself thinking: yet another woman I'll never be intimate with.

Wendy raised her eyes to the ceiling and groaned.

'You ought to think about it,' Art told her. 'Offers like that –' For the second time that day he unexpectedly found himself unable to speak. This time he knew that if he said another word he would burst into tears. What in heaven's name's all this about? he wondered. He shrugged so he didn't need to finish the sentence.

'The best bet would be for me to wear a false moustache,' Wendy said. 'Then with any luck he'll think I'm you.'

The sob cleared, as suddenly as it had come. 'Thank you very much,' Art told her. 'I don't want to go out with him either.'

'Do you want me to give a valuation to the niece of that lady in Mill Park?'

'That's what I've dropped in for. Tell her three thou.'

'*Three* thou? You realise what?'

'What?'

'We'll be lumbered with it, that's what. Nobody else will suggest more than two eight. What are you going to do, list the ghost as a mod con?'

'Our customers aren't superstitious.'

'You were.'

'That's just me. Anyway, I'm off now.'

'Same as before?'

'No. Yes: nowhere.'

'When shall I say you'll be back?'

'I don't know.'

'Tinker tailor soldier sailor this year next year sometime never. I'll say never. He's gone to nowhere and he'll be back never. How's that?'

'It sounds about right,' he said, feeling that sob swelling in his throat again.

Christine was just getting herself a piece of toast when there was a knock at the front door. It was Art.

'What on earth are you doing here?' she asked him. She didn't know whether to push him away or pull him in. They'd agreed early on never to come to each other's houses. Or rather, she'd made him promise.

She pulled him in.

He was big for the hall. He looked it up and down. 'I can get you three two for this place,' he said. 'No, let's call it three five. Three thousand five hundred.'

'For heaven's sake, Art.'

'Oh well, it's neither here nor there.'

'I'll be the guilty party, you mean, and not entitled to any of it. Especially with you coming here in the afternoon. What on earth possessed you? I didn't get the wrong end of the stick, did I, when you rang up to cancel lunchtime?'

'No, you didn't get the wrong end of the stick.'

'You better come through.'

The lounge always seemed chilly and morgue-like on a Wednesday afternoon, as if in suspended animation until the proper time for coming home from work. 'I'll switch the fire on,' she said.

'No need. It feels as warm as toast to me. It's a nice day out. I went into a house this morning, though, that was cold enough to freeze the balls off of a brass monkey.'

Balls, she thought, no escape from them when Art was around.

Sure enough the subject rang a bell for him too. 'I got a hole in one once,' he said. He picked a cushion off one of the brown Habitat chairs to make room for himself to sit on it. The chrome frame settled back like one of those medieval catapults being wound up to fire a boulder. He's a bull in a china shop, she thought. Butterflies took over her stomach. And I'm the china shop. 'I don't think I ever told you about it,' he went on. Her cheeks went hot. 'I don't bring it up a lot,' he explained.

She had got bored with golf quite early on, and it was the last thing she wanted to talk about now. There were other, more important matters.

'It was a fluke of course. It always has to be. You can't even see the flag when you tee off on that particular hole. Nobody can be that accurate. But at the same time . . . I knew I'd done it the second I walloped the ball. Something about my contact, about the crack it made. That little bugger was going home. I stood there with my eyes shut and I saw it pop down, inside my head, just as if I was standing on the green.'

She'd had experience of seeing him on the golf course with his eyes closed, after having given his little ball a fearful whack. He always closed his eyes, hole in one or hole in ten. Lordy, she thought, I bet I know when else he'd do that. She pictured him mooning over her, eyes tight shut. She blew an imaginary strand of hair off her forehead. Oh heck. It made her go shaky.

He might even think the very same thought at the crucial moment: hole in one.

'For a second it all seemed to make sense. I felt as if I was in control. You know what I mean, like as if there was a pattern to everything.'

All based on golf. It was nice to be told the secret of the universe.

Suddenly he let out a fat ungainly sob, as abrupt and uncalled for as if he'd passed wind.

'Art, what is it?'

'I'm sorry. I nearly did that before. At the office. I thought to myself, Wendy will think I've gone mental.'

'Oh my love.' Just like me, she realised. I keep on bawling my eyes out when I'm supposed to be happy. For the first time since the whole business between them began she felt real love for him, a sudden aching in her heart. She got up from her own chair, walked over, and patted his hair. There was still that echo of a duck's arse in it. Art reached up and grasped her patting hand.

'We've got to stop,' he said.

'Stop?'

'This. We've got to stop this.'

'What do you mean?' She knew what he meant. Her heart began beating so hard that she imagined it breaking through her chest. It seemed to beat in her breasts too, making them feel threatening and wayward, as if for two pins she could push them in anybody's face, no matter whose. She experienced the thrill and power and sudden joy of a win on the pools. She bent down and kissed that bushy d.a. of his while he answered. It was a way of stopping herself whooping with delight.

'Us,' he said. 'It's not going to work. It's too – too much of a mess. It'll muck up Trevor's career.'

'Bugger that.' She grabbed his face, and pointed it upwards towards her. It was dangerously near those unruly breasts of hers. His mouth had gone puckered and off-centre under pressure from her pinch. 'His career's not our responsibility. We'll be us. Just us.'

'It'll muck up mine as well,' he said. Because of her grip on his cheeks, he spoke as if he had a mouthful of food.

She let his face go. 'How can –'

'You don't know the half of it. It's a matter of good will. The golf club, Round Table, all that. A whiff of scandal. There's enough delicate stuff in my business as it is.'

She almost pointed out that, as she understood it, he was well known for his womanising, but immediately saw that that was a different matter altogether. There was some sort of strange businessman's scale where you got marks for success at sex but lost them, or even got disqualified altogether, if you ran off with a married woman, especially the wife of a prospective MP.

Suddenly she felt furious. 'What are you saying, Art?' She was so angry that her words began to run all over the place, like spilled marbles. 'Are you saying that you'll give up the plans we had about being together, just because you're worried about what your blessed Round Table is going to think about it?'

'It's because I sell houses. You think about it: what are houses?'

'What do you mean, for God's sake, what are houses?' She screwed up her face in fury. 'Is this some kind of intelligence test, to check whether I'm educationally subnormal?'

'Houses are homes, that's what they are.'

For the first time she could ever remember in her whole life she stamped her foot in rage. 'Aaaah!' she cried. 'How *can* you, Art? Did you go to some estate agents' college where they teach you that type of complete balderdash?'

'An estate agent's got to be a builder of homes, not a flattener.'

'You *what?*'

'Of houses. Of homes.'

'Oh. I was thinking you'd said flatterer.'

'Oh no.' He laughed abruptly. His big strong-looking teeth had edges of brown, as if they were laminated wood which was beginning to wear through. She remembered Trevor telling her about George Washington having wooden false teeth. That must have been in their courting days when he was always reading history books.

She'd said: 'I don't mind you going into politics as long as you keep your own teeth.'

'Do you know,' Trevor had replied, 'you pronounce teeth teef, like in toofy-peg.'

'As long as you keep your own toofy-pegs, then,' she told him.

Trevor had answered something strange: 'Would you still love me if I had to have a colostomy?'

All she'd been able to say in reply was: 'I love you so much I never ever want you to have a colostomy in the first place.'

Now Art said: 'An estate agent's *got* to be a flatterer of homes. Wouldn't get far if not. Flatter yes, flatten no, that's how you've got to steer.'

'And that means you've got to steer away from me?'

He gave her a long look. 'I've got to steer my little boat away from you.'

There was something so incongruous at the thought of Art's little boat that Christine began to cry. She could feel tears slither down her face and then dangle at the bottom of her cheeks in that maddening way drops have, when they refuse to actually drop. She saw Art gazing at them and then, to her astonishment, tears sprang out of his eyes too. Her heart completely melted at the sight. Let our tears mingle, she thought to herself. She went faint at the tragedy of it, and the romance.

'Let's go upstairs, Art,' she said. 'For one last time.'

She should have said for one first time too, but let it go at that.

Six

After he married Christine, Trevor had fallen into a routine of visiting his mother on a Wednesday evening after work. That suited Christine fine. Wednesday was her half-day, so she usually caught up with some chores or shopping, and then went to see her own parents.

Oddly, though, there was something enjoyably secretive about Trevor's visits, as if he and his mother were doing something they really shouldn't. For example, Mum got into the habit of cooking him a proper slap-up evening meal, meat and vegetables, pudding and custard, but later, when Christine asked him if he fancied anything to eat before bed, he would say, 'I'm OK, I had a bite to eat at Mum's,' as if all he'd had was a sandwich, which was what Christine got at her own parents', since they had their big meal at lunchtime. The worst part was, Christine always looked guilty eating her biscuit and cheese because she worried about her weight anyway, and the fact that Trevor was being good showed her up. She never guessed he was stuffed to the gills.

Trevor and his mum would talk nineteen to the dozen. Trevor told her all about the bank, far more than he ever told Christine, since very early on they realised that it was boring if they each trotted home and gave a long speech in turn about their day. He told Mum about the doings of Geoff Cartwright and Alan Thomas, and also of the tellers, Hazel Waite and Ann Cottrell. His mum made out he had a thing going with Ann. The more he emphasised how mousy and timid she was, the more Mum would drive the point home.

'Just your type,' she'd exclaim triumphantly. Her enthusiasm struck him as odd, given he'd always believed she felt Christine wasn't wild enough. Christine could at least speak up for herself.

Mum would imitate the way Ann ate her lunch, though she'd never seen her. She even held her mouth unevenly, to suggest Ann's harelip.

'What a sweetheart!' she said. 'I could eat *her* for lunch.'

Somewhere at the back of his mind Trevor had an intuition of what his mother was saying: Ann was a vol-au-vent, Christine, a meat and potato pie. It wasn't nice as an idea, and he ought to have objected, but it seemed such a minor way of betraying someone, and you needed a little rest occasionally from the strain of being happily married.

Funnily enough he began to have the occasional fantasy about Ann, despite the fact that her sex appeal was zero. It wasn't a question of whether she was attractive or not, but simply that she seemed to give out no signals at all. Perhaps that in the end became a sort of appeal.

Alan Thomas once told him about people who were sexually attracted to vegetable life, especially trees, into which they would drill holes at the appropriate height. There was even a word for it, dendrophilia, though Geoff Cartwright claimed that that restricted it to rhododendrons. On the way to their Friday fish and chips the three of them passed a patch of waste ground, the site of a demolished mill, where rhododendrons had sprouted. They'd grunt and groan with excitement, especially when the rhododendrons were in bloom.

In his murkier moments Trevor would imagine making love to Ann while she stayed as passive as a tree, a small one of course. Not a rhododendron bush: she wasn't leafy enough. Perhaps a miniature weeping willow.

As it happened, Alan Thomas had died suddenly at work one Wednesday afternoon. He had slumped forward over his desk, breathing with a rasping sound. Trevor stared at him in bafflement for a moment, wondering if he was playing some sort of joke. Then he became aware of Geoff rising from his own desk like a vast black besuited bird.

Next thing Geoff was peering down at Alan. He grabbed his head and pulled it back. Alan's grey tongue was lolling out and Geoff grasped it with his fingers and stuffed it back in place. He pressed his moon face to Alan's.

Trevor watched in dazed horror. He's *kissing* him, he thought. Is that what you do at the time of farewell? He thought of something from his days of reading history, Admiral Nelson saying 'Kiss me, Hardy.'

Then Alan slipped from his chair and Geoff toppled down after him, lying on the floor at an angle and shoving his big protuberant mouth on to Alan's again.

Hazel Waite was still in her seat, making a strange honking sound, but Ann had stepped forward, and was standing right by Trevor's desk. Even with horror going on in front of him, Trevor was acutely aware of the slightness of her presence. She can't weigh above seven stone, he caught himself thinking.

'He's giving him the kiss of life,' Ann said in a rapt voice.

Of course he was. Trevor could hardly believe he'd been watching without being able to put a name to what was going on. He felt himself blush with shame. 'Don't want to crowd them,' he muttered. He wondered if you could get a proper seal when the bloke had a harelip.

'Call an ambulance,' Ann told him.

Trevor picked up his phone, hugely relieved to have something he could do.

'What's the problem?' asked the other end.

Trevor explained.

'Are you sure he's not just fainted? It's quite warm today.'

'His tongue is grey,' Trevor said. True enough, though he'd seen Alan's tongue before, and it had been grey then. Still, saying so did the trick, and nobody could accuse him of telling a lie. But when the ambulance arrived, Alan was past help.

Dead people look just like you'd expect, Trevor thought. He

surprised himself by being quite hard-nosed about the whole thing, particularly as he'd grown fond of Alan. What took him aback was discovering that death was perfectly natural. He felt ashamed that he'd been so ineffectual when the crisis had erupted. But Geoff understands what illness is all about, he thought. There were times when having had a colostomy was almost an advantage.

When he arrived at his mother's, however, he felt shaky, though he was also aware of half enjoying the situation.

'Somebody died today at work,' he said. My face must look ashen, he thought proudly. Why did I say somebody, not Alan? Mum knew who Alan was.

To stretch it out as much as possible, that's why.

When he'd explained what happened, his mother said, 'I'm so sorry, Trevor.'

'Oh, well.'

'Sorry for you, I mean.'

'Me?'

'That you had to go through all that.'

'At least it wasn't me who was dying.'

'No, that's the important thing. You've got to hold on to that.'

'What do you mean?'

'I've been meaning to tell you.'

She gave him a long, silent look. He didn't dare speak. Instead, though he'd never done it before and didn't even know he could do it, he carefully raised one eyebrow.

'I've got something wrong with me,' she told him.

'Have you? What is it?'

Again, she didn't reply for a second.

'What is it, Mum?' he said, bad-temperedly. 'You've got to tell me.' For a moment he caught himself wondering if she didn't like coming second best, even to dead Alan.

'You mustn't worry about it. I've got cancer, is all.'

'All? Cancer? What sort of cancer?'

'Women's sort.'

'What do you mean, women's sort?'

'You know.' She mouthed the word: 'Breast.'

He mimed back: 'Breast?'

Then she did something strange. Just like when he was little she hid her face behind her hands then popped it out. 'Boo!' she said.

He actually jumped, then looked at her, appalled. He almost burst into tears.

'Boo!' she said again. 'Here I am! Look, it's me! It's still me, Trevor.'

Now he felt resentful of her, for the first time ever. It's not still you, he thought. It's you with your new boyfriend, cancer. He felt *jealous*, as if the cancer was challenging his own status as her closest living relative.

Fear didn't strike him until a few days later, when Christine had the radio on and they played the Beatles singing about being sixty-four. It occurred to him that his mother would probably never live to be that old. She was only forty-nine. He had never known his father: Mum didn't talk about him. He suddenly understood that life was shapeless and bleak, not just Mum's life, but his as well, everybody's. 'There are no guarantees,' he said out loud.

'It's working OK, isn't it?' Christine said. She'd been joining in the chorus.

It's not the radio that's going wrong, it's Mum, he could have said, but he didn't want to tell her at that stage. It was as if he'd be putting Mum at a disadvantage, especially as she sometimes seemed to resent Christine. Christine's in the right, he thought judiciously, Mum's never been exactly fair about her. But still he wanted to protect his mother for the moment; he didn't want Christine to know she was weak.

When he discovered she had to go into hospital he found himself weeping in bed. It wasn't just the danger or the suffering, it was the thought that she wouldn't be the same mother any more. I've never even seen her breast, her breasts, he realised, at least since I was a baby, and don't want to either. He'd not thought of her as having breasts particularly, certainly as compared to Christine, and other women he happened to look at. She just had a certain shape in her clothes. But he didn't want her to be changed. It was as if some magic formula would be spoiled. Geoff Cartwright's colostomy was a different matter altogether. He'd had it from before they ever met; as far as Trevor was concerned it was part of who he was.

Christine had been in the bath. She came in while he was still weeping under the sheet. 'What are you up to, naughty?' she asked, misunderstanding, and tugged the sheet away. That was the moment when he'd had to tell her.

'She'll be all right, she's tough as old boots,' she told him, which was comfort of a kind. But Mum wasn't all right.

When Trevor collected his mum from the hospital she walked in a constrained way, as if it was her *legs* that had gone wonky. She didn't look him in the face. Something about her eyes he didn't like, as though they'd been seeing what they shouldn't. Just as he'd feared, she was a different person all over, smaller, harder, than before – harder in the sense she might shatter.

'I'll buy you a cream horn,' he said gallantly. She loved all cakes, especially cream horns. If she hadn't had one for a day or two she would quietly moan 'Cream horn, cream horn,' making the 'horn' sound as wild and lonely as if a small wolf was howling it a long way away.

'Goody,' she said.

They pulled up outside a baker's in Top Lane and he bought them one each. It was raining and they sat in the car to eat them. He gobbled his, suddenly ravenous. When he'd finished Mum had only taken a tiny bite of hers.

'You're eating it like Ann eats her sandwiches,' he said.

'Little choochy-face,' she said. She always seemed to coo at the mention of her name, as if Ann was a delightful baby. 'But I think I'll keep the rest till later.' She put the nibbled horn back in its paper bag.

He drove off, looking at the rain blowing against the windscreen through teary eyes, with one thought in his head: doom, doom. It was as if the cream horn was a test, as sharp and definite as litmus paper. She hadn't been able to eat it: she was going to die.

As she grew smaller she became more sharply featured; this didn't make her more distinctive but the opposite. She looked like any dying person, with a nose like a penknife blade. He went to see her every evening on the way home from work. On Wednesdays she still tried to cook him something, but on a diminished scale: fish fingers or Welsh rarebit.

She would toy with her own portion. 'I don't want to be getting fat,' she said once, giving a shrug of her shoulders and a wistful smile as if to say, funny old life. The attempt at self-delusion, or at deluding him, whichever it was, made Trevor angry.

'Getting fat's the last thing you've got to worry about. You make –' he paused to think of an example – 'Ann look fat. Ann at work.'

Why did I say her? he immediately wondered. Christine's slim enough. She's got a good figure. More rounded than Ann's but that's how it should be. Christine's curves showed because she was on the short side, but it was fine that they showed. Mum always managed to suggest she was bulky. 'You make *Christine* look fat.'

'Oh. Well.' She gave a secretive little smile. With her cheeks so thin you could see the whole architecture of smiling, the cords and pulleys that made it possible. The way she'd paused between the oh and the well was anti-Christine propaganda.

He felt himself become furious with her. He didn't know whether it was because she still didn't approve of Christine, or because she wasn't eating, or because she was going to die. Perhaps all three. The worst part about her was that even while she faded away she seemed smug, as though she knew something that was withheld from him. He almost wanted to hit her, weak as she was. He kept on about how wonderful Christine was, how much she meant to him.

She refused to get upset. She squeezed his arm. 'I'm glad it all seems to be working out,' she said, just as if he and Christine were weathering some terrible crisis of their own.

One day she ate nothing at all. She gave him a corned beef sandwich and watched while he got it down. It went hard and lumpy in his throat, but he ate it to set an example. Aware of his gaze, she made one for herself but then put it to one side and bustled about to distract his attention, though she couldn't bustle very well. She looked like a leaf in the wind. 'Mum, you've got to eat,' he told her.

'It's just feeding the cancer,' she replied.

She'd never sounded bitter before, and he fell into his familiar anger. 'I suppose you think you're better than everybody else, don't you?'

She blushed, but then tried to look amused. 'Ooh yes. I want caviare on my butties,' she said. 'I'm too good for the likes of corned beef.' He'd meant she was acting as though she was above eating altogether. 'What's it made of, little doggies?' she asked. 'I bet they get them from the dogs' home and shred them up.'

'What do you mean?' He was shaking with rage. 'Have you gone completely bananas?' Even while he shouted he thought to himself, why did I say bananas? She'll think it's not serious. Why didn't I say mad, utterly mad, so that she would *know* it was important.

In fact she'd often talked about things like corned beef in this way, but it sounded so strange now she was thin and dying.

'I think Mum ought to move in with us,' he suggested to Christine that evening. 'She's not feeding herself.'

'How do you suggest *we're* going to feed her?' Christine asked. 'Squeeze her nose and pop it in?'

Suddenly he couldn't cope with it all. He saw his mother with her mouth gaping open like a little bird in a nest and burst into tears. People seemed to be saying nothing but madness.

'You've got to remember, honey-bunch,' Christine said gently, 'your mum's a proud woman. Having cancer's not going to change that.'

'You're saying that because you don't want her here.'

'I'm saying it because she won't want to *be* here.'

'You don't like her very much, do you?'

'What matters is she doesn't like *me* very much. OK, OK. It's her prerogative. I'm not complaining. It's because she likes *you* very, very much instead.'

'She is my bloody mum, for God's sake!'

'Of course she's your bloody mum, darling. All it is, I'm just saying.'

A few days later Mum was in hospital, in any case, and she never came out again. The funeral was horrible. It took place on a dim March day, with those lowish clouds that never rain hanging over the chapel of rest and a few blown leaves left over from last autumn making scratching sounds on the crematorium driveway. The reverend gave a speech about what a good wife and mother she had been. Trevor had never seen her being a wife and he was the only person who knew about her as a mother, and hadn't discussed it with him. Perhaps Christine had.

The reverend had big teeth that were obviously false, and Trevor couldn't stop trying to picture him going into the dentist to have them fitted, a set of tombstone teeth sitting disembodied on that tray by the dental chair, awaiting their new master. Why hadn't he taken the chance to get normal-size ones made?

Trevor felt laughter shake his chest and to stop it coming to the surface did a sort of cough. People around looked at him. He knew they thought he was trying to stifle a sob, and that only made his chest shake more. To find his sorrow again, he thought about when he started work at the bank, and the way Mum had marched him upstairs to look at his suit, those Chinese mannerisms as she introduced him to the mirror. But even that had the wrong effect. He could feel a sentimental grin appear on his face, as random as if it had been drawn there in lipstick. Then that business about his French O level came back into his head.

What am I thinking of? he wondered. She'd never known about that fib. It was a secret from her the same as from everybody else in the world. But for some reason he felt exactly as though she was taking the secret into the grave – into the fire – with her, as if it was something they'd shared. He felt a kind of panic, sweat starting up in the small of his back. I should have told her, he thought, she was the only one in the world who could have understood. Now I'm stuck with it.

He had cancer on his mind. Her dying slowly before his eyes made him see life as under siege from pink balls of unrestrained flesh. Christine, for example, wearing her large disordered bosom like a disease inside her funeral suit. Breasts were like cancers in any case. It made his teeth zing to think of kissing them.

And he had a cancer of his own, that fib about French. It had been steadily gaining nutrients as his career developed, siphoning off its share of each ill-gotten gain. That's what Mum had said about the corned beef sandwich: it would only have served to feed the cancer. Part of the goodness of everything gets channelled off and goes to building up a monstrous alternative to your everyday life, a pink swaying threatening thing that gets hungrier as it grows until it has the capacity to devour the whole of your existence. For years his fib had been in the background of his life. Since his marriage he had almost stopped thinking about it consciously. But now it appeared from the shadowy place where it had lurked and stood ready to gobble him up.

When he went back to work, the fib came with him. When he sat down with someone to discuss a loan, he would tick off the little exaggerations and evasions the customer made – they all did that, and mostly it didn't matter at all – and then remember his own with such vividness he had to stop himself from saying out loud, 'By the way, I failed O level French, you know. But I faked a pass on my application form to the bank. Can I offer you a loan?'

When he talked to his constituents he told himself, I'm just the sort of liar you expect a politician to be, and that knowledge hurt him so much he felt a physical pain in his heart, since what he believed – his invention, as he thought of it – was that it was much more convenient and practical for a politician to be basically honest. He felt lying was somehow old-fashioned, a technique used by the old school and unquestioningly passed down through the generations. Of course you didn't need a pass in O level French to be a councillor, but it felt as though you did.

Above all, the fib went home with him. Here he knew he could never say it out loud, though he wasn't at all sure why. Christine wouldn't have been particularly shocked, she wasn't the type to be fashed at every incy little thing. But he almost felt he had got married under false pretences, that he wasn't exactly the man she'd thought he was, and that, if he admitted it, he would be letting God-knew-what-else into their relationship. The cancer would spread everywhere: in time she'd begin to suspect he'd had affairs, that he didn't love her, wanted to leave. Maybe she thought these things already. She didn't know his secret, but that wouldn't prevent her from knowing he *had* a secret.

One Wednesday, on a cool April evening a couple of weeks after his mother's funeral, he came home to find the house in darkness. Recently Christine had been going to her parents quite early on her afternoons off so she could be back by the time he got home. Perhaps she'd decided things were back to normal now.

He let himself in, and raised his hand to switch on the hall light. Then he saw a dim glow coming from the lounge.

He tiptoed to the door and turned the handle gently. It made the tiniest of sounds but enough to make him stop breathing in suspense. He stood perfectly still, waiting for an answering noise from inside, but none came.

He took a deep breath as if he was going to dive into water, and shoved the door open. The lounge hit his eyeballs so fast he didn't have time to organise it in his head. Yes, there was everything, corduroy chairs, TV, sideboard with drinks on it, and one small flickering candle. And there was Christine, lying on the settee, her blouse open and her hair hanging hungrily over her face. She tossed it as she saw him and began to take her blouse off.

He watched in appalled silence as she leaned forward, slipped her hands behind her back, and unhooked her bra. She had her eyes fixed on his all the time. Perhaps she could see how shocked he was because she said: 'I know, I know. But you've still got me.'

Her breasts jumped forward in unison. He felt himself flinch. 'I know,' he managed to say. He was in danger of being sick when he opened his mouth.

One of her hands crept down her front, grasped her loose bra with odd precision, whipped it off and threw it over the back of the settee.

She pouted her lips. 'All of me,' she was saying. 'That's what you've got. All. Of. Me.' There was an odd echo of a song in her words.

He couldn't reply. He gazed over her head, at the corner of the room, then nodded.

'Just think,' she went on, determined to get his attention. 'I've never been to bed with anybody else.'

Perhaps because he wasn't looking at her the words seemed to come into his consciousness of their own accord. His breath became shallow, as if she'd told him something terrible. What point was she trying to make? Of course she hadn't been to bed with anybody else, he had always known that, never doubted it. Was she trying to cast aspersions on his mother? There was something a bit vague, murky almost, about *her* past. He'd sometimes wondered about where he himself had sprung from. Once when he'd asked, his mother had just replied, 'From under a gooseberry bush,' with that wide-eyed look of hers, half flirtatious, half innocent.

No, Christine couldn't have meant anything like that, not at such a moment. Nor could she be implying anything about him.

He'd never been to bed with anybody else either, she knew that well enough.

She was talking about herself. She was saying she didn't have a secret. There was something boastful about that, something boastful about her whole welcome-to-the-harem posture. Even though he wasn't looking at her, it, directly, he could sense a kind of triumph. What you see is what you get, she was saying, her bare breasts underlining the point. I am an open book.

It was almost as though she had intuited his lie about O level French. Oh God, he thought, why can't she have a secret too? He had a sense of being alone with his fib for ever. He heard himself speak in a dry, bitter voice: 'I wouldn't have minded if you had.'

Her recoil was visible even though it took place below the bottom of his eyes. The shock must have vibrated the air, stirred the flame of the candle. She'd caught his words as you must catch a stone, an arrow, a bullet. He pictured her bosomy whiteness shuddering at contact with such unexpected hostility. Serves her right. He felt obscurely that he was taking revenge on behalf of his mother.

He kept his eyes fixed above her as she tried to reason with him. Why should she be so perfect? His own mother had been up to goodness knows what, whatever it took to bring *him* into the world. He had lied in his time, too.

He walked out of the room, left her to put her bra back on, put each stupid tit back in its bag. He thought of his mother being buried with only one breast left upon her chest. He remembered that cream horn she hadn't been able to eat and the way the cold rain beat on the windscreen.

He hated himself so much for his cruelty to Christine it made him sweat. None of it was her fault, she was only trying to be a good wife to him. But the fact that he had been unjust made him resent her even more, as if it was *her* fault he was treating her so badly.

★   ★   ★

Geoff Cartwright had a theory about flu. His theory was that it was a very rare disease. Ninety-nine per cent of the times people said they had it, they just had common colds.

Trevor and Geoff didn't talk so much these days. For one thing, they'd stopped going for Friday fish and chips after Alan died. They'd gone the first week after the funeral and had made a little ceremony of it, even stopping to look at the rhododendrons on the waste land as they went past, though neither of them said anything suggestive: it wouldn't have seemed appropriate. When they got to the café, Geoff ordered a large fish and chips, and Trevor followed his cue. They normally ordered 'ordinary' as it was called, which was huge in any case. Large was beyond all reason.

'You can't call it whale,' Trevor said. '*Ordinary* is whale.'

'Only one word for it,' Geoff said. 'Large whale. I reckon that must be a whole blinking cod apiece. All they did, they cut their heads and tails off, and battered the buggers.'

A whole cod and a field of potatoes: they looked at their portions in awe.

'The Alan Thomas memorial lunch, God bless him and all who sail in him,' Geoff went on. He cut a piece of fish and forked it along with a chip. Then he held it up in front of his face. 'To Alan,' he said, 'a good mate.'

Trevor did the same, and repeated the toast. Then they touched portions and ate. Each managed to clear his plate – it would have seemed disrespectful not to.

But that lunch was the clincher, you couldn't follow it. The next Friday he and Geoff just took sandwiches into work, like the others. Going to the café wasn't mentioned again.

Since his promotion to assistant manager Trevor had an office of his own. Geoff was still at the desk behind the tellers where he'd always been, so they didn't get the chance to chat much, except on business. But one day, as he was going past on his way out somewhere, Trevor noticed that Geoff was looking very much the worse for wear.

'Are you OK?' he asked.

Geoff looked wearily up at him. 'Don't tell me,' he asked back.

'Don't tell you what?'

'I look like death warmed up.'

'Your nose is a bit like a tomato, that's true enough.'

'Just as I thought. Normally it's like a potato.'

'Geoff, I think you ought to be home in bed.'

For some reason the suggestion upset Geoff badly. His face went even more flushed than it was already. His tiny eyes looked like balls of snot. Trevor could actually feel the heat radiating up from his forehead. 'Don't say that word bed,' Geoff said. 'I had enough bed when I had my colostomy done. Bed is dead, the way I look at it.'

'I just meant for a day or so. I think you've got a touch of flu.'

'It's only September. People don't get flu in September. People don't get flu any time, not real flu. Well, hardly ever.'

'They say it's going the rounds. That's why Hazel phoned in sick.'

'I'll tell you about flu. People say they've got flu when they mean the common cold. You know why people won't admit suffering from the common cold? They don't want to be common, that's why. It's as simple as that. If everybody had flu who said they had flu, half the population would have been wiped out by now. It's a deadly disease, flu. It killed more people than the first world war. Tell you what, if I succumbed to flu it would carry me off in a matter of hours.' His voice squeaked and groaned as he talked. 'Since I had my colostomy, no resistance, that's the long and short of it.' He stared down at his desk. 'Resistance is useless,' he said in a hoarse German accent.

Despite what he said, the following day Geoff was off work, and the day after that Trevor was too. He was light-headed and feverish. He put up the same argument as Geoff had done but Christine took no notice. As far as she was concerned he had flu and had to stay at home from work.

This was after she had told him she was going to go off with

Art, and it felt odd to be put to bed by somebody you no longer slept with. He had an endless restless day while she was at work, dozing and sweating. Eventually he heard her come back home and begin clattering about downstairs. He felt rather weepy that she didn't come trotting up immediately to see how he was, then equally weepy when she did, bringing with her hot lemon, a couple of aspirins, and a bowl of lukewarm water with which she proceeded to wash his face. Then she made him change his dank pyjamas, and finally she gave his hair a good brushing. He lay back on the pillow with a new sense of well-being, as if he'd miraculously been donated a new head just when the old one was about to explode. He'd never felt consciously pleased to be the owner of hair before.

He found himself waving his weak arms at Christine in a gesture half of beseechment, half of gratitude. She didn't flinch, just did the part of the competent nurse, the firm mother. Even in his groggy state he knew it wouldn't be right to crank the handle and try to persuade her to stay with him after all. It would be emotional blackmail. And there was no percentage in saying sorry – she'd just think it was a symptom of his weakness.

It wasn't long after he was back on his feet that May rang him up and asked him if he wanted to save his marriage. By then he knew for certain that he did.

It wasn't just a matter of the political problems that a broken marriage would cause. Not that those were negligible. One thing that he'd come to accept since formulating his doctrine of political honesty was that practical motives didn't necessarily contradict issues of heart. There was nothing intrinsically cynical about wanting to survive in politics. What people didn't realise was that you could have a complex of reasons for wanting to do or not do something. He wanted his marriage to survive because he wanted to become an MP in due course. He also wanted it to survive because even after all these years he found it difficult to visualise his wife, and if she walked away from him their time together would walk away with her, and he'd be left with a blank. There was a kind of economy to it: he couldn't bear waste.

Also he wanted her to stay because there was a sweetness about her presence. After spending the evening at a council meeting, he would come home, and finding her there waiting for him somehow gave a soft centre to the evening – like breaking open a shell and finding a nut inside it. She was as sweet as a nut. The phrase had gone through his head over and over again while he recovered from his flu.

He had had time to think, over the months, about his anger that she had not had any sexual experience except with him. In fact the problem had focused itself, like sunlight through a magnifying glass, into another phrase: I can read her like a book. It was an apt way of putting it because it was when he was going through those reading orgies of his teenage years that he had met her. Those orgies had themselves been triggered by his guilt at faking his pass in O level French. He was aware of having a very clear way of looking at things – sometimes he wondered if it wasn't too clear, because other people didn't share it, and possibly that gave them greater capacity for living with complication. But he knew it made him effective in handling problems both at the bank and in his political career. If you can't live with complication, you resolve it.

What he had done, in relation to Christine, was ask for something she couldn't provide: a guilty secret in her past to counterbalance his lie about French. Of course, if she'd sowed a wild oat and told him about it from the start it wouldn't have been a guilty secret. What he wanted was the chance to accuse her and hear her lie. But all he'd heard was her telling the truth.

He knew there were other aspects to the problem, but these didn't invalidate his picture, they deepened it. His mother's death had triggered the whole crisis. One way you could describe what had happened: it had turned him savage. So he'd wanted to kill his relationship with Christine to counterbalance the death of his mother. But there was another way, too: his mother had had a past that had now become for ever inaccessible to him. And it was out of that past that he himself had come into the world. So he wanted Christine to have an inaccessible past to keep the symmetry.

All these explanations had flowed through his newly brushed head when he lay in bed with flu. When he was up again they flowed still, flowed so fast and unremittingly that they made him feel he had flu still. All the explanations were the true explanation.

But marriage was in one fundamental way different from politics: knowing the answer, or answers, to a problem, didn't seem to have anything to do with solving it.

Seven

It was a clean ear, basically.

Not fair, to look into it the way he had, but Art couldn't help himself. There was her head on the pillow, with her permy hair looking a bit like yesterday's dinner, and there was her ear.

Ears were a bit much sideways on, but then again, what wasn't, when looked at in the wrong way, or with the wrong attitude of mind? Houses similar, which you learned early on in his game. One man's hovel is another man's cottage, old Toby Penrose used to say.

Marge Bentley's ear was a touch unappetising, sure enough, when looked at this close. More hovel than cottage, no doubt at all about it. But when he examined it closer still, which he did by draping his arm over her chest and grasping her far shoulder in an affectionate manner, he got the all-clear. A bit of dinginess was par for the course, especially with it being situated on the shady side of her head. There was a soft dot of light on the tip of Marge's nose where it just caught the illumination from the window.

She stirred towards him. 'Not again,' she said. 'Man of your age.'

That had been far from his thoughts but suddenly it didn't seem such a bad idea. She had interpreted the way he'd moved closer to look in her ear, and in her business one and one always added up to two. Her eye slid round to check him, make completely sure. It was one of those deep brown, moist kind of ones, far better quality, you'd have to say, than the rest of her, like finding a jewel, a couple of jewels, in a council house.

Marge's was a true council house, inside and out. The bed was all right, tool of the trade, but the wardrobe and chest of drawers were surfaced in brown Formica with a grain on that was supposed to make you think of teak or mahogany. There was bubbly wallpaper on the walls with a repeated picture of yellow trellis-work that had some sort of green plant hanging from it.

'I'm ready for anything,' he said.

'Well, it isn't anything, it's just the usual thing. If you've got the energy to do it two times on the trot, you want to find yourself a hobby.'

'I've already got one. Golf.'

'Two hobbies then.'

'This is my other one,' he told her, sliding his hand from her shoulder and over her front. He didn't explain that this made three times in one afternoon, not twice.

'Fuck off, love,' she said, even while arranging herself, the way women do, so he could get at her. 'Whyn't you go round the pub?'

With Christine it had been an ejaculation of tears.

The preliminaries had been greedy, on both sides, and had taken his mind off the hollow feeling he had deep inside, that sad ache you get in your gut when you feel nothing good will ever happen again, as if you've fallen through a hole in life and found yourself permanently stranded in a late grey Sunday afternoon. But when his climax came, at that exact moment he found himself blarting all over again.

She rubbed her hand up and down his back.

He whispered: 'What are you trying to do, burp me?'

'I love it when you weep,' she whispered back.

'That's nice.'

For a second he was annoyed at her apparent callousness. But then, not. He had loved it too, bursting into tears. It had come upon him in exact parallel with what else was coming upon him, both sensations shivery and warm at once, big and little, sharp and soft.

Those opposites ricocheted round his head. He'd had sex so many hundreds, thousands, of times, but had never tried to put it into words before. Happy pain, that's what it felt like, sweet sadness. At both ends at once.

'I'll never ever see you again, as long as we both shall live,' he said.

'Don't be daft. Costford's not that big a place. You'll come in Smith's one of these days to buy a birthday card, and there I'll be.'

'Not with no clothes on, you won't.'

She wrinkled up her nose, raised her head, and rubbed his chest hair with it, as if to clear an itch. 'You never know your luck,' she said. 'Might be one of our special offer days. A free birthday suit with every card.'

She was full of beans, that's what he thought, caused by the fact that their affair was having to come to an end. Perhaps she knew he was thinking that, because she went solemn straight away, and said, 'You know it's ending because you said it had to.'

'I know.'

'It's not me that's ending it.'

'I know it's not.'

'I'm very glad it happened. And that this part of it happened. Especially this part.'

He believed her, up to a point. But he also guessed she was glad it wasn't going to happen any more. In fact he had an idea she wouldn't have done it at all, if she hadn't known for sure it was only going to be the once.

There was nothing sweet about his sadness as he left her house. She wanted rid of him by that stage, naturally enough, in case Trevor came home early. It was like playing a record at the wrong speed. She went through all the routine – goodbye, it was good, I'll always have a place for you somewhere inside me, no regrets – in a mad rush. She tugged his lapels, straightened his tie, pressed his stomach with her fist. Then they settled into a long final kiss, except it was short. She extracted herself halfway through, put her hands on his shoulders, spun him round, and gave him a gentle push in the small of his back. Suddenly he was in the empty street, conscious of being naked beneath his clothes, utterly forlorn.

Houses everywhere, was what he thought. No end to them, as far as the eye could see. And all he'd do for the rest of his life was sell them to people. It seemed boring beyond belief, he had no idea why. If he'd succeeded in getting fixed up with Christine he would have been in exactly the same position. Falling for a woman wasn't any sort of cure for being an estate agent. He would always have had his living to earn, more so perhaps, since children might have come along and Christine might have had to leave her job at Smith's to take care of them. But the set-up would have felt more special, would have had a point to it.

He found himself walking down towards Tinnington, where the big council estate was, not a part of town he patronised much, given there weren't any houses to sell. He'd come here a few months back, however, with a woman he'd met in a pub. It turned out to be a business arrangement, which was all right by him, in fact a relief because he'd wondered for a moment if he'd been getting himself into deep waters. There was no *Mr* Bentley in evidence but there was a lad around the place who looked no better than he ought to be, Marge's boy, presumably. It was nice to part with a few bob and feel they were all square.

Also, he now realised, it meant you could come back for another go.

It was a matter of replacing what he'd had with Christine: he didn't want it hanging over him. What he had to do was move on as soon as possible.

★   ★   ★

This time he ended up like an empty bottle, worse. He felt a gnawing pain in his lower gut as if he'd tapped into supplies he should have been saving for later. He lay on his back looking up at the ceiling. There was a browning splash mark in the middle of it.

'You had a leak?' he asked.

'You what?' She looked round at him, saw where he was looking, and looked up at the stain herself. 'Oh that. That was a Watney's Party Four. Bloke put the opener in and it went off like a rocket. The bed smelled like a brewery for the rest of the week.'

'Not the worst smell in the world.'

'It wasn't you what had to breathe it day in, day out.'

You could have changed the sheets, he thought.

'I lay here holding my breath,' she added. 'Just breathing enough to keep going.'

'This girl, goes to the doc's for a check-up. He says, Big breaths please. Yeth, she says, and I'm only thixteen.'

'I wasn't so bad when I was sixteen, neither,' Marge said glumly.

They lay in silence for a while. He wondered how many people the Watney's Party Four had been for. Could have been just one bloke who liked to get a few under his belt to fuel himself up. Could have been a proper little party. Christine already seemed worlds away.

'It's still only Wednesday,' he said.

She didn't reply but a few moments later said, 'You know those council flats.'

He gave her a quick look, just with his eyes. 'Which council flats?'

'The ones they're going to build on Prospect Hill.'

'What about them?'

'I want to put myself down for one.'

'You've got a house already.'

'Look at it.'

'It's all right.'

'It's a dump.'

'It's a bit of a dump.' There were some decent houses on the estate where it overlooked Waterloo Road, one of the big arteries into Manchester, but behind them the building got shoddier. The upstairs in Marge Bentley's house was just breeze-block, the doors were plywood, with the outside ones painted that salmon pink you only ever saw on council estates, and dandelions were the flowers that grew best. There was a permanent whiff of cooked cabbage on the wind. 'But it would be a step in the wrong direction, surely.'

'What would?'

'Going from a house into a flat.'

'I remember what my old mum used to say: snug as a bug in a rug. She used to say it in any weather, even hot. She always had a cardy on. She wasn't my mum it turned out, she was my granma. My sister was my mum. I used to think to myself, I wish *I* was that little bug.'

Turned out Marge's son was moving out. Or maybe that was only what she was hoping. Part of the intention behind the Prospect Hill flats was to extract single people from full-sized houses in order to alleviate the family log jam in the council waiting lists. A third of the development was to be for single occupation. Norman Forrester had kept him up to date about all this.

It had been top secret. Art bought the land in his own name, though in part with money put up by Norman. Ostensibly Art'd done it on behalf of a property developer who wanted to put a mixed estate there, houses and shops, not a proposition that could ever have made financial sense in the real world: the place was the scrag-end of nowhere. The developer was getting a favourable arrangement elsewhere in Costford to reimburse him for his trouble. Meanwhile an outline planning application had gone in for the proposal, only to be rejected because the council had, surprise surprise, other uses for the site. Norman's tender for the building work went through on the nod; he and Art would split the profits from the council's purchase of the land.

But that was all years ago. The council had bought the land, sure enough, but only paid half of the amount owing. The rest came due when building work got to a certain point. The arrangement for the building contract itself was even worse, with Norman only getting one third down, another when the second instalment of the purchase price came due, and the final third on completion of the project. Art had quite a bit of money owing to him, but not on the scale of Norman, who was feeling the pinch.

Now, finally, work was under way, but there were constant scares because the government still hadn't given it the all-clear. They just enjoyed having a Tory council hanging out to dry. Norman's building workers, sensing his weakness, had gone on strike for dirt money, and he'd more or less had to go on his knees to get them back at it, not a posture Norman relished. The whole development was a pig's ear, from one end to the other. And to top everything, people like Marge were getting in line for their share. It amazed him that a woman like her could be so up to date.

'Have you been hob-nobbing with some councillor?' he asked her.

'What you mean?'

He nearly said: more knob than hob, but thought better of it. There was no point in getting her back up. 'Guess what,' he said to change the subject, 'I saw a ghost this morning.'

'Did you? A real one? Cross your heart?'

He crossed it.

'It's what you drunk last night, that'll be the thingy.'

'You're the one who drinks Party Fours in bed.'

'Which is gnat's wee. Which was all over the ceiling in any case. What you think I'm going to do, open my mouth and wait for the drops to drop in it?'

'I was stone sober, as a matter of fact. I was valuing a house. There was a little old lady in it.'

'Was it a lady ghost?'

'It was a bloke ghost.'

'Oh.' She was watching him intently now. The sheen on the surface of her eyes seemed to tremble faintly, as if a tiny breeze was blowing across each of them. He wished they were Christine's eyes, though they were more beautiful than hers. The big drawback was Marge didn't have much brain. Also the face all round the beautiful eyes was lined and hard-looking, not from personality, just from life as a whole.

'It was the ghost of the little old lady's husband. She told me he was still alive.'

'Could you recognise him?'

'Yes. Except he didn't have a head.'

'It might have got knocked off in an accident. That's probably what killed him in the first place.'

'That would do it,' Art said. 'It still had a hat on, though.'

'What did it get up to?'

Art sat up, skewed round to face her and gave her a horrible look.

'Oh hot fuck,' she whispered.

'That's about all they can get up to, isn't it? – give you a horrible look. They don't have a big repertoire. They just go boo at you, it's not much of a career. And this one didn't have a face to give a horrible look with. All it did was stand there.'

'Did you run off? I would have been out that house like a rocket.'

'No, I carried on with what I was doing. It went after a while. It just faded away.' It's not exactly a lie, he thought, only a matter of the right words not always being used.

She was quiet for a moment, thinking about it. Then she said, 'It was Fray what bought the Party Four. I don't like the stuff. It tastes tinny to me. He left it lying round the kitchen and this bloke picked it up and brought it in. If Fray gets his hands on him there'll be hell to pay.'

'Why do you call him that? Is it short for something?'

'The bloke?'

'No, not the bloke. Fray.'

'I wanted to call him something nice, that's all. I was only seventeen. They wanted me to get him adopted. I thought, no, I'll call him something nice, and keep him. We always used to have corned beef at home, corned beef and baked beans. We had those tins. I loved the name on them. Fray Bentos. It's just one of them names that remind you of a long way away. I always think about palm trees. And then I thought, well my name's Bentley, it's practically the same thing. The name bloke was a bit funny about it, where you go to sign. I told him it was a family name. I told him we come from Scotland.'

'No palm trees there, that's for sure.'

'I know. I know there's no palm trees there. That's the way I pulled the wool over his eyes.'

Not hard to do, Art thought: who would ever guess the twerp would name her offspring after a tin of corned beef? 'I don't have a say about council houses,' he told her.

'It's a lickle flat what I want. Just a room to sit in and cook. And a bedroom.'

'Or flats.'

'Fray could come and see me. Perhaps he will come in a nice way. He'll be a bit older then. He's getting older all the time.'

Art tried to picture Fray dutifully visiting his mum, holding a bunch of flowers in a fist basically designed for twisting people's privates with. He wasn't a big bloke but there was something solid about him, as if his clothes had been filled to the brim with muscular body. He had a squarish face with big, slightly poky-out eyes like his mum's, except his were hard enough you could trip over them.

'We could have Sunday dinner,' Marge said wistfully.

'Corned beef and chips.'

'No, not –' She balled her fist and banged him on the chest with it. 'You're taking the mickey, you are. Roast beef and York-shire pudding.' Her eyes had that inward look people get when remembering a dream. 'I don't know how to cook Yorkshire pudding,' she whispered.

'Roast beef without Yorkshire pudding, then.'

'Roast beef without Yorkshire pudding,' she repeated, as if she wanted to memorise it to stop herself cooking Yorkshire pudding by accident. 'Then he'll go off again,' she said more cheerfully, and in a singsong voice added, 'First he'll come, and then he'll go off again. Bo-bom.'

'Sounds as if it's the going bit you're looking forward to most.'

'And I'll have a bedroom without Party Four all over it.'

She made it sound like becoming a virgin again.

'It might not be easy for you to do . . . this any more.'

'What you mean, lay in bed?'

'Not just lie in bed. Lie in bed with me. With anyone. With everyone. You know.'

'I thought I might give that up. No offence.'

'Oh, right.'

'Tell you what. When you have a flat, a one person flat, can you – can you have a person staying with you, not like you but . . . ?'

'You mean on an amateur basis.'

'Not paying, yes, that's what I mean.'

'It's like everything else, Marge. You can do what you like as long as you get away with it.'

'It's one thing not doing this. But I can't suddenly turn into Julie Andrews, can I, and just sing songs? You have to enjoy yourself some time.'

'I'll try to put in a word for you if you promise one thing.'

'All right.'

'Not say a word about it to anyone.'

'I thought you was going to say a different thing.'

'That as well.'

*   *   *

I won't say a word about it, Christine told herself as she waited for Trevor to come home. Not a dicky-bird.

She burst out laughing at the dicky, not a nice laugh. There was something sneery and self-satisfied about it. It was also exaggerated. But men shouldn't have those things if they don't want to be laughed at.

Wagging about.

Saying with those little fish mouths: be impressed.

Saying: love me.

Wag wag.

All laughs are exaggerated when you do them by yourself, she thought. Laughs are supposed to be done with other people. When you laugh alone it's at, not with.

Who she was laughing at she wasn't sure.

Could be Arty, bursting into tears just as he came. What number conquest was she, when all was said and done? Hundredth? Thousandth? Did he cry for them all? And if not, why not? There was nothing special about herself, Christine, she knew that well enough. She was ordinary to the point of mediocre, just the usual grade of human being.

Perhaps his tears were a kind of party piece. Maybe his women looked forward to them. They might be his claim to fame.

Or maybe she was laughing at Trevor. What kind of toad would want his wife to sleep with another man?

Even as she thought the word toad she knew Trevor wasn't one. She was the toad.

She said it to herself in the bathroom mirror: 'I'm the toad.' She had quite a square jaw and wide mouth which made her look the part. She stretched her mouth wider still and opened and closed it without the teeth showing. All I need now is to be green, she thought, with sort of knobs on.

But if she, Christine, was a toad, it was Trevor who'd driven her to it.

He had always been a bit of a mummy's boy. Only child of a single parent, it was bound to be a claustrophobic relationship.

She remembered how his mother had looked at her right from the beginning – at least when Trevor's attention was elsewhere – with horrible unforgiving eyes. But of course when she died Trevor was distraught.

He'd wanted Christine to have got up to no good just to take his mind off it, give himself something else to worry about.

You got me to do your dirty work for you, she thought. You bastard. You. You maker of other people into toads. She said the accusation in a croak, and laughed again, in that same nasty way.

Trevor's car drew up outside the house.

She knew it was his without looking, just as she would recognise his footsteps. She took the horrible expression off her face the same complete way that you might take a dress off that you didn't like. The thought made her smooth her actual dress with her two hands as she went to open the front door.

Trevor stood there with his key in his hand, looking as though he'd been caught out with his fly unzipped. As he focused on her, though, his face suddenly shone in that magical way it did sometimes. He must have guessed what I'm going to say to him, she thought, but realised immediately that wasn't it. There was something in his mind already, that he wanted to tell her, some good news. She felt an immediate twinge of disappointment that her own good news had been upstaged.

'I was –' he said.

'What?'

'Going to open the door.' He pushed the key towards her as if she needed evidence.

'Oh well, no need.'

'No,' he agreed. He was the only man she'd ever met with expressive teeth. 'No need,' he said.

'Come in, Mr Man,' she told him, feeling like a mum talking to her toddler. Perhaps that's what we need, she thought, heart sinking, to get us over this: offspring. Trevor had been hinting for years, but she'd never felt the urge. She enjoyed her work too much, and had always been scared of becoming like her own mum and dad.

She led him into the kitchen. It did feel peculiar, almost as if he was a stranger in the house, like Art had been. Perhaps Art was the point. He'd changed the house, so that now Trevor didn't quite belong in it as he had before. All to the good, maybe, in the long run. Perhaps their marriage could do with an injection of strangeness. That might have been what Trevor was getting at in the first place.

'You know that bloke Mr Dobbins. Michael Dobbins. You met him at that do at the Town Hall.'

She picked up the kettle and walked over to the sink. Oh bugger, there was her piece of toast, with a bite out of it, just as she had left it when Art knocked at the door. The bite was a nice clean semicircle, the last bite of an innocent woman. 'Michael Dobbins,' she said reflectively. She picked up the toast by one corner, the way you might a dirty piece of clothing by the point of its collar, or a dirty child by its ear, pressed the bin pedal with her foot, and dropped it in. It seemed to waft through the air in slow motion. Then she filled the kettle and plugged it in. 'Dobbins,' she said again. 'He was wearing a funny hat.'

'He's chairman of the Chamber of Commerce, and the Round Table. He walks everywhere with a silver-topped cane, as well as wearing a funny hat.'

'What about him?'

'Well, he's bought Riley's old store in the precinct.'

'Oh yes?'

'He's opening it as a bookshop.'

'Oh. Blimey.'

'Why do you say that?'

'Why d'you think? It'll be competition. Costford's hardly the bookiest place in the country.'

'His idea is, the more the merrier. You create your own customers. Supply first, then the demand follows. He's done it with his other businesses. He seems to have got pretty rich on it.'

All at once she knew what he was going to tell her. Sod you. You are looking all pleased because something nice is going to happen to me after what I've done this afternoon. Just when I really really needed to give *you* some nice news.

'Good for him.'

'He's going to ask you to be the manager.'

She'd realised it was coming but still her breath went.

'It would be different from Smith's. You'd make all the decisions. Choose what books to have in stock, how many. Michael wouldn't interfere. He would be too busy being important. I'm sure you could ask him for a lot bigger salary.'

'Phew.'

He looked at her, waiting for her to say something more, pleased as punch at being the giver of good news.

'Only . . .' she said.

'Only what?'

'I just thought – Oh, I don't know, this is neither the time nor the place.'

'The time or the place for what?'

'I was just wondering if my career ought to take a back step. A step backwards.'

To her relief he was looking disappointed. She needed to be in a position to cheer him up. It was vital for her to feel she was giving *him* a present.

'Oh?'

'I thought perhaps we should try for a family.'

He went as red as a brick. When he spoke he had a sort of paralysis of the tongue. 'Wad?'

You can try on a life.

She looked in the mirror. Her figure seemed to arrow down towards her ankles, as if she'd lost half a stone and toned her stomach muscles. Just from getting the news about a step up in her career. Her face was serious and managerial.

Collect your cards and bugger off, she said to some shrimpy reprobate who never clocked in on time.

She was a woman who'd spent the afternoon with her lover and whose husband was waiting for her in a dazed state in the lounge at the bottom of the stairs. She was going to be her own boss, more or less. Decisions would become sharp and crisp, unlike the muddy untidy affairs she had to contend with at Smith's, where all the important actions were taken by the area manager.

To her own amazement she tugged her bra up and exposed her breasts, as gawkily as if she was an adolescent all over again. 'Gosh,' she said approvingly. They were big but focused, as if they too had got the message. The unexpected air around them firmed them even more. She breathed in deeply through her nose. How did this afternoon become so wonderful, she asked herself, when a couple of hours ago I was in the slough of despond?

Then she patted her newly flat stomach, pulled her bra back into position, did up her blouse buttons, and trotted down the stairs.

Trevor was sitting in one of the Habitat chairs staring beatifically at the wall. His eyes looked as if they were looking at flowers.

'So,' she said, as if they were in the middle of a conversation, which in a sense they were, 'I don't think it would make a lot of sense, starting a new job, if we're going to, you know, have a try. Try.' I'm playing him like a fish, she thought. It all comes of leading a double life. On the other hand, it's *kind* play. It's for his greater good.

He turned his eyes on to her. 'But how come?' he asked.

'Oh,' she said. 'We just realised. It wasn't practical. And I love you.'

I'm learning so much about the art of lying, she thought. When is a lie not a lie? I didn't finish with Art because I suddenly remembered I loved Trevor. That wasn't it at all.

For one thing I didn't finish with Art at all, he finished with me.

And for another I didn't remember I loved Trevor, I just remembered I didn't love Art. Or didn't love him till I knew it was going to end, when it was safe to.

On the other hand I do know now that I love Trevor. The only snag is that that didn't have any influence on me leaving Art because at the time I'd forgotten it, or at least only remembered in my subconscious.

But. You couldn't get away from two things. She did love Trevor. And she and Art had finished their affair.

'Another thing,' she added, since he seemed lost for words. 'I'm sorry.'

'You've no need to be.'

'No, I am. I should have made allowances. Your mother's death, etcetera. I should have been more patient.'

Another one of those lies that was half a truth. It really was like learning a new language. While she was saying sorry about not being patient she was mentally applying part of her apology to going to bed with Art that afternoon.

Even as the memory entered her head she felt herself blush. She pictured their bedroom, a few hours ago, her cries winging around the room like seagulls. Their bedroom. Trevor's and her bedroom. Her and Art's bedroom. That was how these half-lies worked, when what you said seemed to have the capacity to go in two directions at once.

'I shouldn't have said what I did,' Trevor replied. 'I don't know what came over me.'

'Water under the bridge.' It was a comforting thought. Her own behaviour could float off downstream, along with Trevor's stupid remark.

'Do you really want to, you know, try?'

'Yes, I do.'

'All right, then.' He went bright pink. 'But I think you should still take this job. You never know, we might not be able to have a baby. Or it may take an age.'

'Knowing our luck I'll probably get preggers the first day on the job.'

'On the –'

'At work. My first day at work.'

'We can always get somebody in. An au pair or somebody.'

'An au pair! How much *am* I going to get paid? It's only managing a bookshop, not ruling the world.'

'Oh well, we can cross that bridge when we come to it.'

That's the bridge all our water went under, Christine thought. It'll probably be washed away by the time we try to cross it. Or at the very least there'll be a great troll living underneath. We'll be like the three Billy Goats Gruff. First of all Baby Billy Goat goes trot trot trotting over the bridge. Too small to eat for dinner. Then Trevor Billy Goat: trot trot trot. Too medium sized to eat for dinner. No, not medium *sized* exactly, he's tall enough, but medium in some other way. Medium in every other way. Too medium to eat for dinner. Then Me Billy Goat Gruff. Plumped up and stuffed, courtesy of Art.

Just what a troll wants to eat for dinner.

Trevor was pleased as punch. It made her feel above him, beyond him, superior to him, to see his face all shiny with happiness. It took her back to that sneery mood she'd had before. I've got a secret, I have, she thought. And you can't complain. That's exactly what you wanted me to have.

'No time like the present,' Trevor said timidly, not quite daring to catch her eye.

She looked at him as you look at a naughty boy. 'If you say so,' she said finally, and led the way upstairs.

Eight

While she was looking for her knife, Hilda found herself remembering and remembering something she had never seen happen in the first place.

Alice, pretty as a picture, sits on an upright chair in their little back garden as if she has a book on her head even though she hasn't. Despite being younger, Alice is more rounded than Hilda, who feels like a poor little stick in comparison, and keeping her back straight makes her bosom seem even bigger and more important.

It is a beautiful sunny day, as it usually seemed to be in those times, though abroad it must have rained a lot to make the trenches so muddy and horrible. Alice is sewing. She does it beautifully, her silver needle leaping over the material like a tiny minnow breaking the surface of a pond. Horace the cat prowls round her skirts, tail up and back arched. Bees buzz in the antirrhinums. The afternoon gently passes. The sunshine makes Alice's brown hair look blonde.

Alice stirs in her chair. It is time for tea. There is no Hilda here to prepare it today. Hilda is away, in Liverpool, staying with their grandparents.

Liverpool grandfather: a big gloomy Scotsman with moustaches all over his face, only his pointed chin shaven. He had damaged his leg in an accident in his warehouse, a place where he did what he did. He was in commerce. You can't die of a leg, was Hilda's belief, but strangely he could, and did. Having been away from his workplace for some weeks he began to die, not noticeably at first but more and more as the time passed, till eventually Liverpool grandmother summoned Hilda to help her.

Liverpool grandmother was small and bustling. In figure she was womanly, as people said at that time, which meant her bottom was so big it made her body lean backwards, and her bosom was so big it made it lean frontwards, while in between the two, preventing everything going off in opposite directions for once and for all, was a waist of unconvincing tininess, like a wasp has. The effect was of a little round being who couldn't be taken quite seriously. Hilda had always felt sorry for her, living in the shadow of her husband, who seemed tall and dangerous and pious enough to be her father.

But now, with him dying of accursed Leg, Hilda began to realise that the situation was more complicated than she'd ever imagined. It wasn't that Grandmother liked gloom, but rather she found fun and games inside it, like toys stored in a dark mahogany cupboard.

'Who doesn't want 'is dwink, nen?' she said to Grandfather's big sweating head as it lay on the pillow.

The dark eyes under their furry grey brows looked up at her. He made a dry, dismissive sound.

'What?' she asked, cupping a hand to her ear like a deaf person on the stage. 'What?'

Then, to Hilda's astonishment: 'Me doesn't want 'is dwink,' the dour voice replied. The eyelids half closed, and the face turned away, impatient to concentrate on the scalding Leg once more.

Out of the room tears poured out of Grandmother. 'I can't bear to lose him. He's such a treasure. He's my own boy.' Her bright little face peered at Hilda through private rain, as if in hopes Hilda could pull some solution out of the bag like a conjuror pulling a rabbit. 'I asked them to take it away, but they wouldn't.'

'Take what?' asked Hilda, wondering if in some kind of baby language she was referring to Grandfather going to hospital.

'His leg, what do you think? I told them, I wouldn't mind him only having the one.' She paused thoughtfully a moment, the tears still pouring down, as though visualising this possibility for the first time. Then she looked up at Hilda. 'I would get used to a stump in the course of time,' she said, her chin quivering. 'But they tell me, it won't do. The inflammation has spread along the bone.'

'Oh, goodness,' Hilda said, not liking the word bone.

'He saved my life once upon a time,' Grandmother said, screwing up her face and shaking her head abruptly as if to say, No, No.

Hilda knew this story – it was family legend. Grandfather had had some business on the Isle of Wight and had taken Grandmother with him. The small hotel in Ryde where they were staying had caught fire and he had appeared through wreaths of smoke in his nightclothes, Grandmother in his arms. Hilda had always imagined the heroism involved as of a sternly dutiful sort, but now she learned otherwise.

'"I'll soon have you out of here, my little dandelion," was what he said as he carried me down the burning stairs. He called me his dandelion because I once confided in him that I was nine years old before I learned not to wet the bed.'

My little dandelion, Hilda repeated under her breath, amazed.

By next day Grandfather had become even worse. The doctor came and sat by him. His stern face looked down; Grandfather's stern face looked up. Hilda was terrified to be in the room with them. It was like those moments in school when someone has done something wrong, and the teacher and headmaster have become involved, and even the funny and naughty children have turned solemn. She knew already that Grandfather was dying, but it was almost as if something worse still was at stake, though what that could be she couldn't imagine. Perhaps it was just that death was an even more terrible business than she'd ever thought.

Suddenly Grandfather cried out. It was a hoarse bellow, like a bull, not that she'd ever heard a bull. She had heard a cow on one occasion, when she was taking a walk along Cheshire lanes with her family, and they came upon a herd of cattle being driven towards the gate of a field. One of the cows spotted Hilda with its wild, rolling eye, and roared at her in a shockingly loud voice, its mouth in an O like a human mouth. 'Don't worry about it,' Father said as Hilda burst into tears of fright, 'she's just warning you off her young.'

Grandfather's roar was just the sound pain makes, though strangely it still had a Scottish accent clinging to it. The doctor got to his feet and shooed Hilda towards the door of the room, flapping his hands at her the way you do to tell the smell of burnt food to leave the kitchen. As she got to the door Hilda grasped Grandmother's arm in an attempt to take her with her, but was shaken off. Not for a second was Grandmother's attention deflected from the bed.

While she waited outside on the landing Hilda remembered when she was small, waiting outside the door of the bedroom at home while her sister Alice was being born, how jealous and left out she'd felt.

Perhaps, though, she only thought of that comparison later. What she did notice was the light. The landing window overlooked the street at the front of the house, with the leafy heads of the trees lining it glowing almost yellow in the intense sunshine. Grandfather's bedroom had been curtained, as if letting the day in would add to his agony. What the bright landing sang to Hilda was that another world still existed away from suffering and death, a world out there: a world, she learned soon enough, that had been lost to her while her back was turned.

As Alice stirs in the hot afternoon, she becomes aware of noises in the house. The back door opens, and into the garden steps George. Alice clutches the sewing to her bosom at the sudden man.

George is lean and handsome in khaki. His arm is in a sling. He is carrying his cap with a badge on the front, flashing in the light. He seems official in his uniform, with all the authority of the war behind him.

Alice offers him her hand. George takes it. They both bow their heads a little, as if about to dance.

Alice speaks to George. George speaks to Alice. Oddly, although over the years Hilda has watched the scene time and again in her mind (even though she wasn't there in the first place), she has never been able to recapture the words they say to each other. It's as though she is watching a scene in one of the silent movies she and Petey saw so much of in the years following the war.

George must enquire about Hilda's whereabouts; Alice must explain.

Alice's mouth opens and closes like a snapdragon's does when you press its cheeks. Hilda's name must have been spoken, and the word Liverpool. If she strains towards the memory, cupping her hand round her ear as Grandmother did when listening to Grandfather refuse his dwink, she can almost make out 'Hilda' and 'Liverpool' in the sighing of the breeze and the murmuring of the insects. Her tale is being told in snapdragon language.

The wind goes from George's sails. Hilda can see his shoulders slump slightly. He puffs out his cheeks in response to this facer. Liverpool!

Liverpool, the bees solemnly agree.

Then of course he hoists his shoulders again. It would be rude to remain despondent in Alice's presence. She offers him a cup of tea.

Through the gentle heat of the afternoon Hilda can see Alice miming the offer, as though George cannot hear her either. Alice has put her sewing down on the seat of her chair, and holds an imaginary saucer in her left hand. She picks an invisible cup from it in her right, her little finger rigid as if sending George a terrible, coarse signal.

George stares at the finger, and then a smile of recognition begins to spread across his face.

It seems to Hilda that George's smile is like the fuse on a firework, moving slowly and inexorably to the point where it will trigger an explosion of brilliant white, red, blue, a burst of shocking fire.

The knife was nowhere to be seen.

She went through her chest of drawers, taking everything out of each in turn.

The little undies one first, with its horrid old lady vests and brassières and knickers. Knickers got huge just at the moment when you were shrinking away with age and your bottom was withered like an old orange, too shrunken to fill them out. Unrestrained by buttocks, her knickers rode up to her tummy button and above, like the incoming tide.

Then the little socks and stockings drawer. Poor long-ago Liverpool grandfather: if his little, long-ago wife had had her way, his own drawer would have been full of single socks, and single shoes would have awaited him at the bottom of his wardrobe.

Hilda sang:

> 'You put your left leg in
> You put your left leg out
> In out in out, you shake it all about
> You do the hokey-cokey
> And you turn around
> That's what it's all about!'

He would have had to hop backwards and forwards, supported by his fellow dancers.

She visualised that stern Scottish head with its tufted brows, bouncing like a kangaroo, his mouth beneath the moustaches hymning out the hokey-cokey song. She laughed, then felt a twinge of guilt.

Serve you right, she thought all of a sudden. You deserved to face the prospect of hopping.

Hop to your doom, my bonny.

Fair play, it wasn't his fault he died, and by jingo he'd suffered on the way. But there was no need for him to become all ill at that particular moment. He'd taken *her* life away too, just when she'd been going to start it. It was all right for him: he'd had his own little dandelion to keep him company.

Now Hilda wanted to weep. His dandelion. How brave he'd been, rescuing Grandmother from the fire. And what sufferings he'd had to bear, with that Leg causing unbearable gyp. She had no cause to be cruel and disrespectful, even after all this time.

Then her first big drawer, with petticoats and slips. She laid them on the bed where they looked like shrunken women, much like herself in fact, lying dead over and over again.

This one, heart attack, like poor George. Separated in life, but dead together.

This one, ca-ca-cancer.

> When the moon shines
> Over the cowsheds
> I'll be waiting at the k-k-k-kitchen door

This one, just a waist slip: chopped in half by a railway train.

> Please Mr Porter
> Whatever shall I do
> The train that's come from Birmingham
> Has cut me quite in two.

Then the first cardigan and jumper drawer. One jumper knitted by Cherry, with one of its shoulders somehow bigger than the other, so when she put it on she looked like the Hunchback of Notre Dame, and went round smiling with her face all lopsided.

Hilda pulled it on over her head, now. She couldn't remember a jumper song, so sang:

'I could write a sonnet
About your Easter bonnet'

head bobbing as if she was mental while she did so.

Lastly her other cardigan and jumper drawer, which had her travelling blanket in it too. Still no knife. No knife in any of them. She inspected the empty drawers because it was amazing how you could overlook things. She had overlooked her whole *life*, just because she'd been at Liverpool at the crucial moment.

Her life had been sitting there waiting for her on a garden table in 1918, with the sun blasting away and the bees roaring in the snapdragons. And would you credit it, Alice had raised it to her lips and drunk it down in her place!

George was Hilda's fiancé. That's what you call it, surely, when a hand comes out and takes hold of you.

It had been like being in a heap of oranges and lemons on a barrow, and somebody comes along and picks you out. Of course she didn't have to let herself be picked, but in fact she was so happy about it that she could hardly stop herself from being very unladylike and doing some fruit picking in return. George didn't make it seem vulgar or disagreeable, but somehow witty, like a shared joke, and a little bit wicked. The fact that his other arm was in a sling helped the effect.

And then, when her back was turned for a week or two, Alice stole him from her, and that was that.

The worst part of it was that Alice didn't even seem to like him very much, at least not after they were married. And George didn't seem to like her very much either. It was such a waste.

He didn't settle down well in the aftermath of the war. He worked in his family's grocery shop in Waveney Bridge until his father died, and after that it was his. Alice meanwhile did sewing from home. Then, in the thirties, the shop failed, like many others, and Alice got herself employment at a tailor's. They never had children, whether through luck or judgement. George worked in other shops but didn't hold any position for very long. He didn't look witty any longer, or even wicked, just fat and ordinary. Alice, almost to show him up, got slimmer as time went on, and even glamorous in a common sort of way, with bright red varnish on her nails. The more George ran out of steam, the busier and more full of beans Alice seemed to get.

Once when Hilda went to visit them on a hot summer's day, George was wandering aimlessly over their front lawn carrying the cat. He was in trousers and vest, with a handkerchief knotted in each corner on his head. Hilda remembered how he'd come calling that day when she was in Liverpool, his uniform on and his cap with its gleaming badge under his arm, his other arm neatly in the sling, and she almost wept to see how he'd gone down. There was the sound of humming coming out the open door, from Alice sewing inside with a mouth full of pins.

George looked at Hilda from below his hanky. The cat looked at her too. The cat had the expression on its face that cats often seemed to have, as much as to say, 'Clear off, you. I'm a cat.' George's expression was one he often seemed to have these days also, something shifty about the eyes, as though he was having to peer at her round a corner. Hilda refused to look away and to her surprise he did too. In the distance 'Sing as We Go' was coming from the house in hum form.

An arm rose slowly towards her chest. The fingers and thumb opened, like a snake opening its mouth. Then the mouth shut again, clamped on her left breast like a baby – like May, in the days when she'd fed there. Hilda looked at it in horror. She was conscious of George staring at her face while she looked down at his hand. The cat scurried down to the lawn from his other arm.

Hilda felt a shudder rise through her body. When this had happened all those years before it had excited her, but that had been a different world, a different bosom even, a different George certainly. It was all too late, and it was Alice's fault. She pulled back: the hand came with her. She grasped George's wrist and tugged it away from her. To her fury her breast followed. She let go of his wrist and gave him a shove in the chest. He stumbled backwards and finally released her. Her breast fell back into place. She had a sudden picture of bulky George knocking on front doors and running off down the street, like an enormous schoolboy. It occurred to her, as it never had when she was young, that George made a habit of this behaviour, that he was one of those men women called a pest. Funnily enough even this realisation didn't alter her view of what had originally happened between them, and the understanding that she believed had followed from it.

In the second war, May had gone off to live with George and Alice. It was as though Alice couldn't be satisfied with taking Hilda's man, she had to have her daughter too.

May had been a fat pale ginger baby and had grown up along the same lines. Her legs from the start were sturdy to the point of bigness, there to do a job. Looking at her daughter made Hilda realise your body was simply a sort of personal motor car, something that enabled you to get out and about in the world. If that was the case, then May's was near enough a small lorry, the type builders drove, with ladders and buckets on the back.

May was Petey's baby, that was the problem. It was like having a cuckoo in the nest. If she'd been the product of George, the George of 1918 with his khaki uniform and his arm in a sling, she'd have been a different girl altogether, slim, perhaps even delicate. Lissom, she'd have been, Hilda's favourite word.

It was one thing having a little lorry for a daughter, quite another for her to be parked in someone else's yard. The loss made Hilda want to shriek with rage, on a daily basis. It was Liverpool all over again, except for years and years instead of days and weeks. And except for the fact that Hilda was in her own house. Her home had become exile.

She tried to explain it to Petey. He listened, with that large face of his turned towards her like one of those radar dishes they had at aerodromes. His receding ginger hair was Brylcreemed to the point of blackness. He didn't seem any happier about what had happened than she was.

'But she's grown up, duck,' he said finally, 'so there's not a lot we can do about it. I suppose we should be grateful she's got Alice to keep a eye on her. And it's not much of a place for getting in trouble, Waveney Bridge. Also, who's going to want to drop a bomb on it? Not Hitler, he's got more sense.' He thought about it in his ponderous way. '*I* wouldn't mind dropping a bomb on it, but that's a horse of a different colour.'

With my daughter gone, Hilda thought wearily, I can't even concentrate on the war. Stupid really, but that was how she felt, as if a wireless programme she wanted to listen to was being spoilt by bad reception. People had gone to all the trouble to put on a world war, and she couldn't give it her full attention.

When the war was over, May returned. Perhaps it had been a kind of personal evacuation after all. That was Petey's verdict, anyhow. 'She didn't get blown up, that's the long and the short of it,' he said gloomily. 'Maybe it goes to show she's not as green as she is cabbage-looking.'

May took up residence in the family home as if she'd never been away in the first place. After those years of rage and jealousy Hilda felt astonished that everything could get back to normal so easily. What did I expect, she wondered: that she would return petite and dainty, as if all that had been wrong with her was not being brought up proper in the first place? She didn't know whether to be glad or sorry that May was still the same old galumphing daughter she'd always been. She must have been twenty-four by that time, but there was no mention of any chap. Hilda tried to suggest that it was high time for a bit of courting, but to no avail.

One day they were playing Monopoly with a cousin of Petey's, Howard by name, who had come up from Abingdon to stay with them for a couple of weeks. Howard was a poor crippled bloke who swung himself along on a couple of crutches, and who was no more than five foot tall, though broad in the shoulders, probably as a result of the repeated swinging action. This was a few years after the war, when May was in sight of thirty. She was a secretary in a firm of solicitors in central Manchester by this time.

Not Howard, no, not Howard. He was a good ten years older than May, and a relative, though distant. Still, sometimes during that fortnight Hilda could have wished Monopoly buried in the back garden. She herself was always the top hat, May the flatiron, Petey the racing car. Strangely, Howard habitually took the old boot, even though he had boots himself like lead weights at the bottom of his legs and you wouldn't have thought he'd want to be reminded. What a strange thing for a mother to have to fear, that her daughter, because of having large pale legs, might end up being paired off with a man with hardly any legs of his own worth speaking of. Sometimes Hilda had the thought her life was dogged by legs.

> Big ones, small ones
> Some as big as your head
> Give them a flick, a twist of the wrist
> That's what the showman said.

Nothing was going on with Howard, legs or no legs: that's what the conversation proved. Quite the contrary. But it sent a chill down Hilda's spine all the same.

'Men,' May said, rolling her eyes up towards the ceiling and then rolling them back towards Howard. 'I can tell you for-what about *men*.'

'Go on, then,' he said. He picked up his boot and sent it on five squares, touching down delicately each time on tippy tiptoe like a ballerina, and landing up on Fenchurch Street Station. 'Me own,' he added.

'For one,' May said, counting it off on her finger, 'you have to treat them like a big baby.' She grinned reflectively with her large fishy mouth. My God she's ugly, Hilda told herself. She noticed that a row of yellow hairs had appeared above May's upper lip. Just what she needs, she thought, shaking her head in despair. 'My Mr Tompkin, at the office,' May continued, 'when he's going out to see a client, says, "Just finish it off for me, there's a dear," and passes me his comb. His actual comb! Then he bends his head down towards me and I have to, you know, comb his hair for him.' She rolled her eyes again as she said comb, and did a combing action with her hand. She was all fluttery with excitement. Then she hunched up her shoulders and did a comic frown, as much as to say, what an amazing world! Her eyes seemed bright with joy.

Hilda shut her own eyes in pain. What small potatoes, was her version.

'Not my worry,' Howard said, wagging his bald head. Hilda hadn't thought about him being bald before. Good God, what remained of the poor chap, having been encroached upon from both ends?

'The man ought to have some pride,' Petey said. 'All you need is a jar of Brylcreem.'

'I suppose my chairbacks and pillows needed a jar of Brylcreem as well,' Hilda said. 'Living in this house is like living inside a chip pan.'

'His hair is very fine,' May said. 'It's like a little child's hair. The comb just slides through it.'

'All the more reason,' Hilda told her sternly, 'for him not to take advantage. If he had hair like barbed wire you could make allowances.'

'For two,' May said, ticking it off on her finger again.

Petey was rolling the dice. 'Damn and blast,' he said, 'I've got double four.'

'It's only a game,' Hilda told him, 'no need to swear about it.'

'Leicester Square with two houses,' Howard said. 'Three hundred and thirty pounds.'

'He only has to sit down at his desk and it becomes a tip. I put all his letters in one pile, and all his searches in another, and –'

'Who's this?' Petey asked testily, counting out his notes.

'I wish you wouldn't lick your fingers to do that,' Hilda told him. 'There's years of dried lick on those notes by now.'

'That's because I've spent years paying out rent.'

'I think there's orange juice on one of my five hundreds,' Howard said. He held it to the light. 'And a bit of pith.'

'You're just showing off you've *got* a five hundred, that's what you're doing.'

'Mr Tompkin is who it is, like I said.'

'The one with hair like barbed wire,' Hilda said.

'The one with hair like a child's hair. Oh, I give up.'

'Well, I presume there's more than one bloke in the office. It's Mr Tompkin this, Mr Tompkin that.'

May blushed. Because of her complexion her blush had a rather orange hue. 'That's who I'm secretary to. There's Mr Hammond too. And Mr Baxendale. That's what I'm saying: being men they're much of a muchness.'

'Oh blimey, five,' Petey said. 'That's me on Regent Street.'

'Twenty-six pounds,' said Howard.

'Not that anyone seems interested.' May shook her head bad-temperedly, trying to keep to the point. 'Men, though,' she added, still with a hot face.

'Oh no, fifty-two quid, being as I own all three greens.'

Hilda was about to say: how do you expect us to be interested? Out of your audience of three, two of us are men to start with.

And then she realised.

Howard and Petey weren't men. They were people. You played Monopoly with Howard and Petey. Men proper were remote beings, a wistful distance away, like elves or pixies with their unkempt hair and untidy desks. You tidied them up, and combed them, then you went home and tried imagining, in the depths of your bed, possessing one of your own.

For the first time, Hilda felt a wave of pity for May. She had no earthly chance of getting a husband if she thought men were too good to be true.

'All I want after that lot,' said Petey, 'is to go straight to jail.'

★   ★   ★

Petey wasn't very good at dying, not by comparison with Liverpool grandfather. He lay gasping on his bed like a stranded fish. It didn't help that it was lung cancer, a panicky way to go. He cried a lot too, which made Hilda lose patience, even though she felt sorry at heart.

One day, quite near the end, he said something strange. Hilda had gone down to make him a cup of broth. When she returned his face had changed from its pallor to a deep angry red. He was looking up at the ceiling with dissolving eyes. What he said was: 'Bugger that George.'

Hilda wondered if she'd heard right. She'd not confided her long-ago pash. But in any case, nothing had come of it. George's loss, Petey's gain, was the way to look at it. She put the broth on the bedside table and leaned over.

'Sod George,' Petey said, with real hatred in his voice. 'Damn George to hell and back.' He was still staring up at the ceiling with those desperate eyes, for all the world as if she wasn't even in the room.

'Here's your soup,' she said falteringly.

He continued to take no account of her. The cursing had made him pant, and he lay on his pillow muttering with rasping breaths. She tiptoed out, and for some reason went into the bathroom and locked the door.

George, why George? She sat on the toilet to think about it.

Oh my God.

She realised he thought that George was May's dad. He must have guessed that something lay between them and put two and two together.

True: Hilda had had May as soon as may be after getting married, bang on nine months. But May was Petey's daughter all right, you only had to look at her. She was made of the same raw unbeautiful clay. If the father had been George, the girl would have been lissom. George would have been lissom too, not a swollen old man who pawed at you.

In any case, girls like Hilda didn't get up to that sort of thing in those days, even when they had the notion they were engaged.

Understanding what Petey believed made her more angry with Alice than ever. That woman had taken the girl over to such an extent her own father thought he'd been disowned. He was lying on his deathbed in anguish.

It was difficult to broach the subject without making matters worse.

She went back in the bedroom. The soup was untouched. Even in the last few minutes Petey had become noticeably worse. His eyes were rolled up in their sockets and he was gasping for breath.

She leaned over the bed.

'What about George?' she asked.

He made a little questioning sound in reply.

'Why sod George? Why bugger George?'

Slowly, slowly, he moved his eyes to look back at her face.

'Not George,' he said. 'Jaw. I think it's in my jaw now. I can't eat my soup even. It hurts to talk. So much.' A tear slid from his eye on to the pillow.

'Oh. I thought you said George.' She didn't believe him.

'Sod my jaw,' he said, as if to prove it.

For ever after, Hilda had the odd sense that May had somehow let her father down. That it was *she* who had been unfaithful to him. In fact neither of them had, unless having fallen in love with someone who didn't love you back made you unfaithful.

After Petey, Hilda was quickly wed to Dan Baxendale, the senior partner at the solicitors' where May worked. May was appalled. Her whiskery gob popped like a fish. Serve her right. Those solicitors weren't her private property. And if they were she should do something more useful with them than brush their hair when they went out of the office. If ever there was a young lady totally lacking in va-va-voom, it was May.

Dan had come round about the will. Petey's business was a bit complicated, as he part-owned his butcher's shop in Costford with his brother Cyril. Petey's part had to be valued and sold to Cyril without a family row. Dan did that well enough and in the process he and Hilda came to an understanding. He was a bit older than Hilda and was handsome, at least from a distance. A change was as good as a rest, she told herself, and certainly bed-time was a livelier occasion than it had ever been before. And just having had two husbands was fun in itself. Somehow it seemed to put old George in his place.

> I'm Henery the Eighth I am I am
> I'm Henery the Eighth I am
> Just got married to the widder next door
> She's been wed seven times before.

Dan had been widowed too, and had a grown-up son living in Australia.

Sometimes, when her new husband came home from work, Hilda welcomed him with 'Danny Boy'. He usually came back on the bus with May, who'd wriggle like a salted slug at the song. Then, one day, only four months after Hilda's marriage, May came home alone.

'I've got some very very bad news for you, Mother,' she said.

'Oh yes?' She guessed straight away but for some reason found herself playing a part, as if she expected her daughter to be making a fuss about nothing.

'Mr Baxendale died at work.' She always called him Mr Baxendale, even though he'd become her stepfather.

'Oh, did he?' Hilda replied, still unable to stop herself from sounding as if she didn't believe a word of it.

'He suffered a heart attack. There was nothing anybody could do.'

'I suppose it was you who laid him out.'

'I did no such thing. I sat at my desk and cried my eyes out. Even Mr Hammond shed a tear. He blew his nose that loud way people do when they're upset.'

'It must have been like an abattoir.' Hilda had once told Petey the story of the terrible mooing she had received from a cow when she was a small girl, and in return he confided to her what a slaughterhouse sounded like, the wailing of the damned.

'It wasn't at all like that. It was more like the last trumpet.' Suddenly May burst into hysterical laughter, bawling and cackling both at once. Her face was racked as she tried to suppress the torrents of mirth, as unstoppable and painful as a fit. Perhaps because May used the word 'last', Hilda thought to herself, she's getting the last laugh, and the thought proved prophetic.

It wasn't long before May was going out for meals with Hubert Hammond, the third partner. He was a widower like Dan, with a daughter called Cherry who was going through a difficult adolescence. What help May could be, heaven only knew, since she'd never gone through an adolescence of any kind herself, but now she was taking pride in being a mother to the girl. It seemed quite false to Hilda, like a child dressing up in adult clothes, though of course May was old enough and ugly enough to take on the part, being in her mid-thirties by this time. It was just that she'd never done anything to earn the right to pontificate. The other funny thing was that because Hubert was much older than May, in his fifties, his company made her go all flirtatious and lively. She became at once girlish and motherly, the two things that had been completely lacking from her womanhood, if what was left could be called that.

May began to call Hubert Hub, a coy invitation to marriage if ever there was one. Something about the way she said it reminded Hilda of Liverpool grandfather and his dandelion, not that May had ever known either of them. Hilda tried to imagine May calling him Hub in the office. She wondered if Mr Tompkin still offered her his head to comb.

The wedding was arranged for the spring of 1956, within a year of Dan's death. Though she'd known it was coming, the announcement made Hilda go shivery with indignation. She could feel loneliness gathering around her as if it was a solid substance, something which muffled your voice.

After the wedding Hub sold his house in Altrincham because Cherry needed a fresh start, and they all three lived here with her. Hub had a passion for local politics, and within a few years he'd become Mayor of Costford. Lord and Lady Mayoress, dressed in their custard, Hilda thought darkly.

One day, Hilda bought a whole joint of meat. May usually did the shopping but on this occasion Hilda felt a kind of lust for a piece of her own. She went to Petey's old shop. May always got their meat from Eatmore's, which was closer.

Cyril looked taken aback, and oddly guilty, as if aware he'd got her half of the shop for a snip: she'd given strict instructions to Dan not to haggle. She asked for a modest cut of beef but Cyril insisted on giving her a huge one, and refused point blank to take anything for it. 'That's the advantage of having a butcher in the family,' he said, giving her a wink. He'd always been a nitwit.

She cooked it while all the others were out, just for herself. She didn't bother doing any vegetables with it.

When it was done she took out Petey's old carving set and got to work. Carefully she sliced the whole joint up. An odd thought struck her while she was doing so: she could feel the sensation of the knife blade passing through meat even though it wasn't a part of her body, just dead metal. The beef resisted a tiny amount, then seemed to cooperate, separating for the blade.

The job was intricate and absorbing, like doing a jigsaw puzzle. She was panting when she'd finished, but also, for the moment, felt happy and satisfied. The last thing she wanted to do was eat any of it. Carving had been pleasure enough. She put the meat in the dustbin, buried below other rubbish, so the others wouldn't know, and left the back door open to get the smell away. When she got home May told her off for letting herself get cold.

*   *   *

That's what she wanted now, the chance to carve. Recently the house had become completely drained of knives, not a one in the cutlery cupboard, no scissors in the sewing basket, or even pinking shears, not even nail scissors any more in her bedside drawer – they'd been replaced by a sort of tortoise which munched the ends of her fingers and toes. And the private knife she'd bought herself was gone.

What she needed was edge and point, sharpness in general. Ever since May had married her Hub, words had begun to get stuck inside Hilda and by now it was as though her head had become a round prison like an igloo and they couldn't escape. It made May and Cherry think she'd gone potty. They had no idea she was just the same inside as she always had been. She could think her thoughts and decide what to say, but when she opened her little door they couldn't get out, or if they did they got all jumbled and torn, like a crowd fleeing a burning cinema. The only words that seemed to work properly were in songs, because they were sent on their way and kept in the right order by the notes.

Nine

'I believe you've been meeting with the high-ups,' Geoff Cartwright said as Trevor walked past his desk on the way to his office.

Trevor stopped, thought for a second. It hadn't been sarcastic or loaded.

He wouldn't normally have assumed such a thing, but the remark had hit him while his feet weren't quite reaching the ground, as if he was a hovercraft; and the effect was to make him slowly descend that inch.

He turned. Geoff's head was studiously pointed at the transaction slips on his desk.

'Oh yes. The very high-up ones,' he replied. He'd wanted to say something funny, to take away any possible edge, but he couldn't think of anything.

'I believe at that level they think very bruising thoughts,' Geoff said, still without looking up.

Trevor wondered whether this was his way of asking if he was in trouble. That would be much more Geoff's game than trying to take him down a peg. He nearly reassured him but then thought better of it – he would only sound boastful. 'They've never even slept with a woman – completely above it,' he replied.

Now Geoff did raise his large round head. He looked into the middle distance, and growled softly. Trevor could see his lower lip vibrating beneath his goofy teeth.

'I did that once upon a time,' Geoff said.

'There you are, then. That must be why you're not one of them.'

'Those were the days. That was the day. Unpeeling a Durex, nothing like it. You can keep your blimming bananas.'

Trevor laughed and walked on towards his office. From behind came Geoff's voice, softly, 'Trevor.' Geoff hadn't called him that since Trevor was his junior.

Trevor stopped and turned back. Geoff got up from his desk and walked up to him. 'There's something I want to talk to you about,' he said.

'OK. Come into the office.'

'I'd rather meet after work, if you've got time.'

They arranged to meet in a pub, not the one two doors down but another one in the next road, the Swan.

They made their separate ways to it, almost as if they were having a strange office affair. Geoff got there first and insisted on buying the drinks.

'I'm not supposed to touch the stuff,' he said. 'Cheers.'

'Cheers.'

'Alan's been dead a year, all but.'

'I suppose he has.'

'One thing I never thought I'd do, outlive Alan Thomas.'

'Funny old world.'

'You took the very words out of my mouth. Anyhow, I won't outlive him long.'

'How would you know? How would any of us –'

'*I* know.' Geoff nodded, as if agreeing with a third party. 'I know all right.' He picked up his pint and took a big pull. Trevor had a mental picture of it pouring out of his gut virtually unchanged, like rainwater from a broken downpipe.

Geoff put his pint down and took out a large hanky. For a horrible second Trevor thought he was going to wipe his eyes with it, but he dabbed at his mouth instead. 'It's flared up again.'

'Oh. Bugger.'

'Bugger is right. Bugger bugger bugger.' He put his hanky back in his pocket. 'I don't know whether to take retirement, go on the sick, or what. I've got to look into it. But whatever I do, you won't be seeing much more of me about the place.'

'Don't worry about that. Just get better, is all that matters.'

'I'm not going to get better, there's no point in beating about the bush. I've had my allotted span.' He sighed. 'Any road up, you'll be going yourself, won't you?'

'Me?' For a second Trevor thought Geoff was accusing him of being about to die too, another symptom of his high-speed career.

Geoff spoke very slowly but it still didn't sound barbed: it was as if he was saying, this is the level *I'm* on, where these concepts have to be handled with care: 'People meet the high-ups for one reason, in my experience, to get promoted. I take it you've been given a managership.'

Trevor could hardly bring himself to speak, the whole thing felt so tactless and crass. 'Mm-hm,' he agreed.

'Thought so. Congratulations, by the way.'

'Oh well. It suddenly doesn't seem to matter an awful lot.'

'Of course it matters. I would have liked one. I would have loved one. I would have loved getting an *assistant* managership. Look at me, all I ever got was senior clerk. And I'm pushing sixty. What are you? Not above thirty, I'll bet. That's what they call a meteoric rise. Whoosh.' He did a movement of his hand, like a plane taking off, then sighted along it as if it was a rifle. 'Bang. Right on target.' He lowered his hand and picked up his pint with it. 'Your health. Good luck to you.'

Trevor felt his face burning. 'Thank you,' he said.

'And when I say your health, I mean it.'

For a moment Trevor couldn't say anything more; so he put his hand on Geoff's shoulder and patted it lightly, as if reassuring an excitable horse. 'The thing is, Geoff, the only reason they've done it is because I'm going to be the North Costford Labour candidate in the general election. They want to look as if they're very gung-ho about me, just in case. That's all it is.'

'Oh yes. You're only going to be a bank manager because after that you're going to be an MP. You have a happy knack of making it all sound like nothing at all. You'll make a good polit-ician, you will.'

'Geoff, one thing –'

'Don't take that the wrong way. I mean a *good* politician. Which will make a change.'

'It's very nice of you to say so, but you're jumping the gun a bit. It's quite obvious that the Conservatives are going to win in Costford next time. For me, it'll just be a matter of cutting my teeth for later on.'

'I don't know about that. I'll vote for you. If I haven't snuffed it by then. Funny, having to remember to say that.'

'That applies to all of us.'

'Not in the same way. I *know* I'm going to die soon. I *know* there's not time to do anything more with my life. I'll be gone and forgotten. The bank will be just the same as if I'd never been there, instead of working for them for nearly forty years.'

Trevor felt panicky at the extent of Geoff's bleakness, espe-cially as it was justified. 'You won't be –'

'Oh yes I will. I'm not being morbid. You will too. Well, *you* won't perhaps, because you'll be famous, but everyone else will be, when their time comes. It's not that. It's just – Thing is, I suppose you might say I'm a man of unruly passions.'

Trevor looked at him in astonishment. Geoff was looking directly back at him, very intently. His face looked hot and his eyes were bright. It wasn't a joke.

'Are *you* a man of unruly passions?' Geoff asked him.

There was something cringingly intimate about the question and the whole new manner Geoff had suddenly acquired. The shock of it brought to Trevor's mind a long-ago episode in the school toilets when a boy had asked him to admire his willy. Trevor, who was putting his own away at that moment, was caught on the hop and had no idea what to answer. He didn't know the terms of praise. In the end he mumbled: 'It's very nice.'

To his surprise this turned out to be the right answer. 'Yours is nice too,' the other boy said, adjusted his trousers and departed. Trevor had felt a glow of relief that the gluey familiarity of the exchange was over, but surprised himself by taking his own willy out once more and inspecting it with fresh eyes.

Now, faced with Geoff's intense gaze, all he could say was, 'I – I don't know.'

'Well, I am. Not that I'm in much of a position to do anything about it, with a bag of cack taped to my middle. I'll never have another chance. I'll never be unruly again. No more, not never. Nohow. Especially as I'll soon be dead.'

'You're a married man,' Trevor said. 'That's *usual*. It applies to most of us. You don't need to have had a colostomy to find yourself toeing the line. There's a lot less unruliness about than people pretend, in my opinion.' To lighten the atmosphere he nearly said, 'Even amongst those of us with functioning bums,' but stopped in the nick of time, so all that came out was a little random noise like a smudge on a sheet of paper. Only Geoff was allowed to make a remark like that.

Geoff was still staring at him, listening as if this was information of the utmost importance. Then he shook his head vigorously, like a dog does. 'Have another pint.'

'My turn,' Trevor said, glad of a chance to go up to the bar.

When he came back Geoff took his pint, had a pull of it, then said: 'What I told you before was a pack of lies.'

For a moment Trevor thought he meant he wasn't about to die after all, and felt relieved and angry both at once. He opened his mouth to say something, then put beer in it while he collected his thoughts.

'I've never been unruly in my life,' Geoff explained, and Trevor's heart sank again. 'I can kid along and that sort of thing. But trouble is, I can't look a woman in the eye. You know, you josh somebody, then catch their eye, and you hold the look, and then the mood changes and both your looks go sort of hard. I can't do that. I always end up looking down at my groin.' He looked down at his groin now, as if to illustrate the point. He was sitting back from the pub table, legs apart, and the large groin allowance his trousers always had dangled down rather emptily over the edge of the chair.

'You've been watching too many flicks, is what *I* think.'

'It was poor Alan going like that, gave me food for thought. Do you realise, when I gave him the kiss of life, that was the first time I'd kissed anyone for donkey's years, except giving the missus a peck every Christmas. So many totties in the world, so little time. The main point being, of course, that I've always been ugly. Long before my operation, I *still* was. I've got a photo of when I was a baby. It's going brown with age now. I'm wearing a little bonnet type of affair but my face underneath is enough to give you the screaming habdabs. It looks like a week-old meat pie.'

Geoff scratched his large head. His hair was thin and his fingers made a rasping noise.

Trevor found himself thinking: that head will be a skull soon. 'The main thing is,' he began, and stopped. He'd been going to say, 'You've had a happy married life,' but he didn't have a clue whether that was true or not. Geoff never mentioned his wife except to make music hall jokes about her. 'You've had a good marriage,' he said a trifle uncertainly. He put a bit of cheer in his tone: 'It's lasted all these years.'

'What do they say? Foe de mew, something like that. I heard somebody say it once, but I'm pig-ignorant, I am. I suppose you studied French and God knows what.'

Trevor kept his voice steady. 'A lot of people would give their eye teeth,' he said.

'Perhaps I should have given those rhododendrons a go. But it wouldn't have been as much fun as chasing a totty. How I love that word. It brings to mind white high-heeled shoes and laddered stockings, clopping along the way women do, with their knees together and their feet out. That's probably what I'll think about when I'm finally on it – on my deathbed. Remember what I never had and feel even more forlorn.'

He looked forlorn now, examining what remained of his pint with care. His large head, blobbing out to accommodate goofy teeth and a double chin, made Trevor think of a huge pink teardrop. He felt an urgent need to join in, to say something that would put them in the same boat. It seemed almost cruel to stand aloof. Before he'd even thought, he said: 'I've suffered from that too.'

Geoff's head jerked up. 'Cancer?'

'No, God no. But a sort of restlessness in my marriage. It took a bit of a weird form, in my case. Sort of jealousy in reverse.' Oh God, why am I saying this, he asked himself. But it was a relief to admit it to someone. And Geoff was going to die soon, and would take it with him to the grave. 'I told my wife off for not having had other boyfriends apart from me. She took me up on it and our marriage nearly went kaput.'

'That's a new one,' Geoff said. 'You see, that's the thing about you. You're original. You don't look at things from the same viewpoint as the rest of us. That's how you've got your managership, I suppose.'

'How I nearly lost it more like. I think they'd have thought twice about me if I'd been in the middle of a divorce. They like everything to be safe and settled in our business.'

'Surprising that I didn't do better at it then,' Geoff said sadly.

I'm not going to win this one, Trevor realised.

When Trevor got home Christine still wasn't back. He felt a touch of panic, fancying that she'd got lured away again by Art. Also disappointment: he wanted to break the news of his promotion. He hadn't told her about the meeting, just in case it didn't work out. I should have bought some champers, he thought. But if he went for it now he'd be out of the house at exactly the moment she chose to arrive. Leave it till later. Be the thoughtful hubby in the meantime.

He looked in the fridge, to check what they had in. Mince. He remembered Chris saying something about shepherd's pie. Not exactly a celebration meal but they both liked it, and if the offie had champagne, that would give it a lift. He started to peel some spuds in preparation.

Sure enough after a few minutes there was a ding-dong from the front door. He went to open it.

'Sorry,' Chris said. 'I couldn't be bothered digging in my handbag for the key.'

'You're late,' he said. 'I was just getting some grub.'

'Not the dreaded pea sandwich again.'

'No, not.' He leaned forward to kiss her.

'Ooh, don't bother. You stink of beer. You can't have been in long yourself.'

'I had to have a meeting after work with one of my colleagues.' He didn't say Geoff because he didn't want to go into it all at present, and overshadow his news.

'That's what you call it, is it? A meeting. With a coll-eague. I say I say, a coll-*eague.*'

'What do *you* call it?'

'What do you mean? *I'm* late because I was busy at the shop. I've talked Michael into letting me overstock. Where are you going? Why are you turning your back on me, Trevor?'

'I am not turning my back on you. I am walking into the kitchen.'

'That *is* turning your back on me.'

'I'm walking into the kitchen because I am halfway through peeling some potatoes. I thought I might as well get them finished while we were having our conversation.'

'I can't believe you're being so petty.'

He stopped, turned to face her. 'Petty? What do you mean?'

'I suppose you don't like it because I've got a demanding job now, one I have to put a bit of time and effort into.'

'If you remember, it was me who got you the job in the first place.'

'Trust you to rub that in. You so love to be in charge, you do.

You always want to have the say-so about everything in our marriage. You even pushed me into bed with other men. I mean, another man.'

She stopped, confused. She swallowed, and stroked her hair back with her hand. In a trembly voice she corrected herself: '*Tried* to push me into bed with other men – another man.'

The air between them went so cold that Trevor actually shivered. They stood exactly where they were. He was staring directly at her face; she was looking a bit below his, missing eye contact.

'You did go to bed with him, didn't you?' he asked finally.

She gave a little nod, stroked her hair back again, then replied in a tiny voice: 'Just the once.' Her cheeks were flaming.

'Just the once,' he repeated, as if the words were in a language he didn't understand.

'There's no need to be sarcastic.'

'No,' he agreed.

'I didn't do it until I knew it was all over. Until I knew there was no future in it.'

'Oh, right.' He tried to work out her logic. It seemed to him that was the very moment *not* to go to bed with Art, when it was obvious their relationship had no future. But at the same time Chris had always been a clear thinker.

There was an embarrassed pause. His mind went right back to the beginning of his own relationship with Chris, when they were in the milk bar and he hadn't known whether to kiss her.

'You could have told me,' he said. He wanted to say it in a neutral voice but it came out with a reproachful edge to it, like the complaint of a sulky child.

'No, I couldn't.'

'Oh.'

'It was what you wanted, remember? Me to have a secret. Me to be the mysterious woman, like the Mona Lisa. With a smi-ile.'

She put a smile on her face. Her features were slightly chubby, and for a second she looked so like the Mona Lisa that Trevor almost burst out laughing. The effort not to, made him burst into tears instead.

Chris's smile vanished. In fact her look became hard and contemptuous. 'You shouldn't start these things if you can't cope with them,' she said.

Trevor felt in his pockets for a hanky, but didn't have one. Geoff's had been a yard square. Trevor had a sudden image of him, waddling home to die. He walked straight past Chris, opened the front door, and went out. It wasn't that he wanted to leave the house, just that he had to get out of her sight while he was crying.

In the silent hall, Chris thought to herself: from one point of view, the Mona Lisa. From the other, a toad. There doesn't seem to be an in-between. But the in-between is me.

It was like bringing a drunk home from the pub, not that May had ever done such a thing. Mother sat in the lmp's front passenger seat singing 'Come into the garden, Maud' and 'The Mountains of Mourne'.

Still, May felt able to cope after a whole day without her. The idea was to keep Tuesdays and Thursdays completely clear, with Mother spending the day at Cherry's. Better for everyone. Cherry didn't have to have that feeling of being perched in someone else's house, even if that someone was her doting stepmother. May didn't have that background feeling of responsibility which she had when they did the honours at home. Mother had a change of scene, though who could tell whether that meant anything to her. But picking her up again was like waking from a nice dream and remembering it was Monday morning.

Cherry hadn't helped. She'd got engaged, sort of, to Dave, her body boyfriend.

'What do you mean?' May had asked. 'Are you engaged or aren't you?'

'We didn't say it in so many words. We have an understanding, that's the best way to put it.'

'Agreeing to get wed is having an understanding, where I come from. Not saying so out loud is a misunderstanding. Be warned.'

Cherry pursed her lips and blew air out in an irritated sort of way, as if she was trying unsuccessfully to whistle. 'May, that's not how things are done nowadays. Men don't go down on their knees and say, blah de blah de blah. Women would wee themselves if they did.' May noticed she blushed slightly at the exaggeration.

'More's the pity, then. At least women used to know where they were. There was a sense of occasion about it.'

Cherry opened her eyes wide. Surprise was one of the strongest expressions in her repertoire, for good reason. 'May, don't tell me Hub did that.'

'You mean, do tell you.'

'Yes,' Cherry said breathily, 'do tell me.'

'Well he didn't. What he did do was ask me to marry him in a civilised fashion.' That wasn't quite so, in fact. He'd gone on in his heavy-handed way about sealing the pact, and had used the word nuptials, but if you knew Hub you knew what he was driving at. One thing for sure, there was nothing informal about it. 'You see what I mean about her not being as batty as she lets on,' she added. Mother had started singing 'Here Comes the Bride'.

'The main problem,' Cherry said, 'is that I have a feeling Ben's going to do the honours in the near future.'

'Well, you'd better put him right, hadn't you?'

'I don't think I can bring myself to.'

'If he's all mind, like you say he is, he should be able to think his way out of his disappointment. That's what a mind is for, coping with life's rebuffs.' Whenever Hub came to mind she found herself talking in that sort of vein.

'I'm not a rebuff kind of girl.' Cherry gave May a long, bland look from beneath her hair helmet. 'I'd far sooner buff.'

You're not any kind of girl, May thought grimly, that's your whole problem. You're a grown woman, and haven't realised it yet. 'For heaven's sake, Cherry, you can't marry the both of them.'

'I don't see why not,' she said sulkily. 'Daddy had two wives, didn't he? Mummy and you, one two.'

'But not at the same time, he didn't.'

'I didn't say I'd have my two husbands at the same time. I could marry Dave now, and put Ben on one side for later. Marry him when Dave dies.'

'Who on earth says Dave is going to die?'

'He's pretty well bound to, I should think, going round the world on boats all the time. The *best* way of doing it would be to be married part-time to both of them at once. I could be married to Dave when he's on shore, and Ben when he's gone back to sea. Dave could make me pregnant, and Ben could be a good father to the children. That way Dave wouldn't have to die. It would be far more humane.'

'I think you've been spending too much time with your nan.'

'Oh, I never thought of stabbing anyone. Just waiting for accident or natural causes to happen. Or like I say, alternating the two of them.'

Point proven, as far as May was concerned. There was no point in fashing yourself about it: Cherry was Cherry. Mother was Mother, by the same token, though in one sense that wasn't true at all. She was only a minute fraction of what she had been. What she had been wasn't particularly desirable of course: she'd been strident and greedy, despite her pint size. The best moments during May's childhood were when her mother had a faraway look in her eyes, because then you knew you could get away with almost anything. Perhaps when it happened she was visiting that place, wherever it was, where she now lived all the time, the land of silence, and of song.

May pulled up outside the house and let Mother out of the car. It was a gloomy October afternoon, brownish grey, the light a thickening stew of low-hanging cloud, fog, and nightfall.

'Ooh it's parky, Mother,' May said as they walked up the path. 'Mind the paving.' Not that there was much danger in that respect – Mother hardly had enough substance to touch the ground. She was singing 'Singin' in the Rain', which was one thing the weather wasn't doing at the moment.

The house felt cosier than May expected, given it hadn't been occupied all day. Mother had had her tea at Cherry's, and seemed quite tired, so it wasn't long before May got her to bed. She frisked her first, to make sure that she hadn't acquired anything sharp on her day out. Cherry had agreed to hide all her knives, but she was scatty enough to overlook the really homicidal ones altogether.

May came downstairs and made herself a cheese sandwich. As always, there was paperwork she should be getting on with, above all ward letters to reply to. At her request Glen Parsons, the planning officer, had got in touch with the council solicitor about the civil engineering storage depot that had been perched at the back of her constituents' houses, and an enforcement order had been applied for in the courts. In the meantime Mrs Bradbury had written about how tense the whole problem was making her daughter, and how she needed to concentrate on her A levels, with a view to becoming a doctor. May tried to imagine a seventeen-year-old whose thinking had gone to pot because of bulldozers on her mind. She ought to write, and try to drive those huge yellow creatures out of the girl's head, but after a day in court didn't feel in the mood.

Then there was the problem of the swimming pool renovation at Twining Edge. No sooner had the loan sanction gone through than someone on the Parks and Recreation Committee had started a scare about potential damage to the new fittings by the sub-aqua club, and four underwater swimmers in her ward had sent four identical letters assuring her they didn't represent a threat. The only consolation was she could send them all the same reply, but for the life of her couldn't think what it ought to be. Then there was a letter of congratulation to be done for one of her constituents who happened to be Costford table tennis champion, and had got engaged to a lass who was Bolton table tennis champion herself, with a view to the two of them playing ping-pong together for good, not that she better say as much, given she was trying to behave herself these days. Best wait till she was in a more diplomatic frame of mind.

In court that morning a youth had appeared charged with pinching an electric razor and thirty shilling pieces. He'd hidden the razor under a car, where in due course it had been driven over and squashed flat, and put the shillings in his shoe. His defence seemed to be that the police had no right to search him just because he was hobbling. 'I might have been a cripple, for all they knew about it,' he'd said indignantly. 'But you aren't,' she kept telling him. 'You had all those coins underfoot.' He insisted it was a matter of principle, though what a lad of that ilk would know about principle was more than she could guess at. He didn't shut up till she suggested he show the court his foot.

Enough was enough, for one day. She looked in the *Radio Times*. A repeat of *Dr Finlay's Casebook* was on, and after that, *Dad's Army*.

'Will you have a wee dram, Doctor Snoddy?' she asked herself.

She didn't like whisky and it suddenly occurred to her that since Hub had gone it had never even crossed her mind to stock up on gin. All that faffing about with lemons and tonic seemed like man's work, or something that happened at do's, not a task you should do for yourself. Though she did everything else for herself, not to mention for her mother, and her constituents, and the Costford Tories, and Trevor Morgan. For a second she succumbed to self-pity.

'I weell tha',' she replied, and poured herself a sherry.

Later she dozed in her chair. Glimpses came into her mind of Dr Finlay's sit up and beg motor car pottering through tweedy countryside, of Dr Cameron's grinning face blotting up one dram after another, of Moaning Minnie washing pots in the kitchen.

Later, like a knife cutting its way through her reverie, came a chilling, definite sense that something had gone wrong.

She sat where she was, afraid to move in case she let on she knew something was amiss. On the telly it was *Dad's Army* and Captain Mainwaring was having tea with an attractive lady in a café. She was wearing a blue suit. His round face was pink with emotion and his spectacles looked blind and sad as they reflected the light. Private Pike came in, wearing his long maroon scarf with blue stripes.

May strained her ears to test whether there was a disturbance upstairs. Not a peep. But that might be bad news in itself. Perhaps it had been sudden silence she'd picked up, beyond the burble of the box, and Mother was on the lam in the dark streets of Costford, armed to the teeth.

May put her arms on the chair rests and began to rise to her feet. Then lowered herself again. She'd understood what it was.

She sat and stared at the TV screen, appalled. Yes, that was it.

Captain Mainwaring was at the railway station, saying good-bye to the woman he'd fallen in love with. She leaned out of the carriage window. He tried to persuade her to stay, but there was no hope for it. He was far too ginger. His army uniform didn't help. He waved her goodbye.

The programme was in colour, and May didn't have a colour TV.

'Hello, Cherry. She's all tucked up in her truckle bed.'

'Good-oh,' said Cherry, a bit puzzled.

'I didn't know whether I'd catch you in, after your day of it. Thought you might have gone out on the razzle.'

'In Costie, on a Tuesday night? Some hope. I suppose I could do an evening class in woodwork. We could all hammer together, and sing. Oh no, I've had enough of singing for one day. Anyway, Ben's coming over later.'

May nearly said, perhaps you should take the chance to tell him you're engaged, but bit her tongue. It wasn't her business, and would only irritate Cherry. 'I wanted to ring, to thank you.'

'You don't need to thank me. You pay me. I quite enjoy it. It's better than being a waitress. I look at poor Nan and think: Gather ye rosebuds. Not her, me. *Me* rosebuds.'

'I think what rosebuds Mother was going to gather, she's gathered. I've been watching *Dad's Army*.'

'I have too. Poor old sausage, waving goodbye to the love of his life. But it would never have worked out. She was beyond his reach.'

'Anyhow, it made the programme a lot better. A pleasure to watch.'

'Did it? What did?'

'Colour TV.'

'Ooh, you sly body. You never said. I thought it was time you splashed out. It makes all the difference. The ones I feel sorry for are all those black and white actors who've lost their jobs.'

'Poor them,' May agreed, anxious to put the phone down.

It wasn't Cherry. Who, then?

Of course. The person most in her debt at present, Trevor. He must somehow have managed to replace her TV on the sly. Thing was, they all looked alike as far as she was concerned. When they were switched off, anyway.

May poured herself another sherry, her third. She wasn't much of a solitary drinker, but this evening her nerves needed settling.

Cherry must have been in on it, despite her pretence at surprise. She would have lent him the key so he could let the delivery man in. The aerial man too. What a lovely gesture.

She finished off her sherry. Perhaps she would do some paperwork after all, for an hour or so before bed. Kindness like that brought back your faith in politics.

She got up and switched off her new telly. At just the right moment. In the silence she heard her front gate creak. Here he was, to see how she was getting on with it.

Suddenly there was a horrible thump and smack, a gasp, and then a low moaning from outside.

Ten

'Oh dear,' May exclaimed, 'it would be piddling down.'
She had no idea what caused her to lapse into a coarse-grained way of speech at just this moment – when Trevor needed all the sympathy he could get. It was embarrassing falling over, even if you hurt yourself. In fact, it was almost a relief to hurt yourself: it showed the world that you were a serious faller, not some dilettante.

She'd fallen once in Costford precinct – skidded on something slimy, perhaps even a banana skin for all she knew, and toppled slowly over like a tree. It seemed impossible to believe as she went down that there wasn't the time or the means to stop herself. She had reached out for convenient knobs or handles in the air, which must have made her seem even more foolish. Her cheek had slammed into the flagged surface and she'd broken a tooth. Blood welled up from her mouth and suddenly she felt like a worthwhile person again.

She stepped down the dim path.

Trevor was sitting on the crazy paving, elbows resting on knees, looking as relaxed as if he was having a picnic.

'I was just noticing,' he said in a trembling voice. He pointed up towards the street lamp. 'The raindrops catching the light look like crocuses. Those little gold ones.' Perhaps because she'd been thinking of Costford precinct, May had a sudden picture of standing in a department store with a small child who was clutching her hand and bravely trying to smile through its snivels, periodic sobs shaking its body like hiccups. Who the child had been she had no idea, perhaps a lost one she was trying to help.

'I'm glad you've been making good use of your time, but I'm afraid you've got concussion. I'm going to get you in the house and call an ambulance.'

She bent down and put her arm round his shoulders, but instantly his feet were scrabbling for purchase and then he was springing up, all legs like Dick Van Dyke.

'I'm right as –' he said, and then faltered. For a second May thought he was going to fall again.

'I know,' she said. 'You're as right as a crocus.'

She helped him into the house. When she got a proper look at him, under the hall light, she had quite a turn. There was a swelling like an egg on his temple, and blood had coursed down his face into his collar. She'd once gone with a group of trainee magistrates to the emergency reception at Costford hospital on a late Saturday night, and seen the battered drunks being led in. Their bloodstained shirts had looked so seedy and repellent that she could hardly repress a shudder now, even though this one belonged to Trevor, and the damage had been done in her own front garden. She took his damp jacket from him and hung it over the hall radiator.

'You are in a state. I'm going to –'

'No, I don't want you to, really. I'm all right.'

'If you drop dead you won't be.'

'Well, no. That applies to us all, though, doesn't it?'

'Let me look in your eyes, then.'

He looked down at her and opened his eyes fractionally wider, to help her see. The intimacy of it made her catch her breath.

'I'm not so sure one of your pupils isn't bigger than the other.'

'Nothing's ever sym, sym. Even. The same.' He shrugged.

'You see, you're not right.'

'I'd just like to sit down for a minute.'

She led him into her sitting room and sat him on the settee. 'Put your feet up,' she told him. He swung his legs over and she put a cushion against the arm for him to rest his head.

'That's nice,' he said, shutting his eyes.

'You mustn't go to sleep, whatever you do.'

He opened an eye, the one with the slightly big pupil. 'I thought that was just at the North Pole.'

'No, it's on my settee, as well.'

'Bother.' He opened the other eye.

'I'm very sorry,' she said.

'I don't see what you've got to be sorry about. It was my own silly fault.'

'It was that paving stone that rises up. The cement's gone crumbly round it. I've been meaning to get it seen to, ever since you nearly came a cropper last time. You could probably take me to court.'

'I don't think I'll do that. With what you've done for me. You got me my wife back.' A spasm of pain rocked his features.

'At least let me call the doctor. Old –'

'No, please. Please.'

'The thing is, it'll need cleaning.' She took another look at the bump. It seemed for all the world to be staring back. It was mainly an angry purple, shading to yellow at the centre, surprisingly like a hard-boiled egg in fact. The blood had stopped flowing and was beginning to dry and darken. 'It doesn't look too dirty. Perhaps just a clean cloth and a bowl of water. But it'll hurt like blazes. Tell you what, I'll make you a cup of tea first, to get your strength up.'

She went into the kitchen and made a pot, clattering and banging in order to help him stay awake. When she brought it in he was sitting up again. His shoulders were hunched and his head bowed; from the back he looked like a weary old man.

'I'll tell you what,' she said brightly.

He jumped, then peered over his shoulder, and now he wasn't an old man at all. His eyes had become receptive, in that way they did when he was waiting for a person to tell him something, and he looked all ready to smile. She hurried round the corner of the settee and gave him his tea.

'What I've done, I used the big kettle. So there's plenty of water in it for your head. When it's cool enough I'll bring it in and give you a good dab.'

'Thank you.'

'You won't want to thank me when I'm done. And anyway I need to thank you.'

He raised an eyebrow, in a way that seemed to have become characteristic recently. It rose up the lower slopes of his lump, and he winced.

'You know,' she went on. 'My telly.'

'Your telly?'

'Come on, Trevor, own up.'

'I'm sorry. I don't know what you're on about.'

'Shame on you. What were you coming here for, then?'

'Oh, I wanted – I was just – it doesn't matter. I was just in the mood to fall over.' He gave his enormous smile.

Thank goodness he didn't lose any teeth, May thought. 'Not about the telly? Not at all?'

'Not at all about the telly. I don't know anything about tellies. I just switch them on and turn them off.'

'I expect the water will be about right now. I'll go and fetch it.'

She wobbled off. He must think I've gone daft, she thought to herself. Or got myself pie-eyed. True, there was a whiff of alcohol on his breath, but that was as nothing compared to here. The whole room smelled of sherry, as if she'd put away bottles of the stuff. Indeed she almost felt she had. Serve her right for embarking on that flight of fancy at the council. Perhaps I imagined the colour, she wondered. After all, when you were watching in black and white you didn't remind yourself every moment that it *was* black and white, you got used to it. In some way or other you coloured it in. Possibly that was all she had done. It was like having a psychosomatic illness. She had a psychosomatic colour television.

Private Pike's scarf was maroon. She poured the water into

the old yellow mixing bowl. Perhaps the shade of grey it was on the screen had just suggested maroon. Or maybe his fusspot of a mother had talked about it being maroon.

May imagined it: Private Pike looking sulky while she wound it round his neck. 'I thought I'd knit you a maroon one, to go with your uniform.' Him slouching off.

May couldn't honestly remember. She'd been dozing half the time, when she wasn't sipping sherry ... And of course you would know already that uniforms were khaki and Captain Mainwaring's face would be pink – it was hardly likely to be green, though it might be on some of the colour TVs she'd seen. I wish I could turn the damn thing on again, just to check, she thought, but it's hardly the time.

She burrowed in one of the kitchen drawers for an unused cotton tea towel one of her constituents had given her for Christmas, and which she'd never even taken out of its polythene wrapper. She tucked that under her elbow and carried the bowl through.

'We need to get that shirt off you too,' she said. 'You can't wear it like that. Tell you what, I've got an old one of Hub's. I'll just get it before we mop you up.'

She put the bowl and tea towel on the coffee table by the sofa and hurried upstairs.

She'd given most of Hub's clothes to the jumble when he died: there was no point in being sentimental or, more to the point, morbid. Cherry had been rather shocked. 'It's like him going for good,' she'd said.

'I'm afraid he *has* gone for good.'

'But he was a bit of a dresser, wasn't he?'

'You make him sound like a chest of drawers.'

Cherry gave a raw, high-pitched laugh. 'He *was* a bit like a chest of drawers, dear thing.'

'Anyway, you aren't going to dance about in his cast-off suits, and I'm certainly not, so it's nice to think some person from a council estate will pay tuppence ha'penny for a bit of wool worsted, though they'll probably get it covered in beer and fish and chips before you can say Jack Robinson.'

But despite these sentiments she'd drawn the line at giving away his dinner suit and dress shirt. They'd been worn so often while he was Mayor that she'd thought of them as a uniform, a mark of office.

She scrabbled in the wardrobe almost furtively, as if she was doing something wrong. She pulled the shirt out on its hanger. Luckily Hub had lacked the manual dexterity, as he put it, to cope with detachable collars and cuffs, so the only fussy thing about it was the fly front. May held it against her chest, which was too hilly to tell her anything useful. At least it hadn't gone mouldy, though it did smell faintly damp. She took the hanger out and carried the shirt down over her arm.

She had a sense of having let things lapse. 'Here I am,' she said. 'I hope that water hasn't gone too cold.' She draped the shirt over the back of an armchair and without thinking pulled up the sleeve of her blouse and put her elbow in the bowl, as she had seen mothers taught to do when she visited the baby clinic. 'Not too bad – you only want it tepid. Now, let's have your shirt off.'

Obediently he began to unbutton his shirt. May saw that his hands were shaking. The shock must have persisted, despite his attempt to put a brave face on things.

'Let me,' she said.

When his shirt was open she pushed it back over his shoulders. He wasn't wearing a vest. He was slimly built, refreshing after Hub's lardy expanse, with black, curling hair on his chest. There was some dried blood tangled up in it. He took his shirt off the rest of the way.

'All right,' she said. 'Now lie back.'

She moistened the tea towel while he swung his legs up and settled his head back on the arm. She rested her buttock on the edge of the cushion and he shuffled further on to the settee to make room. She leaned forward towards his head and rested the tea towel gently on his lump. He gasped. She wiped it as carefully as she could, while he lay with his teeth clenched, looking up at her, his beautiful smile rigid, as if it had been caught in a frost. Indeed he was shivering a little, though the room was warm.

'That's done it,' she said. 'Now to get the blood off you.'

She wet the cloth again and wiped his cheek and neck. Then more vigorously, sponged his chest. He laughed out loud at the sensation, though his face was still pale with pain. She squeezed the cloth out, then towelled him with it upwards, noticing the way his chest hair stood on end round his puckered nipples after it had been dried, like cat's fur that's been stroked the wrong way. She leaned towards his head to rub the cloth over his cheek once more. While she was busy doing so she felt her gaze drawn to his eyes and realised they were looking intently back at hers. One of the pupils still seemed a little larger than the other, and she found herself looking at that one with both her own eyes. It was slightly raggedy round the edges, like an impossible black flower.

Then she felt a hand on the back of her neck, her head was pulled down to his, her lips compressed against his lips.

Even while he kissed, his eyes still looked fixedly into hers.

After leaving his house Trevor had walked so fast he didn't have time to think, discreetly weeping as he did so. There was a mist about that was on the point of turning into light rain, so that acted as a concealer, not that there was anybody likely to notice except for a few kids doing their own thing, and occasional older people walking dogs. Crying to yourself was like talking to your-self: you needed to keep it inaudible if you didn't want people to think you'd gone potty. There was an odd phrase May had used to describe whispering politicians: *sotto voce*. That was the way he tried to cry as he walked at such a speed it was an honorary run, *sotto voce*.

The little streets of the estate seemed to fly by almost of their own accord. The sense that he was being propelled by an outside force reminded him of being marched by his mother up the stairs to her bedroom to be reassured his first suit actually fitted. He had no idea where he was going, though he had the strongest feeling he was going somewhere.

Eventually he came out on to Manchester Road, and turned right, as if he was heading towards Costford town centre. There was a row of darkened shops, a little blank factory building with no identification, the entrance to a scrotty park that even from the road had an aroma of dog shit. Then the faint buzzing of electricity from a late-night shop where a man sat reading the evening paper behind the counter. The shelves were half empty: Trevor remembered Chris saying, 'Gawd help him, we've got more in our larder at home.' Beyond the shop was a little cobbled road, Nuffield Street. He turned down it, and after fifty yards took another turn to the right, marked Fontenoy Terrace.

There were dim street lights at intervals, with a halo round each from the damp air, and the cobbles of the roadway gleamed in neat rows except where they were interrupted by black pools of tarmac used to repair the surface. There were bicycles and tufty lawns in the small front gardens of the terraced houses. He came to a halt outside number 14. That's how it felt: like braking a vehicle.

This garden was different. The grass was neatly cut and plants were spaced at intervals in its borders. A cosy light came through the curtains of the front room.

He went up the small path, lifted a door knocker that was like a loop of rope in brass, and knocked twice, gently. He regretted the second one as soon as he had done it. One would have been enough, not quite sufficient to snag the attention, as if he could make a gesture and be let off. Anyway he shouldn't have done either, not straight away. He needed to give himself a moment to pull himself together. All he could hope was that the cold flannel air had wiped away his tears.

The door opened, and there she was. Good grief, she was tiny, smaller even than by day.

She opened her mouth as if to speak, then didn't say anything. He found himself gazing at the scar on her lip, not saying anything either. What on earth am I doing here? he wondered. He'd never visited her before. If asked, he would probably have said he didn't even know where she lived. But of course there was a staff address list at work – there had to be in case of security problems or fire. And he'd lived in Costford all his life, so he knew how the streets fitted together. But still, there seemed something miraculous about arriving at Ann Cottrell's door, as if he'd sleepwalked his way here.

'Hello, Ann,' he said.

She remembered her mouth, and closed it. Then replied: 'What's happened?'

'Can I come in?'

She stepped back. She was wearing very different clothes from at the bank where she always seemed stiff and 1950ish: a woollen pinafore kind of dress, reddish brown, that went right down to her ankles, and a thin yellow jumper underneath. She looked like some sort of elf and this made him feel reassuringly male as he walked past her.

She ushered him into her sitting room. There was a three piece suite, very upholstered, in pale blue. It looked expensive, and he thought with a pang how cheap his shit-brown Habitat chairs would seem by contrast. Three of the room's walls were emulsioned white, and one was the darkest blue you could possibly imagine, the blue of the night sky. There was an abstract picture, in red, purple, blue and white, upon the blue wall, and abstract rugs were scattered on the stripped pine floor. He felt intimidated at all the taste everywhere. It was almost a relief to see the TV on a little trolley, in a bay by the cast iron fireplace with its vase of dried flowers. 'Who Do You Think You Are Kidding, Mr Hitler?' was just starting up. He thought to himself, how can you live in a room like this and take paste sandwiches into work every day?

'Take a pew,' Ann said.

'Thank you.' He sat on the settee. Ann switched the TV off then sat in an armchair, looking as tiny as Lily Tomlin did on *Rowan and Martin's Laugh-In*. She looked at him and raised her eyebrows.

What on earth do I do now? he wondered. There was perhaps four foot of floorboards between them, but it could have been a fast flowing river as far as he was concerned, the sort you had to cross in recruiting advertisements for the army by using ropes and pulleys and things.

How had that Art bloke cleared such a gap to get to Chris? Or, maybe, vice versa?

All over the country at this moment there would be men taking the plunge, finding ways across similar divides, proving themselves to be star recruits for whatever brigade of moustache-twirling philanderers.

And after that had been accomplished, what next? How do you move in on someone when they're sitting down? Bend over, kneel down? Lunge?

Perhaps it would be better to bide one's time till the person stood up, then place oneself right in front of her like the school bully.

Or just speak? That would be one way of bridging the gulf. Mouth some abracadabra that would make her cheeks flush up and her eyes look interested.

He rehearsed it to himself: I've fancied you for years.

Ann, Ann.

Yes?

Ann, I've, I'm sorry, I hope I'm not saying the wrong thing, but I've fancied you for years.

He was a politician, he should find a way of sounding sincere.

He was a sincere politician, that was the problem, or tried to be, which would mean, since he was being insincere, he ought to sound it.

I've watched you nibble your sandwiches like a bunny rabbit until my feet curled with irritation. I've tried to pick up your sexual signals with my little radar set, and got no message at all. The only reason I sniffed around in the first place was because my mother always teased me about you.

Would you like to go upstairs with me, because my late mother thought we should?

'I believe congratulations are in order,' Ann suddenly said in her low, slightly furry voice.

Trevor's heart pounded. For a stupid second he thought he'd managed to transmit a telepathic pass and score an immediate bingo.

'Oh yes?'

'Everyone was gossiping about it at the bank. They said you'd been made up to manager.'

'Ah.'

Now she did flush up. 'Oh,' she said, 'I hope I'm not speaking out of turn.'

He shrugged. He felt his lips giving a judicious twist. 'Ah well,' he said modestly. A possible strategy rushed into his head. It'll mean another branch. Or of course the House of Commons. I'll . . . I'll miss you. The glamour of it, a carrot. The imminent parting, the clincher. We may never meet again in this life. Ships that pass in the night.

He was aware of giving her a rather furtive look. People looked so dressed when they were dressed, Ann especially. She could have been a Victorian woman in terms of the completeness of the cover.

Then, to his horror, a different article of clothing altogether appeared in his line of vision, a miniskirt. It was made of a checked tweedy-looking substance, as if originally intended for a county lady then ludicrously reduced. His eyes moved cautiously upwards till they caught the bottom edge of a sort of fisherman's smock. Then downwards. Two very solid legs, pink in colour, no stockings or tights. A slipper with a pom-pom at the end of each.

'Seen your fill?' came a rather lovely, bell-like voice from far above.

'You – ring a bell,' he replied, clutching at straws. Between her knees he could see Ann's small worried face staring back at him from the depths of her chair.

'It would probably help if you looked me in the face.'

'I didn't know where you materialised from. Caught me on the hop.'

Stupidly he continued to stare at her midriff as if wanting to confirm whether it was really there or not. 'You were just here all of a sudden, like a genie out of a bottle.'

'I got the impression that you were more interested in getting another little genie out of its bottle.'

'Bar!' Ann cried.

Trevor rose to his feet with the exact slowness of a boy at the back of the class when teacher calls his name.

Bar's face was pale, strong-looking, squarish. 'I came down the stairs,' she said in a stage whisper, 'on my little tootsies.' She put a finger to her bright orange lips and shook her head. She had short blonde hair, almost Twiggy-style. 'My name is Barbara.'

'I'm Trevor.'

'I know who you are. Coming the big manager, were we?' She raised her arms to each side and flapped her hands as if accusing him of being a bird. 'What the frogs call it, *droit de seigneur*. Is that what we were hoping?'

'For God's sake, Bar!' Ann cried in anguish.

The justice of Barbara's accusation made Trevor shake. Strangely he felt exactly as indignant as he would have if he'd been wrongly accused. In fact his reaction was so perfect he suddenly realised how he could make use of it.

'I came to see Ann,' he said, his voice trembling with hurt.

'I *know* you came –'

'I wanted to talk to her in private.'

The apparent cheek of this so appalled Barbara that she paused to gulp in air before replying.

Gotcha, Trevor thought. He felt he had just passed a crash-course in lying. 'I wanted to tell her about a colleague who is terminally ill.'

Barbara gently deflated, like a lilo. 'Ah,' she said. She backed away and lowered herself into the other armchair.

Ann got to her feet, went over to Barbara's chair, and pummelled her on the head with the side of a clenched, tiny fist. 'She-gets-so-jealous,-the-sill-y-fish,' she said with each blow.

'I better leave you to it,' Barbara said, beginning to rise again.

'Stay where you are. Then you'll be satisfied no goings-on are going on. She can stay where she is, can't she, Mr Morgan? She'll keep mum, I promise.'

'Of course she can,' Trevor said. He sat down again. Ann perched on the arm of Barbara's chair.

There was a silence.

'Who?' came Ann's soft voice.

'Geoff. Geoff Cartwright.'

She nodded. 'I thought so.'

'It's flared up again.'

'He's the one with . . .' Ann told Barbara. Barbara nodded dolefully.

'He told me tonight,' Trevor said. 'We went to the pub.'

'It's nice that he was able to confide in you. But he knows you're good around illness. Some people are.' She turned to Barbara again. 'Trevor was wonderful when poor Alan had his heart attack. Rushed over in a trice and gave him the kiss of life.'

Trevor almost spoke, then thought better of it. Her memory must have muddled it under duress. Ye gods, he thought, now I can lie without saying a word.

'Of course, he still died, didn't he?' Barbara said, making her tiny gesture of revenge. 'Alan, I mean.'

He undid the buttons of May's coffee-coloured blouse. They were tiny white ones, imitation mother-of-pearl, smaller than shirt buttons, just the size to make his hurrying fingers stumble.

She sat, propped against the back of the settee, as if hypnotised. He'd learned the lesson he'd been struggling with at Ann's. It was a matter of imposing your will. The hand's got to be quicker than the eye, he thought. He had to get this done before she woke up. He slipped her blouse back over her shoulders.

Her bra was deep and large. He put his hands back each side of her ribcage. He had a sense of May's head bobbing against his shoulder, and remembered putting the lead on Chris's parents' dog to take him for a walk, while her old man watched from his armchair through milky eyes, puffing at his pipe. The picture was so vivid that he glanced up and his heart lurched as he made out a nearby form on an armchair; then he realised it was just the shirt May had brought down for him.

Somehow he managed to unhook the fasteners first try. He tended to make such a mess of it with Chris that once she imitated him, hugging a pillow and putting her arms round it with her hands writhing together on its far side like a nest of worms while she pranced round the room cross-eyed. Even at this moment he had time to think: I bet Art whisked it off in a jiffy – but this time, so did I.

May's breasts swung free. Chris was well endowed but not like this. You had a sense of individual weight. They were covered in freckles that merged together in places; the large nipples looked sore with sheer pinkness. He'd never thought of breasts as objects before, not even when his mother lost one of hers. It would have been better if he had.

He grasped May by the shoulders and gently pushed her – lowered her, more like – sideways. Obediently her feet rose, so she was lying on her side, pressed against the back of the settee. Her eyes were shut behind skew-whiff spectacles. She was breathing through her mouth, with a faint snoring sound. She had no capacity to resist. She was completely at his mercy. Gently he took her glasses off and put them on the coffee table. Then he lay beside her and put his face between her breasts.

He felt as if, for the first time in his life, he could say, here is where I am. He closed his own eyes and felt himself enclosed by softness and depth, as if breasts could accumulate and drift like snow.

At some point he was kneeling upright on the settee, unzipping her skirt and pulling it off. Then a kind of corset-cum-suspender belt which he unclipped from her stockings and pulled off. All the time he felt he was sitting serenely inside his head and watching while somebody else's hands did the work. May had opened her own eyes now. Without her specs they seemed small, pale ginger, with slightly pink rims, a little piggish but not, somehow, in a pejorative sense: they reminded you that pigs have intelligent, alert eyes. They looked directly at his face as if trying to learn what the person with the hands was likely to do next.

The hands became his again, as they tugged awkwardly at her knickers. Suddenly her hands were assisting, not in a spirit of cooperation, but just so as to ease them off less uncomfortably. He glanced at a tuft of greying ginger at the base of her stomach's slope, then stepped off the settee, slipped his own trousers and pants off and for dignity's sake his socks, though she still had her disconnected stockings on. He slid beside her.

While he thrust, his hands supported her from behind and the thought slipped into his mind: my Lord, her bottom's large; but it didn't matter in the least, in fact it confirmed his sense that he was in a completely rich and safe place. Once he thought he heard a faint faraway voice cry 'Stop' but it was far too late to take any notice of it now.

It seemed as though his clever fingers had found the hooks and eyes and zippers of her body as a whole or at least of all her body surplus to requirements, and slipped it off her shoulders, down her legs. She became not any person she had ever been before, because she had always worn herself like some great pink and orange dufflecoat, but the person she had once imagined herself to be as she zoomed up a long-ago hillside on the back of a high-powered motorcycle. She had not been naked in this room in all of her life, except perhaps beyond the reach of memory when as a tiny girl she was washed in a tin bath before the fire, and though the radiators she'd since had installed were pumping away the effect was breezy, as if the bright wind in the steeple-jack's tent was blowing upon her once again. When Trevor's hands loomed towards her person she remembered the steeple-jack's arm stretching towards her with that sudden, dis-appointing, tin cup of coffee in its hand, and it was as if that momentary promise, after all this time, had been delivered.

There had never been any hope of delivery from Hub's quar-ter; indeed a cup of coffee would have been a good alternative.

'What do you expect?' she asked him once, when he seemed a bit despondent and apologetic about it. 'We're not exactly spring chickens.'

He must have had some success with his first wife, to have produced Cherry, but as the saying went, once is enough.

When Trevor lay beside May she saw that his pupils were still uneven. Perhaps it created a happy astigmatism by which she appeared attractive enough to be desired. There was no point in fooling herself in any case: this whole episode was the result of a sudden blow to the head. But maybe love was always that, one way or another.

Then she closed her own eyes and found herself far away, in another time, a time she had never properly inhabited before, one in which, after all these years, she was young at last. 'Bob!' she heard herself murmur as she approached her climax. Luckily Trevor gave no sign he'd noticed: with the paucity of men in her life it would be a bit rich to get them muddled up.

Eleven

May watched sleepily from the settee as Trevor pulled Hub's shirt over his head and did it up. He then tied his tie with the sort of rapid efficiency that a hangman might show. The image was fuzzy and made May grope for her spectacles. As she did so she remembered she had nothing else on at all, apart from stockings that weren't suspended and would fall to her ankles as soon as she stood up. She would look completely ridiculous if she sat here with a fully dressed face.

She must look completely ridiculous in any case. The thought of how ridiculous she must look made her want to burst into tears. Her clothes were in a heap on the floor just a foot away, but she didn't dare reach for them, didn't dare move at all, for fear of catching Trevor's attention and letting him see her in that state. Of course, he was responsible for her being in that state in the first place. But what he wasn't responsible for was her body: no one to blame for that except herself, and God.

She held herself entirely still, like you do if there is a danger of wild animals. Also she had a feeling that with such an acreage on display any movement might allow the smell of flesh to seep into the room. Thank goodness for that sherry, she thought.

Trevor pulled up his trousers and snapped his belt together like you do with a car's seat belt. Without looking at her, he said: 'Give you some idea, colleague at work dropped dead a year ago.'

The lump on his forehead was pulsing like a Belisha beacon. I wonder why he's talking in telegram? she thought to herself. There was something manly and decisive about it: perhaps what had happened had sharpened him up. The only flaw in his armoury was lack of an edge. She recalled how Hub prepared for Sunday lunch by rasping the carving knife on the bone, as he insisted on calling it even though it was made of metal, and the image coalesced with what Trevor had been up to only minutes ago. Perhaps I'm *his* bone, she thought, with a little flutter of her heart.

'Oh yes?' she asked.

He didn't reply but stared in the direction of the switched-off TV, lost in thought.

'Oh dear,' she said, in case she hadn't sounded sympathetic enough. The question is, are those thoughts he's thinking in colour or black and white, she asked herself, and almost burst into laughter. Must hold back or I'll lose my disguise. Laugh and I'm naked, she warned herself, naked as the day I was born. Even a podge then, according to Mum.

'Keeled over,' Trevor said finally. 'Boing. I just stood there like a ninny. Not a clue. Someone else had to do the honours. But now what they all remember, it was me who gave the kiss of life. Hero of the hour. It must have been me, because I've made manager.'

'I had a colleague at work keel over,' May found herself saying. 'I didn't give him the kiss of life either. I don't think the kiss of life was invented then. I don't know if kisses of any kind were invented then. He was my stepfather.' She remembered how Hub had blown his nose like the trump of doom as Dan Baxendale passed away.

'So don't expect,' Trevor said, just as if it was a complete sentence. He bent down to do up his shoes. 'I need my jacket.'

'It's on the hall radiator.'

Without another word he left the room. She heard him pause in the hall, to put his jacket on, then the front door opened and closed after him.

Expect what? she asked. He's given me the kiss of life already. Then she burst into tears.

Bugger me, Trevor thought as he stepped out of the house into prickling rain, that puts faking O level French into perspective. He hurried home through empty streets with his mouth clamped into a sort of grin. My God, I'm a one, I am. Nice as pie all this time and now look at what I've got up to: North Costford's Labour candidate rapes Tory councillor shock.

It made him want to laugh. What he had done was so enormous that he couldn't open it, confront it, do anything about it. She'd cried out something but he hadn't listened; and groaned, but he'd taken no notice. That's why dyed-in-the-wool villains are so arrogant and pleased with themselves: what they have done doesn't brook inspection. They can't take it on board. It's like having a huge unportable box of something on the wharf. All you can do is lean on it and moodily smoke a cigarette, or laugh a mirthless laugh like he was doing now, each ha coming out round and separate as bubblegum balls being discharged from one of those bright red vending machines.

After ten years without budging an inch, Chris said: 'Oopsie-daisy.'

That seemed to break the spell, and it couldn't have been more than ten minutes in actual fact. She went through to the kitchen, finished peeling the spuds, put them on to boil, fried up some mince and onions in a pan, then fashioned a rough and ready shepherd's pie. It still needed browning and would probably never be eaten, but she disliked leaving things pending. Then she went into the lounge, turned the telly on, and slid on to one of the Habitat chairs, curling her feet underneath her bum and enjoying the faint bounciness imparted by the metal frame. She watched what came on, without properly noticing what it was and without even considering changing channels. Nor did she think about Trevor or Art or marriage or adultery. She thought about her shop.

Michael, her boss, was a wonder when you got to know him. True, she understood why Trevor sometimes called him the Grand Old Man. He would take a handkerchief out of the top pocket of the tropical suit he liked to wear whatever the weather, a handkerchief made of lawn or cambric or some other long-forgotten stuff, and dab his forehead with it. 'Dirty work, heh?' he would ask while she busily stacked shelves.

But he was active in his own way. As soon as she had agreed to run his shop for him he wanted her there, getting the stock ready. She'd had to point out that she owed Smith's a month's notice. 'I'm the sort of chap who's got ants in his pants,' he told her. He made her creep off after two weeks. 'I'll deal with any comeback,' he told her.

He sat in the little office he had reserved for himself and read the *Daily Express* with the aid of a monocle, or did paperwork for the other businesses he took an interest in. His office was smaller than her own, with only room for his throne, as he called it, and a flimsy whatnot that masqueraded as a desk. He seemed to have no interest in books as such. In the privacy of his office he'd take his shoes off to reveal a pair of expensive silk socks in garish colours, and put a small fez on his head, made of some sort of tapestry.

'He's a secret exhibitionist,' Chris told Trevor.

During her time at Smith's, she had developed certain theories about how to run an independent bookshop successfully, and she wasn't sure how Michael would react to them. She wasn't sure, in point of fact, how independent her bookshop would be. Her main plan was to overstock. The idea was to be like the sort of secondhand bookshop where you have to climb over heaps of volumes to get from one part of the shop to another, even though her books were new. She wanted to communicate a sense of excess.

As she remembered, from her nest in the Habitat chair, what she'd said to Michael, Chris felt herself go pink with sudden pride and pleasure. Excess, maybe that's what I stand for, she thought. Maybe that's the true me.

By having a huge range of different titles, she'd told Michael, you could attract a huge range of customers. And if they came in for a particular book, knowing there was more chance of finding it there than anywhere else, they would stay to buy others. 'Smith's get their margin through bulk,' she said. 'I can't compete with that. I want to get mine through range.'

Michael had accepted it without a qualm, even though his monocled eye bulged like a goldfish in a tiny bowl. Just as well, since she'd over-ordered to start with. Also she wanted a reading club, where customers could discuss books, and perhaps even have visits from authors. She wanted the shop to stay open late several evenings a week. 'Yes, yes, whatever you like,' Michael told her.

Her glee had been tempered with an odd disappointment. Perhaps he didn't really care. Then he added: 'My investment isn't the shop. It's you. What I've invested in is your energy. That's all I ever invest in.' Chris thought it was the nicest thing anyone had ever said to her.

Tired out by excitement, good and bad, and lulled by the sound of the TV, she fell into a sort of doze until she was snapped out of it by the sound of the front door key scratching at the lock. For a second she froze, wondering where on earth she was. I'm in my lounge, she remembered, but whether or not I'm in my marriage is another story.

Quick as a flash she was out of the chair and back in the hall, standing exactly where she had been when Trevor walked out. He opened the door after a bit of a struggle and walked past her without a word. He was soaking wet and she glimpsed a horrible bruise on his temple. She wondered if he'd been so distraught he'd managed to provoke a fight.

'I'm hungry,' she said.

He stopped, turned to face her. The swelling was like a huge searching Dalek eye and for a second she felt a stupid urge to say Exterminate.

'Coming up,' he replied. 'Shepherd's pie, if that's all right.'

'Lo-vely.' The hiccup in the middle was a gasp as she realised he wasn't wearing his own shirt but a strange starchy one that was baggy on him.

It was the weirdest experience. She hadn't planned it and nor, she was sure, had he, but despite all that had happened between them over the last months and during the last hours, they seemed to understand each other intuitively, to be able to dance hand in hand.

She followed him into the kitchen where he stopped in his tracks for a moment, looking in puzzlement at the shepherd's pie. Then, obviously concluding he'd got further with it than he remembered, he switched the oven on and put it in to warm through and brown.

'What's this about the shop, then?' he asked.

'I think, peas?'

'Peas?'

'To go with it. But not marrowfat. Save those for your pea butties. We've got frozen.'

'You're right. With shepherd's pie, peas is correct.' He opened the freezer compartment of the fridge. 'Marrowfat is not correct, but peas in general is correct. Are correct.'

'Carrots would be correct as well. But we haven't got carrots. We ate them all yesterday.'

'Heigh-ho.' For once his donkey fashion of saying yes seemed appropriate to the occasion: 'Carrots would be correct as well. But if we haven't got carrots we can't have carrots.' He found a small saucepan, cut the corner of the packet of peas and shook it airily over the pan. Peas shot across the working surface and poured over the floor. He was obviously drunk. Somehow that thought made her feel drunk also.

'It's like a green river,' she said.

'Yes,' he replied, 'it is. A green ball-y river. Given their shape.'

'That's exactly it. A green ball-y river. That's what it's like.'

'The *mot juste*,' he said. 'Pardon my French.'

'No, no,' she said. 'After you.' She bowed a little and swept her arm, as though to usher him through some imaginary doorway. 'You're the one with the French. Apart from which, you're the one with the balls.'

'*Touché*,' he replied. He dug the dustpan and brush out of the cupboard and knelt down, squashing some peas under his knee-caps in the process. 'So?' he asked.

'So the shop is doing very nicely, thank you very much. I sold Michael my idea about overstocking.'

'Bully for you.' He stood up again, green-kneed and wrong-shirted, and groped for the packet which he had left lying on the side, peas drooling from the aperture.

'Why don't I do that?' She picked up the packet and poured a quota of peas in the pan. 'Tell you a tip Mum's given me. She got it from a magazine. Don't put water on the peas. Put a knob of butter instead and warm them slowly.'

'Ah, good idea.'

'Well, it saves diluting them.'

'Who wants diluted peas? What your mother is, is a whiz in the kitchen.'

Chris gave him a sharp look. He never commented on her parents normally, probably because there wasn't a lot to say for them, and he was too much of a politician to say anything against. Her father sat in his armchair puffing his pipe like a steam train with nowhere to go and no rails to go there on, while her mother waved a limp duster at the world and provided egg and chips or sandwiches. 'No, she's not,' Chris said, 'she's just a whiz with women's magazines.'

'If she can set us on the path to full-flavoured peas her life hasn't been to no avail. In fact it's been full of avail, albeit in a restricted area.'

Perhaps you should get drunk more often, Chris thought. It

seems to make you brighter and harder, less bland. Or maybe you should just get cuckolded more often, if it's that. Though if you're going to get cuckolded again, have someone else do it for you. I've done my share. For the time being anyway.

Walking on thin ice was the phrase in Trevor's mind. It was as if the rest of that evening was built entirely out of thin ice, so that it could be shattered at any point. From his reading days he remembered the Crystal Night in Nazi Germany, when the Jewish shops were looted and destroyed. It had always struck him as incongruous that such a horrible event could have such a beautiful phrase to describe it, but now he realised that if he hadn't learned much more about suffering he'd certainly discovered something about fragility. He pictured his marriage, his career, his whole life, as a delicate, attenuated structure that could be exploded into millions of glittering fragments by one abrupt movement. If he stopped being flippant for a second, if either of them did, disaster would strike.

The solution, they both knew without the need to say anything, was to act as if she'd just arrived home, as if what had been said had never been said, as if he'd never left the house in a tearful rage but had just gone down the hall into the kitchen to get their supper ready. They spent the rest of the evening, of the night as it in fact was, following slow clocks, him like a tramp in wrong and soiled clothes, with a glowing lump on his forehead.

First of all jolly supper cooking. The peas didn't actually do all that well in their butter regime. They shrivelled a bit. He and Chris agreed they looked like small green brains. That made them try to remember what food was good for which bodily function. It was carrots for seeing in the dark, crusts for making your hair curl, and fish for braininess: peas didn't get a look in. 'Perhaps they help you pee,' Chris suggested. 'Or enhance the marrow,' was his thought. The shepherd's pie was hot on the top and rather cool inside, but they wolfed everything down. In lieu of champagne he dug out a bottle of French plonk that had been lying around for ages waiting for some sort of cheerfulness to happen, and they tried to promote it by making up a limerick that rhymed Nicol-ah with knickers-and-bra, but couldn't think of a punch line. The mention of underclothes gave him a physical pain in the chest, the thought of what had happened between Chris and Art, between himself and May, of that taking off and taking off, but luckily you only see the blurriest of shapes through an ice pane.

After they had eaten they took the rest of the wine into the lounge. They didn't switch on the telly. It would be approaching the Epilogue by now, a reminder of true time. Instead they put some music on, Mendelssohn first, followed by Bob Dylan. They talked about furniture.

'I saw an interior recently,' he said.

'Oh yes,' she replied, straight-faced.

He felt himself colour up. 'You know, a room. A – a person's room. On business. Bank.'

She didn't probe but sat waiting patiently for him to say more, looking appraisingly at their own room as she did so.

'It had a lot of . . . I don't know what it had a lot of, but something. Kezzaz. It had a lot of kezzaz. It had a blue wall, and squashy furniture.'

'My dad's just getting used to the Habitat. A change would give him vertigo. What we could do, make him stay at home. He'd prefer that in any case.'

'Alternatively, we could blindfold him on his visits.'

'Yes, that would do the trick. He could feel his way with that blimmin pipe of his, like an antenna. But I've got a better idea still. Why don't we move house? Sell up, and go. Make a –' suddenly she lowered her voice, and he could almost hear a crackle as the surface of things was stressed – 'new beginning. Especially if, you know –' her voice now sank to a whisper – 'we have any luck starting a family.'

'Of course, they don't recommend candidates in elections moving house.'

'Don't they?'

'It makes them look as if they're counting their chickens. Banking on going up in the world.'

'What if they moved into a crummier house than they had already?'

'That might give the impression of losing all hope. Anyhow, you don't want us to buy a crummier one, do you?'

'Not really.'

'Well,' Trevor said, 'who cares what they think?'

That seemed to be agreed: new house. Dylan was singing 'Mr Tambourine Man'. Trevor thought, what a despairing thing a new beginning was, writing off all the past to date. But don't probe, don't investigate it. Out there lost in the dark, his mother's ghost, May weeping over her humiliation, Art ticking off his score. Just accept a new beginning – it's only a matter of usage, of what people say.

'I think it's time for bed,' he said.

It wasn't time for bed, but long after. It must have been approaching two in the morning but they insisted on acting as if it was only eleven. Chris made them cocoa. Trevor went up and used the bathroom. As he was putting his pyjamas on he recalled a story he'd once read about a man who had somehow got himself out of time with everybody else, only by a matter of a few minutes or seconds but it was enough to consign him to a dark empty world where there was no possibility of touching anything or seeing anybody. In a sense he and Chris would be like that. They would stay three hours behindhand for the conceivable future. As long as they did so, her admission would never have happened, she would never have been to bed with Art, he would never have raped May. Perhaps it would mean that they wouldn't be able to make proper contact with the rest of the human race, but in some ways that wasn't necessarily a bad thing. It might help him, and Chris, through the next difficult phase in their careers. There was another thing thin ice was, apart from brittle: hard.

Chris was relieved to find Trevor in his pyjamas when she brought the cocoa up. In his alien shirt and disgraceful trousers he'd looked like an impostor. Even now, the lump didn't belong. In fact, on closer inspection he still looked like an impostor. He took the cocoa and slugged it back as if he was a cowboy in a bar drinking whiskey. Then he strode round to his side of the bed with an odd confidence she found rather attractive.

In bed his new confidence continued. He was crisp, decisive, completely on top, apart from a moment when his forehead brushed her shoulder and he whimpered. She remembered that thought she'd had about the two of them being blank and same-y as a pair of dolls, with just his tube connecting them. This was quite different; indeed difference was what it was all about, that difference she had been aware of all evening. She was being invaded by a hard alien force and had to define her own separateness around it.

She was aware that this was her doing too, the result of the affair with Art. Two men were more than double one: they changed all the maths. It was as if she became aware of Men for the first time, as a plurality, a herd, a species almost. Trevor wasn't just her husband: he was Men. She felt she was a worse person than she had been before, but she was enjoying herself more. Perhaps that was the way of it.

For a long time after Trevor had gone May sat where she was. It was as if she was too embarrassed to move, even though she was the only person in the room. Eventually she put on her bra and pants, then sat for a while longer, her stockings crinkly on her legs. She worried that Mother might wake up, wander downstairs and see her in this odd state, but even that fear couldn't persuade her to budge. In fact all it did was remind her of something that happened years and years ago, the summer after she had met her steeplejack.

She had arranged to go to one of the new holiday camps in Wales with a girl-friend, and had bought a swimming costume to take. She could remember it yet, a beige cotton thing with a little skirt like the ones ice-skaters wore nowadays, and a floppy rose stitched on above the right bosom.

She had gone up to her bedroom to try it on. It was a bit tight but she convinced herself that that made it figure-hugging and provocative. She let her hair down to flop on her shoulders and posed a little, giving oblique looks at the mirror. Then, in the depths of the glass, she suddenly noticed the small intent face of her mother, peering round her shoulder.

She'd felt sweat surge everywhere even though it was cool in the room, under her arms, on her lower stomach, between her breasts, in the small of her back. She was aware of white bulky flesh that seemed to have been abruptly imposed on her from above, of her costume straining at the seams, of the impossibility of drawing breath. For a while she didn't even dare to turn round. Her mother was now looking downwards in a preoccupied way, up to something, but it was impossible to tell from the mirror what it was, with May's own body in the foreground.

Then she heard an odd little sound, like a breath, of something gently landing on the floor, and automatically turned to investigate. Mother was taking her clothes off.

She was doing it in exactly the way a fallen woman might, someone in a burlesque act or brothel. As May looked, Mother had her hands behind her back unhooking her bodice. She then held it at arm's length, and let it drop. Her dress and petticoat were already on the lino. Next the knickers and girdle; finally her stockings. She slid her hands elegantly down each side of her knickers, and worked them down her thighs. They fell to the floor and she stepped out of them, each foot arced downwards like a ballerina's.

May turned her head away, but there her mother was, in the mirror. It was like being ambushed from all sides. Seeing her mother in this state made her think of something they used to talk about at school: the unforgivable sin. They'd spent hours in juicy speculation as to what it might be. Perhaps this was the answer – or at least it was the unforgivable *sight*, the one thing you were absolutely forbidden to look at.

She turned to face midway between the mirror and her mother's actual form, looking towards a blank wall, but immediately found her eyes crawling round to peep at her mother's body. Strangely she didn't even know whether this was because she was herself fascinated by the sight, or because she knew her mother wanted her to look and she still, for a few seconds, had some instinct to keep her happy.

This was the very body from which she had come, and what you had to do in life was walk further and further away from it with the years. But perhaps the time came round for you to have one last look, like visiting your old infant school again, or some house where you'd spent part of your childhood. There were the breasts she must once have sucked, small, shapely, almost hard-looking. Then, at the base of her mother's stomach, luxuriant hair, not a frizzy tuft like her own but a strangely organised-looking growth, as if in some sophisticated untalked-about way, in some secret room at the hairdresser's, one could arrange to have it permed. And concealed beneath those neat waves, the tiny beginnings of that place from which she, May, had first bulged out upon the world.

And then May understood. Mother was doing this to humiliate her. She was doing it out of contempt. She was doing it as a way of asking, why should my body, neat and pretty as it is, have been saddled with a great lump like you? As this second shock hit her, May felt her breasts, her bottom, her thighs wobble, as if not just her eyes but every bit of her plump self was about to burst into tears.

Even her weeping proved ugly as sin, a great hiccuppy bawling that made her panic at the loss of breath. Through red wet eyes May glimpsed her mother doing an Egyptian shuffle dance, one arm outstretched forwards with the hand held flat up at ninety degrees, the other outstretched backwards with the hand held flat down at ninety degrees. Then she bent down, swept up her clothes, and skipped gracefully from the room, the damage done.

May had sat herself on her bed and continued to cry, relieved now she didn't have to worry about doing it uglily. She found herself yanking at the rose on her costume front, pulling and pulling at it till finally the stitching that secured it snapped. She didn't want a cloth flower to ornament her bosom, it would be like fixing a ribbon on a pig. She didn't want her bathing costume at all for that matter, and would have torn it off in her miserable fury except that she couldn't cope with her own naked body for the present.

The outcome was she told the friend she was supposed to be going to Wales with, that she was needed to help her aunt in Waveney Bridge during her annual holiday, and someone else went to the holiday camp in her place. What she'd feared most of all was looking like a saucy postcard.

Funnily enough, May regularly saw her mother in a bare state nowadays. Quite often she had to fish her out of the bath when she'd been using the echoes to sing with until the water had got cold. She was still remarkably well preserved. Her body looked younger naked than it did with clothes on, except perhaps for her bottom which was shrunken like a pale pink prune, particularly when wet. And there were other times and places when she was less than decorous. But any malice on her part seemed mainly ineffective, and May could afford to be brisk with her nakedness.

But sometimes her mother would look at May with those hard intent eyes as she had in the mirror all those years ago, and May would feel sobs rising in her throat and requiring a firm swallow or two before they could be tamped down. She had an idea that her mother had once said she was more like a vegetable marrow than a rose, but that might have been something she'd thought for herself, perhaps derived from the unfortunate flower on her pre-war swimming costume. She never had learned to swim. Hub had been no beauty himself, rather bulky round the midriff with surprisingly spindly legs. But of course the man's attention was directed at you rather than the other way round. Hub hadn't shown enthusiasm for that side of marriage, but May never believed the problem was her lack of desirability. Not of course that that meant she was desirable after all. But the difficulty seemed to pre-exist their marriage, and Hub was many years older than she was in any case. He was a gentleman, and would have shown willing if at all possible.

But tonight –

May tossed her hair, not that it would toss, particularly, and took a deep breath.

Tonight a man *had* become inflamed for her.

How could I have overlooked that? she asked herself in amazement. I have been sitting here in the aftermath, feeling like a dreadful sight to behold, and forgetting completely about what happened before. True, Trevor had received a knock on the head, but the fact remained that he had desired her, for the time it had taken. That was the reassuring thing about how men were arranged: you could measure their enthusiasm on an inch by inch basis, as if on a thermometer.

She remembered the way she'd burst into tears as he left. That must have been happiness, she thought.

Part 2

Twelve

'The problem is,' Wendy said, 'I keep making the breasts look like . . . you know.'

'Like what?' Cherry said. She was bent over her own picture as if her sight had gone on the blink. Perhaps she wanted to hide it from her.

'Breasts.'

'I know. Like what?'

'Like breasts.'

Cherry twisted her head round to look up at her. Her eyes had a little reflection of the window to the right of each pupil, as if they were painted eyes themselves, and had each been given a matching dab of highlight. 'For heaven's sake, Wendy.'

Wendy felt herself colour. 'You know what I mean.'

Cherry obviously didn't, judging by the blankness of her look.

'*Tits*,' Wendy explained. The word came out more forcefully than she had intended, almost like a sneeze, and Mr Burridge at the next easel, who was quite elderly, put a finger in his left ear and wiggled it rapidly about, as if trying to find the trespasser. 'You know,' she went on in a whisper, 'like women's ones.'

Cherry swivelled back to look at the Johnny.

Nick, the teacher, or helper, or whatever he wanted to call himself, fancied himself as a bit of a joker, and made them call all the man models Johnny and all the women ones Doris. The idea was that since they were just members of an art club rather than professionals they wouldn't feel so self-conscious if they lost their own names while doing the honours. Of course they lapped it up, especially the Dorises. Not that it really mattered, because they were never asked to show all they had, rather to Wendy's disappointment. They were kitted out with a useful sheet, which turned all the pictures Roman, if not Greek. One statuesque Doris had held her nerve and tucked the sheet under one of her breasts, with the result that everyone in the room became very serious and devoted to their art so that they wouldn't seem to be taking the bare boob too lightly.

The Johnny who was sitting on the platform at the moment just had the sheet draped over his midriff, as the Johnnies usually did. Wendy had noticed, on her way to the loo, that the people over that side had quite a good view of his bottom crack, which would probably cheese him off when he saw the end-products, being a tax inspector, but from her own angle there was nothing indecent until she found herself making it so.

'The fact is,' Cherry said, giving the Johnny a good look, 'they *are* quite like women's ones.'

'Do you think so? The more I try to get them just right, the more they seem to spring out at me.'

'When you look at a bare-chested bloke on the beach, you don't say to yourself, what a bos-oom he's got, unless he has a ginormous wobbly type of one. But when you look close up, bingo: bosom it is. No other word for it. Nipples, the lot. It helps if there's a bit of hair, of course.'

'Let's see yours, then.'

Cherry looked smartly up at her and rolled her eyes. The little windows stayed still. She really doesn't want me to look, Wendy realised in surprise. She thought of Cherry as being too daffy to be self-conscious.

'I showed you mine,' Wendy said.

'That takes me right back to 2B, or round about. Anyhow, you did not show me yours.'

'I described it vividly enough. Warts and all.'

'Warts is more real than you need. All right, all right.'

Cherry moved her chair back and flourished her arm. In her

helmet cut with her monkeyish face she looked very 1920s, which Wendy had told her once. 'I'm old,' she'd replied, 'but not that old.' Still, she'd looked pleased. What Wendy had been driving at was how she made living in Costford seem less like the end of civilisation.

Wendy looked at her picture, and gasped.

In the middle there was a sort of pink square, rather like a shopping bag, and in the top right-hand corner a smudgy patch of blue.

'What you think?'

'You did an abstract,' Wendy said reproachfully.

'Did I? It looks realistic enough to me.'

'What's the pink bit, then?'

'The pink bit's the Johnny.'

'What about the blue?'

'That's the Johnny's soul, or whatever you call it.'

'But it's not in his body.'

'No. I think it must have got joggled out. By life.'

'Oh.'

'Do you think that Johnny's soul *is* in his body?'

Wendy looked at him. He had a double chin and dark jowls, which made the baldness of his chest seem extreme, like when you peel a hard-boiled egg. There were beads of sweat on his forehead, as if he found sitting still the equivalent of hard exercise.

'No, perhaps not.'

'There you are then.'

'But it's not in the corner of the ceiling, either.'

'I didn't put it in the corner of the ceiling. I put it in the corner of the picture.'

'I give up,' Wendy said.

She went back to her own picture. The Johnny's tits were a mass of rubbing out and pencil marks, so they insisted on being the focal point. What they looked like most of all was those bump eyes frogs and toads have. It was becoming likely she'd never be an artist, unless that turned out to be the next craze, pond things glaring out from people's chests. But sitting in an estate agent's office all week made her restless. Which was what she'd said to Cherry when they met at the Saturday afternoon art class.

It had been the perfect explanation, like saying a password. Cherry talked about the need to aspire. It was as it sounded, she explained, like a church poking up at heaven. The way she said it didn't sound pretentious, just true. Aspiring was Cherry's whole philosophy. She had left teaching to become a waitress because teaching was making her cynical and manipulative, too fond of exercising power over people who happened to be smaller and younger than herself. 'Also,' she said glumly, 'I couldn't control the class for toffee.' They were only seven-year-olds, but seemed to have a dangerous side. They were too young to see her point of view.

Unfortunately the us and them situation had carried over into Cherry's waitressing career. She had a very intricate way of explaining to Wendy how things had gone wrong. She'd recently been for a walk by the River Goyt and noticed the movement of fast-flowing water, the way you could follow individual droplets on their course and see how they would shoot over and around some rocks, and avoid others like the plague. This same phenomenon seemed to happen to a particular table at the restaurant, not the same one every night but varying. Try as she might there was always a table she just couldn't help neglecting; she'd struggle towards it but constantly get side-tracked and eddied, bring the wrong food or get buttonholed by some other customer on the way.

Often the people were understanding about it, but eventually there was a terrible scene. She'd made it worse by trying to explain what was going wrong as she saw it, not using the Goyt example because she hadn't gone on that walk by then, but reverse magnetism. The man had simply seemed not to understand what she meant, so she told him about how two magnets could repel each other, and he'd taken it the wrong way, completely losing his rag.

'He complained to the manager about me,' Cherry said. 'He was under the impression I'd said he was repulsive. The thing was I had, only just in the magnet sense. *Truly* repulsive. I resigned in the nick of time, but it didn't stop me feeling a failure.'

A failure was the last thing Cherry could be, so far as Wendy was concerned. Just seeing her at her easel when she arrived at the art class made her heart lift. She was funny without even intending to be. Wendy liked to be as funny as possible, it made her feel she had a personality, but Cherry didn't try, wasn't even aware of it. She just seemed to live inside a sort of permanent joke, like being surrounded by air or weather.

The best part was, it was catching. Wendy felt funnier herself in Cherry's company. I could fall for her if I was that way inclined, Wendy thought. She'd even told her that, on their way home after the pub last Saturday.

'Woo,' Cherry had said in reply.

'Of course I'm *not*,' Wendy had added hastily. She'd done her falling already, though she didn't want to go into details. And Cherry had too, twice as it turned out. She claimed that it was best to fall in love with two men at once so that one could compensate for the other's drawbacks; plus, it was useful to have a spare.

Nick told the Johnny to make himself decent, then came round to look at everyone's work. 'You need to be more bold,' he told Wendy. He made no remark about the mess she'd made of the bosom. He praised Cherry to the skies.

'Creep,' Cherry said, when he'd moved on. 'He just wants to take me out.'

'Well, you've got brain and brawn on tap,' Wendy reminded her. 'You might as well have art too.' She felt herself go red but Cherry didn't notice.

'I've got more art in my own big toe,' Cherry said.

They stayed on after everybody had shuffled out. That was Cherry's doing – she'd spoken to the janitor last week, and he'd agreed. 'I told him we were so interested in art we needed the extra hour,' she'd told Wendy. 'I didn't mention we wanted to fill in the time till the pubs open.'

Like last week Nick hung around for a while, glancing hopefully in Cherry's direction.

'He's jigging the way my top infants used to,' Cherry whispered, 'when they wanted to go for a pee.'

Finally he came over. 'I don't know about you two,' he said, shaking his head. 'Cherry and Wendy. You almost rhyme.'

Wendy hadn't thought about it before. We're connected by our ys, she told herself, pleased. Given Cherry was ten years older, it seemed a compliment to be compacted together. They were a bit like each other, too, tall and lanky, though Cherry held herself in a rather hunched way, as if she didn't value physical things. Perhaps that was why she'd got herself a bodily man, to compensate.

'I think you better stick to art rather than go for English literature,' Cherry told him.

He took no notice. 'What I was wondering is if one of you would mind being the Doris next week.'

'Yes we do,' Cherry said. 'Mind.'

Wendy almost opened her mouth to disagree. She quite wanted to be a Doris, and it would make a change from the responsibility of doing a picture. The question shot into her head of whether she would have the nerve to show a boob. Answer, no. Anyway it would seem unoriginal. The fringe of a nipple would be as far as she'd go, just a little crescent of darker skin. The fringe of both nipples, braver: wear the sheet like a low-cut gown.

'It's a matter of everyone mucking in,' Nick said.

'Half the women are straining at the bit to be Dorises,' Cherry told him, 'so you might as well use up your volunteers first.'

'But they're ugly, for the most part.'

'Charming. In any case, ugliness is more of a challenge.'

'Well, I tried,' he said.

'I'll clear up in here, Mr Thingy,' came a voice. It was the caretaker, Jack. He came striding in, one normal leg, one heavy-looking one as if he was wearing a caliper on it. He ushered Nick out, no nonsense. 'I won't abide that man mithering me,' he told them.

'Saved by the bell,' Cherry said.

'You spoke too soon,' Wendy told her later.

After pottering around clearing up for a few minutes Jack became confiding. He told them about his job. This building was an annexe of the Town Hall, apparently, even though it wasn't joined on. He lived here, rent free, all services, and got a small stipend, as he called it. But he had to caretake the Town Hall itself too. He wasn't pleased about his job at present.

'They've brought back the hops,' he said glumly. He wore a blazer that seemed strangely out of keeping with his broom, and his hair was brushed so flat it looked as though it had been painted on his head. Given his leg, Wendy thought for a moment that by hops he meant some kind of physiotherapy. 'Mods and rockers on the rampage,' he added glumly.

'Mods and rockers were years and years ago,' Cherry said.

'They're back with a vengeance now. Anyway, what I was getting at, come and look at my quarters.'

'Beg pardon?' said Cherry.

'My flat.'

Cherry looked at Wendy and raised her eyebrows. Wendy raised hers back. This seemed to mean they went, though she'd expected the opposite. Any rate, safety in numbers.

There was a kitchen and dining area, then an archway and a tiddly lounge. No bed visible, thank goodness. Everything was neat and there was no smell, but somehow it seemed stale and unsavoury, as though loneliness itself could make a place go sour.

'It's probably worth about eight quid a week in rent alone,'

Wendy told him. He looked at her in surprise. 'I work at an estate agent's,' she explained.

That pleased him. 'Look at this,' he said, walking over to a small table in the sitting area and picking up a bottle. 'My daughter gave it me.' He unscrewed the lid. 'Have a sniff.' He passed the bottle to Wendy. It smelled like ointment. 'That's malt whisky, that is,' he told her. Then he took the bottle and passed it to Cherry, who took a mighty inhale.

'I thought if I got enough suction I might suck some up my nostril,' she explained.

Jack looked at her for a second while the penny dropped, then turned towards Wendy, smiled and shook his head. His smile was unexpectedly big and baby-like. 'Your mucker's a one,' he said. 'Take a pew.'

Cherry sat down on the little settee and after a moment's hesitation Wendy sat beside her. Jack looked down at them. 'You look like the three wise monkeys,' he said.

Cherry glanced at Wendy. 'No room, Jack, I'm sorry,' she told him firmly. 'Two wise monkeys is all there's space for.'

He'd already gone over to the work surface. 'I'm sure you young ladies would like a cup of tea, after all that art you've been painting.'

'Just the ticket, Jack,' Cherry said. 'No choice,' she whispered to Wendy, 'if we want to get out alive.'

Wendy's heart sank, even though she knew Cherry was kidding. It was the way Jack's small eyes bulged when he looked at her. Cherry had Nick on tap, she had Jack: girls about town.

'I've got some cake. My daughter made it me.'

'That daughter of yours sounds a good egg,' Cherry told him.

'Oh yes, several. Three, I think.'

'She sounds to be a brick, what I mean,' Cherry said in a foghorn voice.

'She did her bit when I got bankrupt, no doubt about that.'

'Did you go bankrupt, Mr Kitchen?' Wendy asked.

'I went belly up and no mistake. I had a small grocer's. It was a total flop.' He seemed proud of the disaster. 'I'll never be able to have a place of my own. No bank or building society will come within a mile of me. For the amount of money I owed I could have been a supermarket. I don't think they got sixpence in the quid when it was done and dusted. If you ask anyone in the business community in Costford, they'll tell you my name is mud.'

To Wendy's surprise the cake had icing sugar and silver balls, as though he'd nicked it from a toddlers' party. He poured the tea and cut them a slice each. 'Tuck in,' he told them.

The cake tasted quite nice, a sponge, but seemed to dry up all Wendy's saliva, so that for a panicky second she couldn't swallow and felt her neck arc forward in a retch. Then she remembered the tea, took a sip and floated her mouthful of cake again. It reminded her of that lovely sensation when you push a boat into the sea, and after a moment the water holds its weight and it's free of the bottom.

'Spot on,' Cherry said, to distract from her struggles. Wendy realised she must have looked like a snake trying to work an antelope down itself.

'It's a good cake,' Jack agreed. 'It's the type of one I like. She always does me one of these.'

'I think I had a touch of hiccups,' Wendy said, by way of alibi.

'Are you all right, duck?' Jack asked, concerned. He put his own cake on one arm of his chair and his cup of tea on the other, rose to his feet, and limped over to her. For a moment Wendy thought he was going to pat her on the back. But he just stood in front of her, hands dangling from his blazer sleeves like large pink gloves. 'Can I fetch you a glass of water?'

'Oh no-o,' Wendy replied, to her irritation actually hiccuping, one of those odd sudden ones that's halfway to a burp. 'Don't worry, Mr Kitchen. Another sip of tea will do the trick.'

'It's funny, isn't it, Jack,' Cherry said, 'you being Mr Kitchen and there's your kitchen.'

Jack turned towards her, then looked down at Wendy again,

as if she could shed light on it. Then he turned back to Cherry. 'Well, I haven't become Mr Sitting Room just because I'm in here.' Saying that name must have made him remember how he'd called Nick Mr Thingy, because he went on, 'You better keep an eye on that art teacher of yours. He'll have you all in your birthday suits when he thinks the time is ripe.'

'We've got his number, don't worry. I'll tell him what *he* rhymes with, soon enough.' Cherry in turn had obviously been brooding on Nick's witticism.

Yet again, Jack looked to Wendy for help.

'I think, sick,' she lied.

'Ah.' He looked cheerful again for a moment, and then groaned, as if in sudden pain.

'Are you OK, Mr Kitchen?' Wendy asked.

He didn't reply but clenched his fist and pressed it against the middle of his forehead, so that he looked like a unicorn with a stumpy horn.

'Mr Kitchen?'

'Jack?' Cherry asked.

'Look at it this way. I have to work all the hours. I have to lock up after those horrible hops. I got this little place, but on an inhabit-only basis. Nothing of mine about it, because I'm person non grata from one end of the financial system to the other. I've no wife or family except the one daughter. The wife cleared off directly my business went kaput.'

'Well, she cooks you nice cake,' Wendy said. 'Your daughter.' She looked guiltily at the piece on her plate, with just the one bite out of it, but there was too much risk of throttling herself or projectile vomiting if she put any more in her mouth.

'Yes, I have cake. That's something to show for my life, cake. The main thing is, what's going to become of me?'

'What's going to become of any of us?' Cherry agreed. She turned to Wendy and said in a whisper loud enough for Jack to hear. 'One of the reasons I have two blokes, as you know.'

'In what respect, Mr Kitchen?'

'Living, for a start. Where am I going to live?'

'What *I* would do, being in the housing business, is advise you to apply for a council flat now. Put your name down. Those Prospect Hill properties, a lot of them are going to be one person. My boss was helping a lady to put her name down only the other day. I'll drop off a form if you like, when I come to art class next week. My boss knows councillors on the housing committee, so he might put in a word.'

Jack nodded, without looking too impressed. 'I know councillors myself,' he said, 'with letting them in all hours of the day and night.'

'There you are, that's a start,' Wendy said breezily.

'Talking of a start,' Cherry said, 'we'd better be off.'

They got up to go. Jack remained dejectedly in his chair. Wendy went over to him, not quite sure how to say goodbye. She felt suddenly maternal as she leaned over him, despite the fact he was a self-pitying old sod.

When they were walking down the road, she said, 'I have a horrible feeling I sort of kissed him when we left.'

'You did.'

'Oh, gorp.'

'But chastely. A teeny little peck. On the forehead.'

'I was hardly going to suck his nose. But even a little one gives me the collywobbles. Why did I do it?'

'You never know what places your lips are going to lead you to. I speak as one who's been to them.'

There was fine rain on the wind. Rain in the dark always struck Wendy as odd, the way it damped you from nowhere. They picked their way towards the same place as the week before, Yates's Wine Lodge. It was on the edge of the market, which was closing down for the day. Street lamps picked out squashed oranges and tomatoes lying like bits of innard on the cobbles. Traders were folding up their awnings and stowing them in vans and little lorries, calling to each other as if they were herding cattle.

The Wine Lodge was brightly lit, and warm as toast. Cherry admired its mezzanine and plastic chandeliers, the fact it was got up to be a proper gin palace. 'I like the way it goes Ya boo sucks, bring on the dancing girls.'

'It seems very respectable to me,' Wendy said. It was full of women with their shopping bags, and middle-aged working men with caps, and scarves tucked into their jacket fronts.

'Perhaps *that's* what's good about it. It says, I'm respectable, even though I drink the demon drink.'

Cherry had a gin and tonic, and Wendy half a pint of lager.

'What's your opinion on older men?' Wendy asked.

'Speaking as an older woman, you mean?'

'You can talk, you have more blokes than you know what to do with.'

'I know what to do with them OK. It's them knowing what to do with me.'

'Anyway.'

'You haven't fallen for Jack Kitchen, surely, after that little snog?'

Wendy shuddered so much it shook her drink. Then she told Cherry about her new feelings for her boss, Art. People had said he was a womaniser, but though he was always friendly and cheerful, and flirted a bit, he didn't try it on with her. He used to go off on mysterious errands, but she hadn't quite been able to imagine him getting up to anything. After a certain age it's not easy to picture men without their trousers on. It was like that feeling you have of being let down when your dad appears in his pyjamas.

But.

Art'd done something rather nice. She'd always thought of him as a hard-bitten businessman, happy to get a bit close to the wind in his dealings from time to time. She'd known him sell a house for less than it was worth because he had a customer ready with a fixed upper limit. And the opposite, when a purchaser was flush. But suddenly he was behaving sweetly to a dotty pensioner who wanted to move to Southport to be near her niece. He'd gone to endless trouble to unload her house, even made it Buy of the Week in his page in the *Costford Express*. The house needed doing up and was apparently rather chilly, presumably the result of damp, but he was on fire to sell it. There was no possible advantage in going out on a limb for the old bat, but he'd done so. It was all to do with him having seen the ghost of her late husband in one of the wardrobes. Her niece brought her into the shop on one occasion, and Art treated her as if she was his long-lost granny, introducing her to Wendy with such ceremony she stood up behind her desk and shook hands. The old girl was gone with the wind, and didn't register; her hand was cold, like her house. Art'd just succeeded in getting a retired solicitor interested in the property.

'Seeing him be so nice suddenly made me realise I love him.'

'Love's a strong word.'

'I know.'

'Oh.'

'I believe I loved him all along but a door was shut on it.'

Cherry picked out her lemon slice and nibbled it. Then she dropped it back in her drink. 'One day in the early days I knew Ben, he'd gone off to some dinner or other and when he visited the next morning to talk about a big book he'd been reading he sneezed garlic at me. After he'd gone I went over to where he'd been sitting. There was a patch of garlic hanging in the air. At least that's what I imagined: like ectoplasm. I bent down to sniff at it, trying to breathe the air Ben'd breathed.'

'Tell you what, that must have been what gave you the idea for the Johnny's soul.'

Cherry gave her a reproachful look. 'If I had to define what love is, I'd say, second-hand garlic.'

'I don't think I could ever go that far, even with Art.'

'Well, the trouble with Ben is he's so platonic. I think the garlic grounded him a little. If Dave ever ponged in that way it would be a disappointment, I must admit, even though I love him too.'

'The nearest I can get to garlic is I used to think Art was coarse-looking. He's got dark stubble, a bit like that Johnny today. And very big features. Big nose, big mouth, ears. Big eye-balls, even. Now I think there's a lovely sort of rubberiness about him. He can even make his ears move, when he wants.'

'Love is love, that's my motto.'

'Thank you,' Wendy said, as if she'd been given permission.

Wendy, in miniskirt and knee-high boots, was all legs angling gawkily away from her chair like a calf's or faun's. Blonde hair curved into each side of her thin face like a pair of brackets, stopping level with her bony jaw. Eyes spidery with mascara; small teeth flashing like semaphore from that mobile, lipsticky mouth. She was vivid and funny from bottom to top, and made Cherry feel heavy-handed and heavy-hearted in contrast, with her spare beloved, her inability to keep her jobs, her continual worrying at the meaning of existence, as though the world was a huge window pane and she a wistful and forlorn bluebottle.

She hated the idea of electric Wendy throwing herself at some dull middle-aged businessman, but there was nothing she could say or do, live and let live being her philosophy. And she had no right to criticise. She herself was a would-be hippie at heart, never within miles of the real thing. For one: too old. Two: not American. Three: lived in a snug house bought with money left to her by her solicitor father. Four: looked after her step-grandmother, on wages from her stepmother. Five: it was too late, now flower power was fading from the world.

She had a sudden picture in her mind of blossom turning to sludge on the pavement when spring is over with. Perhaps my name being Cherry, she thought, makes me liable to such images.

'My old Hilda reminds me of a mummy,' she said.

Wendy had gone into some sort of reverie, perhaps thinking about her estate agent's adorable rubberiness, and gave a little start when Cherry spoke. 'Is she a substitute?' she asked, 'being yours died when you were so young?'

'No, I mean an Egyptian mummy.'

'Oh. They always look pretty horrible when their bandages are taken off, in my opinion.'

That was the drawback to Wendy: she sometimes seemed obtuse. It was because she reacted so fast: the other side to her fizz.

'I didn't mean looks. I meant how she's gone light and dry, as though she could be blown away by the wind. But still herself, unchanged.'

'You make her sound like a Vesta curry. Perhaps you should pour boiling water on her and watch her swell out.'

'She's full size already, that's the point. She was always small. That's what May says: petite. I wish I could be like that, stay the same for ever and ever.'

'Are you happy then, the way you are now?'

'Oh no, I'm not happy. But I'm me.'

'I thought the old girl went round stabbing people.'

'She just flashed a knife on one occasion, but no one was hurt. She's very ineffectual. Of course I let her go off on a wander in the centre of Costie, which was how she got hold of it. I think you can buy them at Millet's. May wasn't best pleased. But you can't tie her up like a horse. And there again everything about her rubs May up the wrong way. She has a way of looking at her as if she's something the cat's coughed up. It's not just her wanting to stab people either, it's the way she sings all the time. In my opinion she's got a rather sweet voice. It's like one of those tinkly bells that you get with Buddhism or one of those religions, a little dry bell. May can't bear to hear it.'

'I'll get us another drink,' said Wendy. 'This dryness makes me thirsty.'

After their drinks they went for a curry to the Anglo-Indian restaurant on Oldham Street, just below the market place. The restaurant was opposite a theatrical costumiers, so called, where shapeless little girls went to hire fairy outfits for fancy dress parties. Cherry had lamb and spinach curry, Wendy one with potatoes and lady's fingers in it.

'They're small for a lady, but that only makes them more lady-like,' she said.

'They're a bit green.'

'That's true.'

Cherry took one. 'They just taste of vegetables in general,' she said.

'That's why I like them. I like vegetables in general.' Wendy took a forkful. 'The problem I've got with Art is, he's very sophisticated. I think he's slept with lots of women.'

'I don't call that being sophisticated. Ben's probably never slept with anyone, and he's about as sophisticated as you can get. Out of a hundred I'd put him about ninety-seven. Once we went on a camping holiday and I lay in my sleeping bag and did sort of little sighs, on the off-chance. He just stayed sitting upright reading his book. I can still see the way his bald head caught the light from the gas lamp. They give off a very white light, and sound as if they're liable to explode any minute.'

'Those sort of heads, you mean?'

Cherry wasn't in the mood for Wendy's wit, though in fact there *was* something almost explosive about Ben's head, full of arcane and volatile material. Dave's seemed safe and solid in comparison, almost like a boulder. 'He had his mouth pursed down, that way people do when they're wearing glasses to read, even though he doesn't wear them. It was as if he was saying, let's leave sexual intercourse to the rabbits of this world.'

'Well, Art is the other sort of sophisticated. He scores about ninety-seven on his type, too. He was having an affair with somebody just recently. My guess is she was married, because he made such a secret of it. Anyway it must have all come to nothing. I think he was really smitten, that time.'

'A bloke like Art just likes women in general, in my opinion, the way you like veg in general.'

'He arrived back one day looking as if he'd been crying his

eyes out, which I've never wanted to do for the sake of veg in general. He was staggering a bit too, like those runners when they've run the marathon and they go yoiks, I've still got to trot all round the stadium. I thought for a moment he was drunk. Then I realised he was just very very sad. So sad. Since then he's kept on being sweet as honey, helping this woman who wants a council flat, and doing all he's done to sell that haunted house in Mill Park. But even when he smiles his eyes look depressed.'

'Has he shown an interest. In you?'

'No. When I got the job, he said he always believed in having professional relationships at work. I didn't know what he was on about at the time, I suppose because he was . . .'

'Old.'

'Old-er. I assumed he was settled, wife and kids.'

'That wouldn't stop him.'

'For goodness' sake, give him the benefit. Anyhow you're a fine one to talk.'

'Don't you start. I have enough of that with May.'

'Perhaps she's jealous.'

'Not of me, she isn't.'

'Of your blokes.'

'No. Anyway, she had my dad, didn't she? I picked him like a fruit, she told me once. Oh no she didn't, it was Dad who said that. She plucked me like a ripe fruit: that's how he used to talk, poor old sausage. But any case, same result. No, who May's jealous of is her own mum, Hilda.'

'I thought you said she sent her up the wall.'

'Think on. She's jealous because she is her mum. Something that May has never been. She was only a stepmum to me. And I'd already got to the stage of being a complete pain in the bum by then. What she needs in life is one of those little babies that wave their legs in the air. Funny part is, I'll probably never have one either, however many men I get engaged to.'

★   ★   ★

As they walked out of the restaurant, Wendy whispered in a hiccupy confidential voice, 'I'm not bothered if folks say he's old enough to be my father. He's so big and lovely, with a sad gaze. His eyes since his last love let him down have got this see-through jelly-y look, like egg whites when you break them in the pan, just that second before the frying gets a hold of them.'

'I like my blokes' eyes to be well fried before I let them look at me, the whites white and the yolks set. And if possible, not too much tomato sauce.'

They walked down the main road bent over with laughter. Each had bulging cheeks as if she'd stuffed a hanky in her mouth. They also walked with each leg in turn crossing over the one before, with trying not to pee. To their left the wedding cake of a Town Hall rose into the night sky. Small lamps strategically set in the grounds made it glimmer whitely in the damp air. To one side, and set a little back, was the annexe where they'd had their art class, its flat roof making it look like a man in a cloth cap.

Music was coming from the main building. Cherry recognised it as Peter Sarstedt's 'Where Do You Go To, My Lovely?'

'Oh God,' Wendy said, 'I wish I hadn't had all that curry.'

'Why? You feeling a bit pukey?'

'No, no. It's just I feel I ought to be eating fish and chips. What you have to do is roll the newspaper in a ball, and chuck it over the wall into the Town Hall grounds. That's what everybody does at the end of an evening. In my circle anyway.'

'I've never done it. What with my father being Mayor it wouldn't have been appreciated, and my stepmother being practically Mayor as well. I feel I missed out on it, though. It makes me realise I never had the happiness of youth, and now it's all too late.'

'Oh dear. I wish I'd never mentioned it. I don't want you to miss out on the happiness of youth.'

'I would have missed it whether you mentioned it or not. And now I've got a second go, I'm too full, same as you are.'

At that moment the main doors of the Town Hall suddenly

opened and a group of youths shot out, exactly as if they'd been vomited. Peter Sarstedt's voice was achingly loud for a moment: '. . . when you're alone in your bed'. The youths scuttled down the drive and spilled on to the pavement, where they looked suddenly confused and directionless.

Without speaking to each other or even breaking their stride Wendy and Cherry crossed to the other side of the road.

It struck Cherry that it must be bred in women by evolution, the ability to turn yourself from a boozy female full of curry and yearning for fish and chips to a smartly clop-clopping passer-by, who by pure coincidence is just happening to cross the road away from a bunch of yobbos who have newly been ejected from wherever they were getting drunk.

She allowed herself one sideways glim as she and Wendy hurried on. She didn't really see anything, hardly a shape at all, just the impression of a limp, passing across the lit doorway of the Town Hall.

Thirteen

Naked greed was the cause of the ruckus, as so often it was. There were a number of things wrong with Jack's job, more than you could shake a stick at. Tied digs for a start, which meant they owned you body and soul.

Tiny amount of stipend for another. One pair of shoes per annum was the limit of what he could afford, and even that had to be from the cash-and-carry where thankfully they hadn't cottoned on to the crash of his business.

The shoes there always seemed much of a muchness, sort of brogue style, with holes punched in in a little pattern, brown or black leather but otherwise no difference. Give a good tug at the lace when you were doing up the bow and sure enough it would snap in your hand. The excess wear he gave the left-hand shoe hardly helped matters, and the last cobbler he took it to renewed the heel on its unworn side, claiming it was as per instructions, which would have left him walking about like the leaning tower of Pisa. Another four bob to get what was done undone, and then done right.

And once you'd got your shoes safely installed on the end of your legs, where are you going to be able to walk them to? As opposed to the daily trudge of work, any rate, with a ring of heavy keys tugging at your belt like a hernia. Living on cake, baked beans and the occasional half-pound of mince still didn't leave enough left over to go on holiday. His daughter, Jan, always offered to take him but he had no wish to be the skeleton in her cupboard.

The solution he'd worked out last summer was to do Chester. It was only seven and a kick by day return, so he'd gone and returned three days in a row. I might as well get to the bottom of it, he told Jan.

The first day he'd walked all round the walls, which he wasn't sure were Roman or medieval, maybe a combination of the two, with a bit of recent thrown in. There was a horse-race track adjacent to them, but unfortunately nothing doing at the time. The second day he wandered round the shops, many of which projected out over the street, with quite a lot of timbering evident. A man in a café told him they weren't Tudor, despite appearances, but Victorian imitations, which seemed a bit of a swizzle, as he later mentioned to Jan. The whole place seemed pretty mixed up, historically speaking. The third day it bally well peed down, without let-up. He went to the café again but the man who'd told him about the imitation Tudor wasn't there, so he went into the public library for a while and read a paper. Chester as a whole proved easier to get to the bottom of than he'd expected, and the great British summer didn't help matters. Meanwhile people he knew were jetting off to Spain, and astronauts were going to the moon.

The worst part of the job was being at so many people's beck and call. Officially he had to report to the Manager of Parks and Leisure, though what the Town Hall had to do with either was beyond him. The annexe had classes in it, so that was more understandable as far as Leisure was concerned, though even there, Education would have been a more logical choice. The manager wasn't a bad bloke but of course he was always off inspecting some flowerbed or other, which left Jack at the mercy of any councillor who cared to order him about.

Some were gentlemanly and considerate, like poor Hubert Hammond, the Mayor as was, who had been so much in a class of his own he seemed to talk a different language, but made it his business to be diplomatic when easing down to your level, like one of those Martians in a cartoon who ask to be taken to your leader. When he died, Jack had said to his widow, May Hammond, or Rollins as she called herself nowadays, 'Give him a month or two to learn the ropes and he'll end up Mayor of heaven,' which had moved her to tears, not that she was anything to write home about herself, with a tongue on her when she had something on her mind. There were others who could come it fairly rough, like the Rate Payer, Bert Colley, who would treat you as his personal servant if you didn't watch it, all in the name of the people of the borough.

And when he wasn't fetching and carrying for the councillors, and letting them in and out at all hours of the day or night, he had to keep tabs on the other users of the building – both buildings, given the annexe was separate. For example the art teacher was true to type, which left it up to Jack to rescue various young ladies from his clutches. And having to weed out delinquents of all ages and sizes from the Saturday night hop was the straw that broke the camel's back.

'I've heard about your shoes,' Ted Wilcox, the council leader, told him, 'I've heard about your holiday in Chester. I've heard your thoughts on the subject of the late Mayor. The late Mayor but several, if you want to be exact. Thank God we're getting to the point at last.'

Ted's grey hair was so shiny it was practically lavender, which wouldn't have taken Jack aback as he'd had him down for a pederast all along, despite his reputation with women. There was an important distinction between looking well turned out in a manly way, which you could do even on a limited income, and wanting to draw attention to yourself by being over-groomed and expensively dressed. The bloke who'd spoken to him in Chester had smelled of talcum powder, which was also a bad sign and caused Jack to be less forthcoming with him than he might otherwise have been. One of the ratings in the navy had used Johnson's Baby Powder, made no secret of it at all but just kept it in his locker, but of course those types tended to lead a charmed life, especially in that service. Nothing more fetching than the square-cut naval shirt and the cap on at a raffish angle, for anyone of the pansy persuasion.

A lot of the trouble at the hop was caused by young lads whose hair was cut so short they could have been in the services themselves. They wore trousers that only went halfway down their calves and were held up with braces, and big boots, also quite military, except they were bright red or yellow. Bovver boots, Jan told him. As far as Jack was concerned they were mods and rockers, though that expression turned out to be old-fashioned nowadays, contradiction though it seemed, and they liked to be called skinheads, which was an accurate enough description. Anyhow they were one contingent, along with the sort of rag tag and bobtail girls who would feel an interest in that type of lad.

The other contingent were as different as may be, twenty-five plus, some in their forties, settled people in jackets and slacks, with the women in frocks down to mid-calf. The skinheads' girls by contrast wore miniskirts so short you could see their knickers, hardly worth getting dressed in the first place, and you could bet your bottom dollar they wouldn't keep them in place till they climbed each into her own little truckle bed at the end of the evening.

Bet your bottom dollar. Ted Wilcox didn't see the joke, just sighed and drummed his fingers. In all probability too close to the bone.

The hops would end up like the prize fights they used to have in the Town Hall in the olden days, before Jack started working there himself. You might as well have had one of those fake cockney announcers saying, 'Hin a hred cahner,' and that type of foolery, which he'd enjoyed as much as the next man in its day. Nothing like seeing a pair of young pugilists knock five bells out of each other, but what you don't want is those sort of goings on at a Saturday night dance.

Money was the root of this evil same as all the others. On that basis he, Jack, ought to be home and dry, given he not only had hardly two pennies to rub together, but in a technical sense possessed an enormous minus quantity, caused by his shop slamming into the buffers. He should be able to get through the eye of a needle without touching the sides, but the same could not be said of the Town Hall at large.

Of course, the hops were originally put on as a community service. Bob Rawnsley, the Parks and Leisure Manager, got fairly stumped trying to find a form of words for the advertising campaign. It was to be on the lines of: *The Town Hall is the Heart of your Borough. Let's let that Heart Beat Again.* Floating above the word *Beat* there were to be little musical notes, and dancing round the bottom of the word little pairs of dancers. The problem was the *let's let*, which read a bit awkwardly, but Bob didn't seem to be able to get round it without losing the gist. Jack suggested *get* instead of the second *let*, but that turned out to be almost as bad. How it was all resolved he never did find out, but the slogan itself was a straw in the wind as to the problem to come. *Beat* brought to mind modern music, the Beatles and all those, not so modern maybe as they once were now they'd gone defunct like the very mods and rockers who used to holler for them, but still a magnet for youth. The dancers in the advertisement sketch, however, were wearing glad rags, black tie the men, long swirly evening gowns the women. They could have been Fred Astaires and Ginger Rogerses in very reduced form. Put your finger on that contradiction and you've got to the core of your problem.

The hops started respectably enough. The very first one was a tramps' ball, which was a good joke, the women all wearing false beards or charcoal moustaches, and smoking their husbands' pipes. Funny part was: made them look more womanish than ever. The husbands appeared much the same as usual, as he explained, to Jan's amusement. For the first few months the hops continued in that vein, not more balls as such but at least proper dances, sometimes to records where Bob Rawnsley himself did the honours, sometimes to a little band called the Mellow Tones that was based at a restaurant in Treadle by name of the Lodge Gates, all middle-aged men who could read music. Bob was unexpectedly good at doing the disc jockeying: he would call a record almost like one of those square-dancing callers, getting everybody into the spirit of the occasion. For some reason he called himself Bo Rawnsley as a stage name.

But of course the novelty faded, and numbers began to decline. Someone in the council decided there wasn't enough appeal to the younger generation, who were the ones with the real spending power and staying power nowadays, so Bob was told the events had to be called discos from then on, and given a younger atmosphere. No doubt in the advertisements the tiny Fred Astaires and Ginger Rogerses were redrawn as boppers.

It was Ted Wilcox who actually did the dirty work, as Bob told it. What about the Mellow Tones? Bob had asked, they're on a fortnightly understanding, with the possibility of more frequent gigs to come. *Mis*understanding as far as Ted was concerned: time they were out to pasture. It gave Jack a melancholy picture of the five of them playing their instruments among trees and meadows as the sun set, like the Last Post only a more syncopated rhythm. Once while out in the hills Jack had had a sighting of the legendary Peak District wallabies against the skyline. It was only a momentary impression, because Jan's husband always drove like the clappers even when just out for a ride, and no one else spotted them at all; there was a bit of joking about mirages and optical illusions, with the kids making out they spotted them too, later the same afternoon in the middle of Glossop. Jack's memory of what he had seen blended with his picture of the Mellows out to pasture till he imagined the silhouettes of musicians bounding slowly over the landscape, tools of the trade clutched in their short forearms, rather like those astronauts leaping in slow motion on the surface of the moon. Of course they still had their regular sessions at the Lodge Gates, but he knew well enough from experience how it felt to be on the receiving end of disappointment as far as making a livelihood was concerned.

What neither Ted nor Bob nor anybody bothered to do was inform the existing clientele of their change of plan. This wasn't oversight, either: they had no intention of coming clean about it. More the merrier, was the line. Given it was Jack's responsibility to keep order and clear up messes he pressed Bob on the point. The idea was to be all-inclusive, to let the whole community come together. They wouldn't be playing far-out pop music, just stuff anyone could appreciate and dance to. That evening back at his flat Jack thought of a comment he should have made: the last time the whole community came together was the second world war.

At first there was no problem that you'd notice, just the usual crowd with a sprinkling of new blood. One beefy young chap Jack noticed that first week who wore braces over his T-shirt, but most of them were just younger versions of the sort they got already. A few more the next time. The music was louder and more penetrating. Then Bob stopped choosing the records himself, and a young fellow took over, the sort of bloke who didn't have two words to string together in a conversation but sat in a hunched fashion, muttering to himself and snapping his fingers from time to time as if trying to tweak something deep inside up to the surface. The deal according to Bob was that one record in three was to be of a softer harmony, with appeal to the older people; the other two, as far as Jack could see, or rather hear, more than made up for it. They were played so loudly that the bits where the music was *supposed* to be loud came through distorted, or maybe it was just beyond Jack's ear range. It sounded like the word blatter being repeated. He asked Bob about it but Bob made two points. One, the Town Hall was structurally sound so wasn't likely to shatter from the impact of the air waves. Two, they had no near neighbours so they were unlikely to get complaints on that score. Jack forbore to point out that he himself was a near neighbour. He would go back to the annexe to rest up for an hour or two before it was time to shut up shop, and discover he was able to hear the din from there. Sometimes he could feel the frame of his bed throbbing. Probably being a single bed it was less stable than a double one would have been and more prone to acting as a receptor, even though his building and the Town Hall weren't physically connected.

More young crowd came the next week and the next, rougher types too, and the music got rougher to correspond. The jockey, named Ade, looked as harmless as a librarian picking you out a book, but he piled on the sound till you could hardly push your way through it. Jack could understand why it was only possible to do such a squeezed, confined type of dancing: they wriggled without moving like flies on flypaper. The whole room, which must have been thirty feet high, smelled of sweat, worse even than bunking on a naval vessel where the ceiling clearance might be no more than five foot and body odours inevitably got tightly packed.

But funnily enough, though some of the older guard got weeded out, quite a number of them continued to attend. It may have been a matter of liking to slum it, or even in some cases trying to bop themselves back to their teenage years, not a temptation that could come Jack's way since he'd been young before being young was allowed. Perhaps some of them hadn't even noticed the change of atmosphere.

A very odd thing had once happened in the old days, with Jack's wife, Loretta. She'd taken a deckchair and gone off to sit in their bit of garden. He must have been busying himself with something in the house. When he went out an hour or two later to see how she was getting on, it had clouded over and was raining, not hard but a definite drizzle. And there she was, still in her deckchair, lost in thought. She seemed as oblivious to the new weather as a bit of garden statuary, but in fact that wasn't the case because when he asked her what on earth she was up to she replied that she'd never noticed before that falling raindrops were white, having always assumed them to be transparent.

It struck him as an uneasy type of thing to say, coming from her; later he decided it had marked the beginning of the end of their marriage, the first sign she was becoming a different person from the straightforward sort of a female he'd got wed to. Their business was just starting to go off the rails, and it was an inkling of what was to happen.

Years later the answer came to him: being the rain is descending there's no time to look through it, hence an opaque effect. The same would probably apply to a dropped bottle or jar, though he didn't put it to the test. But Loretta was long gone by then.

The moral of the story was that he had a nose for trouble, and the hops as currently arranged were asking for it. They had sucked in two sections of the Costford populace that were not compatible. It was like a demonstration he had seen during the war years when the instructor had introduced a piece of phosphorus into water. He'd made it sound as if the two things were expected to shake hands with each other, but of course they didn't, far from it. Perhaps he'd used too large a quantity because afterwards there was scarcely an eyebrow left on the ship. It was a training base in Portsmouth, in point of fact, but in the navy these were always called ships, and after a while you began to believe it yourself, as if the brick and mortar walls were a hull, and the ground they were built on was a very stiff type of sea.

Jack spoke again to Bob, but no joy. The man had looked shifty, true enough, though ostensibly he was cock-a-hoop. The discos were succeeding beyond anybody's wildest dreams, that was the official word straight from Ted Wilcox's lips. Ted himself wouldn't be seen dead at them but that was another story. They were serving a wider range of Costford people, and no group should be favoured over any other, be they young or old, rich or poor, Labour, Tory or Independent. From the way Bob reported, you'd have thought Ted was talking about taking the sacrament of Mass, not about having your eardrums buried under megawatts of rock song. Apparently the hops had been officially declared the council's 'strongest' current activity in some report that had to be made to the central government, overtaking both the new hat museum and the art gallery which had recently acquired a Lowry picture of a factory.

As a last resort Jack had had a word with May Rollins, being that he'd heard her grumble on the subject in the past, but she was very brisk about it. Up to that moment she'd always seemed to him to be a bit of an old lolloper, with tweed skirts and shoes like boats, but on this occasion she was bustling down the Town Hall corridors in a red trouser suit that made her look like a large high-speed strawberry. He prided himself on being nippy but it was all he could do to keep up with her.

She took a similar high-handed tone to the one Ted Wilcox must have had with Bob, telling him that Tories had a live and let live philosophy and believed that what worked, worked. That it wasn't her business to impose her own taste on other people. Given what she'd let slip in the past about the bedlam in the main hall sounding like an abattoir he felt somewhat taken aback, but later on Jan reminded him the election was on its way. It wasn't the right moment for May to show herself as a crotchety old individualist who spoke what was on her mind (which usually took the form of a complaint about something or other, if the truth be told); as Jan put it, the time had come to be gung-ho and busy busy busy.

When it happened he was there and saw it happen. Just as well. It wasn't part of his job to try to put Humpty Dumpty together again, but if he didn't, who would? It was about eleven o'clock, and he'd just come back from a lie-down on his settee, where he could have the TV on to cut down the throbbing. Then he'd got up, made himself a cup of tea, and had a quick sandwich, Mother's Pride and a Kraft cheese slice, bang on. Loretta used to say that eating cheese at night made you dream, but at least if you were dreaming you were asleep. That's what he said to an imaginary Loretta inside his head, as if she'd still be interested in his thoughts on the subject. One advantage of being on your tod, you could eat whatever you wanted. One disadvantage: you had to get it yourself. Then he hooked his key chain back on his belt.

Back at the Town Hall what he did this time of the evening was lurk. He'd have a word first off with whoever was on the door, who would be tilling up by that point, and then with the duty manager, one of Bob Rawnsley's underlings, who was usually sitting in Bob's office off the lobby drinking coffee. Then he would peer into the loos to make sure nothing was happening that shouldn't be happening, even the Ladies. That required a bit of care so nobody could take offence. He would hang around outside, not too close to the door, then when nobody had come in or out for a while and there was nobody in the offing, he would open the door a crack, put his eye there and let it take a dekko. It was almost like using it as a periscope or one of those snail's eyes on a stalk; because he kept the rest of himself so far back no one could accuse him of going to places that were off-limits. Different story altogether in the morning, when Mrs Timmins would often call him in to help remove graffiti from the cubicle walls. A thing he'd learned about women, they were no better spellers or drawers than men when it came to being dirty minded. But he never came across anything untoward going on there, though once in the Gents two or three lads were passing round a marijuana cigarette. He didn't say anything direct, just came in and made out to be testing the taps, and sure enough they turned sheepish, put it out, and scuttled off, one of them calling 'Lettuce leaf, mate,' as he went through the door, and the others laughing as if at a clever joke.

Jack would try the doors of the committee rooms to make sure they were locked. Sometimes, if there'd been a special meeting that had gone on past his resting-up time one would have been left open, and the room'd be being used for nefarious purposes. All you had to do was switch on the light and they'd sort themselves out, heads down and fumbling at their disarranged clothes. There'd been a meeting tonight in point of fact, an emergency session of the housing committee to discuss the dirty strike at the Prospect Hill flats development. But that meeting had ended mid-evening, before he'd gone off.

From now until closing, which was still midnight for the moment though Bob told him they were considering extending it till one in due course – another invitation to disaster – Jack would slip into the back of the main hall for a few minutes at a time, as long as his ears could take the strain. The room was in dimness as a rule, with flashing lights that picked out groups of dancers at random. As luck would have it, the licence extension hadn't come through so the bar at the side of the room was obliged to close at eleven. If they had any sense they'd leave the arrangement exactly as it was. It gave all the customers an hour to sober up before the end of the evening. Fat chance, with lucre involved. At about ten to twelve Jack'd push his way to the front, climb up on the little stage affair, and remind Ade to put on the last waltz, as he called it.

This Saturday there was still about an hour to go, so all he was doing was giving the place a routine once-over. But it's funny how your senses are always alert for a possible kerfuffle. Just as he was about to step back into the lobby, something broke out at the far left, near the stage where Ade was piloting his console thing, a thump, a gasp, odd sounds that added up to trouble. Without a second thought, Jack pushed over towards the bank of light switches on the wall, and snapped them on by feel.

There was a swirl of activity up front. A girl was shouting, and an older bloke, probably in his thirties, was putting his hand on her shoulders. A lad was tugging him from behind, by the collar. The older bloke jerked his head forward to release the grip, and just at that moment another boy, not at all a big chap, delivered a haymaker that went right over the older bloke's head and sent the lad behind spinning over the dance floor. It was so out of proportion to his physique it was like when Popeye'd just downed a tin of spinach.

Of course next thing that happened was the flattened boy's

friends crawled out of their holes to take revenge, gathering round the lad with the punch in a threatening fashion, shouting and pushing at him. The older bloke with the girl was sneaking off through the crowd.

What Jack did was hurry over to the stage. Ade was sitting there looking lost; he told him to be useful and put on one of the mood tracks to create a calmer atmosphere. Where the duty manager was, who knew. Probably hadn't heard a thing as yet. The bar grille was down and padlocked. The young fellow behind there was probably checking the takings and would stay put if he knew what was good for him.

As Jack turned back to go and fetch the duty manager he saw the fellow who'd thrown the punch more or less herding the troublemakers towards the door, helped on by one or two of the other customers who were willing to join him now it seemed safe, like the townspeople did in that film, *High Noon*. Jack scrambled down to give him a hand. It was all about morale, like they used to drill into you in the navy. If you thought you were defeated, you *were* defeated.

Just as they spilled into the lobby, the duty manager made an appearance, face a bit puffy and hair tufted, as if he'd been up to something he shouldn't in the solitude of Bob's office. To make up, he laid into the group, which was only four or five strong when it came to the push, but enough if fists are flying, gave them a good shouting and more or less booted them through the front door. Out on the street, they just looked like a bunch of harmless kids. The lad who'd got laid out was in the middle of them and bleeding from the nose. The problem for him would be which was the way to impress, make a lot or a little of it, nothing in life being simple.

The duty manager was full of praise for how Jack had showed presence of mind, under the impression it had been him doing the herding out. The little bloke who'd really done the business had slipped back into the main room.

Jack spotted him again at chucking-out time, and asked for a word. The lad stood quietly, waiting for it. A thought came to Jack he'd never had before, that folk are usually coming at you, one way or another, or pulling away from you, one way or another, just according to the manner they pose themselves, whereas this boy had a way of being exactly where he was. One of those things you could only appreciate if you saw it.

He didn't seem to be in the company of pals or a girl, solitary bird.

'You box?' Jack asked.

'Box?'

'Yes, you know.' He took up the stance with his fists and moved his feet in a boxer's shuffle on the marbled lobby floor of the Town Hall. He had a little trick which he'd discovered quite by accident many years ago. He could press his tongue against his top teeth and do a sort of half blow, half whistle, and the sound that came out was for all the world the sound boxers' shoes make on the canvas, those little squeaks and groans that always reminded him of the mating song of some obscure bird, marsh warbler perhaps, anything you've never actually heard in the flesh. He did the noise now, as sound effect to his feet movements, making each little curl of sound exactly the right length to correspond with the successive contacts of his soles with the tiles. 'I love the game,' he said. 'I used to follow the service tournaments, and then when they had regular fights here. I even tried it myself a long time ago, but I got KO'd and was advised by those in the know to give it a miss. A glass jaw's a drawback no amount of training is going to cure. Nobody's fault, you can't be good at everything.' He gave his keys a jingle. 'Though I wouldn't mind being good at *something*, aside from going bust and turning keys in locks.'

'No.'

'No?'

'No, I don't box.'

'Well, you ought to think about it, with a sledgehammer like you've got.'

The lad just looked back in silence, with obviously no intention of thinking about it.

'Anyhow, I was wondering if I could have a word,' Jack said. 'If you could wait a minute while I lock up, we could go next door to my little pad and have a cup of tea. I've got a bottle of malt whisky if you'd prefer a drop of that. If you beetle off now, sure as buggery they'll be lying in wait to give you a going over.' He wasn't a swearer by nature, but thought it might put the lad at his ease.

The boy didn't look as if it mattered to him one way or the other. He shrugged his shoulders. 'All right,' he said.

Fourteen

ray Bentley could pick up the signals, he'd had enough practice at it. The Town Hall locker-up was a man in his early sixties, ramrod straight, hair brushed flat, shirt, tie, black blazer, grey flannels, and a real giveaway, the smell of Brut aftershave coming from his jawline, perhaps even from his armpits and further down yet. He almost clicked his heels when he spoke to you, and kept his feet at forty-five degrees while he stood there, ensuring his buttocks stayed tight and round in outline. Then to top it all he did a little dance right in the middle of the foyer. One of his legs stayed rigid, which made the rest of him look like an Indian doing his thing round a totem pole.

That was a new one on Fray, though a couple of times when he was small he'd had to dance with blokes in the privacy of his bedroom. The barman was just coming out of the dance hall with a couple of drunk girls he'd winkled out of some corner somewhere, and all three of them stopped and gawped at the performance. The girls were at that stage when their strings have gone loose and they have to walk about like puppets, but even they were stunned by it. The locker-up didn't notice; he whistled, shook his keys, carried on having his own party.

Fray had no idea whether he wanted it himself. Or even whether he minded, if it came down to a question of just minding. Or perhaps getting something for it, turning it into a cash transaction. His mum used to say, 'You don't mind, do you? It's only to keep Uncle Whoever-It-Was happy.' They were all uncles when he was young. Some people live in cold or hot places; he lived in uncly country. His mum would look at him with those big moist eyes of hers so that his heart would miss a beat and he'd feel himself redden with the urgency of keeping her happy.

In later years he went into the country and saw a cow. He looked at it for a while, wondering why it seemed familiar. The cow looked back at him.

'Have we met before?' he asked it.

He hadn't really.

All his life he thought of things to ask people or say to them, and birds and dogs for that matter, and even chairs and cars and stuff, but he hardly ever said them. He hardly ever said anything. But afterwards he remembered the conversations anyway.

This one was very short because the cow had no answer to give. Not even in the inside of her head. For all she knew Fray was nothing more than some tree that had suddenly sprouted in front of her. After she'd looked at him for a while she just lowered her head and ate another clump of grass. She made it sound delicious and juicy, the way she tore it off and chomped it. The nearest he ever got to noises as appetising as that, was when he put the triangular end of the beer can opener to the top of a Party Four and levered a hole in it, hearing the metal strain and then sort of gasp as it gave way, then another hole the other side, then pour it into the glass and hear its foamy splash which dwindled away as the glass filled up, while the head began to fizz as it formed itself.

Who the cow had reminded him of was his mother. The cow had the same sort of eyes, large and brown and glistening, with a sort of tremble in them when they looked at you which made you tremble in return, deep inside yourself. It was one of those sensations that caught you so deeply in the pit of your stomach it could make you suddenly want to pee.

But after his meeting with the cow he began to see his mother's eyes all over the place. He saw a horse, and he had them too, an even bigger version than the cow's. Then a dog. He even saw a little brown bird with them, probably a sparrow.

Its eyes were tiny, but round, brown and glistening just the same.

At which point it realised he might not be anything more to his mum than a tree or a little pile of turd or a worm in the earth.

After she'd tell him it was only to keep the uncle happy, she would crinkle up her nose and half shut her eyes but still leave the glisten and the tremble intact, and speak with normal-sized mouth movements but her voice turned down to half volume, so what she said came out as a secret between the two of them, 'It's only a bit of fun in any case.' And give him a wink.

After a few times with uncles he had a surprising thought. It came to him out of the blue. You can just be sitting around doing nothing and then give a jump at an idea that's come into your head. Or not even come into your head. It's as if it's been in your mind all along, a thought you've actually been thinking but without any awareness that you were thinking it, like when you get to the end of some piece of work or other and then realise you didn't actually notice you were doing it. Often during his time in the painting and decorating trade, he'd finish a wall or a door then wonder, how did that happen, then?

It struck him his mum had a bit of fun with her uncles the same as he did with his.

He'd thought that they'd played with him in that way because he was young, the way grown-ups might play other kinds of game with you. The idea that they would do such things to each other shocked him to the core. For a while he thought the less of his mother. Then he changed his mind. It meant she wasn't asking him to do anything that she wasn't willing to get up to herself. Also that he didn't have to grow up and become a different person, because grown-ups were as naturally rude as children themselves were. And in those afternoons when he had an uncle in his bedroom and she had one in hers, they weren't separated and mysterious to each other but passing time in the same way, like a mother and son should.

But the trouble with starting in that line when you were

young, and doing it because your mum asked you to, was that afterwards you were never able to tell whether your body liked it or not. He tried it out with girls, of course. He liked the way they didn't have anything at the bottom of their stomachs because it made them neat and streamlined. But tits seemed to interfere with the architecture, as if they'd chosen to build in sheer wobble when there wasn't any structural necessity for it. The big problem when he looked at a naked girl was she didn't seem quite normal.

He told himself, of course she's normal, half the people in the world are made to look like that. What that means, her not looking normal, is just sexy, the sexiness of her being the opposite sex. The other sort of being sexy, the sort he was used to, was just a matter of the parts of the body you could do it with, and didn't involve travelling to a foreign country and trying to discover how things ticked over there.

Because he wasn't even sure if he liked having sex with girls, he turned out to be good at it. It was like learning to drive a car, a question of doing stuff in the right sequence. And because he was good at it he got to like doing it and for a time did it a lot. Also something happened at work which made him feel he'd got himself on the right track.

He worked with this bloke called Decko. His real name was Derek but it had got itself back to front. 'I'm called Decko and I deco-rate,' he told Fray. He was a big bloke with bushy grey hair and a very loud voice. This was the result of his early life as a gutterer, so he said. He'd spent years standing on roofs talking to mates on the ground against a strong wind. First thing in the morning he'd say 'How there, Fray,' so loudly it would practically blast his eardrums, and keep up like that for the rest of the day. His voice was grating, too.

He'd switched to painting and decorating during a bad patch in the guttering business, found it paid a lot better and never gone back. 'People don't mind paying out for paintwork and wallpaper because there's a bit a beauty in it,' he told Fray, 'whereas a gutter's never anything else but just a gutter.' Even hearing him say 'a bit a beauty' was like putting your head in a mincer.

They got on well enough for a while. It was Fray's second job since leaving school. He'd worked in a car repair shop first, and found he had no trouble learning to find his way around an engine, but it all went wrong when a customer said something he shouldn't have said. He was someone who'd been back at Fray's house with his mother, and recognised him. The gaffer had gone home when the set-to took place. Afterwards Fray locked up the premises, put the key through the letterbox, and went home himself, never to return. Nothing more was heard of the bother. The customer wouldn't have wanted it to get out that he'd visited Fray's mother. Fray's P45 and stamp card came in the post, covered in the gaffer's oily fingerprints.

Fray discovered he had just as much of a knack for the painting and decorating trade as for car repair. The first time he did a door he hadn't known you had to do the panels in sequence, starting at the top of each, and Decko began to put him right. Then he looked at the finish and saw how regular it was. 'You sneeped me there, Fray,' he said in a voice like a clapped-out Hoover. 'I was going to tell you you done it all wrong and bugger me it's right as bloody rain.' What it was, paint obeyed him. Wallpaper too: he could picture how it might tangle up when you were handling it after pasting, but for him it always stayed flat and regular. He was able to butt it with that same sure precision with which he fucked girls.

Finding out he had these various knacks made him wonder why he'd been such a write-off at school. It must have been because he never said anything. What the teachers seemed to have been in search of was some sort of social life. He felt comfortable working alongside Decko because though Decko talked a lot himself he didn't seem to worry that he never got an answer, and for Fray it was no more personal than if he was spending his life mending roads with a pneumatic drill. Maybe not a lot had come back to Decko on those roof breezes in his guttering days.

It was an outdoors job that put the kibosh on their relationship, after Fray had been working for him a couple of months or so. Funnily enough, the day before it all went wrong Decko had been up painting gutters. Fray was working on the window frames. It was January and the weather had turned sharply cold. A thin snow began falling, and eventually Fray lost the feel of the brush, having to keep it under control by eye. His feet went so numb they couldn't feel the imprint of the ladder, and coming down he put them through the gaps as often as on the rungs.

The next day it was just as bad. Decko kept his equipment in the garage of his house, all the ladders, paints, rolls of liner, brushes and whatnot. He had a little desk in there too, to prepare bills and estimates on. His van he kept on the driveway outside. The up and under door didn't even open any more: he'd fitted shelves to the inside, and you went in by a side door that needed blowtorching off and doing properly. Fray's previous gaffer used to say, 'You'll never see a mechanic drive anything but an old banger. You get so one car's much of a muchness to the next.' At the time it was a remark that had made Fray look back on the uncles he'd known, how one of *them* was much of a muchness to the next as well. The red paint on the side door of Decko's garage was faded and blistered, and there were ancient splashes on the two frosted glass window panes. There was a loose plastic doorknob you had to push hard to engage.

Fray let himself in. Small hard snowflakes had fallen into his eyeballs on the way over, and made them sting. There was a paraffin stove in the middle of the garage, and he went over to it.

Decko was hopping in the corner. Fray gave his eyes a quick rub and then was able to make out what he was doing.

Decko was dressed in a shirt, paint-stained Fair Isle pullover, and underpants, with his trousers hanging over the upright chair by his desk. His right leg was in one leg of a pair of women's tights, and he was just trying to push his left leg down the other side. The unfilled leg of the tights hung below his foot like a withered limb.

Once an uncle had asked Fray to put on a woman's skirt with nothing underneath it, along with a pair of high-heeled shoes. The skirt sagged a bit on his hips and the shoes were about a size too large, so his feet slid down to the end of them and left about half an inch of space at the heel. 'Do us a walk,' the uncle had said, and Fray tottered across his bedroom, bending slightly in the middle so the skirt wouldn't fall down. He must have looked as if he had stomach ache, but the uncle was pleased.

The uncle took the clothes away with him when they were finished with, but afterwards Fray saw his mother wearing them and realised they'd been borrowed from her. On her the skirt was above the knee, and so tight it showed her stomach falling away and her individual buttocks at the back. The shoes fitted perfectly, one big toe and one next toe showing in the hole at the end of each, with red nail varnish glowing through her nylons. It's just like Cinderella, he thought, but then he re-membered that she must have known all along that he'd worn both them and the skirt, and felt inflamed with rage that she must have known what a dick he'd looked in them compared to her.

Decko's dangling leg suddenly filled out as if it was a balloon being blown up. 'How do, Fray,' he roared. He pulled the top of the tights just over the elastic of his Y-fronts and let it ping into place. His thighs, calves and feet in their stockings looked like linked pork sausages. He pulled a pair of socks on, on top of the tights, then took his trousers from the chair and stepped into them. Fray continued to stare silently at him, wondering if he was like a bloke Mum told him about who wore a peek-a-boo waitress outfit underneath a pinstripe suit to work.

'What you got to remember, Fray,' Decko told him, 'these women are not as daft as what they make out they are.' He couldn't say every word with equal loudness: wim, daft, out, are, exploded in turn in Fray's ears like small grenades. 'Tights are warm and light as a bloody feather. More layers you got on the better, when it's as fucking parky as this.'

He bent down to pull his shoes on and do them up. Then he stepped across to Fray. His hand rose slowly, palm upwards. It was strong-looking, with big knuckled fingers sprouting from it.

The hand cupped itself round his balls and prick, squeezed hard.

Sounds banged in Fray's ears: don't, get, bug, sol.

'What you don't want,' Decko was shouting, inches from his face, 'is get these old buggers frozen solid!'

Fray hit him so hard and fast it was just like not having done it at all. Decko looked as if he'd suddenly chosen to lie down on his garage floor for a rest. One of his trouser legs had got rucked up, and you could just see the pink of the tights above his sock.

Fray let himself out, shutting the wonky door with care. Last thing he wanted was to let the old goat get cold. The snow had got bigger while he was inside but for a while his goolies continued to glow from the goosing they'd got, even without the help of tights. He glowed inside too, feeling strangely happy. What it goes to show, he was thinking to himself, is I've put all that business behind me. What I'm interested in is just women, like other people are. Unlike other people, he also realised, he'd had to chuck away two jobs just to prove it.

There were no repercussions this time, any more than with the last incident. Decko wouldn't have wanted to explain to the police he'd got thumped in consequence of feeling up a youthful employee.

Nearly a year later Fray was sitting at home drinking a Party Four when a thought struck him. It was another one of those surprises you can get just when you're sitting on your tod. He remembered an uncle years ago, who'd ruffled his hair. Fray had thought to himself, 'Here we go,' and got up to head for his bedroom, but the uncle didn't follow, and instead went in with Mum. After a while the explanation dawned: it had just been a friendly ruffle. Now, after a much longer time, a similar explanation came into his head. What Decko had given him was a friendly goosing.

All he'd been saying, poor bashed-in bastard, was, you've got to look after these, my friend, when you're out in poor weather all day long.

He hadn't pulled those tights on to prance about like some ballet star. They were just practical. Maybe other tradesmen who had to work outside in the winter wore them too.

Fray drank his way through the Party Four, trying to keep himself in the same position as he consumed each glass, only his hand tilting when necessary, not wanting to lose his concentration. He felt he was having to think the most difficult thoughts possible, ones that are in a language you don't understand. Not that it made any difference to his current situation whether he succeeded in thinking those thoughts or not. Decko belonged in the past.

Fray had not tried getting another job – there was no future in it for somebody like him.

He didn't get it completely sorted out in his head, but one stupid topsy turvy idea did make itself clear: he wished he'd had it away with Decko after all. What made it ridiculous was that Decko wouldn't have wanted it in the first place. He had a wife in that house of his; it was probably her tights he was putting on.

They called him Decko, Fray thought: I decked him.

What he'd believed he'd achieved by doing that was making it clear in his own mind it was girls he was after. Now he suddenly hungered for the very bloke he'd flattened. He didn't know whether he wanted him so as to keep him happy, as he'd kept the uncles happy in the past, or whether he wanted him because he wanted him. This was the area he never could get clear. But from that point on he lost interest in girls and went back to men again.

Now though it was different. He'd long ago given up working for his mother. Any money he had need of he got by nicking

TVs and hi fi equipment, and selling the stuff in pubs, and he paid towards the housekeeping with that. He was as good at nicking as at his other jobs. He broke in at first by using a glass-cutter and sink plunger, but soon worked out how to force locks and sometimes even pick them as well. He never made a mess or broke anything. There were robbers he heard of who used to shit on the carpet, which as far as he was concerned brought shame on all the rest of them. He had no desire to be seen as half-witted or animal-like, and get himself tarred with the same brush as people who were sick in the head, or didn't know what a bog was.

Sometimes when a lounge he'd broken into was in a terrible mess to start with, he actually tidied it up a bit, for fear of being blamed in the eyes of the police and insurance people for the state of things. He wanted to be appreciated by all parties, so that just as a householder might say to himself, I've got myself a good bloke to mend my car or decorate my house, he might also think, I've got myself a good robber to rob my television set: could have been a lot worse.

Fray was good at selling on, too. Once he knew a punter wanted the swag, which he could always tell by the way the eyes would focus and all friendliness leave the face (something he'd learned to interpret from the expressions of uncles in the past), he would allow himself to be beaten down to the price he'd previously worked out was fair, then stop. He didn't need to say anything, just sort of twitch his expression. He could always tell by the punter's eyes that he'd got the idea – that if he didn't clinch at this point the TV was liable to be stuffed in his gob. It felt economical, elegant almost, being violent without doing or saying a thing.

This was the first of his jobs that proved a success. He had one moment when it all went wrong and he found himself in court, but then a strange thing happened out of the blue. It all turned out right again, and for the first time in his life he was able to think: I was lucky.

Sometimes he would take men back home to his bedroom – his own men, not his mother's, and often he'd accept money from them. It was as though in some way or another he'd gone mysteriously numb in his bum and his cock, despite acute sensations there. His sharpest feelings were coated in velvet or cotton wool, like knives in a box, and money seemed to open the box. It was like on a hot day you know it's hot but you still want to find out the temperature. He could say to himself that was a five quid one, and know what it meant.

This money he never, ever gave to his mum.

Tonight he didn't know whether he was in the mood or not. He was in a funny state in any case. He'd gone to the disco expecting to meet a bloke who owed him some money. The customer hadn't shown, though, and he'd been just about to leave when he saw someone else he knew. It was one of his mum's blokes who'd come to the house when Fray wasn't in, and helped himself to his Party Four.

According to Mum afterwards, he was pissed to start with, and thought it was a good joke, even though she tried to talk him out of it. He even shook up the can on the way to the bedroom, so when he opened it with Fray's own triangle it jetted straight up to the ceiling.

When she told Fray about it, and showed the stain on the ceiling, he felt himself turn into a sort of stone of rage. Other people went all hippy hoppy when they got mad, which seemed to him to waste the energy fury brings. What happened in his case was he became an inch shorter, lost an inch around his middle, became aware of each arm and leg retracting an inch in turn. The shrinkage left him hard and solid.

He stood where he was, listening to his mum, not moving but unstoppable.

I told him, I told him what you. I said, Fray, Fray's who. You don't know who you dealing with. He thought it was a big joke. I said to him, it's not a joke. I told him afterwards, that's torn it. I don't want you here again. Your money isn't as good as the next bloke's, it's worse. And that isn't as good as the next bloke's neither, it's much worse, no use to man nor beast. He hit me when I said that, just a poke, nothing to be ape about. He wouldn't have the strength, him and his army. And it's only a Party Four, when all's said and done, nothing to be ape about. You can take the money for another, go off down the off. It's his money, have it on him. Get level. I didn't want the wanker coming back in any case, not just the Party Four, all the fucking rest of the sod.

Fray knew which one it was, he'd seen him before. Bloke gave him a big wink that time. You could practically hear his eyelids bang together. He must have thought it was funny, saying howdo to Fray when he was going to screw his mum.

He must think everything about Fray was funny.

And here he was at the disco.

He was making himself unpopular even here. He'd stepped in between some lad and his girlfriend, and the lad was giving him a tug from behind.

Fray stepped up, and swung.

The bloke didn't duck. Fray had swung before: they never ducked.

But what happened was the wanker pulled free of the lad who was tugging him from behind at the crucial moment, and bent double with the momentum of it. The lad behind was jerked forward in the process so his head ended up occupying the exact space the Party Four bloke's head had occupied the fraction of a second before, at the exact time to meet Fray's punch.

Fray stood there for a second, thinking about it. He wasn't used to being untidy. In fact, he hadn't been untidy. It was the situation that had been untidy.

There was no point in explaining. Fray didn't go in for explanations in any case.

The Party Four bloke and the girl he'd picked up made themselves scarce: Fray would have to wait for some other time. The lad Fray had hit and his mates fancied their chances for a moment, then thought better of it. But the old man in the blazer was right. They'd jump out at him from the dark if they could.

He went out by the side door with the blazer bloke, whose name was Jack. 'Name of Jack,' he said as they set off, giving his blazer cuffs a quick tug down. He bobbed up and down as he walked, as if going over a chain of little hills.

Fray went with him to his pad. What happened next he'd play by ear.

Back at his flat Jack offered the lad a malt whisky, but he wasn't interested, not even in sniffing it. Just as well: Jack wanted to save it for a rainy day. Anyhow it was a good sign, in relation to the proposal he had in mind.

The lad just stood in the middle of his sitting area. You couldn't say awkwardly exactly, because he didn't seem in the faintest degree discombobulated. In fact, what was fascinating about him was the impossibility of imagining how he would ever get discombobulated, whatever the circumstances. If he was awkward at all it was in the way a pillarbox might seem awkward, plonked in the middle of your house. Although he was a little chap he had the exact sort of sturdiness a pillarbox has, when you saw him up close.

'Take a pew,' Jack told him.

He took no notice, not in an aggressive way, but as if he hadn't heard. In point of fact he didn't seem very ready to take in what you said to him, but at the same time didn't give the impression of being stupid either. He was one of those people who seem to live a long way inside their heads, like a badger or a rabbit or whatnot down its hole. He made Jack think of that joke: 'Knock knock, anybody home?', when you tap on somebody's head with your fist. Not that you would ever do it against this lad's head for fear of suddenly losing your hand, if not your whole arm. Jack had sustained enough damage for one lifetime without chancing on attracting any more. Avoiding that danger was exactly why he'd asked him here.

He'd introduced himself, but needless to say the lad hadn't responded in kind.

'Do you fancy a cup of tea then?' he asked.

The lad looked back with his blank eyes. They were pale green and quite large for his narrow face – stick a few hairs on them and they could be gooseberries. He had mousy hair slicked back, with sideburns to the mid-point of his ears, very white skin, and long fine dark hairs above his upper lip. 'No,' he replied.

'I can't keep calling you nothing,' Jack said.

He just looked flatly back.

'What's your name, then?'

The lad replied something that sounded like Fray. Maybe it was a nickname.

'Well, Fray.' Jack said the Fray quietly, in case he'd got it wrong. 'I've got a bit of a suggestion to make.'

Fray continued to look at him. It was unnerving. It reminded Jack of when he sold his little van, after his business failed. The bloke he was selling it to kept on not replying while they were discussing figures and Jack found himself chipping away at his own asking price, haggling with himself on the other fellow's behalf is what it amounted to. Not that it mattered a lot, since any cash received had belonged to his creditors in any case, but it was upsetting at the time. Jack had felt himself flush up with anger, whether at himself or the other chap he couldn't say. The thought had entered his head that this was why he'd gone bust in the first place.

'You're a handy young fellow to have around. You know how to look after yourself, which not many young blokes can do nowadays. It was different with my lot, with a world war to fight.'

What did I say that for? he wondered. He's giving me a look as if I claimed to have won the whole thing on my own.

'Not but what you could have made two of me even in those days,' he went on. 'What I reckon is, the way those hops are shaping up, that won't be the last spot of bother we come across. And who's going to cope with it? I've got a glass jaw, as I mentioned. None of the others would say boo to a goose. But someone's got to do it. What I was thinking, I could alert my manager and perhaps we could arrange to take you on on a Saturday night, in case of trouble, and other times when we have something on. Doorman, we'd call it. Obviously we'd have to make it worth your while.'

It took a while to sink through Fray's head till it arrived at wherever he actually lived.

'All right,' Fray said at last.

He didn't discuss terms or anything else, not that Jack was in a position to negotiate. But it had occurred to him that some good could come of tonight. If he laid it on thick enough to Bob Rawnsley, and if Bob did the same in turn to Ted Wilcox, they might come round. They'd rather splash out a few quid on someone like Fray than lose the income the hops generated. And he'd make it clear it wasn't part of his job to cope with that sort of bother.

Jack wrote down Fray's name and address. Rather to his surprise, he had a telephone number as well. It would be a rum go having a conversation with him down the wire.

Then something happened which was probably the most surprising thing that had ever happened to Jack in the whole of his life.

Fray took a step up to him. Jack actually flinched, thinking that for some reason he'd decided to give him a biff. But what Fray did give him was a quick kiss, right on the lips, then run a hand over his hair.

Then without a word he was gone.

Jack stayed right where he was, standing in the middle of his sitting area. His lips had gone pins-and-needly, as if they'd received an electric shock. Then suddenly he burst into tears. He could see the drops catch light like pearls, on their way to the rug.

He'd cried a few times in the past, in those days after Loretta had left him, always of course in private. What used to amaze him was how many tears would pour out. After a while his eyes would seem to take it in turns, one resting while the other one wept enough for the both of them.

Fifteen

Trevor Morgan had hardly said a word to May since the rape. What word was there to say?

She meanwhile had taken to looking extraordinarily smart and well groomed, as though by being tightly organised in her appearance she could prevent what had happened from bubbling up to the surface. There was something poignant about the effect. It made him remember all the king's horses and all the king's men trying to put Humpty together again.

He felt – no, it wasn't possible to say what he felt, because he didn't seem to feel as much now as he had before. He was brisker and more efficient as a person – a much better lover for one thing, though that was partly thanks to the enormous, unexpected lustfulness Chris had acquired. Sometimes it was almost like being in a fight, as though bed were a snowy wilderness where you were liable to have bandits or wolves jump out at you. At first he worried about neighbours hearing their cries and moans through the wall but, as Chris pointed out, it would probably just sound as if one or both of them was in severe pain, which was to some extent true, and in any case the house was on the market, so who cared? He would get up the next morning hardly able to walk where his balls had been so manhandled, or rather womanhandled, and would have to check for love-bites in visible places, though there'd be others in locations never to be seen, even by himself, like flags on the moon.

He seemed able to guess when to be aggressive and when to be gentle, sometimes at her prompts, sometimes prompting her:

it was as though all their love-making in the past had been just sketches or blueprints of the real thing.

In politics too he felt he'd gained more assurance, a clearer outline. He hadn't repudiated his creed of honesty and straight-forwardness, but had adjusted it so that it was more practical and liveable with. All that worrying he'd done about his forged French O level now seemed stupid and unrealistic – almost, in a way, pretentious. You couldn't have a political programme that required everybody, including yourself, to be Mahatma Gandhi. It wasn't a matter of asking people to be saints, just as honest as they could be.

In a funny kind of way it was a relief to have acquired a secret that was simply too big to reveal. Sometimes he felt he was con-structed like Dr Who's Tardis. He was an ordinary-sized man who had the enormous crime of rape echoing about inside him.

But just because you contained unmentionables didn't mean you should add to them. He became much more capable of speaking his mind, and had come to realise that his big error had been blandness, a desire to keep everybody happy. That in itself was a form of dishonesty. He still had the odd sense of not quite making contact with other people, like that man in the story who had got out of step in the sequence of time. Perhaps he and Chris were still three hours adrift of everybody else. So much could be dumped down a gap like that.

Oddly, the very thing that now separated him from everybody else also gave him a sense of solidarity with them: we've all got something to hide, he would remind himself. Perhaps because an election was on the way, he found himself thinking quite a lot in terms of sayings. He was using *Join the Human Race* as a slogan in his election campaign, with a squiggly little picture of a puffing but jolly runner hurrying up to a finishing tape. That was at the bottom of his leaflets with the party's national slogan in its place at the top: *Now Britain's Strong, Let's Make It A Great Place To Live In.*

His policy of candidness hadn't actually paid dividends. He'd given uncompromising support to the educational restructuring in the borough and the abolition of the last remaining grammar schools, and drawn flak from those who believed in it in principle but wanted to find practical difficulties to postpone the evil hour. It didn't help not having any children of his own, though he was doing his best to rectify that situation, as he told one constituency meeting. It reminded him of the kind of thing May liked to come out with.

Even worse had been his hostility to the relaunch of the Prospect Hill scheme. His fellow Labour councillors were uneasy at his stance, despite the fact that everybody knew the government were half-hearted themselves about the whole project. But it had, after all, been the brainchild of the local Labour Party in the first place. And there'd been letters in the *Costford Express* from members of the public accusing him of being down on single tenants, who were the largest group set to benefit from the Prospect Hill development, and unsympathetic to the general housing needs of the borough.

May gave a vintage performance at housing committee.

She pointed out that, though a privileged member of the community, she lived in an older house, with inevitable problems: a leak in the bedroom ceiling, a garden path that was becoming a deathtrap – postmen had vanished in it, never to be seen again, paper-boys were swallowed up on a regular basis. She looked at Trevor across the table with triumph in her eyes and a little smile on her lips. His heart thumped in horror, as he waited for her to say, 'And Labour politicians have been maimed by it and transformed into sex maniacs.'

Of course she said no such thing. She simply went on to argue that conditions must be even more difficult in some of the six thousand houses identified as slum dwellings by the borough, and that the combination of a difficult property with difficult inhabitants made the mind boggle, though some would say she was a difficult inhabitant herself. Then suddenly she was sharp and serious. There were people all over the borough desperate to take advantage of an increase in housing stock. At the same time, there was wasted council house space, since not enough accommodation for one- and two-person households was on offer. A census of the council tenants, as organised by the energetic new housing officer, Glen Parsons, had shown that out of 1,835 returns, 965 came from under-occupied dwellings, with 212 existing tenants willing to be moved to smaller accommodation, such as would be on offer in the Prospect Hill tower blocks.

'I was never much good at sums at school,' May said. 'But even I, or even me – I wasn't much to write home about in English either – even poor old innumerate me, can do that bit of addition. And that bit of subtraction, come to that. You put your small households in, you take your small households out, in out, in out, you shake them all about. You do the hokey-cokey, that's what it's all about. The Prospect Hill development is going to provide 297 units of accommodation. Two hundred and twelve of them can be supplied by transfer from existing stock. Larger families can take those places. Add together 297 and 212, and what we get are 509 households happily accommodated.'

May swung her head to give the point a flourish, and large gold earrings came into view. Trevor hadn't noticed her wearing any in the past and suddenly realised she must have had her ears pierced since that terrible night. It occurred to him that the little ginger spikes on her upper lip had been removed also, tweezered off, he imagined, with a little jolt of pain from each one, or even uprooted by electrolysis, perhaps at the same salon where her ears had been done. Her hair, too, was in a different style now, a simple trim below the ears rather than the frizzy perm she'd always had before. He pictured the filing of finger- and toenails, paring away of corns and calluses, expert massage of the bottom from hands like blurred pink choppers, the application of those mud-packs that made women's faces look like images from bad dreams or voodoo islands. May was modifying her body so that it no longer felt, to her, like the one that had been abused.

For one sharp second he felt a squeezing of the heart at the thought of what he'd done. Then his new pragmatism came into play. She was making her own arrangements to cope with what had happened to her: therefore it was the less likely she would ever resort to making it public. In conjunction with time itself, she was reshaping the scene of his crime. It occurred to him that though still buxom, May was already noticeably slimmer than she had been then.

To his amazement he felt a twinge of curiosity at how she would look if he stripped her on her settee again; then a recoil of self-disgust; followed in turn by a recognition on the part of his new self that he couldn't avoid that harsh predatory element in his make-up. It had to be allowed for, accommodated, at crucial moments controlled. It was part of who he was. He mentally shrugged his shoulders at the thought of it, and then realised he'd done so in actuality – out loud, was how he thought of it to himself.

He caught her eyes, and saw that she had seen him. There was a knowing look in them, hard and amused. He hoped she'd interpreted it as a shrug of impotence at the impossibility of making amends, rather than as a shrug of complacency. The reality was it came somewhere between the two.

Then she continued.

'Of course, my good friend Councillor Morgan, who is strongly opposed to the Prospect Hill development, lives in a modern house himself. I don't suppose *you* have any leaks, do you, councillor?'

He felt himself go red. But at the same time his practical, assessing side was telling him: that's all that's come of it, that's all she's going to say, that's the only kind of revenge she's been able to allow herself. Then he was on his feet.

'That's why my house is on the market,' he replied. 'I was afraid of being left out.' One of the bonuses of being harder was that he felt sharper too, more able to come the riposte, even at times be witty. 'As it happens, Chris and I have made an offer on a terraced house, so we might get our share of leaks in due course.' There was a laugh from round the table, even from May.

The terrace was bigger than Ann and Barb's had been, with four bedrooms. Bigger in fact than their current house, which only had two and a half. But the beauty of buying an older property, as this very reference showed, was that it didn't make you look as if you were going ostentatiously upmarket. And it suited the way he felt about himself. It would be more complicated, with a history of its own, not straightforward and lacking in nooks and crannies like their present place. 'I don't think the tenants of the Prospect Hill blocks will be left out either, sad to say: everybody knows how prone to leakage flat roofs are.'

'My Tory colleague is refreshingly frank,' he went on. 'She says she's not very good at maths, and my goodness she isn't. Especially at taking away. Two hundred and twelve of the new tenants at Prospect Hill will be old tenants from elsewhere in the borough. If we deduct that figure from her total of 509, you end up where we started, with the 297 units of accommodation, as she so sweetly calls them – we don't exactly get a picture of chocolate box cottages, do we? – the 297 units of accommodation that we knew about all along. All we've achieved by playing this game of hokey-cokey, as she calls it, is to separate out single people and couples and create a sort of separate ghetto for them, one in which they are going to be piled high, like products on the shelves of a cheap supermarket. But that, I'm afraid, is how the Tories tend to look at their less well-off fellow citizens: as commodities, poorly packaged and insecurely stacked one on top of the other.'

Commodities, he thought: isn't that how rapists think of their victims? No lightning struck, though the sky as he walked into the Town Hall earlier in the evening had been sour and grey. May looked unmoved, perhaps seeing no more in it than the usual name-calling. Which, after all, the small, hard part of himself pointed out, it was. And why not? He believed what he'd said was true of Tories in general, and he was after all a Labour Party candidate. In any case, he understood, one can be a hypocrite from one point of view without being dishonest from another.

'One on top of another,' he repeated, to get his thread back. There was an uneasy shuffle, a slight murmur. Unfortunate phrasing, he realised: people didn't know whether they were expected to laugh or not. Again he tomatoed, no way to avoid it. He imagined what it would be like to be a politician of such iron will he could make those red waters subside, force a reinstatement of pallor.

May might think he was toying with her, deliberately creating an atmosphere of innuendo and bad taste. No, no: his blush would save the day. It was a signal he'd stumbled into this, this – what word for it? – *double entendre* by accident, or at least carelessness, just as on that fateful evening he'd stumbled over the raised crazy-paving in her garden path. 'Each one alone,' he went on quickly, 'each one alone in his room.' It sounded like a line from a song, but he couldn't remember which. 'That is the other major planning error evident in this project. It's not just a matter of its height; it's also a question of its hollowness.

'It's not that I have anything against single persons: it's just that you don't make them any less single by putting them all together. We will have a community of ones whereas I think it would be helpful to have one of allsorts, a healthy coming together of different shapes and sizes.'

Coming together . . . different shapes . . . sizes. Everything you said could tend in the same direction if you let it.

Get on, get past it.

Now a song did come into his mind, as though some researcher in the depths of his skull had been at work since he'd asked the question, and had come up with the nearest thing it could, one of Chris's loves. He saw her suddenly, on her haunches on the floor, leaning against one of the Habitat chairs, singing along with the record. 'Remember the song,' he asked, 'about where the lonely people come from?'' Well, I don't know where they all come from, but I do know where they'll all be sent, if this committee, even at this late stage, doesn't call a halt to the Prospect Hill development. So far, thanks to the dirty strike which has only just been resolved, we don't have much more than four large holes in the ground. Unless we think again, four enormous tower blocks will be planted in them. Those are where all the lonely people are going to be sent. The Russians used to exile the people they didn't want around, to Siberia. Costford will exile them to a Siberia in the sky.'

A ripple of applause. Even May shook her head appreciatively, the way politicians do, as if impressed that a creature from the slime could talk at all, while regretting the fact that it could only spout nonsense. But stupidly Trevor couldn't quite bring himself to resume his seat and shut up. It was an old problem of his, a fear of concluding resonance. Part of him hated to play to the gallery. It was a last outcrop of that false modesty he used to suffer from, and it would have to go. But not quite yet.

'Another point, and I know I've made it before. But once we've built this community in the sky, what about the danger from aircraft descending over that very hill on the flight path to Manchester Airport?'

It was decidedly limp as a point, a kind of fidgety PS. But all at once a form of words came into his mind, and he had his final cadence after all: 'It's one thing building skyscrapers, quite another having them scrape the undercarriage of a passing jumbo jet.'

Now he did resume his seat. Doing so reminded him of something May had once said when she'd been holding forth in some committee or other and Ted Wilcox had asked her rather sarcastically if she'd quite finished: 'The plonking down of my rear end you can take as a full stop.'

Ted himself now got to his feet. 'Well,' he said, giving his mane the briefest of tosses, 'who would have thought an election was on its way?'

Laughter all round. Trevor laughed too: it was a way of saying: I know I sounded self-important.

'And who would guess,' Ted went on, 'that we have a candidate for Westminster in this very room with us?'

Another laugh. Eyes turned to Trevor. He ducked his head, half hanging it in shame, half taking a bow, letting the self-deprecation and bravado cancel each other out.

'I hope this doesn't sound rude, Trevor, but your speech was a waste of time on two counts. One, it should have been made in the hustings, before an audience of about eight hundred voters. And two, it addressed an issue that was decided over three years ago. That was the time for debate, that was the chance for an exchange of views. All that's happened since the decision was made is that the project was put on hold for technical reasons. But this isn't an appeal court. The decision was made, and stays made. The Prospect Hill development exists, even though you can't see its towers as yet.'

'Oh blimey,' Bert Colley said, 'there'll be even more chance of an aeroplane crashing into them if they're invisible to the naked eye.'

After the laughter and applause, Ted resumed, no longer hectoring and sarcastic but in the silky mode that was second nature to him: 'While on the subject, I have an announcement to make. The Minister for Housing is to pay a brief visit to the borough on Tuesday week. He is officially the guest of the Mayor, but he will have an informal meeting with the housing committee in which he will outline the government's thoughts on our housing subvention for next year. This will not be binding, more in the nature of an election promise. But for that very reason it's a chance to make our points to him as firmly as possible. If you don't ask, you don't get. If, as some of us hope, the government is of a different hue after the election it will still do no harm to have some provisional figures in circulation.

'Actually despite what I said just now, this discussion will not include the Prospect Hill housing development costs. That's a delicate and technical matter which will be treated separately. The government will have to revise their original figures because of the delay to the project that they themselves insisted on, taking into account inflation and other factors. It will only upset the applecart and confuse the issue if that topic is broached prematurely. We need to have accountants there in any case to do the details. A lot rests on this, particularly the well-being of the developers and contractors who have been left out to dry all this time, through no fault of their own. So all parties concerned, and that includes parties in the political sense, have agreed to keep mum on the matter for the moment.'

He smiled round the table with some smugness. Mum was the state he liked councillors to be in. He was an operator behind the scenes, a fixer and manipulator. His natural pitch was a confidential whisper. It was a tricky one for him in any case. The Tories had no choice but go ahead with the development because the money had been spent, while Labour, having dreamed it up in the first place, could let themselves be holier than thou now they were in opposition. No wonder Ted hadn't appreciated Trevor's rhetoric. But as Trevor's new internal adviser advised, there's nothing to stop rhetoric from being true.

The Minister was exactly what you would expect, an odious twerp. May looked daggers at his back while she waited on the Town Hall steps with the rest of the Mayor's party as it rained cats and dogs and he stood comfortably in the shelter of the portico talking to that old bonehead on the door, Jack Kitchen. You know a man by the company he keeps, she thought. Talking of which, Jack seemed to have acquired a sidekick recently, a creepy young man who was standing guard with him on the other side of the architrave, a smallish youth with pale, hostile eyes. He reminded her of someone, perhaps because there were a lot of lads knocking about the world, knocking about magistrates' courts in particular, with eyes as hard and dangerous as his.

Really, she would never have wanted the Whitehall level of politics, where the job was to please people at large and let those in the immediate vicinity stay out in the wet. Trevor was welcome to it – not that he'd behave like that himself.

Without suffering from delusions of grandeur she did think Trevor had grown up, somehow, since that odd evening at her house. It was almost as though he'd come scurrying up to her for something he needed, collected it, and taken it home with him. He seemed more settled in himself, with feet firmly planted on the ground. Bully for him, if so; the whole episode had been a tonic for her too. It's not every woman my age who can get the underpants off a charming young man who belongs to the other lot: that was one way she secretly said it to herself. It seemed like a free gift.

Perhaps it was true that a young fellow, at a certain stage in his life, needed sustenance from an older woman, but she wouldn't have believed her past life gave her a claim on that role. She'd managed to get older without having the experience, the particular sort of experience, that the title implied. Of course she'd had a certain amount of experience of other kinds, and maybe that made up for it.

The only pang she felt was to do with this lack. My bloody mother, she thought, she took all the confidence away from me. She was the one who stole the wind out of my sails. Just because I wasn't a china figurine with a little piping voice, she turned me into the ugly duckling. A forceful phrase came into her head: she wanted to squash my possibilities.

Not that May had any illusions at all of ever being a swan. Being a woman was quite enough. The fact that she'd felt exposed and emotional afterwards, while he got dressed and left, sitting there with nothing on but her stockings, too *much* of a woman if anything at that point, naked and womany and large, now seemed part of what had been achieved. It made her feel the free gift was all the more of a gift for not being completely free.

The point was, a man needed another mother, at a certain stage, providing something his own mother could never give to him, rather in the way that Cherry said she needed a spare fiancé. In Trevor's case his own mother had not long died. Breast cancer, of all things. On top of that his wife had been up to what she shouldn't with another man, and had only been rescued by the skin of her teeth – of May's teeth, come to think. No wonder Trevor had come rushing and stumbling round to her house in confusion and need, falling flat on his face in the process.

For a woman it was a different story, had to be. You weren't looking for another mother – heaven forfend, as Hub used to say. One was quite enough. No, you were looking to *replace* your mother, to *be* a sort of mother in your own right, to comfort and sustain and give. She felt she'd finally extracted herself from the terrible prison her own mother had tried to keep her in for life. Better late than never.

'Better late than never,' she said, as the Minister finally disappeared into the maw of the Town Hall and the Mayor deemed protocol permitted them to follow, for all the world as if it was Black Rod who'd been knocking at the door. Some of the men climbed the stairs straight-legged, their trousers were so wet.

Jack Kitchen gave all the members of the party a salute in turn, a strange affair with two stiff fingers pointed at his forehead like a small boy pretending to shoot himself with an imaginary gun, probably something learned in the Scouts and never forgotten. The young gargoyle on the other side of the door did nothing but stare.

Vol-au-vents and cheese straws in the huge cool Banqueting Room, where the assembled dignitaries rattled around like stones in a tin. A couple of schoolgirls in waitress dress carried trays of Cyprus sherry about in trembling hands. Dingy chandeliers twinkled above. May had tried in the past to get them cleaned but never got anywhere. It would cost a hundred pounds, apparently, and lead to hostile comments in the press.

The Mayor made a welcoming speech. The Minister responded with one of his own, talking in the usual platitudes about the need to get a roof over everybody's head. You would imagine that the people of Costford bedded down in a field. Then there was a reception line. The Mayor did the introductions, first to the Minister's little helper, and then to the man himself. Trevor was in line immediately in front of May, and had quite an exchange, the Minister holding his hand in a prolonged shake as they talked on. May took a step back so they wouldn't feel crowded. It was an important moment for Trevor. She fancied the Minister's hand was giving him a hoist, as he climbed towards the top of a long ladder.

Not that, in truth, he was as near the top as he might be, at present. The Tory candidate for North Costford, blond, pink, featureless, a dismal nonentity who had been drafted in from the Cheshire countryside, was ahead of him in terms of voters' intentions, everybody said so. It was mainly a matter of the national trend, of course, though May had a slight feeling that the confidence and maturity Trevor seemed to have gained when looked at from close quarters took a hectoring and uncomprom-ising form when he was on the stump. It was probably also a symptom of inexperience, a matter of trying a touch too hard. It could even be for the best if he lost out on this occasion, in any case. He was still very young, and might well make more of an impact if he turned up in Parliament next time around.

Then it was her turn.

First of all the monkey, who did a little bow and said he was delighted to meet her.

Then the organ grinder, who informed her she had a wonder-ful town here. As he said so, his eyes gave a mischievous look. 'What a pity there's not time for you to show me the sights,' he said. His slimness and good looks were as London as a red bus; even the flirtatiousness had a patronising aftertaste.

'What sights would they be?'

'Well, your viaduct for a start.'

'Oh yes, my viaduct.'

'I understand it's made of millions of bricks. And then your hatteries. The Mayor's chauffeur was wearing a Costford bowler, I found out.'

'I have one myself.'

'Do you really?'

'It's maroon, of course, for the more female wearer.'

'I wish I could have seen you in it. I'm sure you look charming.'

'I could have done with it today, that part's true enough, when I found myself stuck out in the rain.'

'Oh, your weather.' He rolled his eyes. 'No need to show me that,' he said, wriggling neatly off the hook.

She plodded away with a vague sense of having been teased and bested, and by the time they got to the committee room where they were going to talk turkey, as Ted put it – himself a man who had no intention of saying a dicky-bird if he could help it – she felt bad-tempered. After a quarter of an hour of sitting while the Minister trundled out meaningless figures in conjunction with vague claptrap she could bear it no longer.

As she got to her feet she was aware of Ted's underwater face mouthing silently at her. Bert settled back in his seat to enjoy the show. Trevor leaned forward alertly, as if this was a lesson he needed to learn. Perhaps it was: how not to behave.

'This reminds me of a reception at a shotgun wedding,' she said, 'where nobody mentions what's on everyone's mind.'

'May,' Ted called, in a sort of whispery shout, 'we've agreed –'

But she was off.

She talked of procrastination, of blowing hot and cold. She said that the trouble with hole in the corner deals was that if understandings were consigned to a hole they could conveniently be buried. She said, giving Ted a fishy look, that postponing decisions at election time was a recipe for disaster. She was not talking about do-goodery, she pointed out, she was talking about honouring business transactions. People had put up good money, and were waiting for a legitimate return. At the other end of the scale, it wasn't a question of whether the deserving poor were either deserving or poor, that was a matter for another day, and a different forum. Or perhaps best left to God Almighty. But rightly or wrongly they'd been made a promise of a better, more elevated – she gave Trevor a look – way of life: it was the duty of everyone in this room, as elected public officials, not to squash their possibilities. The point was that the council had long ago committed itself, with government support, to the Prospect Hill development: now was the time for delivery.

Ted whimpered out loud at one point, with the horror of it all.

The Minister was deep in consultation with his sidekick while she spoke. There was something panicky about their huddle that showed they hadn't a clue how to respond. She could tell them exactly how they would. In fact she did tell them how they would. She told them they'd say something equivocal and wishy-washy and then scurry back to London as fast as their little legs would carry them. But her remarks would be on the record, out in the open, and it would be all the harder for them to dodge the issue in the future.

So the council's position would be strengthened, and nobody would have lost out – except for May herself, if Ted carried out the threats he'd previously made.

And he certainly looked in the mood to do so. He was staring at her with eyes like screwdrivers, and kept tapping his front teeth with a pencil as if to test how sharp they'd bite. The Minister might be Labour but he was in power, and Ted did not like anything to obstruct his connection with power. Never mind, May thought, he's a closed-door politician, and I'm a woman of the people. In the old days she'd taken pride in being wayward and uncompromising, a 'character' as it was called in political circles, difficult but essentially harmless. But now she felt she could go one better. Recently she'd felt much more purposeful and in touch, as though she'd developed an instinctive rapport with the ordinary Tory in the street, or more appropriately, the living room.

'It is time this whole sorry business was sorted out and brought to a conclusion,' she concluded. 'Could I suggest that the Minister forgets for a moment about his correct strategy as a

Labour politician, and takes note of the slogan of his local party candidate. Join the human race instead – or, if by any chance you've done that already, make the effort to remind yourself that you are a member of it.'

She sat.

And then something happened which froze her to the marrow.

Trevor got to his feet.

It was as though, by using his words, she'd said some terrible abracadabra and accidentally summoned him, her golden boy, her political genius, out of the safety of his bottle.

Sixteen

Perhaps it was going to be a good day. There was a phone call from Mr Tompkin, the retired solicitor who was interested in buying Edith Barker's property in Mill Park, the haunted house as it was known by Art and Wendy. He asked if they could make an appointment for him to take a friend round it the following afternoon.

'That's an example of how you do house selling,' Art told Wendy when he rang off.

Wendy looked up at him. She had a funny way of baring her front teeth like a hamster when she was being slightly sarky, which was often. The effect reminded him of someone posing for a photograph while staring directly into the sun.

'I'm not sure I want to know this,' she said.

'It'll help you if you want to be an estate agent in your own right. Don't you have any ambition?'

'Oh yes, I've got ambition. One of my ambitions is to not be an estate agent in my own right.'

'If you ever change your mind, a good way of selling a house is to price it on the high side.'

'Ah.' She gave him an amused, rather wary look, and lightly scratched that dip where her neck gave way to her breastbone. There was a little mark there, and he leaned forward and took her hand away from it. Her head went back sharply, like a pecking chicken's, and she half shut her eyes in that expression when somebody is trying to pull a fast one and you're part on your guard, part amused at their cheek – a look he got quite often from vendors and purchasers alike.

He leaned towards her neck. Just being so near a woman's body made him whimper slightly, but he turned it into a murmur of enquiry, like a doctor. 'Mmm, just a freckle,' he said.

'I beg your pardon.'

'You were scratching it. I thought it might be a mole. You mustn't scratch a mole. It's liable to give you cancer.'

'A mole?' She wrinkled her nose in distaste. 'A mole? You could inspect every inch of me and not find a mole on my entire body.'

'All right,' he said.

'All right what?'

'I'll inspect every inch of you.'

Her bright lipstick paled with the ferocity of her blush. 'You'd better take my word for it.'

'Worth a try,' he said, feeling shaky as if it was a near miss, not that he'd been intending to get anywhere. She was staff, after all, and in any case he hadn't got over Chris yet. He kept reminding himself that sex wasn't the same as love, so even if he'd loved and lost there was no need to let that cramp his style. That had been why he went off to Marge Bentley's the very afternoon he'd had to end the affair. Since then, however, he'd lacked heart or energy to go out on the chase.

But this moment of proximity to Wendy made him feel oddly nostalgic, as if he'd not been to bed with anybody for years and years. One day he'd be an old man shuffling through some bedroom shop, seeing them all lined up, the singles, three-quarters, doubles, king-sizes, putting a buttock on the edge of some and giving a little bounce to try the springs, remembering the long lost days when they were the tools of his trade, his real business in the world, and he could perform his own acrobatics on them like gymnasts at the Olympics. What I do, he thought, is that, number one, golf second, and sell houses to keep the show on the road. Only trouble is that in time terms the order is reversed. 'Anyway,' he added, 'I don't picture you as a mole. How I think of you is a daddy-long-legs.'

'Thanks a bunch.' She looked quite pleased though and her long legs stirred under the table. He pictured them gently rasping together, like an insect's.

'What you've got to remember is that people set themselves upper and lower limits when they go off to buy themselves a house. Same with a car, anything expensive. If you price below their low limit, you miss them. If you up a property and get it within a particular person's band, then you've got two advantages. First they haven't got anything to compare it with, because all the similar properties that haven't been upped are below their range so they've never gone round to have a ganders at them, and second, it's cheaper than everything else they see because it's at the bottom edge of what they're going for. So it looks a real bargain just because it isn't a real bargain. Funny old business.'

'I don't like that kind of funniness very much.' Perhaps to avoid scratching her freckle again, she put each hand over the far side of her neck, and gently rubbed it, which left her pointed elbows covering each breast, smart girl.

'The more we get out of Mr Tompkin, the more chance old Edie's got of buying herself a place in Southport.'

'How I'd rather it, is they both do well out of the deal.'

'I don't think it would be worth the name of deal, in that case. More like a non-event. But with houses most people do all right in the end. If you've got your fingers burnt just wait a year or two, and you'll catch up. What old Tobe used to say: in this business, wounds heal themselves.'

'But what about the ghost?'

'The ghost was a dead old bloke's hat, as you know.'

'I mean the chill of it, when you walk into the hall.'

'It was probably just a goose walking over my grave that morning, as I went in. In any case, Mr Tompkin is a retired solicitor.'

'What's that got to do with it? Just because he was a solicitor doesn't mean he deserves to have a hallway that chills him to the marrow.'

'I don't think you'd say that if you knew solicitors as well as I do. But what I was getting at is, being a solicitor, he's bound to get himself central heating. End of problem. As things are, you've got that cold air gnawing at Edie's bones and making her rheumatics go ape. And it may be what's causing her to be a bit touched in the head. Cold makes your brain seize up, like when animals hibernate. Put her in a cosy little bungalow with sea breezes next door to her niece and she'll be as right as rain. Probably end up on *Brain of Britain*. Remember, she's the one who's our client. She's the one we take responsibility for. Did you hear about the dumb blonde who went on *Brain of Britain*?'

'I expect so. But it's nice you worry about your clients' mental health.'

'All part of the service. Talking of which, I'd better nip round now and warn her Mr Tompkin wants to have another look tomorrow. You could give the niece a tinkle, let her know what we're doing.'

The bell went and a customer came in, a plump jowly man in a Gannex raincoat.

'Good morning,' Wendy said, and got up to walk round her desk. As she set off she seemed to stumble and almost fall. She supported herself on the filing cabinet for a moment.

'Are you all right?' Art asked her. The customer was absorbed in the house details on the display boards.

'I was sitting with my legs crossed. I must have cut off the blood supply. My left leg's gone completely numb. It's like not having a leg at all.'

Art let his eyes run down her legs, trying to make his gaze seem clinical and helpful. 'They're both there all right.' They were gawky and angled at the best of times, part of their charm. 'Perhaps it could do with a rub,' he suggested in a low voice.

'I think not. I can feel the blood pouring back in. It's just like filling a kettle up at the sink.'

He carried on looking at her leg. It was perhaps more unlike a kettle than anything else in the universe.

Then she stepped forward towards the customer, sweetly limping. 'Can I help you? Oh goodness, it's –' She pressed her hands together over her nose and mouth. 'I nearly said, the Johnny,' she went on in a little ashamed voice.

The customer turned towards her, his doughy face lighting up like a low-wattage bulb. 'I'm surprised you recognised me with my clothes on,' he told her in pleased, fruity tones.

Mrs Barker was standing by her gate, watching the world fail to go by. Mill Park was a cobbled cul-de-sac, ending in an actual park where Art could just pick out a keeper sweeping up the autumn leaves. He was struck by the horrible impossibility of the task. You might as well sweep up the world. How depressing it must be to have a job you could never actually finish. You just did it for a while, then stopped.

Mrs Barker looked at him without recognition at first, or rather, he realised, she recognised him but didn't know where from. When he told her Penrose's, the estate agents, she did a little girlish skip with pleasure, muted by arthritis. He wasn't under any illusions – nobody ever skipped because you were an estate agent. It was because she was relieved to have him nailed.

'I just came to tell you, Mrs Barker –' he began, but she'd already turned away from him and begun walking up her path to the open front door. 'All I –' No good, she was inside the hall, holding the door and waiting for him to follow.

Bite the bullet. He would have to spend time getting in her head what was planned for tomorrow afternoon, or Mr Tompkin and his companion would find themselves being sent packing. As he went in she croaked the word tea at him.

The hall chill descended, serious and enveloping, like when you jump into water that's far colder than you ever expected and the breath is knocked out of your body. Though of course he was expecting it to be far colder than he expected, so he couldn't make a fair judgement.

The kitchen felt like a refuge, though it was beaked up with cups and plates and the floor had the original quarry tiles laid directly on the soil. The shelves and cupboards were cheap deal things with a wartime look about them, covered in Anaglypta. He'd made the point to Mr Tompkin that it was far better to be in the position to total a room than have to reconcile yourself to someone else's taste. There was a slight smell of urine: this was where Edie spent her time.

She filled the kettle. 'Len's down the park,' she said. 'He'll be back later.'

He had a lunchtime meeting with Norman Forrester in the golf club. It would be about Prospect Hill, as usual. They had both had money tied up in it for years, but Norman's investment was on a much bigger scale and he was feeling the pinch. Since he fancied himself as a smart operator, his pride must be hurt too. 'I can play old Ted Wilcox like a bloody trout,' he'd once confided to Art. But despite the endless delays Art always expected Norman to be in a good mood, and he was always wrong. The funny thing was he knew why he made the mistake, but that didn't stop him making it. Norman had a bit of a beer pot but wasn't what you'd call a fat bloke except for a couple of double chins, and these always gave Art the impression he was smiling. As luck would have it, his mouth was quite small, so however miserable his lips looked there wasn't enough of them to alter the overall effect.

One thing for sure: today he was madder than a wet hen.

'If I could scrag that fucking tosspot he'd know he'd *been* scragged,' he said for starters. 'Pardon my French,' he added with a nod towards Bertie who was glaring at him from the optics.

'Which tosspot would that be?'

'Which one do you think? That pinko lefto candidate for MP, some hopes, sodding Trevor Morgan.'

'Got up your nose, did he?' Art held up his hand in the

direction of Bertie, put his thumb and forefinger about half an inch apart, as if gently holding a silverskin onion, and then popped it in his mouth.

'Good idea,' Norm said. Bert came over with a little dish of onions and put them on the table. Norm looked at them in surprise. 'What're these little buggers about, then?'

'You're a gent, Bertie,' Art said. He prodded one with a cocktail stick and put it in his mouth.

'I thought you were asking for proper grub,' Norm said. 'You fill up on those and you'll have no hope of getting your secretary into the broom cupboard this afternoon.'

'Shows how much you know. These are an aphrodisiac, in my experience.' He put another in. A sudden picture of that daddy-long-legs tangled amidst brooms made him pause, and the second onion remained between his teeth like a nut in a nutcracker. Then he swallowed it in one and rinsed his mouth with whisky.

'Scrag's all right,' Bertie told Norman, 'and tosspot's OK. But we have to draw the line at f-u-k-i-n-g.'

'I thought you were giving me the menu for a moment,' Norman said.

'Macaroni cheese. Plaice and –'

'Macaroni cheese'll do fine. What about you, Art?'

'I'm not hungry.' In point of fact his stomach suddenly felt hollow and echoey but with sadness, not hunger. He thought of Wendy's legs rasping under the desk, of her delicious hobble, of her in the broom cupboard just as if she'd really once been in there, even though they didn't even have a broom cupboard. They seemed to him not just the most beautiful legs in the world, but the embodiment of the beauty of the world, and he would never touch them or even come near, because she was staff and in any case much much too young. He munched another onion viciously because it was there and she wasn't.

'You could have fooled me.' Norman nodded at Bertie, who went off. Norman leaned across the table towards Art. 'Do you think he really can't spell fuck?' he whispered.

'I think he was just trying to be brief,' Art said.

'What you expect with a Labour councillor is at least they'd support council housing. But oh no, not this one, with that big arsey smile of his. First of all May Rollins, who should know better, gets the minister blokey all cranked up and wild eyed, then that young twerp comes wading in to finish the job. Anyone'd think they were working hand in glove. All they had to do was wipe his bottom for him – you wouldn't think that was too much to ask when there's a million or two at stake. They'd rather upset the applecart, and show what big bad councillors they are. At least May Rollins was trying to shake the money loose. That bonehead Morgan seemed hell bent on getting the Labour government to chuck out a Labour project. It beggars belief.'

'As I understand it, it's not that Trevor Morgan is against council housing, just high rise. What was that thing he said, that was all over the paper?'

'I oppose blocks of flats. I support flat housing. He just wants to be a clever dick. Next thing, he'll say he thinks the *earth* is flat. May as well be, from his point of view. What was that other thing? The sky is a road, then some drivel about the flight path to Manchester Airport.'

Bertie brought over Norm's macaroni cheese. As he always did, Norm tucked the big linen napkin in his shirt collar like a toddler's bib. It's *his* mouth that's an arse, Art thought as he watched it open, not Trevor Morgan's with that great chorus line of smiling teeth. He thought of Trevor's face zeroing in on Chris's. He felt a pang of jealousy, then realised he wasn't feeling jealous about Chris, but suddenly, frantically, jealous about Wendy, jealous because she was alive in life in such a way he could never touch her.

Norm sent Bertie off for another pint for himself and a whisky for Art.

'Anyhow,' Art told him, 'I think he's cooked his goose. The Labour Party's going to give him no back-up for his election campaign now he's embarrassed one of their ministers. It's not the way to build up your career, making a member of the government walk out of a meeting in a tantrum.'

'The thing is,' Norm said, 'he's come near cooking my goose and all.' His jaw moved up and down with unlikely speed, as if he'd had some sort of automatic chewer installed. The drinks came, and he took a quick, agitated swig of his pint without even a glance at Bertie. 'These shenanigans are going to prolong the issue even more and God knows when I'm going to see a return. To top it all, I've had to give a rise to the bloody construction workers. I tried to keep them to the original agreement, but they got round it and went on a dirty strike. Said there was nothing about dirt in their contract. I said, there's nothing about going to the toilet either, but I expect they'll want to do that.'

'The council'll pay up in the end, when the dust has settled. They've got no choice.'

'I don't know why you're taking it so calmly. You're out on a limb, same as me.'

'I take things as they come, me. And I'm not in it for such a whack as you are. Anyhow, I'm going on my holidays in a couple of weeks.'

'Are you, by God,' Norman said. 'Funny time of the year for it.'

Art drove straight past his office when he returned from lunch at the golf club. He was trembling with need.

He'd only make a fool of himself with Wendy if he went in, talk and talk and not say anything. There were women who lapped that type of thing up, enjoyed flirty conversation, but Wendy had a sharp, sarcastic edge that would make him feel obvious and pathetic.

The viaduct up ahead looked exactly as if it was taking an enormous bite out of the centre of Costford. He drove under it, past the precinct, and took the Tinnington turn-off at the bottom of Prospect Hill. The grey day had become almost bright: that tantalising sort of autumn weather where the sun looks like an eye with a cataract over it.

As before, he parked a street away from Marge's, and walked the rest. There was no sign of life in the numb afternoon but for some reason he felt as timid as a teenager going into a chemist's shop, and to calm himself cast an estate agent's eye over the gardens that he passed. Gardens, *neighbours'* gardens, he'd told Wendy, were ingredient *x* in your sales pitch, didn't merit a mention in the property description but could be instrumental in setting the tone.

There was the occasional smart garden even on the Tinnington estate, pruned and tidied for the winter. Others had lost heart and had tufty lawns and overgrown beds, and the third sort had never tried in the first place and had gone one of two ways: two-foot-high grass or beaten soil with bits of cars or children's toys, even rotted underwear, scattered over them.

Marge's garden had been the middling type on his last visit but to his surprise was now practically smart, the lawn having been mowed and the soil in the flowerbeds scratched up to a consistent rough finish and weeded. All it needed was a few plants and it would be away. It gave him a pang to guess she must be on her best behaviour in the hope that it would improve her chances of getting a transfer to Prospect Hill.

He knocked on the pink front door. Knocked again. Eventually a blurred head appeared in the tightly frosted window and the door opened. She had curlers in her hair, a shiny gown, green nightie showing beneath, bare feet. A quick glance at them reminded him of her ear that last time, not dirty but not quite convincing either, feety feet, slightly yellow in the daylight, when what you wanted were pink ones dusted with talc. He found it hard to imagine Marge tidying up her garden, whatever the odds of getting something out of it.

'Sorry,' he said.

She opened those lovely eyes of hers wide, not to show surprise, more as if to get who it was standing there. 'Oh,' she said.

He felt a touch peeved she'd taken her time to work out who he was, but maybe the blokes started to merge together when you'd been in her game a while. Perhaps one of them was in her bed at this very moment. 'Is someone here?' he asked.

'What? No, no one's here. Fray's out.'

'I didn't mean Fray. I meant –'

'Oh. Oh no. I was just having a kip.'

'I see.' My God, when you went to bed for a living it seemed a bit much to do it in your own time too. But bed was maybe all she knew about.

He followed her into the kitchen. She took a fag from a packet on the kitchen table, lit it with the gas lighter, lit the gas with the lighter too, and filled the kettle. Like the garden, the kitchen had improved: only a plate with a bitten sandwich on, Marmite by the looks of it, and a dirty cup, just her lunch things in other words. She was obviously turning over a leaf, despite her current undress.

'Any news?' she asked. 'It was in the paper about that government bloke running off in a huff.' She spooned tea into a pot that looked like a country cottage with a thatched lid.

'Yes, that threw a spanner in the works.'

'Fray was there, you know.'

'Was he, then?'

'He was on the door. He said the government bloke came shooting out like a rocket. He rushed down the steps then just stood out in the rain, waving his fists and swearing. He was in a terrible state, according to Fray.' She filled the pot with boiling water.

'So I heard.'

'Do you think that'll put the kibosh on it?'

'No, no, the whole thing's been signed and sealed for years. It'll have to go ahead.'

'I don't know what my chances are,' she said glumly through her cigarette.

'Your chances are fine. I gave your name to your councillor, or rather I got another councillor I know personally to give your name to him. He'll've passed it on to the housing officer. I'm willing to bet your number'll come up.'

'Folk've been talking about them blocks everywhere you go. I think lots of people got their heart set on getting one of the places up there.'

She poured the tea, got milk out of her little fridge, and passed him a cup and the bottle.

'Help yourself,' she said. She took a stainless steel sugar bowl from the shelf and put it in front of him too. 'Fray got me that,' she told him.

'Did he really?'

'From the Co-op.' Art tried to picture Fray queuing in the Co-op to buy a sugar bowl. More likely nicked it. Still, at least he'd nicked it for his mum. 'He said he didn't like spooning it out of the bag because it sprays everywhere. You know, the paper of the bag flicks the spoon, type of thing, while you're pulling it out.'

'There's two sorts of list, new tenants and relocations. You'll be on the relocation list. It means you've already got a council property but you want a smaller flat. You'll take priority because it's to their advantage to move you. They can give you a one-bedroom flat and move a family of four or five in here. That takes pressure off them. Assuming Fray doesn't want to go with you.'

She stubbed her fag in her saucer. He offered her another one, but she shook her head and wafted the air in front of her mouth. He took that as a promising sign, getting herself into gear for him.

'Fray won't come,' she said. 'He's moving out next week. Going to stay with a friend of his. Older man.' She gave Art a straight look. 'He's always been that way, Fray has, ever since he was a little chap.' She inclined her head towards the hall door, and raised her eyebrows at him.

★   ★   ★

She only had to take off her gown and she was ready to go, in her working gear, so to say. As she climbed into bed he glimpsed her bottom through the semi-transparent green nylon of her nightie. Green, he thought, who on this planet would go in a shop and buy a green one? Answer: Marge. Her legs beneath were pale and lean with a tiny mauve web of veins on the inside of one thigh. Her bottom was up to standard, quite neat in fact, but it struck him it was just a bottom, so what? Everybody had one. Even men had them. He took off everything except his underpants and followed her.

'You been eating onions,' she said companionably, as he lay facing her.

'Sorry.' He rolled over on to his back. 'Tell you what,' he said, 'you've painted out that Party Four stain.'

'You're the only one who's noticed.'

'Houses are my trade, remember.'

'Fray painted the whole ceiling, a week or two ago. Decorating was *his* trade, once upon a time.'

'Very handy.'

'He's a different lad these days. He did over the garden last weekend. He tidies up in the house, I don't know what all.'

'I thought somebody must have been having a go.'

He wondered as he spoke if she might take offence, but she just lay thoughtfully a while then said, 'I don't know what's got into him.'

'You'll not be wanting to part with him, this rate.'

'Oh no, I'll be glad to see the back of him. I know it's not what you should say about your own boy. But he has a way of looking at me sometimes that makes my hair stand on end. He's a funny lad. And any road I want a snugger place, just to me own.'

'Like that bug.'

She turned to face him. He felt her hand slide into his pants. 'Yes,' she said breathily, 'like that little bug.'

She squeezed him rhythmically. He peered round at her face. Her eyes were open, thinking of other things, thinking of her flat.

It occurred to him that he was thinking of other things too, and he made himself concentrate. That was exactly what he always loved about sex, the way it stopped him thinking about anything else. But this time it didn't happen. I'm thinking about thinking about it, he realised.

After a while she took her hand away. 'Just have a rest for a few minutes,' she said. 'We'll have another bash in a bit.' She turned away and instantly seemed to doze.

After they'd lain quiet for a while he gently slid his pants down, raised the bedclothes a little, and peered down. It was swollen but not stiff. Never had it let him down before. He'd always had a no-nonsense attitude to it, and it had repaid him by having a no-nonsense attitude back. But something had happened. Chris had started it, though the immediate effect of breaking up with her had been to make use of it as if there was no tomorrow. But Wendy had finished it.

He continued to look despondently, while Marge snored gently beside him. The last thing he needed was for it to turn into some kind of thick pen only good for writing true love, the way kids did on bus shelters and trees.

Seventeen

Ted Wilcox rang May first thing. So first thing, in fact, that she was still in bed. Normally she was up with the lark, but today she had nothing on till late morning and had arranged to drop Mother off at Cherry's at ten. In the meantime the old bat would be happy pottering round her bedroom, talking and singing to herself until breakfast. So when the phone rang, May slipped on her dressing-gown and hurried downstairs to answer it.

'I was wondering if we could meet,' Ted said.

It was funny to hear that soft voice on the phone. He was usually so confident and insinuating. The big trick was to make people think that you'd never learned to raise your voice because everybody always snapped to attention when you opened your mouth. And of course they'd then prove his point by being quiet and still so as not to miss what he was bleating on about. He was a man you had to approach ear first.

Now, though, there was something uncertain in his tone. She knew exactly what the problem was: he couldn't decide whether to be conciliatory or menacing, bawl her out in that whispery way of his, or build bridges. She had stepped seriously out of line by her speech to the twerp from London, and compromised the nice little behind-the-scenes agreement Ted had set up. On the other hand, the twerp from London was one of the enemy, a member of the Labour government; she had been pushing the cause of the tower blocks, the jewel in the crown of the Tory group Ted headed, the jewel in *Ted's* crown, in other words.

Above all she'd triggered poor Trevor Morgan's rush of blood to the head, and damaged his chance of winning North Costford for the Socialists.

She mourned that last fact, of course. The only way to account for it was that Trevor was still so emotionally involved with her that he hadn't been able to stop himself following her cue in bringing the matter into the arena, even though doing so would inevitably alienate the Labour powers-that-be and ensure no bigwigs came in support of his election campaign. He'd contrived to appear in the national papers, fighting his cause in the wrong corner altogether. It was a tactical error strangely out of keeping with his political instincts, and just went to show that passion could blind a man. But Trevor's loss was Ted's gain. He should be cock-a-hoop.

'Oh yes?' she asked noncommittally.

'Perhaps lunch?'

'Sorry. I've got something else on.'

'Oh. Really?'

'Yes, really. I have a lunch date already.'

'A date?' There was a sneer in the question. Trust Ted to home in on a word. He had a knack of testing everything you said for signs of weakness, like those people in cowboy films who bite coins to see if they're genuine. It was what he would regard as leadership. What he wanted was for her to say 'It's only . . .' It's only a constituent, it's only my stepdaughter, it's only an old girl-friend. He wanted her to apologise for making an accidental comparison between herself and the red-blooded sort of female who might have a lunch engagement with a man-friend, the sort of female Ted himself might have an appointment with.

'That's right,' she said firmly. 'A date.'

'Oh.'

'Some other time, perhaps.'

He tried to pin her down but she was in no mood to be pinned. Mother's thin voice floated down the stairs: '*Que sera, sera*, whatever will be, will be.'

'It's important that –'

'What is it they say abroad?' she asked. *'Mañana.'* A Hub expression, of course. *'Mañana* is another day.'

'The future's not ours to see,' Mother's voice added obligingly.

As she went back upstairs May said it to herself several times over: 'A date. *A* date. A *date.'* She hung her dressing-gown behind the door and slipped back into bed. She clasped her hands behind her head on the pillow. 'A date.' The coin was genuine all right.

The date in question was with Maurice Tompkin, from the solicitors' office where she used to work as a secretary. During her marriage to Hub she'd only seen him once a year, at the works outing, as Hub insisted on calling it, the annual dinner the partners had in the Midland Hotel in Manchester. It was a ghastly occasion as far as May was concerned, even by comparison with some of the occasions she had to attend as wife of the Mayor. The worst part of it was that Mother used to insist on going in her capacity as widow of the senior partner-as-was, Dan Baxendale. She'd only had time, in her short marriage, to go to one works outing as his wife, and May hadn't been able to attend that one, being still a secretary.

Dan had invited her, in point of fact, but she'd felt her mother's hard gaze and said she'd rather not.

'No, it's hardly a do for the younger set,' Dan said gracefully, but her mother's look had lingered, and what it said was: You've no place at it, being just a secretary there while I'm a *wife.*

May had felt like Cinderella getting a glare from one of the Ugly Sisters, except in this case it was she who was the ugly one while the Ugly Sister was smart as paint, radiant in triumph. In May's experience it was always the Ugly Sisters who got the good looks when they were being handed out. It was the Cinderellas of the world who ended up looking drab and plain.

Even after the tables were turned, with Dan Baxendale dying and May marrying Hub, she still felt at a disadvantage, going along in a threesome, with Mother contriving to look as if she owned the shop. The only consolation was that Maurice

Tompkin, who was unmarried, always brought his own mother with him as his guest, and would throw May sympathetic looks from time to time. His mother had shifty, hostile eyes and always seemed to have on a dress that was full but limp, like a wilting tulip.

Maurice's mother had died a few months back. He'd sent May a formal notification and she'd written in reply; after that he'd taken to telephoning her about what was going on. He was selling their house in north Cheshire in order to buy a new one in the Harper area of north Costford. He'd found one he liked and wanted to go ahead, but felt he needed moral support from a friend, so asked May if she would be willing to look round it with him. Since she drove and he didn't, she was going to pick him up. Then he would treat her to lunch somewhere, and after that they'd go round the property. It was a date, however much Ted tried to nibble at it.

As she lay there, anticipating, May gradually became aware that something strange had happened.

Sometimes, when May was lost in her thoughts or her work, she would realise that she'd been listening to Mother singing for a long time without knowing she was. Once, one terrible time, the same sort of thing had happened with Hub.

It had been the middle of the night and she was fast asleep, dreaming. In her dream someone was saying something, and then she became aware that what they were saying was 'May, May.' Even this, though, got itself entwined in whatever the dream was about and didn't seem to entail her doing anything. And then, after what must have been ages, she realised that the words weren't coming from her dream but from outside it, and she had to drag herself up up up into wakefulness, being as clumsy and heavy in sleep as in true life. Finally, there was Hub beside her in bed, saying her name quite quietly so as to wake but not startle her, a strained edge to his polite, civilised voice that made her heart turn to stone.

'What's up?' she'd whispered.

'Oh, I expect it's a bit of –' he told her, then gasped and moaned terribly.

But this time, as she lay in bed thinking about her date, it wasn't something she'd been hearing that broke her reverie but something she'd been looking at: the damp patch on her ceiling.

Or rather, the place where the damp patch had been.

Maurice Tompkin's house was a comfortable Edwardian semi in Alton. He contrived to swing open the front door in a way that left his arms apart in greeting. She had rather expected him to look, with her older eye, nondescript and spindly, though still a date. Your partner didn't have to be Gregory Peck in order for it to count. In her early days as a secretary she inevitably looked up to the solicitors, and saw Maurice as a sensitive, delicate type, too good for this world. Since that time, of course, she'd had ample cause to take a more realistic view, having had one solici-tor as a stepfather and another as a husband.

He was thin, of course, and his hair was thin too, so that the scalp showed through, but he seemed animated and bright-eyed. She'd always thought of him as less pompous than the other partners and a certain freshness still lingered. He was wearing a sports jacket and flannels rather than the usual solicitor's suit, and had on a shirt with a thin red stripe, and a deep red tie.

'Don't tell me you're Labour,' May said.

To her surprise he pinked up a little. 'Liberal,' he confessed. 'I used to keep it a secret in the office.'

He ushered her in and poured them both a glass of sherry. The living room was full of dark mahogany furniture. 'Mum's taste,' he explained, and then in a whisper, as if Mum was still listening from the afterlife, 'I'm going to get shot of it.'

'Are you, then?'

'She spent her life polishing it.' Suddenly, almost impatiently, he started talking in a normal voice, as if he was tired of being discreet about her. 'Whenever she walked past something she would inspect the surface, then huff her breath in disapproval, and rub at it with her sleeve or her handkerchief. And for what? One of these house clearance chappies will offer twenty-five pounds or thereabouts for the job lot. I've come across the same thing over and again dealing with wills, people telling me with quivering lips how much old so-and-so loved his things, as if that meant all the rest of us had to love them too. To be honest, I'll be happy to make a fresh start. My taste's more towards the Scandinavian type of furnishing. I'll probably buy in a lot of pine from Habitat. Mum was bad-tempered a good deal of the time, and I always see this furniture of hers as frowning at me. She was a terrible nag. Unlike *your* charming mother.'

'My mother isn't as charming as you might believe.'

'I always thought she showed mine up at those horrible do's they used to frog-march us to. She was so petite and pretty, chock-a-block with bone structure.'

'She's all very well to look at. Handsome is as handsome does, as they say.'

'Anyhow, we've got better things to talk about than our mothers, at our time of life. Between ourselves, that's why I'm so grateful mine's passed on. It's like being let out of prison. Let's go off and eat. That'll help us change the subject.'

As they were about to leave, Maurice did a very strange thing. He whipped something from his top pocket and held it out to her, bowing as he did so. The flourish reminded her of Hub at his most ceremonial, but there was a far more provocative, even sexual, element in it. The way his head was pushed in her direction was brusque and thrusting. Then she realised that what he had in his hand was a comb, and his head was being offered to her, as a reminder of long ago, for a combing.

Now his hair was short, and grew in almost random clumps and tufts, the way seagrass does on a smooth sand dune. Instead of taking the comb, she placed her hands on each side of his head. The gesture was instinctive, perhaps to stop it pushing any closer to her, but he remained still when her hands were in place, and she too stayed as she was for what seemed like ages, her heart pounding. His skull between her hands felt full and fragile, and somehow important. She wondered if there was a religion in Africa where you were passed an ostrich egg and had to hold it with reverence. Perhaps because of that idea she found her own head moving forward, and before she could stop herself she had kissed him solemnly on the top of his.

He raised his head and she let her hands fall to her sides. His cheeks were slightly pink again. My goodness, he's become rather excited, May thought, feeling rather excited herself.

They had lunch in a wine bar, where the Welsh rarebit was called *croque monsieur*. It was nice, though. Maurice ordered a bottle of wine, then looked doubtful and agonised. 'I forgot you were driving,' he said.

'I'm a JP, remember. Most of the police in these parts know me. Anyhow, it's only an lmp. It wouldn't count. It's hardly like being run over by a serious vehicle.'

'It's quite a small house, too,' Maurice said, 'the one I'm going for.'

'A house lmp, you mean.'

'That must be what I mean.'

'Well, there's only you.'

He smiled. 'It's a cheap house, May.'

'Is it, just?'

'The firm went down the plug-hole. You didn't know that, did you?'

'How could it have done? You were solicitors, for heaven's sake.'

'It changed a lot since Dan and Hub's time. We had a couple of fly boys in as partners. They got involved in all sorts. Property dealing, mainly. Do you know a man called Norman –'

'I know Norman.'

'Well, they were hand in glove with him over those Prospect

Hill transactions. You know how that all ground to a halt. Along with a lot of other things. Most of them ground to a halt as well. The upshot was, money was lost, and the investment I had for my pension got dragged into it, not to mention that I find myself retired a long time before I expected. I've got a few private clients, people I've known for years, that's all. So I'm having to buy for less than I sell, and invest the rest.'

May looked at him sadly. He was the first solicitor she had ever known not to make money. You may look like a candle flame, she thought – which was what she'd decided he did look like, maybe on account of the red shirt and tie and a certain attractive tendency of his lean body to flicker somehow, so you couldn't quite pin him down – but there was no need to get yourself snuffed.

'But,' he went on, 'it's a challenge. Between ourselves, it's a little gem. I don't think the estate agent has any idea. It's an eighteenth-century worker's cottage, just like that row the council are pulling down to build an old folks' home.'

'What Ted Wilcox said, when that demolition order came up at planning committee, was: are we concerned about old houses or old people? He always manages to end up on the side of the angels.'

'Bully for him. Anyhow, the more they demolish the past, the more valuable will be what's left. And even the council can't demolish Mill Park. Its position is too noticeable. It's a lovely location, and you only have to step into the house to realise it's got atmosphere. I think some of that must have percolated through even to the estate agent. It's got a ghost, he informed me.'

'Is that so?'

'No extra charge. And guess what? the ghost is called Len.'

'It's funny you should tell me that.'

'Why, do you know him? It?'

'No, but I had an odd experience myself this morning.'

'Oh, tell.'

Suddenly, May didn't want to. It was as though she didn't have the words to describe it. Also, it seemed silly. She didn't want to be lumped with Maurice's estate agent.

'It doesn't matter.'

'Oh. Anyhow, what I want to do, is do it up. The cottage.'

'That can be an expensive business.'

'Myself, I mean, do it up myself. I'm perfectly capable. It's my hobby, as a matter of fact. I did all the repairs on Mum's house.'

'Did you, then? In that case, I *will* tell you.'

'That's my reward, is it?'

'It's just you might be able to tell me something in return. Give me advice.'

'I'll try,' he said, eyes narrowing.

'No, I don't mean legal advice,' she said hastily. He looked relieved. She realised he was afraid of something serious cropping up and spoiling their day. 'It's do-it-yourself advice I want. Or ghost advice.'

'Ah, well. Only problem, I don't even own my own ghost yet. Len's the property of the current title-holder till it all goes through. But the promising part is, he doesn't have a head, according to the estate agent.'

'Mine doesn't even have a body.'

'I see. But none of them do, when you think about it. No call to feel short-changed.'

'It's only a patch of damp.'

'That so? Shaped like a spectre, you mean.'

'What's a spectre shaped like?'

'Like a person in a shroud. Like a person in a sheet, holding his arms aloft.' He held his own arms briefly aloft. He had a bit of *croque monsieur* on a fork at the end of one of them, and a knife at the end of the other. 'Woo-oo,' he said softly. Someone at the next table, who was sitting in front of a pile of whitebait, gave him a quick look then returned to the massacre on his plate. 'I am the ghost of Len,' Maurice added in a low, sepulchral voice.

His little act would never have been performed by Dan

or Hub in a million years. They wouldn't have done it even if they'd been spectres themselves. Perhaps they now were, grey-flannel ghosts indistinguishable from professional men in life, hardly aware of being dead. Far too well behaved to jump out at you.

A lump in her throat stopped May speaking for a second. Then she said, 'No, no. It just looks like a patch of damp.'

'Perhaps it *is* a patch of damp, in that case.'

'The thing is, it's gone.'

'Gone?'

'It was on my bedroom ceiling, right over my bed. I would lie there and inspect it. And then today I realised it wasn't there any more. I thought at first it must have been repaired as a surprise by one of my stepdaughter's fiancés who said he'd have a bash when he had a moment, but it turns out he's on the high seas. Suddenly recalled, she told me.'

'Isn't it funny to think about it?' Cherry had asked: 'recalled to the deep blue water? I told him about that poem, "I must go down to the sea again, To the lonely sea and the sky."'

She spends too much of her time with Mother, was May's thought on the subject.

'I see,' Maurice said. 'What colour is your ceiling?'

'White, like they usually are. I'm just a common or garden girl, I am.'

She blushed at the vanity of calling herself a girl, even a common one. She wouldn't have dared to make the claim in the old days. The word 'girl' would have seemed like a title belonging to people who were fresh as daisies, pretty as pictures, while she'd just been a girl in another sense altogether, like at primary school, where they used to have BOYS written up above one of the entrances, and GIRLS above the other. That was the only sort of girl she'd ever been: not a boy.

Who *had* been a girl, was her mother. Still was, almost.

But now, in company with her solicitor man with a head like a precious egg, she thought, blow it, I'll be a girl with the best of them. Being not a boy is the whole trick, exactly what's required. Common or garden will do nicely. There was room in the world for cabbages and swedes and Welsh rarebits. I've got legs, she thought, I have a bosom. She wished she'd realised that earlier on in life.

'The bit where the damp was is just as white as the rest of it,' she told Maurice. 'Whiter, if anything.'

'I see.' Maurice thought about it for a moment or two, letting the forkful of *croque monsieur* bump rhythmically against his lips. 'Let me ask a question. Was the damp grey damp or brown damp?'

'What's the difference?'

'Grey damp would mean what you're seeing is just wet. Brown would mean the damp has stained, and the ceiling's got discoloured. So if it was grey, it might have just dried out, for some reason.'

She wished she hadn't asked, because now she knew it mattered she found it impossible to recall whether the damp had been grey or brown. Greyish-brown, she guessed. For two pins she would have told him about the strange thing that had happened to her television, the way it had become a colour one all by itself, without her buying an aerial or a new set, but thought better of it. This was their first date. She didn't want him to think he was going out with a madwoman.

'Grey, I think,' she said finally.

'That's all right, then. Some rainwater must have found its way in, and maybe it doesn't any more. Perhaps the timbers swelled and sealed themselves, or a bird's nest got in the way, I don't know. Just count your blessings no damage was done. And let me look at it some time, to see if it needs fixing.'

'That's very kind of you.'

It would, of course, mean a visit to her bedroom. She sensed that thought lying between them like another, unseen, meal on the table.

Suddenly, a few tables away, a rumpus broke out. May saw a

full glass of red wine rise high into the air, hang there intact for a moment, then plunge down and smash to smithereens on the table below, scattering wine and shards of glass. The woman sitting there rose to her feet, wailing, her hands over her face. The man she was with stayed put.

'Thtung!' the woman called out.

'What she say?' a woman at another table cried frantically. 'What she say?'

'Thtung! Thtung!' the standing woman shouted, with that panicky maddened body language you use when people aren't getting it in charades.

'Stung? Or tongue?' the other woman demanded.

The standing woman stamped her foot and did a shriek of rage and frustration.

'It's both!' a man shouted. 'Her tongue's got stung!'

The woman nodded her head desperately.

'It must have been a wasp,' the man said. 'What it's doing on the go in November, Gawd alone knows.'

'For heaven's sake,' the other woman called. 'Keep your tongue out of your mouth. Hold it with your hand. It's liable to swell up and choke you.'

'You want to go to Casualty,' the man said, 'straight off.'

The stung woman nodded again. She was holding her tongue out of her mouth with both hands now. It looked swollen already, to May's eyes, though she wasn't used to seeing a tongue extended to that length. It must be horribly slippery to get a grip on.

The stung woman peered down at her husband. She was making incoherent shrieking noises at him. He looked up at her, downed his wine, and got to his feet. She rushed out of the wine bar, hands still clutching her tongue, him following.

'Good grief,' Maurice said. 'I'm sorry. I wanted this to be just right.'

'It's hardly her fault,' May said, 'getting stung like that.' She was touched that Maurice took the occasion so seriously.

'I mean her husband, the way he finished off his drink. He was completely uncouth.'

'He could at least have helped her hold her tongue,' May said. 'It must be a business, stopping it sliding back into your mouth. Especially under stress. But I think he was out of his depth. He finished his drink to buy a bit of time. Some people need to wait while their reflexes get under way.'

At that moment the manager came in from the kitchen, carrying a tray. He stopped at the table and looked at the detritus in horror, hardly able to believe his eyes. 'What an absolute disgrace,' he said to the room at large. 'A bloody disgrace.'

'They don't expect incidents in Alton,' Maurice said. 'It's not that sort of a place. But I can't afford to stay here, whether or no.'

Her verdict on his prospective house: dinky, but a lot of charm. It felt fresh and airy, despite its small size, perhaps even a little cold.

'Not to worry,' he told her. 'It'll be quite different when it's inhabited.'

'It's inhabited now,' she pointed out.

'Well, hardly.'

That was true enough. The vendor had invited them into her kitchen with a lean pointing finger. She reminded May of a poem, the way Cherry's fiancé's return to sea had reminded *her* of one, in this case the old rhyme: 'Come into my parlour, said the spider to the fly.'

I don't think I like old ladies very much, May thought: my mother, Maurice's, and now this spidery thing. She was wearing a strange dress, too big for her, that looked to have come from the Victorian period, navy blue with white dots, and a kind of white ruffly bib-thing at the front. It was a relief when she'd made it clear she was going to stay put in the kitchen while they did their tour.

'She never moves around enough to stir up the air,' Maurice added. 'It's her niece who's organising the sale. Mrs Barker just sits in that kitchen and waits for her Len to come back from the park. But as the estate agent suggested, I can install central heating. I'll do it my own self.' He looked flushed and chipper at the happy prospect.

He must have been one of those boys who built things with Meccano, May thought. And why not? The thought of George, with a handkerchief on his head, knotted in each corner, came into her mind. There were worse ways of being a man than the practical version.

How odd that Maurice can do up a whole house yet not comb his hair.

Then the thought struck. Of course he could comb his hair, or could have, when he'd had hair to comb. It was just that he'd wanted an intimate moment with her. The only way he could approach a woman was to make her into a mother, being so saturated with his own.

What a fool I was, she thought, I could have had him for the plucking.

She'd gone through life assuming men would take the initiative, and when they didn't, assumed that they didn't want to. But maybe they'd just been shy. Maybe they didn't know how to make their move.

Why on earth would Bob the steeplejack have gone to all that trouble to take her up a mountain just to give her some Camp coffee in a tin mug?

I was so ready to jump to conclusions, she thought sadly. I had so little confidence myself that it didn't occur to me that men might have lacked confidence as well. That was what my mother did to me.

Only Trevor, unexpectedly and wonderfully, had had the courage of his convictions, but if he'd managed to feel desire for her, at his age and in his position, it wasn't too far-fetched to believe other men could have felt the same.

Not too many: she wasn't a fool. But probably Bob, who'd taken her to his breezy tent.

And Maurice, charmingly offering his head.

I won't turn it down this time, she decided. She remembered as a child being sent to gather eggs for tea from the chicken run, how smooth and self-contained they'd seemed in the dirt and the straw.

As they came back downstairs there was a knock on the front door. Maurice made as if to answer it, then stopped himself. 'Better not jump the gun,' he said.

Mrs Barker came out of the kitchen. Her old face opened up in a smile. It looked like a wrinkly apple with a bite taken out of it. 'That'll be Len now,' she croaked. She pushed past them to the door.

'Her life must be full of disappointment,' Maurice whispered.

'Oh my Lord,' said May, instinctively putting her hand over her mouth.

'What is it?'

May turned from the open front door to Maurice, who was looking at her appalled, shocked by her shock. It occurred to her that for a second he must have believed she'd actually seen Len, minus possibly his head, standing on the front door step. She would have been happier if she had.

Who it was, was Art Whiteside.

She should have known, of course. She'd seen the Penrose sign outside when they arrived, but had been too busy anticipating the house, and thinking what it might be like to have Maurice living within a mile or so of her, to remember that it meant Art.

'Hello, Mrs Barker,' Art said, striding in while Mrs Barker wittered confusedly on the doormat, no doubt wondering where her Len had got himself to. 'Hello, Mr Tompkin.' Art's big smiley face fell as he took in May, but not half as much as hers had, and he recovered in a second. 'Hello, councillor. I didn't know you were a friend of Mr Tompkin.' He said it rather as if he didn't expect her to be the friend of anybody.

It made May cringe to think how she'd blackmailed him to stop his affair with Christine Morgan and then promptly had one of her own with Trevor. What a hypocrite she was. She owed him an apology, but of course this was exactly the sort of thing that couldn't ever be apologised for, no matter how sorry you were. And it occurred to her she wasn't as sorry as all that.

In fact she wasn't sorry one bit. She felt awkward about what she'd done, but when push came to shove wouldn't change a thing.

'We go back a long way, don't we, Maurice?'

'Dear little hallway, isn't it?' Art said. 'I always think you get the atmosphere of a place as soon as you step through the front door. What this one says to me is: welcome. But it is a bit of a squash, with all of us.'

'I'll take you into the kitchen,' said Mrs Barker, dignified now she'd adjusted to the absence of Len.

Art tried to usher them in her wake, establishing himself as the man in charge of the occasion.

'Maurice and I need a word together,' May told him. 'We'll join you in a minute.'

'Of course, of course,' Art said oozily. 'In fact, I'm delighted to hear you say that.'

'Oh really?' Maurice asked him. To May's relief it was obvious he didn't like the man one little bit. And why would he? Maurice was thin and finely chiselled, while Art looked as if he'd been bought at some wholesale warehouse by the pound. They inhabited different universes.

'It sounds as if you're making your mind up, for better or worse,' Art said. 'Music to my ears. The thing is, I'm off on my hols.'

'Is that right?' May asked. 'It seems a funny time of year for it.'

'I took my late mother to Southport about this time last year,' Maurice said.

'Oh yes,' Art said. 'That's where Mrs Barker's hoping to move to.'

'Just for the day,' Maurice went on. 'While we were there my mother said something very unusual. I thought so, anyway. There were big waves breaking, in a wind. She said the surf reminded her of those frills you sometimes get on slugs.'

There was a short pause, while Art took this in. Put that in your pipe and smoke it, was May's thought, which she sent in Art's direction. Also: poor Maurice's mother doesn't sound to have been much better company than mine is. He seemed proud of her though, even while being glad she was dead.

'We're not staying in these parts,' Art said. 'We're off to the Canary Islands.' He dropped the 'we's in like little pinches of spice, making sure May understood that he wasn't still mooning over the loss of Christine. 'It would be nice to get things tied up before we go. I'll leave you to your deliberations.' He went through into the kitchen, on big tiptoes as if to emphasise that he didn't want to disturb their concentration.

The closing of the door left May feeling oddly intimate with Maurice.

'I've made my mind up,' he said.

'Offer two hundred below the asking price,' May whispered to him.

'I don't know about that. She's a bit –'

'Don't worry about her. It'll be the niece doing the business, remember. And Art. I know Art of old. He always works with a large margin. He's that type.'

Cherry's town house was very small but had won some sort of prize for its design. Its main claim to fame seemed to be that the sitting room was upstairs, above the garage. Her front door was green, meticulously painted last weekend by that bodily fiancé

of hers before his sudden recall to his ship. Cherry had all but
introduced May to the door when she dropped Mother off this
morning, explaining what a tiny brush the fiancé had used to get
right into the panel edges, how he'd poked his cheek out with
his tongue, as if sucking a humbug, from sheer concentration on
the job, how he'd just worn ordinary clothes, and didn't get a
speck of paint on them.

While she waited on the step May thought about Maurice's
mother looking at Southport's slug-like sea with mean, jaundiced
eyes. From above came the sound of her own mother singing
'We'll meet again' in a quivering little voice. Anyhow, I saved
Maurice fifty pounds, May told herself.

Cherry opened the door. Her cheeks were flushed, and her
eyes had that guilty look that people with open natures tend to
get when they know something you haven't heard about yet.

'Oh yes?' May asked, as if they were already in the middle of a
conversation.

'I'm sorry,' Cherry said.

May nearly said, I don't know why, she's still singing, but managed to keep her lip buttoned.

'It's Aunty Alice,' Cherry continued. 'Her neighbour rang, an
hour ago.'

'Kicked the bucket, has she?'

'Well, not quite. She's given it a bit of a kick.' Cherry wiggled
her shoulders in that way she had, one after the other, much like
a footballer lining up for a slog. 'Quite a bit of one. A heart
attack, Mrs Briggs says. A bad heart attack.'

'I don't expect anyone ever has a good heart attack.'

'They've put her on a machine.'

Suddenly May felt tears slide down her cheeks. My mistake,
she thought, I shouldn't have tried to brave it out. Those hands
of Alice's, lovely as they were in her heyday, fluttered about in
her head like pink-tipped butterflies. And now Alice was on a
machine. Luckily Cherry had turned her back to lead May up the
stairs to the sitting room.

Mother wasn't there.

'She's in the spare room,' Cherry said. 'She went for a lie down, and hasn't come back out yet. I haven't told her.'

'She sounded as if she knew, what with her singing that horrible song. Even in the war I always thought it was about *not* meeting again. It didn't help with Vera Lynn being a baritone.'

'I think Grandma's prophetic. By the way, I had a bit of trouble with her this morning, when we were in the precinct. She attacked a postman. I ended up saying something very silly.'

'She didn't stab him, please tell me.'

'No, she didn't have a knife on her. But I think she thought she did. She kept whacking him on the shoulder with her clenched hand. He looked very surprised.'

'What was it you said to him?'

'I told him she thought she was a dog. With him being a postman. He was a bit po-faced about it. He said, "Perhaps you better keep her on a lead, then." He was one of those people who don't rise to the occasion. Oh, I'm sorry. I know how you must be feeling.'

'I've always thought of her as my real mother. Alice, I mean. You know how your father never knows for sure he is your father? With the milkman always being a possibility? But a mother always knows for *certain* she's the mother because she's the one who had the baby in the first place. Well, I always thought my mother had her doubts. I think she thought *Alice* was really my mother. That she'd been lumbered with me. That's how I felt as well, like a cuckoo in the nest. Not but what Alice isn't a graceful sort of woman too. But at least she's always been open to me. I nearly said, her heart's in the right place, but I suppose it isn't any longer. I better get over to her.'

'Do you wish she *had* been? Your mother?'

'Yes. Not but what I could do without George being my father, though. Petey was far nicer.'

'You know what they say, you can't choose your parents.'

The sound of 'I'll be seeing you in all the old familiar places' came through the wall. The very sweetness of the words sounded like an insult, with no sincerity behind them.

'I could stab *her*, given half a chance,' May said. 'With or without a weapon.'

Eighteen

May thought, seeing Alice's coffin on its trestles at the
front of the Chapel of Rest, what a relief.

It was the wrong thought to have and she tried to
find another one. A spot of sadness would come in handy, she
told herself, but try as she might she couldn't dredge any up.
When she looked there the cupboard was bare. She felt sad
because she couldn't feel sad, which wasn't the same thing at all
as feeling properly sad.

Aunty Alice was the only person she'd ever truly loved, and it
was tiring to love someone for so long, a relief when you didn't
have to any more.

Everyone was singing 'Abide with Me'.

Except Mother, who chose not to sing now she had the chance
to do so without getting on people's nerves for once in her life.
She just stood there with a little smile on her lips. For some
reason she had brought an umbrella with her even though it was
a sunny day with a touch of frost in the air. People had stamped
in the car park of the crematorium, preparatory to entering the
chapel, to get the circulation going in their legs, to emphasise to
themselves that they still had circulation, and still had legs.

All around in the gardens of remembrance were tablets and
broken columns, gravelled patches with inscriptions on plaques
and plinths, trees and benches *in memoriam* to people who were
now no more than names and dates, while cars and lorries roared
past outside, up Costford High Street. There was a touch of
white on the distant fells, where hoar frost or even early snow

had settled, but the air in the car park was sharp and clear, and Hilda had swished her unnecessary umbrella from side to side as if it was one of those offensive weapons that had become so dear to her of late. Now it was leaning against her chair seat and every once in a while she would twist round to adjust it, as though changing gear in a car.

It's not that I'm not going to love anybody again, May realised. I probably love Trevor Morgan a certain amount as it is, in a ships that pass in the night sort of way. And then of course there's my egg. Her heart fluttered at the possibilities he opened up.

It was premature to say she loved Maurice, but she was perfectly prepared to do so in the near future. He had offered to come to the funeral with her, which was thoughtful of him.

'You helped me buy my house,' he explained.

For a second she'd felt a little indignant at the way he seemed to want to compare the two things, but then it occurred to her that in one respect they could be equated after all. For Maurice the house in Mill Park was a new beginning, and perhaps Alice's death meant the same for her.

May had always wished she was Alice's daughter, and now she didn't need to wish it any more. If she had been her daughter she would be an orphan now: it would be done with and she would have found herself all square, no different from the other people in this world who weren't Alice's daughter.

That was how she could think of herself in the future, as Aunty Alice's orphan rather than as her own horrible mother's child. Let one door close and another open. Alice being dead, no harm could be done.

But Alice didn't deserve to be treated like this, as though her death was a cause for celebration.

May tried to concentrate on the coffin, reminding herself that Alice was really and truly lying inside it.

Alice had only done one thing in her life that May disapproved of, and that was being George's wife. It had seemed a sin that she could have accepted such a poor thing for her own. May remembered her bringing over the photo album she'd compiled with those arthritic fingers of hers, with its endless pictures of George in his garden, George on the beach, George standing beside their car, or holding their cat. Alice couldn't have put it together out of love but must have been prompted by the loneliness of old age, a need to convince herself that she'd had a life behind her, a desire to manufacture a happiness that had never really been hers.

But Alice *had* had a life, one that couldn't possibly show up in a photograph. She should have had the courage of her convictions.

There'd been a quality about her you could only glimpse, a flicker of wings, a suggestion of petals in the breeze, something that was edge-on to the forward plod of existence, a sudden dash of colour May had caught from time to time out of the corner of her mind. A touch of beauty, of style.

Whatever it was had been trapped by old age and taken away by death, and it was a relief not to have to look for it any more. I wanted to be her and now I can be content to be me, May told herself.

The vicar said: 'Our sister Alice, beloved wife of George, who passed away some years ago, now reunited in heaven.'

George, my foot, May thought.

Wintry sunshine but the smell of rain in the air. *I'm dreaming of a white Chriss-muss* sang in Hilda's head so loudly it almost passed her lips, and she had to keep them tightly buttoned while everybody else sang 'Abide with Me'.

No thank you, you've abided enough for one lifetime.

Alice had come all the way from that summer garden in 1918 to end up here in a chilly chapel in Costford Crem, but a fat lot of good that was to Hilda now. You couldn't put the clock back, that was for certain. George had been in his grave for years, since long before he actually died. Slim, handsome George in his uniform, with his arm in a sling, had been buried inside fat useless George with his drink and his betting and his bankrupt shop. He was all spoiled.

Alice's death was as if she was saying Here here, you can have it back now, I'm done with it, shoving some mangled thing at you and rushing off home.

The vicar stood at the front like Mr Snowman, with a white cassock and tombstone teeth. He even had a carrot for a nose.

When they filed out of the chapel the weather had turned. Quietly as she could Hilda sang 'Singin' in the Rain'.

The car park looked as if a quaint party game was going on, or even one of those minuet sort of dances they did in the classic serials on TV. Everybody rapidly shook hands with everybody else, the whole crowd puckering and throbbing with movement like a sea anemone with tangled arms in a rock pool. The tarmac was wet and puddled, with icy rain falling so steadily May could hear it drumming on the rim of her bowler. Where it had come from goodness only knew; the morning had had such snap before they entered the chapel.

People she didn't even know came up to commiserate, and say Alice this, and Alice that. Before the funeral these remarks had made her feel uncomfortable because she hadn't been able to think what to say in reply. It was a matter of trying to squeeze somebody's life into a single sentence. But now the memory of other funerals came back to her, Petey's and Hub's especially. All you had to do was say something nice and cosy. There was no need to compare it with the real person. The real person wasn't there any more. You just needed to say this and that back.

She was so busy doing so she didn't notice a strange hand grasping hers for a shake. No, not strange, familiar, that was the strange thing about it, a large warm hand despite the weather.

She hadn't been taking people in – many of them, Alice's neighbours in Waveney Bridge, she didn't know in any case. And the brim of her hat cut out the faces of taller people.

The hand belonged to Trevor, Trevor Morgan.

She looked up at him through the white, sleety rain, hoping the redness of her face would be killed by the maroon of her hat.

'Trevor,' she said.

Trevor wasn't at all embarrassed. 'Hello, May. I'm sorry we have to meet in a place like this.' He gave her his full smile but very speedily, so she wouldn't think him cavalier and tasteless in the circumstances.

'I – I didn't know you knew Alice.'

'Alice?'

'Alice. Aunty Alice.' She waved at all the people around.

'Oh, I see. No, I didn't know her as a matter of fact. But I'm, you know . . .' He didn't look at a loss for words, just amused at the awkwardness of the situation. He did seem more assured than he ever was before, more grown up, May told herself.

'She passed on.'

'I'm sorry.' Trevor didn't sound insincere, or even sincere, just happy to say the right thing.

'Whoever she was,' May added for him. She couldn't resist being naughty, she felt so cheerful all of a sudden.

'Your aunt, that's who she was. So I'm sorry. Was she . . . ? Did she . . . ?' He waved his hand to summon up the relevant issues of life and death.

'Oh yes, all that. Yes, yes.'

He nodded.

'She was a wonderful woman,' May explained.

He raised his eyebrows to take that on board. There were beads of water in them, and in his hair, catching the light like pearls.

She was, she *was* a wonderful woman, May reminded herself. But here in this crematorium car park they were all wonderful women, or wonderful men, just by dint of being dead. It was a coincidence that Alice really had been one.

'What you should have is a hat,' she told him.

'I couldn't wear one with your . . . panache,' he replied.

'That's just what my Hub would have said. I learned my lesson when I got soaking wet the day our friend came up from London. You know.'

'Yes,' Trevor said. 'He was a one, wasn't he?'

'He wanted me to show him our famous viaduct.'

'Did he just? That's odd. His constituency's only about forty miles off.'

'I think he wanted to make the point that where he was really coming from was London.' Which you would have done well to keep in mind, she added mentally.

'I suppose so.'

'He also wanted me to show him round the hattery. That's where I got this one in the first place, straight off the production line.'

'Like getting a loaf fresh from the baker's. Lucky you. I've been caught out.' He looked ruefully round at the weather.

'It happens to the best of us.'

He suddenly sagged, as if the rain had got through to him, but then was chipper again.

'I thought it was going to be a fine day.' He raised his eyebrows, widened his eyes behind rain-flecked spectacles, and gave that smile of his once more.

'Didn't we all?' she asked. At that moment she became aware of her mother's screechy voice singing 'Singin' in the Rain'. 'Just what we need,' she added. 'I better fetch her.'

He bowed his head a little by way of saying goodbye, then merged with the crowd in that way he had, going smoothly backwards into anonymity like an ice skater in a grey worsted suit.

From beneath a flowery umbrella floated Mother's voice:

'What a glorious feeling
It drives me insane.'

You and me both, May said under her breath.

★　　★　　★

When he saw May, Trevor's heart had lurched for a second. I'm supposed to be able to calculate the odds, he reminded himself, the new me, hard-headed. Nothing was going to come of what had happened between them, there'd be no logic in her having saved her revenge for this particular time and place, however much you were supposed to serve the dish cold.

But her appearance here was unexpected and ominous, like a vengeful ghost's. Surely she hadn't known Geoff Cartwright?

Then it dawned. One service was over, the next about to begin. The mourners for Geoff Cartwright and those for whoever it was that May knew were merging together on the waterlogged tarmac like the steel teeth at the top of an escalator. People nodded to each other, shook hands even, who weren't actually attending the same funeral.

May hadn't noticed him. She was meeting and greeting, very much in charge, definitely slimmer and more elegant than she used to be, except for a strange hat that looked as if it had been spannered into place.

If he stayed at the far side of the car park she would notice him eventually and from then on they would catch sight of each other out of the corner of their eyes. It would seem tantamount to saying they were stuck with what he had done, marooned like shipwrecked sailors.

No good for her, that, any more than for him. There was an economy in the world of feelings, as in all the other worlds. He recalled something Kennedy had said, about the secret of being President. Don't waste emotions on things you can't change. He had taken a deep breath and walked over to her.

They stood, caged by the rain, talking in nervous little spurts. He just hoped he wasn't adding to her unhappiness.

Eventually she went off to collect her dotty mother and soon after that the Aunty Alice people drifted away, and the Geoff Cartwright shift was called into the chapel.

For a moment after he entered, his new forthrightness deserted him and he looked downwards, sideways, anywhere but at the coffin on the stage thing at the front. Finally he looked up.

The coffin, almost comfortingly, had a bulky, double-breasted look to it, suggesting Geoff had not wasted away too much before he died. I should have visited, he thought. He wondered why he hadn't. It was almost as though he'd been waiting for an invitation.

The thing was, he'd not expected him to go so soon, despite their conversation in the pub. There was a lot of him to die, it would be like invading Russia.

And he'd feared reminding himself of that last time they spoke. That very same evening he'd had his row with Chris, gone to Ann's, raped May.

Almost as if by the power of thought, Ann slipped into the pew beside him, just as 'Abide with Me' began. They mouthed hello as Ann slipped off her wet coat. She was wearing a silky little lilac dress, not the sort of thing she wore to work, and black stockings or tights, mourning tights. Geoff would have preferred laddered ones no doubt, but still it was nice to think the forlorn old goat was being remembered in an article of clothing that contained a woman's legs.

Trevor remembered how he used to try to catch a sexual signal from her. Now he knew she was lesbian there was no difficulty – it was like finding the right wavelength on a radio: the foreign burble of another sort of sexuality came through loud and clear. She grasped his shoulder, pulled his head down towards hers, whispered in his ear, warm breath from the damp little face, the words slightly lopsided from her harelip. She smelled of rain and underneath that of perfume, something positioned oddly between flowers and hospitals. In his experience perfumes hardly ever smelled simply nice. That wasn't, presumably, the point of them. Sex itself wasn't exactly nice. That wasn't the point of it, either.

'How're things?' the whisper said.

He turned his head to her little ear, which she lifted accommodatingly towards him.

'Fine,' he whispered back.

It wasn't exactly true, but what else could you say at a funeral? He had been at his own small branch of the bank for the last few days, and that had gone OK. Just as well, given he would probably be there for some considerable time, if not ever. His political campaign was in ruins, as far as he could see. The Health Secretary had been going to make a brief visit to Costford on his way somewhere else: he had cancelled without explanation, though as far as Trevor could work out he was still going to the somewhere else. Some of the people in the local party were hardly speaking to him. He'd been ridiculed in the evening paper.

Oddly, this hadn't dented his confidence. He still felt he'd taken the right line. It was as though, for some arbitrary technical reason, the right line wasn't going anywhere. In coming to terms with who he was and what he'd done a few weeks ago, he had achieved a new, crisp definiteness, and one of the ways in which you knew you were being definite was when you found yourself going in a different direction from other people. In fact when the *Costford Express* interviewed him he'd made his words harsher and more provocative than ever, telling them that the four Prospect Hill blocks would be two fingers to the town twice over, in reinforced concrete form. 'Like gesturing with both hands at once,' he'd said.

All that had achieved was to earn a sneering editorial, saying he was jeopardising homes and jobs while pursuing mirages. It was headed, WHEN IS AN AEROPLANE LIKE A WINDMILL? and the answer was: When Trevor Morgan tilts at it. He felt he'd worked out a doctrine of success that was everything it should be except successful.

In other areas, in *the* other area, bingo.

One night he and Chris had gone to bed and had their usual exuberant foreplay, or what had become usual in the weeks since their crisis. They were celebrating in any case, having got an offer for their house, and had taken a bottle of champers and two glasses up to bed with them. At a certain point in their love-making, Trevor became aware the moment had arrived.

Two important things had come together, and his new prag-matic self picked up on their convergence: new place to live, lust-fulness as if it had only just been invented. Rhetoric unrolled headily in his brain as if he was at a political rally, making a speech.

If he was saying that something fruitful and positive can come of aggression and assertion, this was the opportunity to prove it.

If he was suggesting that one should bring one's doings as a whole, good and bad, plus and minus, into a sharp focus, turn them into something powerful and effective, make them move onwards, now was the moment of truth.

If he was laying claim to a new, thrusting, approach to his existence, here was the point to start.

As they had sex he had a sudden memory from when he was a small boy using a pea-shooter, that sense of a slight obstruction in the tube waiting to be fired, hitting it with a lump of breath as tangibly as kicking someone up the backside, the cork-out-of-a-bottle feeling as the pea cleared the orifice, so specific that your lips registered the exact millisecond when it exited the O and began to negotiate the larger air beyond.

This process could be just as deliberate, as directed. He focused his attention on one tiny tadpole waiting to make a child. Whatever happened to the other millions, this one was going to go all the way.

It chimed with his personal campaign motto: *Join the Human Race*.

In the middle of Chris's orgasm her features flickered in sur-prise as her body registered that something new had happened to it. New was the word for this whole phase of his life, of their lives – all three of them.

The vicar had taken up his place at the front, the same one as at Trevor's mother's funeral, with those clacking false teeth of enormous size, and a red nose registering the cold. 'Let us remember the life of Geoff Plowright,' he began.

Nobody put up their hand, nobody called out *Cart*wright.

Perhaps it got the whole thing over with. How long did it take for a name to get illegible on a tombstone? Hundreds of years. This vicar could do it in seconds.

Suddenly Trevor recalled what Geoff himself had said about being forgotten and, abruptly, burning tears sprang out of his eyes and down his cheeks. He was aware of a small hand creeping into his and giving it a squeeze.

In the dark chapel doorway stood the vicar and Geoff's widow, shaking hands with the mourners.

Trevor avoided saying thank you to the vicar, indeed saying anything. He didn't even smile, but looked him hard in the face for a second. Not that it did any good: the vicar just thought he was grim with grief, and patted his shoulder. Come to think of it, he was.

He moved on to shake hands with Geoff's wife, and here he had a shock. She was an elegant middle-aged woman with fine features. She was wearing a grey suit with the skirt down to the knee, and her calves were slim and shapely. Her stockings had a faint haze of darkness which accentuated their curves. She had a little black hat rather like a beret, and blonde wavy hair with touches of grey, clipped neatly round her ears. She regarded him gravely with dark blue, almost violet eyes.

'You're Trevor,' she said in a low, almost husky voice.

'Yes. How did you know?'

'Geoff described you to me.'

'He must have been very good at word pictures.'

'To tell you the truth, I've seen your photo in the evening paper. You're famous.'

'I'm just a local busybody.'

'You were a good friend to Geoff. He talked about you a lot, Trevor.'

Trevor looked at her, embarrassed. He'd expected a sort of

pantomime dame, and felt he ought to apologise for his mental image of her. Geoff's fault of course, barbarian that he was. He'd made no attempt at a word picture in *her* case. Unless of course he was just being a joker, taking it for granted that everyone knew that his remarks about his wife, about women in general, were off the top of his head, a running gag because it was common knowledge he was married to a beauty.

Good friend, nothing, Trevor thought, I didn't know anything about the man. I didn't even visit him when he was dying, though I knew he was frightened stiff. In his heart of hearts he knew he'd resented Geoff for giving him the beer that had brought down all the disasters of that evening on his head.

'I'll miss him,' he said lamely.

'So will I,' she replied in a soft, heartfelt voice.

'He was very . . .' He couldn't think exactly what, and let his voice tail off, hoping it would sound as if he'd been checked by emotion.

'I know,' she replied, intuiting something that wasn't there.

In the car park he found himself with Ann again.

'I didn't expect Geoff's wife to be like that.'

'Oh, Joyce is lovely. Barb and I went to their Christmas party last year. Joyce said, Orge everyone, orge. She said, Orge, damn your eyes, if I remember right. Geoff came in dressed up as Father Christmas. He was quite a Father Christmassy kind of bloke, in my opinion. He gave everybody a present.'

I wasn't asked, Trevor thought sadly. He felt like a child, missing out on the jelly and ice-cream.

'Orge is not a good word to say to Barbara,' Ann added reflectively.

The point was that Trevor had been an assistant manager, and his presence at the party would no doubt have made people feel awkward. Hard to orge in those circumstances, even to be Father Christmas. Perhaps the Cartwrights hadn't held parties in those days when he too was a clerk. Still, Trevor felt a sudden restlessness, a desire to prove himself, to show he wasn't a man who could be overlooked.

'Did you notice a public telephone here?' he asked Ann.

The *Costford Express* editor sounded surprised and amused, the way a bloke would sound if he made a casual proposition to a girl at a party and she said yes. Not that Trevor had ever done such a thing but he felt nowadays he could have. He felt he'd been around, gained experience. And one thing experience should tell you: it was dangerous, politically, to give a newspaper editor a nice surprise, especially one who'd already ridiculed you in public.

Keith Dobson had a massive, bald, almost cone-shaped head, and wore small metal-framed spectacles, like a surgeon might. Trevor pictured him at the other end of the phone, his lenses flashing neon from the tube on his office ceiling, his lips curled down slightly in a knowing smile, an affected carnation in his buttonhole staring straight ahead like an innocent pet. He was formidable. Trevor felt like a poker player pressing on with a mediocre hand because he'd got so far there was no way back.

It was just an open-plan telephone in the chapel hallway. Ann waited nearby, having shown him it, not sure whether to stay or go. Her presence made him feel busy and resourceful. He put the phone back on its rest.

'Photo shoot,' he explained.

'Oh yes?'

'Up where they're building the flats. I'm going to have my photo taken, looking disapproving. You know how people do in the papers, when they're opposed to something. They have to put their hands in their pockets, hunch their shoulders, and scowl.'

'I'm sure you'll look very fetching.'

'They wanted me to do it before, but I said no. I didn't want to be a one-note politician. But it strikes me that that's what's happened anyhow, so I might as well bite the bullet.'

She thought for a moment. She was a thoughtful sort of person. Trevor wondered why *she* never got promoted. Perhaps she thought *too* much. That was how he could have consoled Geoff, telling him he was too big for the bank, they couldn't really cope with him: their loss.

It didn't matter any more. All that restlessness and frustration was in its coffin, waiting to be burned to a cinder. In some ways that was a consolation, for all concerned: things only ever mattered to a certain point.

God, I've got hard, Trevor thought.

'Isn't it a bit self-defeating?' Ann finally asked.

'In what way?'

'Well, you can't stop them being built, so it puts you on the losing side.'

'You're quite right. That's what they tell you not to be, in politics, on the losing side. But you've got to trust your instincts, and mine say there's still a bit of mileage in this business. So I'm going for it anyway.'

She gave him a long look. It had some admiration in it, but also, perhaps, sympathy. Even pity. A horrible thought came into his head and made him feel cold all over. Perhaps it was possible to trust your instincts even when you had the wrong ones – even when you had none at all.

It was sleeting when Trevor drove up to the top of Prospect Hill. The towers were rising side by side in skeletal form, just girders at the moment, and only to about the fourth floor of each, a quarter of their final height. Big yellow diggers and cranes stood around like grazing beasts. Not much seemed to be going on at present.

Keith Dobson was standing beside the prefabricated site office. He looked enormous in a black duffle-coat. Trevor had read somewhere about those long swishing coats the cowboys used to wear, roundabouts they were called. Keith's had the same sort of cascading menace about it, with toggles from hell. Standing beside him was a shrimpy photographer hunched in a suede car coat.

Trevor parked and joined them.

'Would you bloody read about it?' Keith Dobson said, glaring at the weather. 'It's still only November.'

'Have they come to their senses?' Trevor asked.

'You what?' Keith replied grumpily.

'Not doing a lot, are they?'

'The girdermen are not allowed up if there's a danger of ice, the bloke told me.'

The bloke, or a bloke, came out of the office at that moment, carrying in each hand a bunch of hard hats like yellow melons by their straps. Keith took the biggest one and squashed it over his coat hood.

'Bloody hell, Keith,' the photographer said. 'You look the next best thing to God.'

'Being the editor of the *Costford Express* is the next best thing to God,' Trevor said. 'From where I'm standing.'

Keith belched. 'Better out than in,' he said.

That's your level, Trevor thought. He remembered his mother in her final days, when she'd become very flatulent, just part of the endless humiliation of her illness, saying in a little girl voice, 'Pardon me for being so rude. It was not me, it was my food.' She'd had a singsong intonation as if she was doing her times tables. And of course it wasn't her food. She wasn't eating anything.

'I'll stand in front of it and give two fingers, shall I?' Trevor asked, feeling the anger in his voice. 'With both hands. By way of illustration.'

'Ooh, dearie,' the photographer said in Frankie Howerd style.

'This has really got your goat, hasn't it?' Keith said. The God he was runner-up to must have been some God of the insects, with a gleaming, compartmentalised head. It wasn't difficult to work out that this was a man set on destroying Trevor's career. Given the balance between Labour and Tory voters in the borough and the sensitivity of his position as boss of the local rag, he would normally be discreet and hedge his bets, but he'd got the scent of blood in his nostrils and had every intention of getting credit for forecasting Trevor's demise.

I'm letting him do it, Trevor thought. A lamb to the slaughter. What's got into me? 'I believe in speaking my mind.'

'Speaking it's one thing. Making rude signs on the front page of my paper's another. Tell you what, though, you could do a Churchill style V for victory. That's the next-best thing. Everybody always knew he was really saying up yours.' The snow was falling properly now, and what you could see of Keith's face, beneath the hat and inside the hood, had the blotchy crumbling look of severe cold. Oddly, Trevor didn't feel it at all at present. Numb, probably.

'But it's *not* a victory, that's my whole point.'

'Tell you what. Why don't you hold up both arms, with your forefingers pointing skywards. We'll get the rising towers behind you, to back it up. It'll turn your whole body into one big fat rude gesture, and nobody will be able to take offence.'

It was a put-up job. He had intended to pose him like that all along, pointing at the empty air. If doubts hadn't weevilled their way into Trevor's brain long before this they would be doing so now. What was being suggested was a perfect image of ineffectualness. If there was ever a time for a politician to have an instinct it was now. Every political bone in his body said to walk away.

I know what's going on, Trevor thought: my instinct is telling me to override my instinct. 'OK,' he said.

'We better get a move on,' the photographer said, 'the light's going already.'

Trevor looked at his watch: not quite four. But it was true, darkness was already inveigling its way into the air. He remembered the black sheen on Geoff's widow's stockings. What a mind I've got nowadays, he thought, that can jump from wintry twilight to a woman's legs. It was as though that horrible episode with May had set some beast free inside him, something that was best kept chained up. My mother would be proud of me, he thought.

And then he wondered.

He'd always thought of his mother as the raffish one, with her obscure past, her constant tendency to suggest that he should take more risks in his life. But what risks had he ever seen *her* take? There'd been no blokes on the scene all the time he could remember. She had never gone for nights out. She'd made him feel staid and unadventurous, but for all practical purposes she had been exactly the same herself, despite constant hints at a disgraceful past. And perhaps, unconsciously, that was how she'd wanted him to feel. She used to pretend she wished he'd fallen in love with Ann Cottrell. But she knew nothing about her – except that Trevor had described her as timid. *Chris* wasn't timid. She'd proved it.

He became abruptly cheerful. That was why he'd found himself willing to play fast and loose with his own political career: he'd become an adventurer, at this late stage. It was a matter of moving on from his mother's death, of moving on from his mother. It was more important to do that than to be successful.

'Better let the dog see the rabbit, then,' he said.

Keith Dobson took hold of his elbow, and they walked together to a likely spot. Keith had suddenly become companionable, as an executioner might, taking you to the gallows. No point in being petty about it.

'Good enough,' the photographer called out. He spun his camera into position on top of the tripod. Keith scuttled back to join him. 'Just the ticket,' Keith called out. 'Now let's see you do your Moses on the Mount of Olives impression.'

'It was Mount Sinai,' the photographer said, eye glued to his viewfinder.

Trevor held his arms aloft, forefingers pointing upward. He wanted to look angry but also amused at this way of showing it, so as to appear to be making a comment on the very photograph he was starring in, as if to say, I'm sorry to have to resort to this nonsense to make my point, but there's no alternative.

He became aware of the sound of an aircraft approaching him from behind. They passed over every minute or two, preparing to land at Manchester Airport. It would make the point better if it was included in the picture. He looked angry, then amused, and wondered how to weld those two expressions together.

The roaring grew louder. The falling snow seemed to tremble in time with it, like a trick light effect at a disco. Louder still.

Keith dropped to his knees. His enormous head was looking raptly upwards, as if in the throes of a religious experience. The photographer kept behind his camera but tilted it upwards in parallel with Keith's face. The roar was enormous now, the biggest sound Trevor had ever heard. He wanted to spin round, put his arms protectively over his own head. But he held his ground, maintained the pose he'd struck.

The earth began to pulse and throb in response to the deep bass notes of the plane's engines. The bloke from the site office ran out the door and threw himself on the muddy, snow-splattered ground. From the three men Trevor could see, and others he couldn't, came a snivelling wail, like the crying of the damned.

Nineteen

Art had looked good by the pool: and in the bedroom, for that matter.

It had all been a bit whirlwind and that was the first look she'd got at him, in Lanzarote.

Wendy had put in her resignation. Never do that unless you mean it, her dad had said when she started work, good advice probably but she didn't take it. He was one of those silent worldly-wise type of dads, very impressive, but you only had one life.

She'd told Cherry that she didn't intend to heed the advice. Cherry replied that the only advice worth taking was not to take any, then spent half an hour advising her against trying to throw herself at Art.

Wendy didn't appreciate the way she said 'trying'. There was an aspect of Cherry that could get right up your nostrils.

Meanwhile Cherry's Dave had painted her front door for her, then buggered off to sea, while Ben was more austere than ever, and had taken Cherry to Manchester to hear Benjamin Britten's *War Requiem*.

Wendy tried to get over to her that if Cherry could have more than one bloke on call at any one time, it surely meant that she didn't take either of them too seriously; in which case, why was it such a big deal *her*, Wendy, taking a chance on an older man? That was barking up the wrong tree, however. Cherry took both the men in her life extremely seriously. In fact she took pretty much everything extremely seriously.

It crossed Wendy's mind that she didn't love Cherry quite as much as she'd thought she did. A week before, she would have said quite truthfully that she loved her more than anyone she had ever met, bar Art of course. But niggles had set in, precisely because Cherry didn't approve of the Art business.

Cherry was so pleasing because she was herself through and through, but now Wendy had begun to feel that was her limitation also, it made her narrow and inflexible. Like that time she had told the customer he was repulsive in a strictly magnetic sense, causing her to eddy and eddy away from him however much she'd wanted to serve him his food. That was funny but from a certain point of view it made you want to smack her. She was one of those people who made you laugh because she didn't have a sense of humour herself.

Wendy had resigned that day Art had inspected a freckle on her chest, or claimed to be doing, on the grounds of possible cancer.

Inspected her *chest* more like, or as much of it as he could.

She'd been wearing a blouse under a wool cardigan, not a lot of access there. He always joshed her about but that was the first time he'd got to the threshold of something more intimate. She'd felt the warmth of his breath on her neck, even fancied she could feel it inside her blouse, creeping down towards her cleavage. Then he'd snapped out of it, almost as if he was waking up from a trance. He'd let out a little groan, then tried to cover it up with his usual joking.

He left the office and was gone for hours. When he returned he was in a state. His face looked red and swollen. My goodness, Wendy marvelled, aren't men a giveaway. Poor lamb, she thought.

'I'm going to have to leave,' she told him.

He stared at her, baffled. 'Is it time?' he asked.

'I don't mean to go home. I mean leave. Resign.'

His mouth dropped open. 'Why?'

'My legs keep going weak.'

'Your legs?' He said it in a hoarse whisper. 'Oh yes, you nearly fell over this morning, didn't you? What's the matter with them? Have they gone . . .' She could see he was floundering for the right word, not quite ready to adjust from thinking sexual thoughts. 'Funny?'

'Funny? What do you mean, funny? How can legs go funny?'

'I don't know. Not working properly.' His face was even redder and he looked sweaty about the eyes.

'They're not a couple of sausages, you know.'

'But you said they went weak.'

'Well, they'll soon be cured. All I need to do is toddle off on them.'

'Oh.'

'You're not with it today, are you?'

'I am your boss, you know. I don't think you ought to talk to me like that.'

'What it is, I'm in love.'

He blinked, like a schoolboy might, when life's too much for him. 'Who with?' he asked.

'Who do you think?' Wendy nodded. He nodded back, as though it was a nodding lesson.

He had a little speech all ready in advance, it turned out, despite being so taken aback by their conversation. 'Something fishy there,' she told him, after complaining about how he'd got it all off pat.

What he'd said was, their age gap was wide enough for him to be her dad.

That he was a bloke who'd been with lots of women.

That he'd just had a serious affair, and had hardly got over it, hadn't got over it. (He said he'd tried to snap out of his feelings for the person concerned by visiting a woman he knew, on the Tinnington estate. He didn't say prostitute, but explained he gave her money. Wendy liked the delicate, roundabout way he put it. It was as if he was trying to protect not Wendy but the woman herself, whoever she was.)

That he thought he was getting into a serious phase of his life. He didn't know whether that was a good thing to say or a bad thing to say. It meant he didn't want to trifle with her affections. But at the same time it meant that at her young age she might be getting more involved than she wanted to.

'I want to,' she'd said.

Her resignation wasn't accepted, for the time being. He told her he was booked to go on holiday. It was originally planned to be a honeymoon type of thing with the other woman. That was very frank, almost too much so, as Wendy told him.

'I didn't cancel her booking,' he said.

'Didn't you?'

'It's a new link, Manchester Airport to the Canary Islands. I got an opening offer. It was two for the price of one, if you were one of the first bookers. And I was. I got tipped the wink by a friend of mine, bloke called Norman Forrester, who always has his ear to the ground. Those offers are only there for those in the know. After the bust-up I thought, letting it stand is no skin off my nose, and it means I can claim two travel allowances. You know how you're only allowed to take fifty pounds out of the country with you? I treated her to her fifty, but it seemed silly to cancel the pesetas when we broke up. I could say she fell ill on the day, and no one would enquire about the money.'

'So you've got a spare seat on the plane?'

'And a double booking at the hotel.'

'Dearie me.'

'So I could change the booking to your name.'

'And I could have the fifty pounds' worth of pesetas.'

'Yes, you could. Of course I might deduct it out of your wages.'

'The amount you pay me, that'll take till Crimble.' She reflected a while. 'God knows what my mum and dad will say.'

He was looking at her anxiously, his eyes bright.

'All right,' she said eventually, 'it's a done deal.'

Lanzarote looked alien, with its stretches of volanic ash. But the sea was navy blue and there was warmth in the sunshine.

Wendy did try going in the sea once, just to say she'd done it in November. She had orange goggles, bought by Art in the town at a little shop with whitewashed walls, that seemed to specialise in hula-hoops. She put the goggles on, not worrying about the poky-eyed look they gave her. She lay face down and saw something horrible sliding along the bottom of the Atlantic, a sea-cucumber according to Art when she described it. Dawn, half of a couple they'd made friends with, agreed with her about its horribleness.

'My idea of a cucumber is one that stays where it's put,' Dawn said, while they were all having drinks together.

Dawn and Rhodri lived in London, where they ran some kind of import/export business. They were in their early thirties. Being midway between Wendy's age and Art's they acted as a sort of bridge, and made everything normal and problem-free.

Rhodri was a Welshman. He originated in Bangor, and was very patriotic about it.

'It's all very nice,' he said, waving at the island and the ocean in general, 'but it isn't Bangor.'

He told them the story of the shepherd from the hills above Bangor who won a sheep-herding prize and had to go to London to get it. '"A lovely place," he said when he got back. He was a little bloke who always wore the same old tweed jacket and flat cap. "But an awful long way from anywhere."'

When Dawn made her remark about cucumbers, Rhodri said, 'Vegetables grow to a surprising size in Bangor, due to the climactic conditions.' There was a vegetable research station there, where he'd worked in his school holidays, looking into the bigness of the crops, presumably.

After her encounter with the sea-cucumber Wendy kept to the hotel pool. An elderly waiter with tired feet used to bring them drinks. There was a charcoal stove on a raised terrace with purple flowers clinging to the wall behind it. The stove was lit in the evenings and they did mainly fish, fresh tuna or sardines. The flowers were bougainvillaea, which could never have survived in a place like Costford. Wendy stared at them in fascination. They were living proof she was abroad.

She and Art had a double room.

'I know you don't like them,' he told her.

'Don't I?'

'You told me once that if you got married you would have a bedroom to yourself.'

'Ho. I must have said that to get you going.'

They had sex together so often it became almost decent, like some sort of sport you might do for your health. They would retire to bed in the afternoon, leaving Rhodri and Dawn on their sun loungers.

'Oh lor,' Rhodri would say, 'going for a siesta. We always used to have to have a nap back in Bangor, when the sun was shining. There was an old sofa in the library of the vegetable station, where I'd stretch myself out from time to time.'

Wendy had been worried about Art taking his clothes off. They hadn't done anything intimate before coming on holiday. There had only been a little over a week to wait, in any case, and without saying anything they both understood it would provide a necessary formality to be discreet before then.

One night in her bedroom at home, trying to summon up the courage to tell her parents the next day about what was planned, Wendy had found herself looking at it all in a strange light. She imagined herself and Art to be tiny people, children or even insects, going through the rituals of life at an advanced speed because of their small size: a week of courtship, then a little marriage, followed by two weeks of wedded life. After that, who knew?

Her father had said nothing when it came to it, but crumpled slightly as if in pain. 'He looked just as if I'd stuck a knife into him,' Wendy told Art.

So, on the first day of their holiday, the moment came. They were in a chalet that belonged to the hotel. The great unveiling, Wendy thought to herself. That had been what Cherry always said when some Johnny or Doris went off behind the screen to strip and put their sheet on.

Her heart was in her mouth. She had a horrible fear that it would all be a terrible let-down. Art looked fine in his T-shirt and shorts, with strong arms and legs and a manly-looking chest, but she felt scared that beneath his clothing he'd prove a sudden, awful let-down, white and wrinkly. She remembered as a little girl getting lovely parcels at Christmas, then opening them to find just ordinary things inside.

But no, he was well built, muscular and very hairy. His chest was developed. You could see he wasn't in his first youth, of course.

'Don't worry,' Art said, catching her inspecting look. 'It's all in working order.' And it was.

Apart from all the sex there was a lot of conversation too. Art was quite dissatisfied with his existence. 'The way I see it, there are three needs in life,' he told them, Dawn and Rhodri included, over drinks on the terrace before they had their evening meal one night. 'Food, shelter and reproduction. In the end, that's your lot. Being an estate agent, I'm supplying one of those three, to the population at large.'

'I'm sure if you tried harder you could help with one of the others at least. If not both,' Rhodri said, winking at Wendy. She felt herself colour up.

'I suppose it's not everybody who could say that they're sup-plying *one*,' Art said reflectively.

'Well, no, Dawn and me couldn't say it. We're importing small wooden elephants, for example, with little ivory tusks. Nobody could say they were food or shelter or reproduction, could they? They're just wooden elephants, that's all they are.'

'So from one point of view I'm doing one of the big three things. But from another point of view I don't think I'm doing anything useful at all. I'm not *building* houses. I'm not producing anything.'

'You're like a butterfly,' Dawn said, 'fluttering by.'

'Here one minute, gone the next,' Art agreed glumly.

'We're all butterflies together,' Rhodri said, 'a blimming great flock of them, doing bugger-all useful. We're all of us here today and gone tomorrow.'

'I suppose so,' Art said, not sounding convinced.

Wendy loved the idea of Art being an estate agent in a rage at his profession. If you've got to be an estate agent, be a dissatisfied one, was her verdict. She wondered if the reason he was such a sexual kind of man was out of frustration with his career, even though he seemed to make bags of money at it.

Once Art talked to her about Dawn's bikini. It was made of light nylon fabric that went very clingy when wet. Dawn had been lying in the pool on a lilo with her legs a little apart, and he said about how the material went in and out with every detail of how she was down there. He said it when he and Wendy were in bed together, just as an observation, but it made Wendy go hot with embarrassment and, she noticed, lust. She'd been interested too, looked as much as she dared in Dawn's direction. Just checking up, was how she'd thought of it.

Art sees all women in the same light, she realised, the point of view being the between-the-legs one, or as near as he could get to it. Yet she was sure he was a true romantic, that he had really loved the woman he had been having the affair with before, that he really loved her, Wendy, now. His sweat, as he lay beside her in, or rather on, the bed during the warm afternoon, smelled slightly of onions, which she didn't mind. It was to do with his age, she knew, even though she'd not been this close to an older man before. It was quite pleasant in its way: she'd always enjoyed savoury things.

'I'm the only person I've ever known who liked school

dinners,' she announced out of the blue. Maybe she said it to get on safer ground.

'Is that right?' Art asked.

Then she started to talk about Cherry with her two fiancés, how wonderful she was. But that led to her telling Art about something that had happened at the last art class they'd gone to together, the Saturday before she flew off on holiday.

Nick, the teacher, had asked for volunteers to be a Doris. To Wendy's amazement, given what she'd said on the subject previously, Cherry got slowly to her feet. She patted her hands downwards as much as to say, I know, I know, don't bother to applaud, someone's got to do it.

Behind her a woman called Jennie Summers had begun to rise to her feet also, one of those florid handsome type of women with wavy blonde hair, pushing forty. When she saw Cherry stand up, she dropped back into her seat again and tried to look as if she'd just been getting herself comfortable, standing up so as to untangle her buttocks ready for sitting back down on them. Her face was ablaze at having almost been an unwanted Doris, the humiliation of it, because there was no doubt from Nick's gleeful reaction to Cherry that he would give *her* pride of place.

But of course Cherry had been dead against volunteering, mainly because Nick was so keen on her doing so. It was Wendy who'd been interested in the idea. Nevertheless, off Cherry went, behind the screen, as if she hadn't a care in the world. And when she came out again she was naked to the waist.

She walked to her place in the front of the room with her hips swaying, which wasn't the way she normally walked. Although she was lovely looking, to Wendy at least, she usually held her arms and legs as if she couldn't really be bothered having limbs, as if she'd like to stow them away somewhere. Wendy had assumed that was why she'd needed to acquire a body fiancé as well as a brain one. If so, he'd done the trick. Wendy imagined a huge pot balanced on Cherry's head. The sheet hung down to her feet like an African woman's skirt, while her breasts looked bold and confident, with the nipples out.

Wendy didn't tell Art that bit. But she did say how sneeped she'd felt. It was a left-out sensation, like discovering your best friend was going to a party you hadn't been invited to. You could cut the atmosphere of the art class with a knife: people began to paint as though their lives depended on it. They had painted hard when that previous Doris had her breast out; now they painted twice as hard. Grey rain was beating against the windows of the Town Hall annexe, drumming on the flat roof.

Wendy painted eyes on Cherry's breasts where the nipples should be, while the proper eyes looked in a different direction. In her role as a Doris, Cherry never looked towards her once.

'I said to her afterwards,' Wendy told Art, 'that she'd told me she didn't want to do it. "Did I?" she said. "I just thought to myself I might as well get it over with. It was a spur of the moment thing." Pah. She can keep all those fiancés of hers. I think she's selfish when it comes down to it. Or self-centred, anyhow.'

'I'm glad she was the Doris and not you,' Art said gallantly. 'I want you all to myself.'

'It's not her being the Doris that made me choke. I expect we'll all get to be Dorises in the end, or Johnnies. But it was leaving me in the lurch like that. It made her look as if she was a good sport and I was out in the cold. I felt as if she was grinding me underfoot.' Suddenly she welled up.

'Don't fret, darling, you'll show her your stuff in the end. You'll show all of them.'

'I thought you wanted me all to yourself.'

'I want you to be happy, that's what I want.'

'Anyhow if I do get to be a Doris, what's left for me to do, that Cherry hasn't done? I haven't got four tits, you know, or three even.'

'Thank God for that.'

'Oh piss off, Art. You think you're such a bloody clever-clogs.'

She felt stupidly furious, and completely forlorn. She wished immediately she hadn't said clogs, it was a soppy word. She felt about two years old, floundering about with no idea why she was feeling all the horrible emotions that were rising up in her. She knew in her heart of hearts that if she had been the Doris first she would never have dared show her boobs. She'd had it all worked out in advance, her own pathetic little plan: half of each nipple, maximum. That made it worse: Cherry had such spark, compared to her. It was all to do with how much younger Wendy was than Art, than Rhodri and Dawn, than Cherry herself. She was younger than everybody, and she felt out of her depth.

One evening at the end of their holiday, Wendy found herself sitting alone on the terrace with Rhodri. Art had gone up to their room to put a pair of long trousers on because the mosquitoes were biting, and Dawn had gone off to the loo. Wendy and Rhodri had gabbled away quite happily, along with the others, for the duration of the holiday, but now suddenly it became difficult to think of things to say. She wondered if it was because she and Art were going home the next day. It was like famous last words.

She imagined lying on her deathbed, not able to think how on earth to get it all over with. Out of desperation she confided this thought to Rhodri. It was better to have a conversation about not being able to have a conversation than have no conversation at all.

'This bloke,' Rhodri said, 'on his deathbed, all his friends and relations standing around him. He was a lecturer at the University of Wales at Bangor, lived in quite a posh house, the sofas always plumped up, like. At a certain point they realised he hadn't been very active for quite some time, and wondered if he'd already croaked it. "Feel his feet," one of his pals said, "nobody ever died with warm feet." Quick as a flash the dying bloke's eyes popped open. "Joan of Arc did," he said, and then his eyes shut again and he passed away. Very satisfying that must have been, to end with a quip like that. They always have very high calibre staff at Bangor, even the dead and dying ones.'

Of course they would, Wendy thought to herself, big brainboxes to go with the enormous carrots and turnips that grew in the area.

'I think I'll go to the loo as well,' Wendy said, rising to her feet. To her surprise Rhodri stood up too, so abruptly that his chair almost toppled over. She stepped round the table and he did too. It was only then she noticed that for the time being there was no one at all on the terrace except for the two of them.

Rhodri stepped right up and put his arms round her. He was a bit stout so they weren't as long as all that by the time they'd cleared his body, and Wendy had the odd sense of being embraced by a penguin. Instead of putting her at her ease, though, the idea made her stupidly frightened.

Rhodri plonked a kiss half on, half off her mouth. It's just a silly kiss, she thought, it doesn't matter, but somehow it seemed to, it seemed to spoil the arrangement that had held all holiday, she and Art, adult couple, Dawn and Rhodri, friends, another adult couple. I thought I was being taken seriously, was what came into her head.

'It's been a lovely holiday,' Rhodri said. He was trying to sound sentimental but his eyes were hard with desire. What they were asking was: how much of you can I get hold of, in the time I have at my disposal?

'I should cake-o,' she replied as breezily as possible.

'Look what I see, a holiday hug,' came Art's big voice. 'Soon as my back is turned.'

Wendy swivelled to look at him, still within Rhodri's arms. He was beautiful, so tall and big, so trousered.

'That's it,' Rhodri replied. He released Wendy, stepped over, and clapped Art on the shoulder. 'We'll miss you pair,' he said.

You old so-and-so, Wendy thought. It was as if Rhodri was saying: I could as easily hug one of you as the other, or both; all the same to me.

'Tell you what,' Art said, 'one of those little perishers got me right on the bum.'

'Oh, that's the best bit, from their point of view,' Rhodri said. 'It's like a rump steak. Come to think of it, it *is* a rump steak.'

When you see it out of a plane porthole the world looks just as if it's in a bubble, like one of those snow-shakers, except that the world from this particular plane was a hot one, the Atlantic Ocean with slow metallic-looking waves on it.

In Wendy's mind the holiday was a bubble holiday. She said that to Art.

'The trouble is,' he said, 'I want my life to be only bubbles now. I'm tired of the bits in between.'

'One bubble after another. It would be like a pearl necklace.'

'Beads'd do, I'm not fussy.'

'I'll be your bubble,' Wendy said.

'Ta,' he said, picked her hand up and kissed the back of it. 'And every evening, after a long day labouring over a hot estate agency, I can come home and prick my little bubble.'

'Yes, you can,' she said reassuringly. 'And I can come home after a long day labouring too, and have my little bubble pricked.' Home, she thought, does he mean we're going to shack up together? Home was likely to be a big idea to an estate agent.

She felt joy and fear both at once. A house, what was it? Was it a bubble too? Or did it turn into the everyday world which you needed a bubble to escape from, one of those little bubble cars? Hell for leather, down the hill, across the blue horizon, over the sea to Skye.

A big G and T, which Art had ordered for her from the hostess, had sent her a bit addled.

She remembered her father, after she'd told him about the holiday, looking as if he'd been stabbed through the heart, trying to remain erect and dignified but ashen-faced, telling her she was too young to settle down. Going to the Canaries for a holiday hadn't seemed much like settling down at the time, but perhaps he was right after all.

Wendy had discovered she wasn't an ideal flyer. She felt the need to concentrate on the wings, keep them in position. Otherwise she had a horrible suspicion they were liable to snap off. She read her Georgette Heyer to take her mind off it, though of course she didn't really want to take her mind off it, given mind-power might be the key to survival, for all she knew.

It was a crime novel with butlers and people in. Her mother had given it to her to read on holiday, and she'd dutifully kept it with her when lying on her sun lounger by the pool. She'd hardly looked at it at all but as the time passed it had bloomed a bit like a rose does, its pages fluffing out and the whole book swelling to two or three times its original size. The process of flowering hadn't made it any more interesting, however, and as she read now she couldn't repress the occasional groan. Always, vibrating through the pages, was the low throb of the plane's engines.

'If you don't like it,' Art said, 'why don't you read something else? You can have one of my Hornblowers if you like.'

He'd brought all the Hornblower novels by C.S. Forester with him, and had read them enthusiastically while they were lying on the terrace and Wendy was letting her mind wander or talking twaddle with Dawn – Rhodri, porky though he was, being the big swimmer of the lot of them and constantly shooting around the pool, just coming up from time to time to spout.

Art told Wendy he took the same books on holiday with him every year. It didn't seem to occur to him to read anything different. He took pride in the fact that he didn't read them at other times for fear of spoiling them for his holiday.

Wendy had wondered how many different women he'd taken with him in the time he'd kept to the same old Hornblower. Funnily enough that didn't make her fear him being unfaithful. Quite the opposite. It seemed a sign of essential steadiness.

'No, it's all right,' she told him. 'This book's so boring,

it's almost interesting. It's like as if it's come round the other side.'

As they drew near home the cloud beneath grew thick and joined-together. The sky around them was deep blue, almost violet. The sunshine felt mellow coming through the porthole but Art said that outside it was minus God-knew-what.

'Perhaps heaven's like that,' Wendy said. The scene looked just like the heaven you saw in cartoons, with angels sitting on the top of puffy clouds, except here there weren't any angels.

'Heaven?' asked Art.

'Perhaps heaven's as cold as . . . I don't know what. Cold as hell.'

The hostess came round pushing a trolley-load of goodies for sale. She looked too groomed, with her little blue hat on top of her hair-style, to be doing something so mundane.

Art bought Wendy a bottle of perfume.

'That's nice,' Wendy said, 'and it hardly costs any more than in a shop. Think of the convenience of being able to buy it on board an aircraft in flight.'

'You're so sharp, you'll cut yourself,' Art said.

It was something her mother used to say to her, and to her amazement Wendy felt homesick tears well up in her eyes. Suddenly it was as if she'd been away from her parents for months, years almost, as if they were dim, remote people left behind by time, tottering around in the far past.

She thought of her dad with his ramrod back and his ramrod soul, dignified to the marrow. He even made a dignified comment about *Top of the Pops* once, something about the singers not sounding sincere. And her jolly mum who flapped around all day at her chores, who was busy as a bee yet strangely relaxed inside, either because her soul was at peace or more likely because she had no soul at all.

Wendy wouldn't mind her not having one: it made her seem

more valuable still in a funny sort of way, properly contrasting with Dad, balancing him out, as if she was saying, I'm not superior to my time and place, being on earth is good enough for me, I'm happy to be ordinary. But not having a soul also made her vulnerable. Wendy thought of those words in the funeral service: ashes to ashes, dust to dust, and imagined a time when her mother would be nothing more than a particular sort of dust, and her dad would be in a grim kind of heaven, just where he ought to be, but somehow deserving better because he was after all her dad and she loved him.

She couldn't work out which was sadder, him being immortal or her mother being mortal: both were miserable ways to end up, and she felt a desperate, panic-stricken urge to get home and save her parents from their respective fates before it was too late.

She realised all children must feel like this – your parents brought you into the world, and it was your job, in return, to try to stop them leaving it – but she'd only just become aware of it herself. It had taken till the present moment to sink in. It was something she'd learned by going off to the Canaries, and now she had to get home as fast as she could to make up for lost time. I think I must be a very late developer, she told herself, it's taken me all this time to understand what I've got, and how it would feel to lose it all.

'We're going down,' Art said.

'You what?'

'Beginning to come in to land.'

Sure enough the plane was on a forward tilt, and when she glanced up at the porthole there were thick white swirls outside it, smoke, she thought for one horrible second, and her heart began to pound hugely in her chest. Then the shade shifted to grey and immediately after went almost blue or purple, the colour that threatens rain, the Costford colour, and she realised they were merely descending through cloud cover.

At that moment the captain's voice came over the loudspeakers.

'Fasten your seat belts, ladies and gentlemen, boys and girls, we are commencing our descent.' He said it very melodiously, with an odd stress on *are* as if someone had argued that they weren't. His voice was cultivated and plummy.

'He sounds as if he did his piloting lessons at Eton,' Wendy said.

'You wouldn't want riff-raff like us pair flying a plane,' Art told her. 'It's all a matter of stiff upper lip.'

'I suppose it's his stiff upper lip that makes him talk funny. My heart's beating so hard I feel as if my eyes are going to jump out their sockets. I could do with wearing those goggles I bought.'

'That's just because we've lost a bit of cabin pressure. You do sometimes when you come in to land. You need lots of pressure to keep your eyeballs in place. When it drops they have a tendency to bulge.' He leaned into her, bulged his own, and did that strange thing he could do with his moustache, commanding each bristle to stand to attention by sheer willpower, even making them vibrate slightly. 'They're not the only thing that bulges.'

'Thank you very much,' she said, 'I know just what you mean by riff-raff now.'

All at once they were through the cloud.

There was the edge of the Peaks below them, with glistening grey dry-stone walls and grey-green grass, sliding down to a plain and then the whole of Manchester, a great dank tangle of roads, houses and factories, chimneys poking up like long pink fingers. Overhead the clouds were fat with rain.

Within a minute or two the plane was approaching Costford, one wing dipping horribly down and down so that the other, presumably, could rise horribly up and up. Some more patches of low cloud abruptly fogged the porthole and then it was clear again. Little streets came into view, almost recognisable, as if you could just snap your fingers; some way ahead Wendy could pick out the long meaty expanse of the viaduct.

The captain's voice came over the intercom.

'Ladies and gentlemen, we've run into a little problem. Please remain calm. Stewards, emergency procedure.'

There was a great hiss as everyone drew their breath in at once. 'Oh my God,' Wendy said.

'Now you know why his accent needs to be so posh,' Art told her.

The hostesses had scurried to the ends of the aisles. Wendy looked sideways to the porthole. It had clouded up again. Oh ef, this time it wasn't cloud at all. As she thought that, she also thought: I can't say fuck, even just inside my own head. Even now.

Whimpering noises began to come from here and there in the aircraft. A baby started bawling.

The captain's voice came through again, still sounding calm, almost bored: 'Passengers, will you please adopt the emergency position. This is just a precaution in case of a bumpy landing. Bend forwards and place your head as far as possible between your knees. The stewards will help you if you find it difficult.'

Sure enough the hostesses had started down the aisles, pushing people's heads down.

'Oh fuck,' Wendy said.

'I'll tell you something,' Art said. 'Once I scored a hole in one. I gave the ball a mighty whack and as soon as it took off I knew it was going straight down the hole, even though at that distance I couldn't even see the hole as such. Sometimes you just know things.'

'I don't want us to go down a hole. I want us to land.' Wendy's voice was quivery.

'That's what I'm talking about. I know we're going to land. I just know it. We're going to get to that runway and land on it, sweet as a nut.'

He put his hand to the back of her head and pushed her gently forwards. There were bowed heads all around. Wonderful, she thought, we'll all end up looking as if we died straining on the loo.

The very fact that she'd used the word *die*, even though it was only in her own mind, generated a huge fear inside her. It was like having a bomb ticking away in your stomach.

The plane began bouncing suddenly and she heard people scream. She did too, or at least cried aaaagh! not so much because she had to, but simply in order to join in, be one of them. She did it below the level of prevailing noise, like in church, singing hymns inaudibly.

Actually she felt glad, it was so comforting to be touching the ground, not to be up in the air any more. She knew the ground was the dangerous bit but it was also where she belonged, it was home.

She raised her head and looked out of the porthole, and realised to her horror that there were houses and patches of waste land and strange curvy roads with little toy cars on them, still below her. It hadn't been the ground at all but a patch of hard air, like the spot of turbulence they'd run into on the way over to the Canaries, only this time caused, she imagined, by the aircraft going through the air at the wrong angle, like a yacht she'd once been taken for a ride in, which suddenly hit the waves head on so that they went smack smack smack as if they were made not of water but something hard like tarmac, and shook her till her brains rattled. Just ahead rusty girders groped at them from the tower blocks they were building on Prospect Hill.

She put her head back down between her knees.

A strange whining sound came from the engines, then a horrible grating noise, and then suddenly silence. The passengers were silent for a moment too, and then began bellowing again, and weeping aloud. Above it all came the Eton tones of the pilot: 'Please keep calm, everybody. We're shortly coming into land. It may be a bit bumpy so hang on to your hats.'

Fuck you, she thought, it's my *head* I need to hold on to.

Somebody started to say, in a quavering, high-pitched voice, 'It's not fair, I've got a baby.' It was infuriating to hear her, the way she spoke sounded so exaggerated. But how do you exaggerate being in an air crash, with a baby? Dying was the one thing you couldn't exaggerate. Perhaps when you died the pain was so terrible that you could never tell it to anyone. Maybe that's what dying was, intolerable pain which you couldn't return from. Perhaps everybody who had ever died had suffered so much pain it was impossible to imagine it. You could get to the point of no return, and that's what being dead was.

Once, when she was seventeen, she'd gone on a fairground waltzer with a boy called Andy. She was under the impression that she'd been on one before in her life, but when it started off she realised, no, she hadn't. It had turned into an utter nightmare. The world was all bits and pieces sliding into each other and breaking apart again, leaving nowhere where she could live at all.

She'd started to scream, then the sound of her own screams had panicked her, and she'd screamed even more. Andy had his arm around her and a huge grin on his face which suddenly flew off and shot away across the fairground to vanish in the distance, fluttering out of sight like a blown paper bag.

'Stop it! Stop it!' she'd cried. Andy started waving frantically and then a fairground boy swung towards them over the intervening machinery and stood on their little car thing, stopping it spinning on its own spindle by the way he distributed his weight, though of course they still went round and round on the long arm of the ride until it all came to a halt, but that was all right, she'd known she was going to live.

This was like that, the plane a waltzer they were stuck in, but with no fairground bloke able to swing over and put a stop to it.

'Always somebody,' Art's head said from between his kneecaps.

She heard her voice say 'What?' as if it was a voice in a different country or time or galaxy. She raised her own head slightly to turn and look at Art. Beyond, on the other side of the aisle, a fat woman hadn't been able to get her head between her legs at all, and was just leaning forward with her bosom and stomach like a great squidgy filling to a sandwich, a look of complete forlornness and self-hatred on her face, realising now that her life had always been heading for this moment when she needed to be slim, thinking how huge and unnecessary her unfoldable bottom was.

'Special pleading, doesn't it get on your wick?' Art's head replied. Then, in a mimicky singsong voice: 'My baby, my baby.' Sure enough, somewhere behind them, the mother was still calling out.

'But it *is* her baby,' Wendy whispered.

'We're all in the same boat. And you could say us grown-ups have got more to lose.'

Through mists of terror she caught a glimpse of an estate agent, arguing, cajoling, putting his case; experienced a sudden jolt of hate and love for him.

Then felt rather than heard a low-pitched thunder.

She woke into silence.

Her first thought was, it must be Monday already, time for work. Her heart sank. Then she remembered: she'd fallen in love with her boss.

Then she remembered she'd come back from the Canary Islands, and her heart sank more. Back to the real world.

She remembered a house they'd been in the process of selling, the haunted one, and wondered what there was to do next on the transaction. The bloke had said yes. He was a weedy little man with wispy hair. He'd beaten Art down a little but was still paying over the odds. With any luck the deal would be in the contractual stage by now, outside her sphere of responsibility.

'I won't have to get my hands dirty,' she said out loud.

'What, love?' came a voice.

She opened her eyes. She was in the body of the plane. It was darker than before, and things seemed bent, out of shape. The whole structure was leaning to one side. Her seat felt wrong and she realised its back was broken. People were filing out. A little man was kneeling on the seat in front of her, peering down. He wore a fireman's helmet that was too big for his head.

'It's like a Panatella tube,' she said, wanting to be helpful, to explain.

'What is, duck?'

'The plane. My dad has one every Christmas. I trod on it once. When I was about seven. It got all bent. It still had the cigar in.'

'Blimey. Was he put out?'

'He forgave me. He always forgives everybody.' She began to cry.

'Well, nobody trod on this lot. It come down a bit short of the runway. Its engines failed and it didn't quite make it. What I want you to do, darling, is just keep on looking at me. Your dad isn't doing too well. We'll have to get him off to hospital.'

Oh God. She turned to look at him.

It wasn't her dad, it was Art. A huge wave of relief swept over her. Then she saw that his head was lolling and one eye was half out. She remembered their talk about bulging.

'What's happened to him?'

'Shock wave,' the fireman said. 'You never know where it's going to pop up. Just keep looking at me, missy.'

The fat woman from the other side of the aisle pushed past him, another fireman propelling her from behind, and limped towards the exit at the far end.

'You were saved by your seat taking the strain of it,' the fireman said.

'He's dead, isn't he?'

'That's not for me to say. Look on the bright side, eh?'

She felt a striped sensation, part sadness for Art, part relief. What sort of relief? she wondered.

Relief at not being dead herself?

Further down the plane, the baby bawled indignantly.

No, not that.

At it not being her dad who had gone?

Not exactly that either. That was just part of it.

What it was, she didn't have to worry about Art any more. That was a horrible feeling to have but she couldn't help it. She hadn't wished anything bad to happen to him, so it wasn't her fault. She hadn't let him down in any way.

But now she could just go home and be how she was, except sadder. She'd been let off the hook.

Twenty

O ne of May's constituents had suffered a bereavement.
May had read about it in the evening paper. The dead
man was an amateur parachutist who had pulled his
ripcord a few seconds too late – three, to be exact, according to
the secretary of his jumping club – and had been found by a
farmer in his field, with his legs spread and his left arm outstretched. He must have looked as if he was doing semaphore,
silly apeth. The Manchester Airport plane crash was warning
enough that you didn't need to go looking for trouble.

But his mother was a party member who did a little bit at
election time, so a thoughtful letter was in order.

May felt unwilling to settle down to write it, even though
she'd always been a one for getting on with her business. Too
much death, she'd had her fill of it. First Alice's funeral, only a
week ago, and Art Whiteside dying in the plane crash that same
day, not that he was much of a loss, and if one person had to
meet his Maker out of everyone on board it might just as well
have been him as anyone. Then Joss Carpenter, one of the old
stalwarts of the council, was taken off to hospital with cancer of
the bladder.

She had gone to visit him yesterday afternoon. He lay there
with his big yellowish head on the pillow looking like some Hal-
lowe'en pumpkin that had succumbed to the last throes of
despair. Not even producing a copy of the unconfirmed council
minutes for him to read between the lines of, did the trick any
more. He had lost interest.

That's what he said, 'I've lost interest.'

She told him that her grandmother had given a recipe for onion gravy on her deathbed, but to no avail. She didn't say the word deathbed, remembering at the last minute that it would hardly be tactful. She just said: right at the end of her life, long after she had stopped cooking herself, as if cooking was the main point of the story, rather than the old girl passing away. In politics you learned to think on your feet, and to give what you said a bit of a tweak when necessary.

'Sod onion gravy, May,' Joss had said in reply. 'Pardon my French. I can't imagine how your grandmother kept up her interest in it right to the end. You don't have onion gravy on your dinner in heaven. You probably don't have dinner at all. I can't imagine anything being cooked up there.'

He lay still for a while, breathing in an odd snory way. Illness was a funny thing: she wondered why bladder cancer should have the effect of giving him noisy breath. Then he spoke again. 'I don't even know if I'll go to heaven.' Tears slid from his eyes down on to the pillow.

'Of course you will, Joss,' she told him, though the thought of a heaven with Joss in it struck her as a bit odd. It was typical of him that he should be so concerned about getting membership. She remembered how peeved he was that his waterworks had prevented him from taking up the offer of free golf lessons.

Still, she had time for the poor old buffer. She recalled the way he always used to say, 'A word to the wise,' when he wanted to dish out the dirt on something or somebody. But the fact of the matter was, she was liable to be fonder of him than God would be, being a fellow councillor. She was prejudiced on his behalf.

'Not that it matters either way, for the time being,' she reassured him. 'You'll be sticking round here for a while yet.'

Again, he seemed to take an age thinking it over. Then he said, 'I've got something I want to show you.'

His puffy, liver-speckled hand crawled across the counterpane towards the bedside table, almost as though its fingers were legs, perhaps belonging to a lobster or some such thing. He reached up and picked a picture from the table.

It was a photograph in a frame that had been lying face downwards. May realised from the way he handled it that that hadn't been out of disrespect but the opposite, because it was too much of a treasure to be on public view.

He passed it over to her.

An elderly couple, standing by a wall. It looked as if it dated from the 1940s. Not another one, May thought, remembering Alice's album. She felt irritation – no, more than that, anger – at Joss for being so unoriginal. The old dears were even squinting into the sun just as George had done in that photo where he was wearing a handkerchief with a knot in each corner on his head and carrying the blessed cat in the crook of his arm. You'd think if you were going to die in the near future, you'd at least try not to go through exactly the same motions as everyone else.

'That's my mum and dad,' Joss whispered.

'Is that so?' she replied, trying to sound less sarcastic than she felt.

Joss held on to the picture in his clumsy chubby fingers, like a baby with a precious toy. She had a vision of that hand of his scuttling across a vast empty ocean floor, looking for some lost burrow where it had once been happy and safe. The image was so vivid and unexpected it made her gasp, and then she felt her eyes fill with tears and her throat go chock-a-block with sobs; she had to pretend to have a coughing fit in order to let them out.

Maurice had been waiting for her outside the hospital, Cherry having agreed to babysit for the evening. He noticed straight away she was a bit upset and asked her where her favourite place was to go for a meal. No competition, as far as she was concerned: prawn cocktail, steak, chips and salad, with ice-cream to follow, in the Berni Inn at the end of Top Lane. Maurice asked her if she was sure. He would obviously have preferred something a bit more high-class, like that wine bar they'd been to in Alton, despite his need to count the pennies, but he'd have to put up with it. She'd been in need of comfort food. 'Let them eat steak,' she told him. As it turned out he had the chicken, not being much of a steak man, as he put it. In fact she slightly regretted the choice herself. It wasn't that the steak was tough, just that her teeth didn't seem as handy as in days of yore.

Tempus fugit, as Hub used to say. It was him who used to quote that French queen too.

Still, Maurice praised her new winter jacket, made of velvety material in a raspberry shade.

It never rains but it pours, was how she felt about all this death death death when she picked up the pad of Basildon Bond the next day and sat down to write her condolences to the poor dear whose son had perished in a parachuting accident.

The first page of the pad had a drawing by her mother on it, a stick man in soldier's garb, even wearing puttees, with his arm in a sling, and large boots. Rather incongruously he was surrounded by flowers, with a big babyish sun sending down rays from above. Mother was in her bedroom at present, which gave May a breather before she needed to take her over to Cherry's and go off to court herself.

May tore out the page, and carefully wrote her address in the top right corner of the next one. Luckily with condolences it wasn't necessary to go into detail – all she need do was commiserate on the tragic accident. You couldn't pretend there was a silver lining either, unlike the Manchester plane crash which had saved dear Trevor Morgan's bacon. Even allowing for the fact he had a magic touch, that photo in the *Costford Express* had been nothing short of a miracle, with Trevor standing in front of the partly built tower blocks pointing up with both arms extended at the aircraft roaring just over his head. On its middle page the *Express* had written a long apologetic editorial headed TIME TO EAT HUMBLE PIE, where it admitted Trevor had been right to deliver his warnings all along. 'This time we were lucky. The Prospect Hill tower blocks have not yet been completed, so the faltering aeroplane was able to clear the tops of them, landing just short of the runway at Manchester Airport. As a result there was only a single casualty, however tragic that nevertheless is for Mr Arthur Whiteside's family and friends. Next time a faltering jetliner might plough into a skyscraper, a skyscraper unwisely positioned on the top of a hill, with catastrophic consequences . . .', and more of the same. You could almost hear the low rumble of supporters' feet as they pounded back to Trevor's side again. He'd been a prophet in the wilderness. He had told the truth in the face of incomprehension and hostility. The *Costford Express* wanted the authorities to think again about the Prospect Hill development, despite the need to get on with slum clearance and cope with the council's accommodation problems.

Trevor had saved his political career and disposed of his rival in love, at a stroke. The piece describing Art's death was FLUKE SHOCK WAVE KILLS LOCAL ESTATE AGENT. Given the aircraft had come down shy of the runway, its wheels folding up on contact with the soft turf, and had scraped along on its bottom till coming to a standstill, the only fluke involved was the absence of a shock wave in respect of the other passengers.

Ted Wilcox was speechless with rage at the serendipity of it all. Of course nothing could be done to halt the project at this stage. All he was able to promise was a red warning light on the tops of the buildings, and negotiations with the airport on the subject of flight paths. He had looked daggers at May across the committee room as if it had all been her fault. There'd be no more talk in the near future about meeting together to build bridges.

Anyone would think it was she who had attacked the project, instead of speaking on its behalf at every opportunity. All she had done was try to get the whole thing sorted out, and persuade the government to spell out its investment in the development. It could be argued that, given it was her peroration to the little rat of a government minister that had caused Trevor to rise up on his hind legs and commit political suicide, at least temporarily, she had almost done her own party a power of good.

Unintentionally, as it happened. For the life of her she couldn't muster any support for the plump North Cheshire nonentity who was standing in North Costford for the Tories. She'd had to go to an election rally a few nights ago at the Harper Moor Conservative Club to demonstrate her support, and listen to a singer called Norma Leon belt out a piece of tosh entitled 'Calypso Blues':

'His eyes are blue
His hair is white
It shows you that
He has things right.'

The song was about Edward Heath, of course, but James Hunter, the local candidate, chose to take the references on board for himself, pointing to his eyeballs with the first line, his pale locks with the second, and doing a kind of soft-shoe shuffle during the rest of it, while curvaceous Norma shimmied alongside him. It was one of those moments when May wondered what she was doing in politics. And given Trevor's resurgence it was a dance of doom in any case.

But still, it wasn't her fault that Trevor was able to rise from the dead. Even Ted couldn't blame her for that.

Dear Mrs Pollock,
   I was so sad to hear of your son's tragic accident. Please accept my sincere condolences.
   Yours very sincerely,
   May Rollins

There – nothing to it when it came to the push. She folded it, put it in the envelope, did the address, affixed a stamp. Done. She screwed the cap back on Hub's old pen and went upstairs to fetch Mother.

Who was all ready for the off. Hair brushed, neat dress, not a peep out her. There were days when you would hardly realise she was next best thing to an imbecile.

Outside it was a nice sunny day, with a bit of frost on the lawn. If the old bat had been in songstress mood it would no doubt have been 'Oh, What a Beautiful Morning', but she kept her lips buttoned and the only sound from her was her heels tapping on the path. May herself had almost put on her furry ankle boots, to keep her feet warm in court, but then thought blow it, and slid into a pair of heels too, so that together they made a bit of a symphony on the crazy-paving. She was going to meet Maurice later, and wanted to be at her best.

She eyed her new garden bench as she went past. Mrs Bradbury, cock-a-hoop that the civil engineering firm had moved away from the bottom of her garden, had bought it for her. It looked a bench too many at present, standing askew on the lawn as if it had been dropped there from outer space. There had also been a letter, explaining how stressful Mr Bradbury's professional life was, and how he could at least now sleep at nights. You probably need to have a fine-tuned brain to sit in a car-school car all day, was May's thought. Also how the daughter had written the best biology essay the school could remember, all on account of no longer being troubled by heavy-duty machinery.

May hadn't replied and thanked her in turn yet. Death took precedence, was the way she thought of it. There had been a card from the neighbour too, with a goldfish on the front and a simple message inside: 'Thanks to you he didn't die in vain.'

'Remember the paving stone, Mother,' May said. There were days when she'd as soon the old girl came a cropper and broke her neck, but today wasn't one of them. She had a bereavement letter in her handbag and enough death and destruction in the previous few days to last her for the time being.

Then she noticed.

The delinquent paving stone wasn't proud any more. It was flat as a pancake, lying on an even keel with all the others.

She looked up and down the path, just to make certain she hadn't lighted on the wrong one, thinking to herself, How can you lose a whole blooming paving stone?, but of course she hadn't. No, it was the right one, sitting in its place as nice as pie.

She opened her handbag, took out her reading specs, put them on and looked down at her path. Mother was waiting patiently by the Imp. It came to something when you had to wear glasses to read a slab.

No, it was flat, flush with the others, and the surrounding cement was intact. You'd never have known it had been a bother.

Yet Trevor Morgan had almost brained himself tripping over it.

May shook her head. It seemed to have settled back in position. A puzzle, but no point in worrying over it. Sometimes your paving showed itself to be more obliging than you had any right to expect.

Cherry had two young men. It was her policy.

That's what she'd told Hilda. 'It's my policy, Grandma.' The two in question were the naval vessel and the brainbox.

Having two seemed a good policy to Hilda. She could have done with that policy herself. It would have enabled her to have both George and Petey to herself, no room for Alice at all. Alice could have kept on sewing, in that hot garden long ago, where the snapdragons whispered.

George would have been kept for best, in his smart army uniform and neat sling to put his arm in. When you took him out he would have clicked his heels and saluted. You would never have played with him for long enough to get all scruffy and misshapen. His nice soldier's hat wouldn't have been worn out or mislaid, no hanky with a knot in each corner. When finished with for the time being he could have been put away, before he got spoiled.

> O soldier soldier, won't you marry me
> With your musket, fife and drum
> O no, sweet maid, I cannot marry thee
> For I have no coat to put on

So off she went, to her grandfather's chest
And she brought him a coat of the very very best
She brought him a coat of the very very best
And the soldier put it on.

George would always have had his coat of the very very best, while Petey would have been perfectly fine for everyday use.

Cherry's vessel had gone away to sea. And when Dave went he had given her a little present for a keepsake. He had bought it far away, on one of his voyages. It had a carved horn handle.

It was a kni.

That's what she'd said.

'He is sweet. He gave me something to remember him by. It's a lovely little kni—' Then she'd stopped. She went pink. She added, because she was going to say it anyway and she didn't want Hilda to notice she'd stopped halfway through a word, 'It's got a lovely carved horn handle.'

She'd said this part in a tiny voice, like a snapdragon might, and then changed the subject.

But from that moment on, Hilda had known it was in the house somewhere.

Poor Wendy had been sent home after a few days. As she'd told Cherry: with the best will in the world, they can't let you stay in hospital when there's nothing wrong with you.

'I think they should,' Cherry told her. Wendy was propped against her hospital pillow, surrounded by grapes. She had received a huge bunch from the Mayor and Corporation of Costford, enough to start a winery. 'You've just been in an aeroplane crash. That's a good enough reason.'

'But I wasn't hurt.'

'A crash is enough without you actually being hurt. You know, my dear old dad had a dreaded lurg when he was at university, and missed his finals.'

'Did he? Hub? I'm surprised. From what you've said about him I thought he had a jumbo brain.'

'You're thinking of Ben. He's the one with intellect. There was a poem I did for A level, which had a line in that I think about when I think about him. "His mind moves upon silence." I believe that's how it went. That's how Ben's mind moves too. Upon silence.'

'He doesn't sound much company.'

'It suits me, when I'm in the mood. Anyhow, Dad wasn't like that. I don't think he could think at all. It was just he knew such a lot. He had the kissing disease, he told me. God knows what that is. I used to think his lips must have fallen off. But of course he had done loads of work during his course, so they gave him a pass anyway. It was called an aegrotat, that was the name for it. That's what I think you should have, even if you haven't got a scratch on your body. An aegrotat, to let you be ill, on account of being in a crash and all you went through. I don't see why you should be penalised just because you didn't lose a leg or anything.'

But no aircrash aegrotat was awarded, and home Wendy went, after a couple of days. She then insisted on going back to work the following morning, but that hadn't been a success. There was a lot to do, with Art being dead, but she was over-taken by sadness before lunchtime had even arrived, and had to go home, weeping. Cherry tried to visit her every day.

Grandma had been on her best behaviour today. She had only broken into song a couple of times, and now she was happily ensconced by the radio, listening to Sandy MacPherson on the seaside organ.

'I'm off out for an hour,' Cherry told her.

Hilda sat and thought about it.

'So I hope you'll be good.' Cherry hated talking to her as if she was a child. The old lady looked back at her with bright knowing eyes, for all the world as if she was aware of the funny side of it. 'I don't want May on my back,' Cherry added in a warning tone.

A few minutes later, while Cherry was brushing her hair in the bathroom, she heard Hilda singing 'We'll Meet Again', in that honeycomb voice of hers. She was punting it out with Sandy's backing, but the choice seemed a promising sign.

Wendy was lying on the settee in her parents' lounge. Her mum showed Cherry in. 'Here she is,' she whispered, as though Wendy was beyond coping with normal volume.

'Hello, Wendy.' Cherry whispered too, so as to be consistent.

'Hello, Cherry,' Wendy whispered back, for all the world as if there were another Wendy somewhere further on, and that was the one who needed protection from decibels. But it was a sprightly whisper.

'How are you feeling today?'

The sprightliness instantly evaporated, and Wendy's whole face went as wobbly as a blancmange. 'Not very happy,' she replied.

'Oh dear.'

'I'll go and make you both a cup of tea,' Wendy's mum said, and scuttled off.

'What is it?' Cherry asked when she was out of the room.

'Can you smell me?'

Cherry leaned forwards and sniffed. She had a heady perfume on, too old for her if truth be told. But perhaps it was a sign of recovery.

'Art bought it me,' Wendy said. 'On the plane. It was in a glass bottle.'

'They're always in a glass bottle.'

'It survived the crash. And Art didn't.'

'Oh. Yes.'

'Look what I've drawn.'

Wendy passed over a pad of cartridge paper.

Cherry flipped it open. On the first page there was a prone body, with a broken aeroplane in the distance and smoke spiralling up. Oddly enough it was exactly as you would draw an aeroplane crash if you'd never been in one.

The man's body was naked. His face had a bristly moustache. He also had an erection, with a sort of flag fastened to the top of it. Maybe it was an estate agent's sign.

Cherry looked at it in amazement. Wendy watched her watching, as if trying to read some sort of message in her expression.

Cherry had the feeling that any response would be seen by Wendy as very significant, so didn't dare say anything at all. She tried to look as if she had a reaction without giving a clue as to what it might have been.

'I got the idea from you,' Wendy whispered.

'Did you?'

'When you did that Johnny's soul. In your painting that time. The day we ended up going to the caretaker's flat.'

'Oh yes?'

Wendy pointed at the flag. 'What I thought, darling Arty had his soul in his knob.'

Cherry looked at her in horror. Wendy looked back up at her. It reminded Cherry of her teaching days, when some child would look up at her for approval.

'I mean,' Wendy continued, 'I think he was very sincere. I think he had a very sincere sort of soul. He had a very sincere sort of knob, come to that.'

'It looks as if he had a big one,' Cherry said, trying to sound judicious. 'Assuming your picture is in proportion.'

'Oh yes, it was big all right.'

Cherry passed the pad back with a shaking hand. 'He would have made a good Johnny,' she said, trying to give a lift to the atmosphere. She felt sad, bereft, as if it was she who had lost someone in the crash; as if she'd lost Wendy.

'I've got a great big laugh lodged in my chest,' Wendy said. 'It's just stuck there. I don't know what to do about it. It's one of those laughs that's the next-best thing to a heart attack.'

'Perhaps you should let it out.'

'When he died, I thought, goody, I can go back to my mum

and dad. Isn't that horrible? And now, when I think about him, I just think demeaning thoughts, like about his knob.'

Suddenly the laugh burst out. She gave a cry, almost as if in pain, and then huge vibrating ha-has that reminded Cherry of her record of the laughing policeman when she was a girl. Then, after a few seconds, Wendy's face seemed to fracture. Her features slid and blurred like a frost-crazed window pane, and then she was weeping her heart out.

'It's all right,' Cherry said, squeezing her arm and stroking her forehead. It wasn't all right, of course. A man had died. But that wasn't Wendy's fault, however guilty she felt. He'd had a good holiday, by the sound of it, and from what Wendy had told her he'd been dissatisfied with his life and his future prospects in any case.

Wendy's tears seemed a promising sign, however racking they were. It was a stage, and she would get beyond it. Of course it wouldn't do to make a practical observation of that sort, any more than to say anything about the danger of putting all one's eggs in one basket. All Cherry could do for the present was to give her silent female support. But it was good to do that, good to feel, as she did in her heart of hearts, a kind of relief on her own part, that Wendy had come back to her after her travels.

Wendy was calmer when Cherry left.

Cherry herself didn't remain calm for long. When she got back home she found that Hilda had gone.

It was all done now, but he liked to check.

Whatever work he was in at the time, car repair, decorating or robbing, Fray always liked to do a good job, and make sure afterwards that everything was clean and tidied up.

In court that time Miss Rollins had said, Not Guilty.

She'd had a conflab with the clerk first, him giving Fray one of those looks. He had on a black gown, which made him look like a vulture, with a big narrow nose and thin twisty neck. His eyes were grey and hard. But Fray had had looks like that often before. Hot with lust yet hating him at the same time. As much as to say: being as I can't get you to bed, in my position as clerk of the court for my part, and you being a robber for yours, I would like to drop you right bang in the shit by way of revenge.

Fray liked to get things right, whether fucking girls he didn't desire, or fixing carburettors, or even, at seven or eight or nine years old, pleasing uncles in his bedroom; but now his robbing had gone wrong the way all the other things in his life had gone wrong, and he was nabbed.

'Not guilty.'

Her eyes were hard, too, like those marble chippings you see on graves, glowing in afternoon air and making you feel it was just as well not being dead.

But their hardness had been on his behalf.

She had said it without sympathy. He'd thought she was saying the opposite of what she was. He could feel himself shrinking, the way he did with anger, arms and legs retracting, his flesh compacting till it was hard as iron.

When he was little he had gone to another boy's house after school. He could only remember doing that the once. The boy's mum had given him a smile but there was a sort of shudder tied up in it. Every time she had to be near him he could sense she held her breath, and at tea she had to send her hands towards him with sandwiches or cake as if through thick and gluey air, disgust turned almost solid, only a fear of bringing things to a head, of saying something sharply rude in front of her own boy, giving her the strength to do it.

The boy had an electric train set. Fray watched in fascination as it went the rounds, everything miniature and perfect, in fact everything perfect because it *was* miniature, a world too small and detailed to have room for horribleness.

The boy's name was Roger. Roger made the train go fast or slow by operating the transformer. It had a pointer on it that you turned on a dial. What Fray had to do was switch the points. You flipped a little lever and the train took a different track. He loved doing it at the last minute, so that the train was all set to go one way then found itself going the other. Just one movement of the tiny lever and the engine and all its carriages were abruptly shifted.

That's how it felt when the magistrate said Not Guilty. Fray was all set to go one way, off to prison, and suddenly his life switched direction, back into the open air.

Part of him couldn't keep up with it. He walked out of court with the clerk chuntering in his wake, the magistrate looking at his back with her ungiving eyes, and he felt as hard and solid as granite. I'll get you, you bastards, was what he felt.

He stood outside the court and when Miss Rollins came out he followed her home. If the clerk had come out first he would have followed him instead. The next day he hung around in her road waiting for her to come out of the house. Over the course of a few days he worked out the set-up. She lived there with an old girl, obviously her mother, and before she left the house a young woman would arrive to take care of the old bird.

He didn't do anything for the time being. He knew better than that. It was a question of biding his time, and one thing he was good at was biding. Every now and then he came back to the house and had a sniff about.

Miss Rollins got into the habit of taking her mother off with her some days, dumping her with the girl, presumably.

One Tuesday, after the two of them had gone, he broke in.

He wasn't sure what he intended to do. He certainly didn't plan to smash the place up, it wasn't his style. Steal her TV was one idea. Bit of tit for tat. See how she liked being on that end of it.

He went into her lounge and switched it on. To his amazement it was a black and white one. He wouldn't be able to sell it in any self-respecting pub, or even give it away.

He went upstairs, found her bedroom. He could tell which was hers. The other one had the drawers poking out, and the bed was all bulging and rumpled where the old girl must have been sort of nesting in it, using it as a den. Miss Rollins's was neat and tidy.

Fray approached the bed, lifted the pillow, picked out the nightie from under it, shook it out full length. He could steal that.

He opened the drawers in her chest and took out her undies. He could steal those too.

He remembered her as she had been in court, with a vast grey dress and a horrible blue hat pulled down almost to her ears, wearing her clothes as if they were a suit of armour.

He held a huge bra up to his chest. It drooped down like a great double catapult. He did it up at the back and then pulled a pair of her pants on over his trousers. Now he wandered round the room with a snarl on his face and his fists in the air, all his movements jerky and unsexy, beginning his revenge, like an Indian on the warpath or someone leading a conga.

He went up to the wardrobe and opened the door, still doing his odd harsh dance. More clothes inside, her dresses and two-pieces. He stepped in among them.

He could wait here. He could stand among the dresses, with their faint smell, some sweetish perfume or other along with something more medical, mothballs or disinfectant, until she came home and went to bed. And then, in the dark, in the middle of the night, when she was snoring in her bed, he could . . .

What could he do?

He could rape her.

He could do it meticulously, competently, expertly, out of sheer hatred. He could show her what was what.

He stepped inside the wardrobe, into the dark, and pulled the door shut.

The house had been silent before, but it was more silent still now, and the air was warm and intimate. It was as though he had stepped inside the clothes smells too, gone past the added flavours and arrived at a human odour that only travelled an inch or two beyond the surface of the garments, flesh, sweat, half unpleasant and choking, half enjoyable and reassuring.

It was only after he had been standing there for some minutes that he remembered.

She had said Not Guilty.

She'd flipped the lever and the points had switched.

He stood for a while longer in the dark, trying to get his head around the idea. Not guilty. He would have to take another kind of revenge altogether, the sort where you repay one favour with another.

TV, no bother. He was used to getting hold of those. It would need a colour aerial, but he had experience of clambering about at the top of houses, could snitch one of those and fix it up for her.

He stepped out of the wardrobe. Above her bed he noticed a damp patch on her ceiling, exactly like the Party Four one above his mother's bed. He could sort that out too. As he left the house he tripped over the rising paving stone.

It wasn't till he was halfway down the street that he realised he was still wearing her bra and knickers on top of his own clothes. Luckily it was one of those quiet residential areas and no one was about.

It took longer than he expected to do the jobs. He had his Saturday work at the Town Hall, organised by Jack, plus extras for special occasions. Then he was asked to do a spot of security at a new bookshop that had opened in town. They were organising a club for talking about books on a Tuesday evening, and had straight off run into some bother with skinheads. The precinct was deserted at that time of night, with all the other shops long since shut.

Nothing much was going on, as it turned out. The skinheads had got into the habit of standing in front of the shop window, pressing their noses against the glass.

'They look like a row of pigs,' the woman who ran the shop said. 'Their noses go like horrible blobs, with two nostrils in the middle, and they've made themselves as bald as coots. They frighten some of the old dears half to death.'

She paid him to come for the last half hour, and then walk everybody towards the buses. The second time he was on duty the skinheads duly showed up and squashed their noses. Fray stepped out, tapped the nearest one on the shoulder, and when he turned round rammed his finger in his eye. Off they went, the one with the big red eye crying like a baby.

The following week there was a big do at the shop. It was supposed to be held at the music store further along the precinct but that had suddenly gone bust. A free record of Hylda Baker singing 'Nearest and Dearest' had been offered to every couple in Costford who'd been married twenty years or more, and who turned up with their marriage lines to prove it. Having had the event dropped in her lap, Christine, the woman who was running the bookshop, had decided to make an evening of it with readings about married life and books for sale on the subject, and asked Fray to help out.

Middle-aged people stood about in the shop, with their fat tits and bellies and false teeth, in their cardies and tight tired jackets, faces and bodies falling to bits, hair falling out or growing grey or sprouting in thick tufts from their ears, noses big and black-heady, proud of not running away with other partners, just as if other partners would want them.

But that's where Fray met Christine's business partner, Michael Dobbins.

Michael was a different story altogether from Jack Kitchen at the Town Hall. Jack had been like one of those skinheads, content to peer through a window, not up to really doing anything. When Fray approached him he would look at first excited, then busy, then so energetic he could have been plugged into the mains, anything so he wouldn't have to look Fray in the eye, hopping about that way he had.

Michael insisted that Fray escort him home at the end of the Hylda Baker evening, 'for safety's sake'; and well he might, with that sort of teacosy thingamijig on his head. Once at Michael's flat, all sorts of things happened.

One of them was setting Fray up in business. Michael believed in facilitating, was how he put it. He had facilitated Christine's shop, because he thought she'd make a go of it. He also thought there was a big future in security: for shops, factories, especially for discos and clubs for young people.

He talked about years ago, when people believed you could turn ordinary metal into gold. What they were really waiting for was the arrival of modern business. It was just the same as all those people sitting on horses for years, centuries, waiting for cars to be invented.

Fray had never heard anybody talk like that. He felt that he'd never heard anybody talk at all, just grunt.

In security, Michael said, you could turn a slightly iffy background into an asset on your application form, and end up making money for not doing anything, just being who you were, what you were.

'All you need do is look a bit smartish,' Michael said. This with that thing, fez by name, on his bonce, embroidery and sequins sparking in the light. 'Wear something that calls to mind a uniform. When you get other people to work for you, have them wear the same thing.'

Other people working for him: that seemed pie in the sky. But already it was starting to happen. Michael had got him an arrangement to act as night-watchman at Rabbit Confectionery, the sweet factory out at Heslop. Fray did it four nights a week. Michael found him someone else for the other three. Old pal of mine, Michael had said. He was a big bruiser called Jimmy with cauliflower ears and the brains of a flea. Former pugilist, Jack Kitchen said, delighted at the find.

They both wore black short windcheaters and black cord trousers, Michael's idea. 'Gives you a silhouette,' he said, though Jimmy's silhouette was like a boulder.

Fray had been on duty at the Rabbit place all night. Nothing had gone on. Nothing ever went on, which was just as well as his arm was temporarily up the spout. The only person who ever stole sweets was Jimmy, who stuffed himself the nights he was on duty.

The day before yesterday Fray had finally bumped into the Party Four bloke. Fray was just going back to Michael's flat, where he was living now, about nine in the evening, when he'd come face to face with him in an alleyway next to Hillgate. It was one of those moments, nothing to be said. The Party Four bloke didn't even look especially scared, just pissed off, like a bloke in a picture Fray had once seen, who was just going to be shot. At a certain point all you can do is be completely fed up.

Fray fetched him a single wallop.

No missing this time. It would have knocked his head off if he hadn't flown gracefully backwards like somebody in a high dive competition.

But the blow had done something to Fray's arm. His limbs always seemed to retract on him when he got mad, and this time his arm wouldn't seem to go back to normal when it was over with. It had got itself pulled or twisted, and now killed him, even when just hanging loose.

He had made himself a sling on the sly, just a scarf knotted together. He wore it on the bus to work, then took it off when he went through the factory gates and reported in. Then when no one was left about he slipped it on again.

He'd got back to Michael's flat by about seven this morning, and kipped for a couple of hours. He had an appointment at eleven – another friend of Michael's who owned a garage and was having some bother with vandalism. He put his gear on to go there, give the right impression, but wore his sling on the way. He went to Miss Rollins's house first, just to check that the slab had settled right. He'd cemented it in yesterday afternoon, and as far as he was concerned it was even-Stevens from now on. TV, stain on the ceiling, crazy paving: that was enough to pay back one verdict of Not Guilty.

A cool, sunshiny day. No one about. He peered at the path from the gate, then nipped in just to make sure the cement was hard dry.

He was testing it with the toe of his boot when somebody flew at him.

There were arms round his neck, and he glimpsed a blade. His own arm in its sling screamed blue murder. He swatted out with his left hand.

It was an old lady, buck naked, pink as a shrimp. She had a horn-handled sheath knife in her hand. It was just as well he'd had to use his wrong arm or he'd have killed her. As it was, she ended up in a heap on the driveway, scratching at the path with the tip of the knife. She looked up at him, her eyes squinting against the sunlight. Fray could see her ribcage and her tits hanging against it like shrivelled fruit.

'You rotten bastard, George,' she said, in a whiny little voice.

'Fray's the name,' he told her.

May dashed into the house, Cherry at her heels, Maurice out on the street locking her Imp, perhaps being tactful in the face of family business.

'Thank God,' May said, seeing Hilda in her armchair wearing a nightgown. Then she froze.

A youth, dressed in black, arm in a makeshift sling, was sitting on the settee.

'I thought I better wait with her,' he said. He held up the knife. 'She went for me with this.' He had cold direct eyes that rang a bell, eyes that she'd been looked at with before.

'Did she –?' May asked, pointing at the sling.

'Oh no. I'm OK. I better be off.'

'But won't –?'

'No, don't worry. Never saw a thing. I'm late for a meeting, any case.' He went off.

'It's time I did something about you, isn't it, Mother?' May said, looking at her sadly. 'This can't go on.'

'I hid it right under my mattress,' Cherry put in.

Hilda didn't look at either of them. She started snapping her fingers rhythmically, though not with enough pressure to actually make snaps. Then she rose to her feet and began slowly to dance.

'You put your left leg in,' she sang, in her little-girl voice:

> 'You pull your left leg out
> In out, in out, shake it all about
> You do the hokey-cokey and you turn around
> That's what it's all about.'

Acknowledgements

The lines from 'Silver Dollar' by Clarke Van Ness and Jack Palmer on p.70 are reproduced by kind permission of Anglo Pic Music Ltd.; the quotation from 'Easter Parade' by Irving Berlin (© copyright 1933 by Irving Berlin; © copyright renewed; international copyright secured; all rights reserved) on p.133, is reprinted by permission; the quotation from 'I'm Henery the Eighth I am', words and music by R. P. Weston and Fred Murray (© 1910) on p.142, is reproduced by permission of Francis Day & Hunter Ltd, London WC2H 0QY; the quotation from 'Where Do You Go To, My Lovely', words and music by Peter Sarstedt (© 1968) on pp.214–5, is reproduced by permission of EMI United Partnership Ltd., London WC2H 0QY; the quotation from 'Whatever Will Be, Will Be (Que Sera Sera)' words and music by Jay Livingstone and Ray Evans (© 1955 Jay Livingstone Music/St Angelo Music, U.S.A.; Universal/MCA Music Publishing Ltd, London) on pp.278–9 is used by permission of Music Sales Ltd; all rights reserved; the quotation from 'Sea Fever' by John Masefield on p.286 is used by permission of the Society of Authors as the Literary Representative of the Estate of John Masefield; the quotation from 'Long-Legged Fly' by W. B. Yeats (*Collected Poems*, Macmillan, 1965) on p.347 is made by permission from A. P. Watt Ltd on behalf of Michael B. Yeats. Thanks to: Tracy Brain, Barry Day, Jean Day, Jeffrey Denton, Suzannah Dunn, Tessa Hadley, Jules Hardy, Paula Hutchings, Richard Kerridge, Michael Schmidt, David Thomas; to my agent, Caroline Dawnay, my editors Christopher Potter and Catherine Blyth; and to Marian, Will, Sam, Helen and Jo.